"Al Pessin escorts you through thrills and chaos,
writing with the sure hand of authority.
This guy knows his stuff."
—**Richard Castle**, *New York Times* bestselling
author of the Nikki Heat thrillers

"*Sandblast* is the definition of a terrific military
thriller: straightforward, precise, and devastating. This
timely, realistic story—with its authentic and knowing
voice, and courageous main characters—propels
readers to the peak of white-knuckled brinksmanship
and will be awarded top marks by fans of
Alex Berensen and Vince Flynn."
—**Hank Phillippi Ryan**, Mary Higgins Clark,
Anthony, and five-time Agatha Award winner

"In *Sandblast*, Al Pessin has crafted a taut action-thriller
that really pulls you in. You'll feel like you're right
beside the main character, on an increasingly perilous
journey filled with impossible choices that threaten to
change him at his very core. The plot is highly original,
and I felt like I was there. It's a great book."
—**Henry V. O'Neil**, author of the Sim War series

"*Sandblast* is tense, believable and relevant. Pessin calls on his years in the Pentagon and White House press corps for the keen details that bring this tale to life. There's a high emotional content here, too, as we follow the almost impossible quest of a likable and massively outgunned hero."
—**T. Jefferson Parker**, *New York Times* bestselling author of *The Last Good Guy*

"So exciting, and so terrifyingly realistic, you won't be able to put it down. If you like complex international thrillers, keep Al Pessin on your short list of must-read authors."
—**D. J. Niko**, international bestselling author of the Sarah Weston Chronicles

"*Sandblast* is an aptly titled nail-biter of a thriller that opens at a pulse-rattling pace and only ratchets upwards from there. Al Pessin not only knows how to tell a story, but his journalistic background imbues this tale of an Afghan-American Army officer infiltrating a terrorist organization with compelling authority."
—**Les Standiford**, author of *Water to the Angels*, director of the Creative Writing Program at Florida International University

"*Sandblast* vividly depicts a close-to-real scene, (which) makes the story more entertaining, real and educating."
—**Ali Ahmad Jalali**, author, Afghan ambassador to Germany, former Minister of Internal Affairs and presidential candidate, Distinguished Professor, Near East South Asia Center for Strategic Studies (NESA) at the National Defense University, Washington, D.C.

"Al Pessin brings a lifetime of frontline experience to a novel that could have been taken from today's headlines. Utterly compelling and a cautionary tale for our times."

—**Retired Admiral James Stavridis**,
author of *The Leader's Bookshelf*,
former dean, Fletcher School at Tufts University,
former commander of NATO forces
(including those in Afghanistan),
and frequent media commentator

"The author writes with incredible authenticity . . . exceptionally well plotted . . . complex and consistent . . . each chapter adds a new hook . . . the story will appeal to a broad range of readers. We met the people, felt their anxiety, sweated with them in their decision process. This is a deeper story than it appears . . . the inner turmoil of [the] protagonists propels the story. The reader is pulled along, seeing lives lived, lost, and changed. [Faraz] is a heroic character of sequel deserving merit."

—**Statement of the judges,
Royal Palm Literary Awards**,
given by the Florida Writers Association

SANDBLAST

A TASKFORCE EPSILON THRILLER

AL PESSIN

PINNACLE BOOKS
Kensington Publishing Corp.
www.kensingtonbooks.com

PINNACLE BOOKS are published by

Kensington Publishing Corp.
119 West 40th Street
New York, NY 10018

All Kensington titles, imprints, and distributed lines are available at special quantity discounts for bulk purchases for sales promotions, premiums, fund-raising, educational, or institutional use. Special book excerpts or customized printings can also be created to fit specific needs. For details, write or phone the office of the Kensington sales manager: Kensington Publishing Corp., 119 West 40th Street, New York, NY 10018, attn: Sales Department; phone 1-800-221-2647.

PINNACLE BOOKS and the Pinnacle logo are Reg. U.S. Pat. & TM Off.

First Pinnacle premium mass market printing: April 2020

10 9 8 7 6 5 4 3 2 1

ISBN-13: 978-0-7860-4671-3
ISBN-10: 0-7860-4671-6

Printed in the United States of America

Electronic edition:

ISBN-13: 978-0-7860-4672-0 (e-book)
ISBN-10: 0-7860-4672-2 (e-book)

FOR AUDREY

PART ONE

CHAPTER 1

When the young Arab man in a business suit got out of a black cab and breezed into the lobby bar in late afternoon, no one took any notice. This was the Marriott Grosvenor House in London, a haven for visiting delegations and business barons from around the world, in a city with a sizable Muslim population. No fewer than five of the hotel's cable channels were Arabic satellite networks.

Mahmoud ordered apple juice and took out his *Times*. If he had been arrested at that moment, and there was no reason to do so, there would have been nothing incriminating on him at all.

He perused the newspaper and sipped his juice. Mahmoud had left a message for a bellboy he'd befriended at a mosque in South London. The message said he would be in the hotel and needed a small favor. It asked the young man to please meet him near the service elevator off the lower lobby at four o'clock. He checked his watch, 3:55.

Mahmoud put a five-pound note on the bar and took the stairs down one level. The bellboy was already there.

"I was surprised to hear from you, Mahmoud," he said. He did not appear to be concerned. The two were about the same age and had met several times. They were both five feet, seven inches tall, clean-shaven, and had olive complexions and similar builds. Men at the mosque had commented that they looked like brothers.

"My friend!" Mahmoud greeted the bellboy with a handshake and a smile. "I'm sorry to bother you, but I need your help."

"Of course. I will help you if I can."

"Thank you, thank you. But, well, this is a confidential matter." He looked around to be sure no one else was in the service hallway and then, as if he didn't know exactly where he was going, Mahmoud pretended to notice a large utility closet, its door ajar.

"In here," he said, "Just for a second."

Now the bellboy gave him a suspicious look, but it was too late. Mahmoud pushed him into the closet and closed the door.

"No, wait!" said the bellboy

"Shhh," said Mahmoud, "I have something to show you."

"No, I will not . . ." The bellboy continued to protest, but Mahmoud reached under a shelf and removed a small packet, ripped it open, and pressed a cloth to the young man's face. The bellboy passed out before he could make another sound.

Mahmoud paused. He had impressed himself; it had all gone as it did in practice. No problems. No hesitation. That gave him confidence for the work yet to be done.

Under another shelf, he found the second packet—this one with a pair of plastic gloves and a carefully forged hotel nametag. It said "Mahmoud." Why not?

Mahmoud put on the gloves, removed the young man's uniform and put it on himself—dark blue trousers with a black stripe down the sides, a white shirt, and a pullover tunic matching the pants. It fit well, as expected. He replaced the bellboy's nametag with his, and made sure the passkey was in the pants pocket. Mahmoud took the money and two handkerchiefs out of his own trousers, now crumpled on the floor.

He opened a large plastic garbage bin and tossed in his clothes and the young man's nametag. Then he hefted the bellboy into it. The head faced Mahmoud with closed eyes, then lolled to the right.

Now, Mahmoud found the final packet under a third shelf. He took out the gun, screwed in the silencer, put it against the center of the bellboy's forehead, and fired. The young man's head jerked back and his body convulsed. Mahmoud was briefly startled. But he composed himself, put the gun and the gloves into the bin, and made sure to properly seal the lid, protecting his hands with the handkerchiefs.

Mahmoud cracked open the closet door and peeked into the hallway. Still clear. He left the closet, locked the door, and took the service elevator to the ninth floor.

Using the dead bellboy's key, he went into a small storage room filled with cleaning supplies, linens, and other housekeeping items. In the back of the room was a stack of yellow plastic buckets labeled "floor wax." He removed the upper rows until he could access the bucket at the bottom left. He opened it. It did not contain floor wax.

Seeing the black backpack in the bucket made Mahmoud pause again. Until now, he had been remarkably calm. He went through the motions of capturing and killing the bellboy as he had in dozens of practice sessions. He put the bullet into the young man's head as easily as he had fired an empty gun at the head of his trainer at the safe house, again and again. He understood now why the man had made him do it so many times. But looking at the backpack, he realized how close he was to his goal, how close he was to performing the will of Allah. He caught his breath, felt his heart race.

Mahmoud removed the backpack and put the lid back onto the bucket. He restacked the other containers on top of it and left the storage room. Carrying the backpack by its top handle, as a bellboy would, he returned to the service elevator.

On the sixth floor, he headed for Room 626. The door was open and a handwritten sign read "Delegation Baggage." No one was inside. Across the hall, several men worked behind a partly open door labeled "Control," but none of them paid any attention to Mahmoud.

Room 626 was almost empty. All the furniture, including the bed, had been removed. There were a few suitcases and other bags on the floor along the far wall, under the windows looking out on Hyde Park. The bags had delegation tags on them, each with a name, a list of destinations and room numbers, and a small American flag. The tags were tied to the luggage with white strings. Mahmoud untied a tag labeled "Mr. Goff: Brussels, Kabul, Baghdad, London" and tied it to his backpack.

He opened the top zipper. His heart pounding now, he removed several books to reveal a metal box and reached down its side to feel for the switch. He flipped it. A red light flashed once. He put the books back in, closed the backpack, put it behind the other bags, and turned to leave. He had been in the room less than a minute.

As he left, one of the men across the hall saw him. "Hey," said the man, "Where's that other guy?"

"Went home sick," replied Mahmoud, "Can I help you, sir?"

"No, it's okay." And the man went back to his work.

Mahmoud went to the public men's room on the main floor, where he stashed the bellboy's tunic in the trash bin. He went out on the far side of the hotel, toward the park, and hailed a taxi. Within seconds he was lost in the traffic, on the first leg of a trip that would crisscross London via taxi, bus, and train before it took him back to the safe house.

Mission accomplished.

As the afternoon wore on, civilian officials, military officers, and the journalists who were traveling with them dropped their luggage in Room 626 to be sent ahead to the plane while they finished their work. Nearly everyone had an extra laptop in one of their bags. Many had other equipment—codecs, recorders, mixers, modems. By evening, when the security team came to take the bags to the plane, they were overflowing into the corridor.

Mahmoud's bag, with its metal box and tangle of wires, would have drawn attention at any normal airport security checkpoint. But it would not stand out among these bags packed with electronics that belonged to known, vetted, and trusted holders of delegation credentials.

At midnight, a police escort led the way as the delegation's motorcade rolled through a misty drizzle into Northolt Royal Air Force Base, forty-five minutes west of London. Its plane was already loaded and ready for the overnight flight to Washington. The aircraft was an impressive-looking, but aging, Boeing 747 configured for government use, white with a wide blue stripe along its fuselage, an American flag painted on its tail, and UNITED STATES OF AMERICA emblazoned on its sides.

A small, shivering team of British officials lined up on the tarmac to offer farewell handshakes and small gifts of English tea. The tired delegation members and their press corps managed weak smiles and quick thank-yous before dragging themselves up the stairs onto the plane for the last time this trip.

After takeoff, some tried to go to sleep in their seats or grabbed some floor space to lie down. Others worked on their laptops and shared the few Internet access cables. In keeping with tradition on the final leg, the boss's favorite beer was served, with pretzels.

Three hours later, when the explosion ripped the plane apart, most of the passengers were sleeping, including the secretary of defense.

CHAPTER 2

Bridget woke up with a start, as she always did, a legacy of her combat tours. The clock read 0428, two minutes before the alarm setting. She reached for Will but he wasn't there. Then she heard the water running in the bathroom.

As soon as she moved, her cat Sarge started crying for his breakfast. She got out of bed and slipped into the oversized white T-shirt that lay in a heap on the floor.

Even in that, she looked pretty good. At thirty-eight, she was five feet, six inches tall and had an athlete's body from running and exercise. Her skin was on the pasty white side, an occupational hazard. She didn't get much sun. But that only accentuated her pale blue eyes. Even her just-got-out-of-bed light brown hair somehow worked, frizzed out a bit, the ends dancing on her shoulders.

At the bathroom door she saw Will from behind, with a towel wrapped around his waist. He was shaving. She ran her fingers through her hair just as he noticed her in the mirror.

"Morning, kiddo," he said.

She smiled. "Hi." Her tone was noncommittal, which seemed about right. She gave him a peck on his shoulder blade as she squeezed by. The manly shaving cream smell gave her ideas, but she knew there wasn't time.

The toilet's small alcove provided a modicum of privacy. "Taxi at zero-five?" she asked, largely to cover the sound of her peeing.

"Right."

Bridget could see part of Will's chest reflected in the mirror. His muscles were highly toned after years of rigorous physical training, and she caught glimpses of his impressive arms as he shaved. His freshly clean, milk-chocolate skin enhanced the effect like a permanent tan.

Lieutenant Commander Will Jackson was a Navy SEAL. It was part of his job to stay in shape, and he did his job extremely well. In thirty minutes, a taxi would take him to Joint Base Andrews, east of Washington, D.C., where he would meet up with his team and depart for downrange training and deployment, probably to Afghanistan. Bridget was not allowed to know his destination, officially. But she had a pretty good idea. She did know this would be his fifth tour, and he would be gone about six months.

Bridget squeezed by again, making sure her breasts slid across his back. She wanted him to miss that.

"You have time for a cup, right?"

"Yeah, sure. Thanks."

Bridget moved toward the kitchen and struggled for something more to say. She couldn't ask where he was going. Same for "When will you be back?" "What's your plan?" and any other question she could think of.

It was a rare bit of awkwardness in their three-month relationship. They had kept it pretty casual. The occasional romantic interludes over dinners or walking along the C&O Canal in Georgetown had been natural, and no one made too big a deal about them.

They had both known this day would come.

Arriving in the kitchen, she went with the safe bet, raising her voice to be heard over the running water, "Supposed to be good weather for flying today." Gawd! The weather? So lame!

"More excellent information from the Defense Intelligence Agency!" he shouted back. "Of course," and she could hear that little smirk coming onto his face, "I'm not confirming that I'm flying, or to what destination, if any, or what the weather will be like there, if there is a 'there.'"

"Fucking navy!" Bridget yelled.

Will laughed, and nearly nicked himself on the last pass of the razor.

By the time Bridget delivered the coffee, Will was sitting on the bed in his boxers and T-shirt. He pulled up his second sock and stood to take the mug.

They were standing irresistibly close, and they kissed. It was intimate, but not passionate, and they had a one-arm-each embrace as they tried not to spill their coffees.

"Grrrrr."

"Yeah," he said. He took a sip and met her gaze. "I'll miss this."

"Don't get too mushy on me now, sailor."

"No, I mean the coffee. They serve us shit downrange."

"Asshole," she said, and she smacked him on one of those muscular arms.

"Yeah, but you knew that."

"Yes . . . I . . . did," she said, pausing a little between each word and separating from him. She went to brush her teeth.

He admired her body as she walked away. "Nice ass. Can I see it?"

"Not anymore," she said, but then it felt harsh.

When Bridget came out of the bathroom, Will was fully dressed in jeans, a gray cotton crew-neck sweater, and sand-colored combat boots. He was cinching the flap of his desert camouflage duffel bag.

"Aw, Will, this sucks," she said, letting her guard down for a change.

"Yeah, but like the man once said, 'I'll be back.' " His Schwarzenegger was not very good.

"I thought your travel plans were classified," she teased as she sidled up to him, still wearing just the T-shirt.

They kissed again, more deeply this time. Her hands explored his back, and his slid down to that ass he liked so much. She didn't mind. It was safe. They had made the boundaries clear, yet again, and the taxi was due any second.

His phone buzzed. There it was.

"Well," she broke the kiss and leaned back in his arms, "better not be late for your first day of school."

He chuckled.

"You think I'm cute, don't you?" she said.

"Nah." And there was that smirk. "The army always makes me laugh."

She pushed him away in mock anger. He shouldered his duffel and picked up a small backpack. He took a final look around to be sure he had all his things.

Will gave Bridget a resigned smile. She moved aside so he could pass, and followed him to the apartment door. He opened it and turned back to face her. "See ya, kiddo," he said.

She gave him one more kiss, and a hug that said, "Yeah, see me again, will ya?" As he backed through the doorway, she said, "Stay safe out there."

"Yes, ma'am," he answered, and he flashed her a salute. One more smile and he turned for the stairway and was gone.

Bridget listened to his footsteps as he went down the stairs. She heard the outside door slam. And she waited until she heard the taxi pull away. Only then did she go back inside.

Leaning against the door, she let out a long sigh. She allowed herself just that moment.

Then she went back into the bedroom, dressed quickly in her workout clothes, grabbed her oversized work purse and prepacked garment bag, and headed for the gym.

Her martial arts instructor was going to have a rough morning.

Bridget put her bags in a locker in the women's dressing room and walked through into the Pentagon Officers' Athletic Club at 0530. It was not a quiet time there. More than half the aerobics machines were already being used by soldiers, sailors, airmen, marines, and Defense Department civilians, many of them wearing

T-shirts with service colors and slogans like "America's Air Force, No One Comes Close" and "Pain is the Weakness Leaving Your Body."

The free-weight area was also getting crowded, with already-muscular men working on their upper bodies and legs. There were a few intrepid women as well.

The gym was functional, not fancy, but the locker room décor hearkened back to an era of wood grain and white-shirted stewards. TV sets hung from the ceiling, tuned to news and sports channels.

Bridget found Jack flirting with the receptionist. "Ready?" she said, without the usual "good mornings" and "howya doings."

"Sure," he said, looking surprised by her abruptness.

She took off for her warm-up run on the track around the perimeter of the gym, leaving Jack sprinting to catch up.

"What's with you this morning?"

"Nothing, just want to get started," she lied and picked up the pace.

"Right," Jack said, falling behind and clearly not be-lieving her.

After a few laps, they went into a side room where mats covered most of the floor. This room also had a TV, but the sound was off.

"Okay," Jack said, "Let's start easy."

He assumed a defensive stance and Bridget attacked him. They fought for a few seconds and separated, then went again.

After three rounds, Jack said, "Take a break."

"I don't want a break."

"Take one anyway," he ordered, rubbing his left shoulder and breathing hard.

Bridget could tell Jack was dying to find out what was up. But he wouldn't. The wall around her made that impossible for all but a very few. That's the way it had to be for an attractive woman in a building where twenty-five thousand men worked.

Thirty seconds later, she said, "Come on," and they were at it again.

She threw Jack to the floor hard, and he raised a hand for her to stop. "Working out some anger, are we?"

"Sorry, Jack," she said, avoiding the question. She offered him a hand and he stood.

"So, what's up?"

"Nothing."

"Right," he said in a tone that made clear she was not fooling him.

Standing near the middle of the room, Bridget could see the TV over Jack's shoulder. A "Breaking News" banner came onto the screen, and then a shot of the White House press room, with the presidential seal hanging on the lectern. The seal only appeared when the president himself was going to speak.

"What the . . . ," Bridget said.

"Huh?" Jack said turning to see what she was looking at.

She jogged the few steps to the TV and turned up the volume, just as President Andrew Martelli walked into the frame.

He was tall and thin, and seemed to be moving in slow motion. His suit was impeccable, his tie was perfect, and his gray hair was all in place. But his face foretold what he was about to say.

"My fellow Americans," he began. Then he stopped, as if he hoped he wouldn't have to go on. But he did.

"I have very tragic news to share with you this morning. It is my sad duty to tell you that the plane carrying my good friend and our secretary of defense, Roderick Bates, is missing. Its last contact was over the North Atlantic, and I must tell you that all our technology and all our experts lead us to believe that it exploded in midair."

Bridget felt as if all the blood had been drained from her body. She involuntarily grabbed Jack's arm.

"This is a great loss for our country. Rod was a wise adviser and a great leader of our Defense Department. I knew him for more than thirty years. Rod's wife Cathy was also on board, a wonderful woman and a great champion of our military families. And we lost dozens of our military personnel, civilian officials, and members of the press.

"We do not yet know the cause of the explosion. But if this was an act of terrorism, our enemies can be assured that our response will be swift and strong. We will provide more information as soon as we can. For now, I ask you all to pray for Rod, Cathy, and the others, and their families. This is a time for America to come together, as the great nation that we are."

Bridget did not hear that last part. She was already sprinting for the locker room.

By the time Bridget came through the double set of steel doors into the shared DIA workspace at 0615,

Tommy was already there, abusing his keyboard. It seemed like he had been born there, but in fact he had been working at the Defense Intelligence Agency only twelve years, after retiring from the army at age forty-five as a master sergeant. He was twenty pounds overweight and balding with a bad comb-over. And that morning, he looked particularly terrible. He was sweating, his broad face was flushed, his shirttail was untucked, and he was using his stubby index fingers like hammers.

Bridget had known Tommy O'Regan for fifteen years, since he had been the top sergeant in the first platoon she commanded. He was the one who had really taught her how to be a soldier and a leader, and years later he had convinced her to come to the agency after grad school. Bridget was his junior by nearly twenty years, but also once again his boss. He was the hard-bitten old softie uncle she had never had. But at that moment, she was a little bit afraid to approach him.

"Hi," she tried, from a safe distance.

"Fuck, fuck, fuck, fuck, fuck!" he said, hitting a key with every word. That was unusual. Tommy was much more likely to say "heck" or "darn" than anything stronger.

"Tough morning, I know," she said, trying to lower the temperature. Bridget needed him to calm down. There was a lot of work to do, and she thought he might give himself a heart attack.

"'Tough' doesn't nearly cover it! I knew most of the people on that plane. So did you! Those bastards!" Tommy stopped, then continued in a lower voice, "Those fucking bastards." He looked as if he might cry, but it passed. "We gotta hit 'em back, and hard."

"Absolutely. Let's dust off some old options and

when the rest of the team gets here we'll brainstorm some new ones."

"Sure, okay. Fucking bastards!" And he returned to the abuse of his keyboard.

Bridget went into her office and booted up her computer. She rated a decent-sized office for the Pentagon, which meant something more than a cubicle. She even had a small round table with four chairs. But she didn't have a window. No one did in the second basement.

This was the DIA's Operations Directorate, and Bridget was chief of the Central Asia Division. She supervised a staff of intelligence analysts, what the press called "dot connectors." They collected, categorized, collated, and prioritized the mountain of factoids and alleged factoids that came in from troops and agents in the field, from wiretaps and Internet monitoring, and from other intelligence agencies, U.S. and foreign. It was Bridget's job to determine whether their analysis was right, and to conceive, plan, and run clandestine operations to act on the information and generate more dots.

She and her team were among the people who should have prevented the attack on the secretary's plane, should have noticed some change in the patterns of terrorist communications, some movement of the key players they tracked worldwide. But they hadn't. Worse yet, that wasn't unusual. The terror groups had gotten too good at covering their tracks—using throwaway cell phones, satellite phones, and other evasive techniques, leaving fewer patterns to notice.

Bridget had arrived at DIA three years earlier via West Point and nine years of active duty as an intelligence officer, including two tours in Afghanistan. It was there that she became disillusioned. From her vantage point, she could see they were chest-deep in shit and the tide was against them. It hadn't been an easy decision to leave the army, but she told herself she would find another way to serve.

So, having more than fulfilled her commitment, Captain Bridget Davenport, holder of two combat badges, numerous commendations, and an impressive array of ribbons on her uniform, resigned her commission and enrolled in Georgetown's national security program.

Four years later, she was Bridget Davenport, Ph.D., author of *Impediments to Counterinsurgency: Cross-Cultural Perceptions of Religion and Democracy in Afghanistan and Their Impact on U.S. National Security Strategy.*

She counted it as four years, three apartments, two boyfriends, and one cat. By graduation, only the cat remained. Grad school had not changed her relationship pattern, nor her desire to serve, but it had given her some distance from the frustration. She rejected breathless entreaties from corporations and consulting firms, taking Tommy's advice instead, and went right back to work for the Pentagon.

Bridget logged on to the classified network and accessed the aircraft manifest. Of course she had known people on the plane. Christ, she could have been on it! She hadn't volunteered only because the trip ran through Will's final days in town. Bob Jenkins had taken the DIA seat. Oh my God! Bob! He had two little kids! Or was it three now? Jesus!

Bridget felt a chill, and beads of sweat formed on her forehead. She didn't like it when her emotions got out of control. She closed the manifest and got up to hang her suit jacket on a wall hook.

Even on this terrible day, she had The Look.

The Look was essential for any woman hoping to make it in the defense establishment. Today, it was a white silk blouse open not quite enough to show cleavage, and a knee-length, gray, pinstriped skirt that rode up almost to mini length when she sat down. Her high-but-not-too-high heels completed The Look.

She might as well have worn a sign: "Formidable Executive. Notice Me, But Don't Mess with Me Just Because I'm a Woman in a Man's World."

Bridget caught her reflection in the glass of the desktop frame that held a picture of her parents. "Not bad," she said to herself. Then she realized that's what Will would have said, but in a dismissive way to make her smile. Now it did the opposite. She'd be going home to Sarge and no one else, and coming back to her job in the bureaucracy tomorrow. Will was living the life she had left behind—exciting, exotic, stimulating, but also dangerous and sometimes almost impossibly difficult.

As Bridget sat back down, her classified email lit up. U.S. government intelligence services had picked up a claim of responsibility for the plane bombing. The translation was preliminary. The authenticity had not been confirmed. But chances were, it would prove out.

In the name of Allah, brave fighters of the jihad
have delivered justice to the murderer Bates and
his evil cohort. They have crippled the Infidel
war machine that seeks to destroy the true Faith,
and struck a great blow for Allah. We call on the

Infidels to withdraw from the Holy Lands or
they will face more of Allah's wrath.

It was signed by Ibn Jihad, "Son of the Holy War,"
the shadowy terrorist leader who had united the commands of the Taliban and al-Qaida. U.S. intelligence
said he was somewhere in eastern Afghanistan, moving
almost nightly to evade efforts to find him.

She thought about Will. He might be heading to that
same area. He could already be in the air. Helluva day
to deploy.

Around 0700, Tommy knocked on Bridget's door. He
had tucked in his shirt and looked as if he had washed
his face. Overall, he was much more like himself.

"Come in."

"Hi. Sorry about earlier."

"No problem. We're all upset."

"Thanks. Listen, I got something for you to look at."
He held out a file marked "Classified: Top Secret."

"What's this?"

"It's Sandblast. Got rejected a long time ago, before
you came on board. I'm thinking maybe now . . . ."

"Okay, thanks," she said, taking the file. "Tommy, do
you think this was the MTO?" MTO—Pentagon-speak
for major terrorist operation. The intel community had
been getting indications one might be in the works for
months.

"Hard to say for sure. It'll take a while to figure
that out."

"I know. Just looking for your best guess."

"My guess is no. I think they're looking to target

civilians, probably multiple locations. That's what the Israelis' source said."

"But now he's gone."

"Disappeared. Lends credibility to his story."

"But not confirmation."

"Correct. But Mossad's info is usually solid. And we know jihadi chatter is up. Hitting the plane would have been a close-hold operation. But multiple targets would require some coordination, and a jump in intercepts, like we're getting."

Tommy pointed to a scattergram on Bridget's desk. The classified page had clusters of dots divided into quadrants indicating time and geographic area. Each dot represented the intercept of a phone call or email among suspected terrorists.

"Wish we knew what it all meant," Bridget said.

"Me, too. Thousands of calls, a dozen languages, and the key conversations coded."

"Yeah. Well, thanks, Tommy. I'll have a look at this file. And leave the door open, will ya?"

He did. But the usual noise of the office didn't filter in. Most of the staff had arrived, and people were busy. But there was none of the buzz, none of the banter about military services or sports teams. No one was even lingering by the coffee machine. The Pentagon was a house of mourning.

Once Bridget started reading the Sandblast file, she couldn't stop. In fact, it had been rejected twice as too dangerous and too much of an escalation. But Tommy was right. Now, it might fly. It might be exactly the counter-strike everyone was looking for.

Who came up with this? Did they have someone who could do it? Would he agree to take it on? What would his chances be?

There were lots of questions, lots of reasons not to do it. But Bridget liked the boldness, the shoot-for-the-top audacity, the high reward that might come with the high risk.

But it was easy for her to like it. She wasn't the one who would have to do it. She was, in fact, the one who would have to find the guy to do it.

CHAPTER 3

At the army training ground in the California desert, the newly formed platoons and their lieutenants were practicing combat tactics. They would deploy to Afghanistan in a few months, carrying the proud banner of the 101st Airborne Division, the Screaming Eagles.

The visiting major surveyed the scene from an observation deck. A captain handed him a pair of binoculars and pointed toward a group of men taking cover in some bushes to their left. "Peters and Abdallah are in that unit, sir. Dombrowski is farther out, behind the trees."

The major tried to pick out the men he was there for, but at this distance it was difficult. "Send them to see me as soon as they're finished," he said. He handed back the field glasses and left.

When they came to his borrowed office a few hours later, still dusty from the field, the major didn't introduce himself. "Men, you've been selected for some specialized training. I can't tell you much about it, but you leave tonight for the east coast. Tell your parents, wives, girlfriends, whatever that you'll be out of touch for six to eight weeks. Tell them it's classified, blah, blah, blah."

In military-speak, they'd been "voluntold." Any of

them could have declined, but the option was never exactly presented. They had been chosen, and they would be doing this now. The major could see their confusion. "Listen, this is an honor. We picked you three out of the whole brigade. And don't worry, you'll be back before it deploys. We need you men for this, so go pack your gear, make your calls, send your emails. Be back here at 2300."

"Yes, sir," they said, and they went to do as they had been told.

The major was not there when they returned for their flight, and they were the only passengers on the small military transport plane, aside from the crew and a security detail.

The three young lieutenants went through a battery of physical and mental tests at Fort Meade, Maryland. They had their skills, loyalty, and leadership tested. A week later, they were split up, and Lieutenant Faraz Abdallah sat through several lengthy interviews, during which he revealed everything the instructors asked for.

He also went through two endurance tests, and had an extensive physical. He heard one of the doctors say, "No tattoos. Good."

Faraz wondered how the others were doing. He didn't know they had been sent back to California, having unwittingly played their parts in a performance meant only for him.

At the end of the process, the trainers sent Faraz out on a seventy-two-hour field-survival exercise. When it was over, a rescue team picked him up where he had collapsed on the bank of a small creek and took him to the base clinic. He was exhausted and dehydrated, completely broken down physically and mentally, and he had a variety of cuts and bruises. But he had passed the test.

At the clinic, they let him take a shower, eat a light meal, and go to sleep in the first real bed he had seen in weeks. He had no idea what was going on. He was just glad it was over, and too tired to notice he was the only patient in the clinic.

The next morning, after a good breakfast, the staff gave him one of his uniforms, freshly cleaned and pressed, and led him to a small room that had all the charm of a police interrogation cell. In the middle, there was a square, gray steel table with two matching chairs. The major he'd seen in California sat in one of them.

The major stood, smiled, and offered his hand across the table. "Lieutenant Abdallah, how are you?"

"Better now, sir," Faraz responded.

The major was short and trim, with a shaved head and bright white teeth. His bony fingers delivered a strong handshake. He invited Faraz to sit, but still did not introduce himself, and there was no name tag on his uniform. Faraz noticed what he assumed was a two-way mirror, covering nearly the full width of the far wall.

"Congratulations," began the major. "You made it. I'm about to offer you entry into one of the military's most elite units. But you have to want it. You have to agree to take on one of the toughest missions we have."

"I joined the army for tough missions, sir," Faraz replied.

"Not like this one."

* * *

As the major began to explain, the team behind the mirror attempted to size up Faraz. They were a Special Operations officer, a CIA official, a psychologist, and a psychiatrist. But it was the woman from the Defense Intelligence Agency taking copious notes who would ultimately decide whether this young lieutenant she had found in the army database was up to the task.

Bridget had hoped for someone with more experience—a couple of combat tours and an intel background would have been ideal. But that person didn't seem to exist, not with the other requirements. The more seasoned men who fit the key profile characteristics were too old, had kids, or were desk jockeys. And contradictory as it might seem, the ops people had convinced her they needed someone who had never been to Afghanistan, so there would be no chance he would be recognized.

Still, this guy was about as green as they came. He had combat training but no deployments. From her perspective, he'd been a soldier for about fifteen minutes. And here she was considering sending him on a mission that could turn the tide of the war or cost him his life, or both.

She consoled herself that the shrinks concluded there was a decent chance he could handle the stress. He had been near the top of his ROTC class at UCLA and received outstanding evaluations from his army training. He was smart, motivated, had excellent leadership skills, and passed all the physical and psych tests with flying colors.

But now, all of that meant almost nothing. For this mission, his primary qualifications were that he was a young, unattached ethnic Afghan, and spoke fluent Pashto, the language of Afghanistan's large Pashtun community, which dominated the Taliban.

If he accepted, and if he succeeded—and those were both big "ifs"—this might turn out to be the most significant mission of the war. That's why Bridget had fought so hard in the weeks after the plane bombing to get it launched, over her boss's objections. General Hadley thought it was too dangerous and had too little chance of success. He only relented after the scattergrams showed another increase in jihadist chatter, and word came from the White House that the normally taciturn president was near apoplectic, demanding more solid intel on the mystery MTO and anything else out there.

As soon as Hadley sent Sandblast forward, it captured the imagination of folks all the way up the line, as Tommy had predicted. Bridget got her green light, and started the process that had found Faraz.

She had to admit Hadley wasn't completely wrong, though. This was likely the most difficult and dangerous assignment any soldier had been asked to take on in a long time.

And that was saying something.

Faraz had difficulty believing what the major told him. He didn't know how to feel about it or how to respond. The major sent him back to his clinic room to consider his options.

"Take your time," he said in a magnanimous tone. "Take a day, two if you need it. And remember, all this is classified up the wazoo."

"Yes, sir. Thank you, sir." Faraz rose, shook the man's hand and was led back to his room.

There was little need for that last reminder. A plan like this would be known only to a handful of people. And who was he going to tell, anyway? He saw only the clinic staff, and he had no phone or other way to communicate with the outside world.

Sitting on his bed, it was difficult for Faraz to get his head around what the major had asked him to do. A big part of him wanted to say yes. But this? God, not this!

"We want you to join the Taliban," the major had said.

Faraz thought he should have figured that out. He had expected to use his language skills in Afghanistan, but this was a bit more to the point than he had anticipated.

"We need intel on any MTO," the major had continued. "And we want to hit Ibn Jihad."

The hairs on Faraz's arms had stood up. That was the heart of it, a direct response to the killing of the U.S. defense secretary. And they wanted him to make it happen.

Ibn Jihad was an Afghan, with ambitions that ranged far beyond the Taliban's original goals for Afghanistan. He saw his country as the vanguard of a global jihad, and he was using the worldwide reach of al-Qaida and the combat experience of the Taliban to launch a new offensive in Afghanistan and a series of attacks on targets in the West.

In addition to the bombing of Secretary Bates's plane, U.S. intelligence had linked Ibn Jihad to an attack at the Eurotunnel terminal in France and nearly a dozen other operations. And he was only getting started. The acronym-crazed and foreign-name-averse U.S. military called him "IJ."

The plan the major laid out was simple, really. All good plans were, went the cliché.

Faraz would be inserted into Afghanistan, walk out of a remote area looking for work, attend a few mosques, get noticed by a Taliban recruiter, and allow himself to be sucked into their world. A tribal leader in a small village near his insertion point, newly on the Pentagon payroll, would vouch for his cover story—poor family, parents dead, he and his brothers and sisters farmed out to relatives in a refugee camp in Pakistan.

If he could convincingly avoid becoming a suicide bomber, maybe, eventually, Faraz could get some high-value information.

In the meantime, he would not risk making any contact with his handlers. No reports. No check-ins. No high-tech comms gear. He would be on his own for months, maybe years. He could use the contact protocol for only three purposes—to call in a strike on Ibn Jihad, to provide solid info about an imminent MTO, or to request emergency extraction. That last was not guaranteed.

It would be a difficult and dangerous life. Faraz would live like a poor Afghan, eating little, sleeping in the dirt, allowed no contact with his former life. He would have to participate in terrorist activities, maybe even kill people, all in the service of a greater good.

But that was not the worst part. That was not close to being the worst part. The worst part was that Lieutenant Faraz Mohammed Abdallah of San Diego, California, would have to die first.

* * *

Faraz had always done everything the army had asked him to do. That included the call he had made to his parents two weeks earlier, as the major had instructed. He told them he'd been selected for a special secret training program, and wouldn't be able to call or write for several weeks. He had told his mother not to worry, but he knew she would. His father, on the extension in the bedroom, had wished him well, sounding overwhelmed with pride, and told him he loved him.

Faraz couldn't remember the last time his father had done that. Was that the last time he would ever speak to them? No. No way!

Amir and Faiza Abdallah fled Afghanistan in the early 1980s, during the Soviet occupation, and built a new life in San Diego. Amir's Ph.D. in agricultural engineering from Kabul University was no good in the United States, so he had taken a job driving a truck for a seed company, and spent time talking to the farmers on his route. After a few years, he started a small seed company of his own. Faiza volunteered at the Islamic Center and taught Pashto to refugees' children.

The couple raised their American-born son to honor his native culture. They spoke Pashto to him and sent him to Koran classes, where he learned some Arabic. They also taught him to love the country that had saved his parents and had given him a life they had only ever dreamed of.

Faraz had always wanted to be a soldier. He never went through the fireman phase or the bus driver phase or any other phase. Someone gave him a set of toy soldiers when he was very young, and he played with them constantly.

Then there was Johnny.

His cousin was five years older than Faraz and was his friend and mentor. Faraz remembered the day Johnny came to visit after he finished basic training, his uniform pressed, the buttons shiny, his shoes buffed to a high polish. For young Faraz, it was as if the President of the United States himself had come into their humble home and bent down to give him a hug.

Johnny's mother was Faraz's mother's sister. Her American husband had insisted on giving their son an American name, the better to help him fit in. So, he was Johnny Jones. You couldn't get much more American than that.

Johnny stood out in the family, lighter skinned and taller than anyone else, and more easygoing and self-confident, no doubt the influence of his father. And he had taken a special liking to his younger cousin from the beginning, volunteering to babysit and to take the boy to movies, playgrounds, and the zoo. In later years, he shared the joy of fixing cars, more than once getting into trouble for the grease Faraz brought home on his clothes. Johnny and his dad even took Faraz to his first major-league baseball game, to see their beloved Padres.

Johnny taught Faraz big-boy slang and swear words, and shared wisdom about all things. One day, after much begging and on a promise of absolute secrecy, he taught the boy how to ride a motorcycle.

"It's golden!" Johnny would say whenever things turned out right, or when he thought he had figured out what was wrong with a car. When he told Faraz how the girl he had his eye on said "Yes" when he asked her to the prom, he said, "Aw, little man, it was golden! You shoulda been there!"

And when Johnny told Faraz he was joining the army,

he said, "It's golden, little man. Get in shape, serve the country, get free college. Golden." And he had flashed his big smile.

Whenever things went right for young Faraz, he said they were "golden," too.

His mother could not have any more children, which even at an early age Faraz understood was a heartache. So, Johnny was his parents' surrogate second son, the brother Faraz could never have.

In the privacy of his room at the clinic, Faraz tried to focus on that day Johnny came to visit—the uniform jacket he let Faraz try on, the walk they took to the local park, where everyone made a fuss over the young soldier. It had been spring 2001. Johnny was on leave before his first deployment to a base in Germany. He was not quite nineteen.

Faraz could picture the meal his mother had prepared that day—Kabuli pulao, a mountain of seasoned rice stuffed with lamb chunks, almonds, and raisins. It was Johnny's favorite, and therefore it was Faraz's favorite, too.

"I want to be a soldier, too," Faraz had gushed over dinner.

"You'd be a great soldier, little man," Johnny had replied. "But you gotta study hard first." He had the big smile on.

"Oh, there are many things you could be when you grow up," Faraz's mother had quickly added.

"Many things," his father echoed.

After dinner, there were hugs all around.

"Be well," said Faiza.

"Stay safe," said Amir.

"Next time, bring your gun!" said young Faraz.

"Well," Johnny had said. "I'm not sure I can do that, but here, try this on."

Johnny took the black beret from his belt and put it on the boy's head. It was oversized, but Johnny made it work, and tilted it to the right angle. Faraz held it with both hands and ran to a mirror.

He saw the stylish curve of the material, the black patch in the front with Johnny's unit insignia, a screaming eagle, in the middle of it, under the word "Airborne." He caressed the soft material, then ran back into the living room beaming.

"Wow, Johnny. This is the coolest thing ever!"

"Keep it, little man. Take good care of it while I'm gone."

"Really?"

"Sure."

Faraz threw his arms around his cousin. "Thanks, man! Really, thanks!"

"Johnny, you can't give that to him," said Faraz's mother.

"Don't worry, Aunt Faiza. I can get another one. I want him to have it."

"You will spoil the boy," said Faraz's father.

"Aw, we did that years ago, didn't we, Uncle Amir?" They all laughed.

"All right, gotta go." Johnny hugged his aunt and uncle, then held out his right hand for a low five, which Faraz delivered with all his might, even as he held the beret in place with his free hand.

Then Johnny turned and left, crossing the front porch and making a neat series of taps as his hard soles hit each wooden step on the way down to the walkway. He got into his father's Ford and paused to wave and flash one more smile at the family gathered on the porch before he pulled away.

But it was impossible for Faraz not to think about another day, less than a year later, the day he came home from school to find his mother crying on the sofa.

"Why, *mohr*? What's wrong?"

Faiza didn't seem to know how to tell the boy. "Wait for your father to come home," she said. But he had gotten it out of her, and he joined her in heaving sobs on the sofa.

Johnny had been in one of the first units sent to Afghanistan after 9-11, and he had been among the first to die. It was a firefight with the Taliban. He had fought bravely, they were told.

Faraz thought about Johnny's flag-draped coffin at the mosque, about the large crowd, most of them not Muslims. He remembered the speeches by men in uniforms just like Johnny's saying what a fine young man he had been, how everyone who knew him liked and respected him, that his family should be proud. They called Johnny a hero, an American hero.

And Faraz remembered the tears—his mother's, his aunt's, his own.

Later, at the house, they let him hold the folded flag while the other kids came over to touch it. One of the soldiers told him to be careful not to drop it. That was hardly necessary, but he hugged it more tightly all the same.

It had taken a long time to get back to normal after Johnny died. Faraz's mother wore black for a year. His aunt wore it for the rest of her life. As a boy of fourteen, Faraz returned to normal activities—school, homework, sports—but he held a sadness inside that made him feel older, more serious.

Now, whenever anyone asked what he wanted to be when he grew up, he said, "Soldier, for sure," and he meant it.

Much as his parents tried to dissuade him over the years, they could not overcome Faraz's feeling that the best way, the only way, to honor Johnny was to volunteer.

His parents' only success was to convince him to go to college first. So Faraz volunteered for ROTC and for every bit of additional training and every difficult assignment that came along.

And now this.

He wasn't sure he could do it. Everything he had believed and everything he had become over the nine years since Johnny died pushed him to do it. But another part of him, a deeper part, told him he could not.

The last thing he ever wanted was for his parents to have to endure again what they had experienced when Johnny died. Of course, he knew he could be killed in combat, like Johnny was. But he couldn't accept lying to his parents, putting them through the worst thing that could ever happen to them, if it wasn't true.

Faraz wanted to take on this mission, to do whatever the army needed him to do. He had never imagined it could ask too much of him. But this might be the "too much" he had never imagined.

For two days, Faraz turned it over and over in his mind, but it always came out the same. He pretended he had said "No" to the major, and that felt terrible. The very idea of declining an assignment was a huge weight, particularly when he realized there was probably no one else who could do it, and when it was clearly so important.

Then he pretended he had said "Yes," and that felt worse. That weight he could not bear.

When Faraz went back to see the major, he couldn't meet his eyes. He felt awful and looked about as bad. As soon as he walked into the room, the major and all the people behind the mirror knew what he would say.

"Sir, I want this mission. I was made for this mission. But, I'm sorry, sir, I can't let my family think I'm dead. I can't do that to them. I think if I did . . . I don't know, sir . . . I couldn't live with myself."

"I understand, Lieutenant. Would you like some more time?"

Faraz paused. But now that he'd said the words, he was even more sure of his decision.

"No thank you, sir," he said. His voice was barely audible.

CHAPTER 4

Behind the mirror, there was an enormous letdown. They adjourned to a secure conference room to talk about it, and the major joined them.

"Maybe the mission can be designed so we don't have to fake his death," said the psychologist.

"No, too risky," said the major.

"Agreed," said Mary Larson, Bridget's counterpart from the CIA. She was Bridget's age, but more buttoned-down and by the book. Her version of The Look was wool pants and a high-collared sweater, with her black hair close-cropped.

At the head of the table, Bridget sighed. The grand plan was falling apart before it could even get started. "I'll talk to him," she said.

"No," Larson said. "Out of the question. We can't break protocol and then go forward. Let it go. We have other scenarios." They all knew she was right, and also that the other scenarios were not nearly as good.

"I'm going to meet with him," Bridget insisted.

"No!"

"Listen, Mary, my party, my rules."

"Miss Davenport, this is way off the reservation,"

said the major. "You endanger yourself and him. I urge you not to do it."

"I'm doing it." Bridget was not a big rule breaker, but she hadn't come this far only to take a "no" from Faraz without a fight.

"Come up with a cover ID for me," she said to the group. "Keep him here until tomorrow. We'll talk strategy at 0800 and I'll meet with him at 09."

"Bridget, you really need to think about this," Larson said.

"I already did," she shot back. And she left the room before they could try again to talk her out of it.

Bridget headed for the base hotel. She was confident that sending Faraz on this mission was the right thing to do. It might be their best shot at an equivalent response to the plane bombing, with the added possibility of stopping an MTO. But she wondered whether she would do it, whether she would allow the army to tell her parents she was dead.

She also knew that even if Faraz succeeded in the training, it was impossible to say what his chances were of accomplishing the mission. Conceivably, no one could.

The question was whether he had a chance in hell.

He seemed earnest enough. He met the basic criteria. But this could easily be a suicide mission, successful or not, and she had to admit she was not particularly comfortable with that.

Bridget met Faraz in the same secure room where he had seen the major. The team behind the two-way mirror was ready. He stood when she came in.

"Good morning, Lieutenant," she said, trying to sound upbeat and holding out her hand. "I'm Kylie Walinsky from human resources."

Faraz shook her hand. "Good morning, ma'am."

More than three million people worked for the Defense Department, including civilians, troops, and contractors. A database search revealed there was no Kylie Walinsky among them, no real person for him to give up, if it came to that.

But offering a name made her a friendlier and more sympathetic character than the major had been. Being an attractive woman didn't hurt, either. She looked him straight in the eye and smiled like they were old friends.

"Please sit."

"Thank you, ma'am. How can I help you?"

"I understand we need to get you back into your training course. How was that going?" Bridget wanted to get him talking, get him comfortable.

"It's good, ma'am."

"It was a bear when I took it," she said.

Faraz was impressed. "You're army?"

"Yes. Nine years, two tours downrange. So, how's it going?"

Faraz smiled. "It's a bear, ma'am." Bridget smiled, too.

She asked him about some aspects of the training, and gave him a few tips.

"Thank you, ma'am," he said again.

Bridget hesitated, creating a brief awkward silence. She looked down at the table.

"Ma'am?"

She looked up. "Faraz, I'm not from human resources."

"Oh?"

"I was behind the mirror when you met with the major."

Faraz sat up straight. His eyes widened. The stress of what he'd been asked to do and what he'd decided slammed back into him.

Bridget let it sink in, let him remember what he had tried to forget. She looked directly at him. Now, it was Faraz who looked down.

"Ma'am, I explained all that to the major."

"I know. I want to discuss it with you again."

Faraz looked up at her. "Ma'am, I really want to do that mission." He paused and looked down again. "But I can't."

"I understand. It's asking a lot. I don't know if I could do it, either." That was true, but she also needed him to think of her as someone a lot like himself.

"Ma'am, is there any way to do it without saying I died?"

"Sadly, no. It's too dangerous   too dangerous for you and for your family."

Faraz sighed, but this time he looked at her and spoke with confidence. "I'm sorry, ma'am."

That sounded definitive. Bridget had to find a way to keep the conversation going so she could look for some sort of opening. "Tell me your concerns, specifically," she said.

"It's not fair to my parents," he said. "I'm their only child. We're very close. I can't put them through that again."

"Again?"

"Yes, ma'am. When my cousin Johnny died, it nearly destroyed my mother. He was one of the first in Afghanistan in '02."

"Oh, Faraz, I'm so sorry to hear that." Her sympathy was genuine, as was her surprise. How could the team have missed that? "You were just a boy."

"Yes, ma'am. He was my idol. He used to spend a lot of time with me. When he was killed, it was really hard for me . . . much worse for my parents, especially my mother. Johnny was the reason I wanted to be a soldier. But as I got older, memories of the day he died almost kept me out. I never wanted to put them through that again. And I can't do it if it isn't true. I'm sorry, ma'am, I just can't."

"I understand." Bridget had to regroup. "This would be hard for anyone, but I can see how it's especially hard for you."

"Yes, ma'am. Thank you, ma'am."

Bridget thought she might have to excuse herself to consult with the team. Then she saw her opening.

"Faraz . . ." She paused, not sure how to say it, not sure whether she should.

"Go ahead, ma'am."

"I hate to ask you this, but what do you think Johnny would have done?"

Behind the mirror, the team breathed a collective sigh of relief. Even Mary Larson was smiling.

Late that night, Faraz thought about Johnny again. He thought about his parents. He thought about the scenes of death and destruction he saw almost daily on television, people killed and maimed by crazy terrorists who were trying to retake control of his ancestral homeland, and would strike at America whenever they could.

He thought about himself, too, about what he wanted to do with his life. It suddenly seemed as though it had been a rough road to twenty-three. He'd always felt like he grew up quickly after Johnny died. Now, it seemed, maybe too quickly. He was so determined to fulfill his plan that it had been a long time since he'd examined it. And now that he had achieved some of his goals, he hadn't stopped to think about what came next.

He had wanted to be a soldier. He had achieved that. He asked to join Johnny's old unit, the 101st Airborne, and he'd done that. He requested combat duty, and soon he was to lead a platoon in Afghanistan.

But then what? Rise in the ranks, have a career, maybe make colonel someday? That'd be awesome. The little boy with the funny name would never have believed it. That boy who envied Johnny his American name, his fair skin, and his long legs. That boy who the white kids at school thought was black and the black kids thought was white. What do you mean you don't celebrate Christmas, and not Hanukkah, either? What's wrong with you?

Things changed for the worse on 9-11. After that, they all seemed to have figured out instantly what he was. Muslim! Terrorist! More than once he had gone home crying or sat outside the principal's office while his parents held hushed-tone meetings inside. He was not the only Muslim at the school, but still it felt like everyone was looking at him, hating him.

The situation at school improved after Johnny was killed. It was his cousin's final gift to him. Faraz went from suspect to hero overnight. But it wasn't until college that he really started to feel like a regular American, as if his ethnicity didn't matter. The feeling was even stronger in the army, where people seemed to care mainly about the sparkle of his rank insignia.

Now, they wanted him to go back to being the "different" boy, to embrace the dark skin and funny name, to use the language he had long resented having to learn. He was being asked to truly become Faraz, and then to put Faraz aside and become what the kids at school had said he was—and to stick a knife in his parents' backs at the same time. This was not part of his life's plan.

But this mission—this was something special, something unique, something only he could do. He could take the fight directly to the fucking assholes who ruined Afghanistan, enabled the bombing of the twin towers, forced the United States into war—the fucking assholes who killed his cousin. This could be one of those golden moments Johnny used to talk about.

But his parents . . .

Faraz was up nearly all night, then fell into a fitful sleep.

When the nurse woke him it was already 0800. He was embarrassed to have slept so late. But she told him not to worry. He still had an hour until his meeting.

In the shower and over breakfast, Faraz had the same conversation with himself he had been having for the last several days. Which would be worse, letting the army tell his parents he was dead or saying no to this mission?

His answer was shifting.

As he prepared for the meeting, he stared at himself in the mirror. He was of slight build, but muscular from his training. His face was narrow, and his nose stood out. He imagined himself in traditional Afghan clothes like the outfit he had had as a boy.

He could do this.

When the thought of his parents followed, he was now somehow better able to deal with it. He was talking himself into believing that his parents' sadness would fade over time, that they would get on with their lives, proud of their son, the hero.

He imagined asking Johnny for advice, and his cousin saying, "It's okay, little man. This is bigger than all of us. It's golden."

At 0900, Faraz had one question for Bridget. "Ma'am, if I do this, can I go home someday, come back from the dead?"

Bridget hesitated. The team had not discussed that. She had to make a call, had to say what he wanted to hear so that he would say what she wanted to hear.

"Yes," she said trying not to sound tentative. "It would be tricky, but we can find a way to make that happen."

Faraz took a deep breath and let it out. There are not so many junctures in life when a man has the ability to choose between two distinct paths, two destinies. These were his final few seconds holding that power. But he knew which way he was going to go. It felt awful, but it also felt right.

Looking straight at Bridget, he nodded. "All right, ma'am, I'll do it."

"Thank you, Faraz. This is an incredibly brave thing you're doing. You have my admiration."

"Thank you, ma'am."

CHAPTER 5

Faraz walked into the village in mid-morning. The simple buildings were the same color as the earth. People went about their daily tasks, leading donkey carts laden with goods, sweeping the entryways of their homes. Women covered head-to-toe in chadors labored over open fires.

The men eyed him closely as he passed. He nodded and smiled, offering the traditional greeting, *"Salaam alaikum."* Peace be upon you.

It was hot, mid-eighties with the sun still rising, and more humid than Afghanistan was supposed to be. Around the village, bushes gave way to a dense woodland of willows and southern pines. And there was a patch of brightly colored wildflowers, including Virginia creepers and black-eyed Susans.

In the middle of the village, three men approached and blocked his path.

"Who are you?" one demanded in Pashto.

"My name is Hamed, brother. I have just arrived from a camp in Pakistan. I have come to look for employment opportunities."

"No! No! No!" shouted the chief instructor from behind a donkey cart, also speaking Pashto. "Not 'employment opportunities.' 'Work!' You came to look for 'work!' Keep it simple. You just blew your cover and got yourself killed. Now try it again!"

This was the simulated Afghan village at the U.S. Army's Camp Shelby in southern Mississippi. The villagers were carefully vetted Afghan-Americans, who enacted a variety of scenarios to help train troops preparing for deployment. Right now, they were having a laugh at Faraz's expense, although they knew him only as Hamed.

After he accepted the mission, Faraz had made all the usual preparations for deployment, except reviewing his life insurance and death-notification information. The team didn't want him to face those forms and perhaps reconsider his decision. He'd filled them out when he went on active duty only a year earlier, anyway.

He surrendered his IDs, his bank-account information, and his credit cards. A technical team deleted all photos of him from the Internet. They even took away his name. Everyone involved in the training called him Hamed, so he would get used to it. He memorized his cover story and practiced providing correct details in response to casual questions asked at random. What was the name of your mother's village? How many goats did your father own? When did your grandfather die?

Faraz expected the training to be hard, but it wasn't. There was a lot of studying. There were one-on-one seminars about Afghan village life, farming, history and traditions, and about life in the refugee camps. The shrinks talked to him about guilt and motivation and being secure in who he was and what he was doing. They gave him a crash course in the psychology of covert operations.

He was on a diet and wasn't allowed to exercise much, except for some running. He shed muscle and grew a scraggly beard. He spent time in the sun, where his already-tan skin darkened. A dentist came three times to stain his teeth so they wouldn't have that American pearly whiteness. And he hiked the base's wooded areas in sandals, and sometimes barefoot, to beat up his feet.

Faraz reviewed a bit of Koran, but not too much. They didn't want to make him too smart for his cover story. He spoke only Pashto, and his tutors insisted that he speak simply and make grammatical mistakes, as a country boy would. He expanded his rural vocabulary and learned some countryside slang.

Now, he was midway through the second week of mission simulation. The trainers were constantly trying to trip him up, to get him to use the intellectual language his parents had taught him, to make mistakes in his cover story, to act like a foreigner in an Afghan village.

At first, he made many mistakes. But he was a quick study. Much of it came naturally as he drew on his boy-hood experiences speaking Pashto to older members of the Afghan community in San Diego and visiting the homes of people more traditional than his parents.

Whenever he did well entering the village, someone invited him to stay in their house. The role-playing continued into the evening and through the following day, with the lead instructor whispering behind the scenes to order more and more complex tests.

One day, someone new came to the village and denounced Faraz as an infidel spy. The villagers locked him in a goat shed overnight with no food or water. In the morning, they dragged him out, tied him to a tree, and lined up a firing squad.

Faraz begged for his life, and his pulse was thumping, even though he knew it was an exercise. When the "boom" came, he felt as if his heart stopped. Then they all had a good laugh about it until the order came to start again.

The trainers helped transform Faraz into what he might have been, save for a twist of fate and some fast action by his father thirty years earlier. He became a skinny but tough young Afghan, who spoke poorly and had little education, no money, and no prospects.

In short, he became prime fodder for a terrorist recruiter.

Two weeks later, Bridget drove her rented car north from the New Orleans airport, across the long bridge over Lake Pontchartrain and through marshy lowlands into Mississippi. The reports were good, but she wanted to check on Faraz's training, see his transformation for herself.

After convincing him to take the mission, Bridget had experienced some buyer's remorse. She was aware of the responsibility she bore. Operation Sandblast had become her baby. Her boss, General Hadley, had even been calling her "Sandblast" around the office. Her reputation was on the line, but there was more to it than that.

Bridget couldn't help but like Faraz. He reminded her of herself fifteen years earlier, maybe too much. He was young, driven, and eager to be challenged, like she had been. But also like her, maybe he was too driven, virtually possessed by some inner drive to serve, a compulsion to live up to something. For Faraz, it was pretty clearly his cousin's legacy. For Bridget, though she hated to admit it, it was the need to show her father she could do whatever the boys did.

As the countryside gave way to strip malls and giant

Walmarts, she thought about how shocked her dad had been when she told him she was applying to West Point. He was a retired air force senior master sergeant, and he had considered every airman at any base where he was assigned to be "my boys." He had often told young Bridget it would be a fine thing if someday she married one of them. Years later at graduation, they both choked up when he pinned the second lieutenant's bars on her shoulders. Dad stepped back, snapped to attention, and gave her her first salute.

With the benefit of hindsight, Bridget could see the reasons she had chosen the path she had—at least she thought she could. She also thought maybe Faraz was on a similar path, and that she had taken advantage of the same . . . the same what? Was it a character flaw? Was it the hubris all young people have—that they are invincible and always right? It was possible she had pushed him to go in way over his head. If he died, it was on her.

Bridget had run plenty of operatives in her army and civilian careers, and lost a few of them. It was always hard, but she would tell herself they were key players in their generation's great battle of Good vs. Evil, that their deaths had meant something. And she would remind herself that they had known the risks and volunteered anyway.

But she felt differently about this guy. Maybe it was his boyish face, his dark eyes, the little smile she had seen only once. Maybe it was his willingness to try the impossible, as she had once wanted to do. Maybe it was that even if he succeeded, he lost—he would have already devastated his parents and changed his life forever.

Maybe it was that she had lied to him about more than her name. Her promise of a return to his family was thin, at best. It would be difficult to arrange, and quite possibly worse for his parents and himself than not doing it. But she had promised, and she resolved to try to fulfill her promise . . . if Faraz made it home.

The main gate of Camp Shelby loomed in front of her. Bridget reached into her purse to fish out her ID.

The next morning at ten, it was already almost un-bearably hot and humid as Bridget stood with the major, hidden among some trees on the edge of the village. At first, she didn't notice Faraz among the other Afghans when he entered along the main road. It wasn't until he stopped to talk to a man, and others began giving him sideways glances, that she realized who he was.

"Wow," was all she whispered. After that, she was riveted on his every move. When another young man picked an argument with Faraz, and voices rose, she was able to hear him. But it didn't sound like the guy she remembered. Speaking Pashto seemed to change the tenor of his voice, his inflections, even the way he carried himself and gestured as he spoke. "Unbeliev-able," she added to her commentary.

"Yes, he's done well," said the major. "And what's important is that the lead trainers think so. He could have convinced you or me after two days, but my guys are much harder to please. They think he's ready."

"It really is amazing to see."

"He passed all the written tests and psych evals, too."

That was all well and good, Bridget knew. She also knew that although her team had planned every aspect of the operation right up to the time he would enter Afghanistan, that was only the beginning. Once Faraz was launched, the rest depended exclusively on him—his strengths, his intellect, his ability to innovate and survive. And she knew she would have little idea, probably no idea, how the operation was going for months, possibly for years—possibly never.

As she watched his argument with the Afghans escalate, one of Hadley's criticisms echoed in her brain. "He'll never pass muster with the jihadis in country, even if he has the look and the language." Bridget wondered. Even if he fooled them for a while, could he keep it up for weeks and months? He could be found out, interrogated, tortured, broken, and forced to tell all he knew before dying an agonizing death, and her team might never find out. Or they might know all too well if the Taliban put Faraz on public display or used information he gave them to attack Americans.

Now that Operation Sandblast was happening, the many reasons *not* to do it felt more compelling. When the acting secretary had asked, Bridget put Faraz's chances at fifty-fifty. Others put them considerably lower. This would be a tough assignment even for an experienced covert operative. But Faraz was a freshly minted lieutenant, completely unaccustomed to all he would have to deal with, working alone inside enemy territory, in extreme danger, pretending to be someone he wasn't.

As much as Bridget thought she knew about Afghanistan, she also knew there was much she would never fully understand. She could only hope that Faraz could navigate the roiling sea of Afghan culture, buffeted by the winds of radical Islam, traditional values, Western interference, and Allah-only-knows what else.

There were lots of "hopes" and "ifs" here. That was bound to be true of anything so daring. But this mission had far too many of them. And she had pushed, pulled, cajoled, guilted, and virtually seduced a fine young man into accepting it.

She sighed. "I'll sign off," she said to the major.

"We will, too. Arrange the transport and insertion. We're just about done here." And he walked away, leaving Bridget hurrying to follow him out of the training area without being seen.

She had wanted to meet with Faraz, to offer him some encouragement, to become his stateside touchstone. But she knew that was a bad idea. She'd taken enough heat for meeting with him at Fort Meade. Let him focus on his new identity, and let Kylie Walinsky fade from his memory.

The next morning, Faraz was called into a makeshift office in one of the faux Afghan homes. The major was there, along with some other officers he had not met. The major stood, picked up a shallow, rectangular woodgrain box and walked around the desk.

"Attention to orders," he said, and they all snapped to attention. "By order of the secretary of defense, Lieutenant Faraz Abdallah, U.S. Army, is hereby commissioned as an officer of the Defense Intelligence Agency Special Operations Bureau, with all the rights and privileges characteristic to that unit. Congratulations, Lieutenant."

The major shook Faraz's hand and gave him the box,

while the others applauded. Faraz opened it. It was lined with green felt, and held a diploma, a copy of his new orders, and a unit arm patch and pin for his uniform.

"Thank you, sir," he said.

Just that quickly, the major reached forward and took the box back, slamming it shut. "Of course, we'll have to keep this for you," he said.

"Oh, right, sir," Faraz said, momentarily confused. But he realized he shouldn't have been. The small crowd laughed and applauded again. They'd all been through the same ceremony.

"Lieutenant," the major continued.

"Yes, sir."

"That's the last time anyone will call you that for some time. This mission is a Go."

"Yes, sir. Thank you, sir." The small crowd gathered around for handshakes, pats on the back, and kind words of "good luck" and "good hunting." But, Faraz could barely acknowledge them. The major's announcement had hit him hard—goosebumps, then nausea. There was no turning back, now.

Faraz returned to his room to pack his duffel. Nearly all his army clothes and supplies went in, except for a few items he had in a small backpack for traveling. A soldier was coming shortly to put the larger bag into storage.

The last item in, folded carefully on top, was Johnny's beret. Faraz smoothed it down, savoring the feel of the material he'd first caressed a decade earlier. Now it lay proudly next to his own, the two Screaming Eagle insignia glaring at him, side-by-side.

He gave the cord a sharp pull and tied the bag closed. That was the last he would see of his real life for a long time, maybe forever. He picked up the backpack and took a last look at the duffel standing next to the bed.

Then he turned and left the room, heading for the flight line.

The day Faraz left for Afghanistan, two army cars pulled up in front of a modest home in a San Diego suburb.

The small houses were close together and neatly kept, their yards carefully trimmed. Middle-aged trees provided some shade as two young mothers pushed strollers along the sidewalk, chatting amiably. Across the street, a retiree walked his dog.

The three officers in dress uniforms appeared out of place on the warm evening as they emerged from the cars. Two young soldiers who had driven them hung back, ready to help with whatever happened. The officers—a doctor, a chaplain, and a young captain trained in casualty notification—walked up the path to the house.

Faiza collapsed at the front door almost as soon as she opened it. Amir, still chewing his dinner, ran from the table.

"What did you do?" he demanded of the officers.

"Let's help her up," the doctor said, keeping his voice even as his training required.

"Sir, may we come in?" asked the casualty officer.

"Yes, yes," said Amir, well behind his wife in understanding that his world was about to shatter.

"May we sit down?" asked the casualty officer.

"Certainly, certainly," said Amir, leading them to the living room and helping his wife to the sofa. She was in a daze and said nothing.

"What's this all about?" asked Amir. "Is Faraz . . ." The question caught in his throat as he realized what the answer would be.

Amir sat down slowly next to Faiza. She buried her head in his chest, breathing in small gasps, unable even to cry.

The casualty officer said the words that had to be said.

"Mr. and Mrs. Abdallah, it is my sad duty to inform you that your son, Lieutenant Faraz Abdallah, died in a training accident at Fort Meade, Maryland, earlier today. The secretary of the army has asked me to extend his deepest condolences."

CHAPTER 6

It was the second day of walking in the mountains. Faraz thought he was in good shape, but he was lagging. He saw his guide stop below the next ridge and turn to look for him. Faraz waved. The guide did not acknowledge, but turned again, planted his walking stick and climbed out of sight.

Faraz shook his head and continued, his sandals slipping on the rocks. The guide was not much for company. Faraz worried that the man could turn him over to the Taliban as easily as deliver him to the insertion point. But he had been assured the guide was trustworthy, and at this point, completely lost in the mountains, there was little choice but to follow.

They hadn't seen another person for more than twenty-four hours. The best mountain trails that connected Pakistan to Afghanistan were well-traveled by smugglers, bandits and fighters. So they had taken a particularly circuitous, long, and difficult route, frequently walking through areas where there was no path at all, as far as Faraz could tell.

He carried only a bedroll and a small satchel containing a threadbare brown sweater and what was left of his food and water. At least it didn't weigh much. Most U.S. troops who entered Afghanistan carried thirty pounds of gear, some of which he could have used on that mountainside, specifically socks, combat boots, and a map. A pack of crackers and peanut butter would have felt like a gourmet meal, and could have also gotten them killed if they'd encountered anyone looking to make a buck by reporting them to the Taliban.

Later that day, they began their descent, and the next afternoon they saw the clutch of huts perched precariously on a hillside above a fertile valley. Faraz had no idea when they had crossed the border. Around here, it was more of a concept than a line.

Speaking Pashto, as they had all along, the guide told him to wait under cover at a safe distance.

Faraz sat behind a boulder, camouflaged by bushes. Their thorns cut him through his thin cotton trousers. He took off his traditional tan woolen hat, a *pakol,* worn, seemingly, by half the men in Afghanistan. It was kind of like Johnny's beret, Faraz thought, but at the same time completely different. He gnawed on his last bit of food—a stale piece of bread.

Three tense, chilly hours later, the man returned. "Come," he grunted. Without waiting for a response, he turned and headed back down toward the village.

Faraz caught up after a few paces. "Is it clear?" he asked.

"Yes," said the guide. His conversation skills had not improved.

They entered the village at dusk, walking side-by-side along a dirt road. Several grubby boys stopped harassing a dog to ogle them. A toddler wearing a threadbare

T-shirt and nothing else ran toward his ramshackle home shouting, *"Mohr! Mohr!"*

The two men passed the boys and entered the largest hut, in the middle of the cluster. It was dark, and it took Faraz's eyes some time to adjust. The only light was a small fire in the center, vented through a hole in the roof. At least it was warm compared to outside.

Slowly, the scene came into focus—an earthen floor scattered with some rough carpets, an old man on a homemade wooden chair near the fire, a teenaged girl in a long dress preparing tea, her scarf pulled across her face. A baby lay in a hammock hung between two sticks stuck into the ground on the other side of the fire.

The man was studying Faraz. His deep-set blue eyes and red-tinged gray hair revealed that he had one of Alexander the Great's soldiers in his lineage. He was impossibly thin, and his face was sunbaked and deeply wrinkled. The decades of farm work on the stony, hard-packed mountainsides had not been kind. And his brown turban was filthy. Faraz guessed it might actually have been white one day. He could not have guessed the man was barely sixty years old.

"Salaam alaikum," the sheikh said offering the traditional greeting. Peace be upon you.

"Alaikum salaam, sayyid," they both responded. And upon you, sir.

"Ahlan wa sahlan," said the man, surprising Faraz with a bit of Arabic. It was appropriate, though: This is your home, and we are your family. It meant: You are safe here, under my protection.

He gestured for them to sit on a carpet in front of him. They all waited silently as the girl served tea. Faraz looked at her dark brown eyes, the only part of her face he could see. For an instant, he thought she might be smiling at him under her veil. But then it was gone.

The girl took the baby and withdrew, pushing aside a hanging carpet that served as the hut's back door. Faraz saw a smaller hut behind the main one, and caught a glimpse of the sheikh's wife preparing their dinner. He could hear her shushing the children who had come from every house in the village to see what all the excitement was about.

Switching to Pashto, the sheikh said, "You are Hamed." It was the only name the man knew for him. The sheikh seemed to be testing this young American's Pashto. It must have been beyond his comprehension that a man could come from America and speak Pashto like an Afghan.

"Yes, *sayyid*," Faraz responded.

"You had a good journey." The sheikh tended to tell more than ask.

"Yes, *sayyid*."

"And your family . . ."

Faraz told the cover story. He was the eldest of five, originally from a village not far from this one. His father died, in a well-known American drone strike, while he was visiting relatives in a neighboring village. His mother died a few months later, giving birth to his youngest sister at the refugee camp. His younger siblings went to live with various family members. He had left to find work.

Faraz passed the first Pashto test.

Faraz knew a lot about the sheikh, too. He had no love for the Taliban. They had marauded through this area several times, taking what they wanted, including two of his grandsons. He had never seen them again. They also forced him to let his eldest granddaughter, then fourteen, marry one of their fighters. He had never seen her again, either. Faraz imagined the sheikh must have been afraid they would come back someday for the girl who had served the tea.

"Now we pray," said the sheikh.

Faraz and the guide helped the sheikh out of his chair, and the three men went out the back of the tent to a well, where Faraz pumped water for them to wash. Back inside, they unrolled three prayer rugs that were stored in a corner. The sheikh indicated the direction of Mecca. They knelt and prayed, pressing their foreheads to the ground.

When they finished, dinner was served. They never saw any women except the teenager, who brought plates of meat, rice, and vegetables. Faraz reasoned that there must not be any young men left in the village. If there had been, one of them would have served, rather than the girl.

The sheikh bragged that his wife had slaughtered a lamb as soon as the guide announced himself that afternoon. And he ate with gusto, reveling in the apparently rare treat.

There was more Pashto testing during the meal. The sheikh took the lead. Faraz knew not to ask any questions. Afterwards, the sheikh assigned a boy to take Faraz and the guide to a hut with mats, blankets, and a small fire. They settled in for the night, but Faraz wasn't sure he could sleep. He had just had dinner in Afghanistan. Holy shit. This was happening.

But he did sleep, exhausted from the trip and the stress.

* * *

When he awoke at dawn, the guide was already gone.

The boy came to fetch him for prayers in the sheikh's hut, followed by breakfast of homemade bread and cheese, served by the girl. Faraz thought he saw her looking at him as she served the sweet tea. Any new young man in the village would be a curiosity. But he dared not speak to her, or even look at her. He only offered a quiet *"deyra manana."* Thank you.

"Hamed, you will leave today," said the sheikh. "Akram will show you." He tilted his head toward the boy, who was waiting near the door.

"Yes, *sayyid.*"

"He will take you close to the town. From there . . ." The sheikh's voice trailed off. He shrugged and looked toward the hole in the roof. *"Allah hu akhbar,"* he said. God is great.

"Deyra manana, sayyid."

After breakfast, Faraz used his most polite Pashto to thank the sheikh for his hospitality. The sheikh gave him some food and water for the road. *"Ma salaamat,"* he said. Go in peace. The sheikh placed his hand on his chest. The gesture meant: You are in my heart.

Faraz went with the boy to retrieve his satchel and they set off for town.

It was an hour-long walk, and Faraz tried to engage the boy in conversation. But Akram had apparently been told not to speak with the stranger, so they walked in silence.

Faraz took in the expansive view of the valley. It was an important moment for him. As a child, he had heard stories about Afghanistan's beautiful scenery, its rich history, its food, and his extended family. His parents had instilled the pride of the nation in him. No one had ever conquered and held Afghanistan, not even the mighty Soviet Union.

He once thought he might never see Afghanistan. Then, after 9-11, he was sure he would, but only wearing body armor and carrying an M-16. Now here he was, much as he might have been, walking a mountainside footpath in sandals and local clothing, unbathed, unprotected, unsure of what lay ahead.

Faraz thought about Johnny and about his parents. How would his father feel to know he was in Afghanistan? He pushed such thoughts away.

The road widened, and they exchanged greetings with a few people as they passed by, some with donkey carts, most on foot. Faraz was focused on talking and acting like a country boy. They walked through a couple of villages but didn't stop.

Then, the road split. To the right, it continued to hug the mountain. To the left, it descended into a valley and turned alongside a stream. In the distance, Faraz could see the road pass through some farm fields and enter the town. He could see the minarets from the main mosque in the market square. He knew the town well from the maps and satellite images he had studied during his training.

"That way," Akram said, pointing to the lower road. *"Ma salaamat, Hamed."*

"Ma salaamat, Akram," Faraz replied. *"Deyra manana."*

Twenty minutes later, he paused on the edge of the town to collect his thoughts. He had been unlikely to get caught while crossing the mountains, and the village had been a safe zone with the sheikh's protection. But now, he was on his own with the enemy. He was going to become one of them. One mistake was all it would take for him to have his throat slit and his body hung from a bridge.

Suddenly, Faraz didn't want to be that close to death. He broke out in a sweat. He sat on a rock and took his water from the satchel. He imagined this was how World War I soldiers must have felt as they were about to go over the edge of the trenches.

No matter how brave you were or how strong or how young, it was not a good feeling.

But like the doughboys, for Faraz there was no going back. There was only forward. So, he put his water back into the satchel, stood up, took a deep breath, and forced himself to put one foot in front of the other to carry him into the town.

Faraz wandered through the narrow lanes in the general direction of the square. It was Friday, and the town was crowded.

He passed shops selling all kinds of items, and it struck him that none of them were things he had ever thought he would want or need—steel pipes, old appliances, metal cookware, wood-fired stoves.

He got some curious looks from shopkeepers and people passing by. But the town was big enough that seeing a stranger was not cause for immediate alarm.

The market in the main square spilled into the nearby lanes and Faraz had to slow down because of the crowd. First, he passed the bakeries, then the clothing stalls, then the vegetable sellers and, as he emerged into the square, butchers to his left and spices to his right, with food stands in between. Charcoal grills were lit and vigorously fanned as cooks prepared kebabs to sell after midday prayers.

He walked through the rows of spice merchants, with their carefully sculpted mounds of powder—a rainbow of yellow, brown, crimson, and orange among other colors. The vendors leaned forward with long metal scoops to offer tastes to the women passing by, every one of them accompanied by a man, and all wearing black, blue, or brown chadors, with a screen to see through. He couldn't even see their eyes. Many had a clutch of children in tow.

Several particularly ragged-looking men were selling goat and sheep heads, and had pots of soup boiling and ready to serve in metal bowls. The heads lay cheek-to-cheek on wooden shelves and overflowed at odd angles from barrels, their lifeless eyes surveying passersby with disdain. Understandably so, Faraz thought.

Near the mosque were the sweets, neatly stacked in geometric towers—gooey baklava and hard squares of sugar embedded with pistachios or peanuts, and his favorite, candied dates. He nearly bought one, but he realized such an extravagance by an evidently poor young man might draw attention. He also remembered how little money he had. He would need it later to buy something more sensible to eat for dinner.

He mounted the steps of the mosque to take in the view. With his clothes, his *pakol,* and his complexion, he looked like he fit in. But he had never felt so foreign. In his mind, he might as well have been wearing a "USA" T-shirt. He thought someone could easily walk up to him and say, "What the hell are you doing here?" He imagined the police, or the Taliban, hauling him away.

But nothing happened. He stood there unmolested, unnoticed, as men started to enter the mosque and two women settled on the steps with their children for a picnic.

Then, a loudspeaker crackled above him. Someone hit a microphone hard three times and blew into it.

"Allaaaaaaaah hu akbar!" came the familiar chant blasting over the speakers high in the minarets. God is great! It was time for prayers. Throughout the town, other muezzins from other mosques competed for worshippers, calling out from their inferior sound systems.

"Allaaaaaaaah hu akbar!" Hurry to prayers! Hurry to triumph!

Faraz turned and mounted the last few steps, left his sandals with the growing pile near the door, and went inside. The mosque had high ceilings, with windows around a small dome in the middle. The once-white walls were cracked and unadorned, except for fluorescent light fixtures and some framed Koranic calligraphy. A hodgepodge of old carpets covered the floor, mostly in shades of red with geometric designs. Faraz noticed that unlike in America, there was no area for women, no way for them to join the men in prayer.

Faraz did what his training suggested—he followed a random man and took the place next to him. Then he knelt and started saying his prayers.

An imam gave a sermon about what in America would be called "family values," with a few swipes at the "occupiers," who he said were threatening Afghanistan's Muslim way of life.

After the service, Faraz stayed behind as the worshippers filed out. He looked at some Koranic verses that hung in one corner, near a folded table and chairs. He guessed that was where they held study sessions.

He was running out of verses to pretend to read, and thought he would have to leave the mosque with nowhere in particular to go. But he saw the imam talking to a man near the door. When the man left, he approached.

"Salaam alaikum," he said.

"Wa alaikum salaam." The imam was fortyish with a trimmed black beard. He was taller than Faraz and nearly as thin. To Faraz, he looked like he was impatient to get home for lunch, perhaps weary from years of poor young men asking him for favors.

"Pardon me, my brother," Faraz began, fretting over every word. "I am a poor boy from the camps, and I am new to this town. I am sorry to ask, sir, but I have no money. Is there somewhere I can get something to eat?"

The imam gave him the once-over. There was always reason to be suspicious in this part of Afghanistan, but thanks to the work of his trainers, this young man looked and sounded authentic. His clothes were pathetic, and his satchel barely held together.

"What is your name?"

"I am Hamed Anwali, sir. I am an orphan just returned from the camps." Faraz had practiced that line hundreds of times.

"Do you have relatives here?"

"No, *sayyid*. I came to look for . . ." Faraz checked himself. " . . . work. There is nothing for me in the camp."

The imam looked around the mosque. Faraz imagined he was hoping to pawn him off on someone else, but the place was empty.

The man sighed. "Come with me," he said, and turned for the exit.

Outside, they gathered their sandals and the imam led Faraz to his home on a lane behind the mosque.

When they entered the front room, several small children shouted and ran over, hugging their father's legs and asking when they would eat.

"Soon, soon," the imam said. "Now, go and help your mother."

The children ran for the kitchen, clearly imagining that their help would speed the arrival of lunch.

The room had no furniture. There was a large carpet that nearly covered the entire floor, with cushions along the walls. The house was concrete, and the green paint in the main room was peeling. In some places, the poorly made building material had fallen off, leaving rough gouges behind. There were a few of the framed Koranic calligraphy pieces on the walls, like in the mosque, and one small window, next to the front door, with a black curtain drawn across it. A single bare light bulb dangled on a wire that came through a hole in the ceiling.

Two men in turbans were already in the room, and the imam made introductions. He invited all of them to sit on cushions where they could rest their backs against the wall.

The men ignored Faraz as they shared town gossip and news of the war. One of them had heard on the radio that the Americans were planning to increase bombing. This drew condemnation from everyone.

More men filtered in, and Faraz saw some of their wives hurry from the front door to the kitchen without speaking to the men, their children close behind.

Each man walked around the room, embracing or shaking hands with all the others. Those who had rifles leaned them in a corner nearest to where they sat. Others laid their pistols next to them on the floor. A few showed off by checking their cell phones, then quickly put them away.

Faraz resolved to speak only when spoken to, and no one spoke to him. After the first few arrivals, the imam stopped introducing him, and Faraz blended into the crowd. There were shopkeepers, looking relatively smart in well-pressed traditional clothes with Western-style sport jackets. There were farmers from the market, wearing clothes more similar to Faraz's country outfit. And there were Taliban fighters dressed all in black, with their signature black and silver turbans, and bandoliers across their chests. One had a particularly bushy beard and a potbelly that strained his shirt. He was the most senior commander in the room, but Faraz thought he'd have been booted out of the U.S. military thirty pounds ago.

There were about a dozen men by the time his host's eldest sons started to bring the food. First came salads— hummus, eggplant, cucumbers, and tomatoes—served with naan bread.

They waited for the imam.

"Oh, Allah, bless the food You have provided us and save us from the punishment of hellfire. In the name of Allah."

There were no personal utensils or plates. The men passed around the bread and tore off small pieces to scoop up the salads.

The conversation continued and became heated, especially on the subject of the war. One man said the

Americans would never leave. The commander shouted him down, insisting the infidels would be killed or driven out like the vermin they were.

The meat came out. Platters of chicken and lamb with some roasted vegetables and rice. Faraz had stumbled into the best Friday lunch in town.

He was hungry, but he made sure to be the last to take food from each platter, and to take only a little.

"Eat, boy," the imam said. "We do not serve like this every day!"

The other men laughed at the young visitor too shy even to eat. They laughed with their mouths open, showing their half-chewed food and their bad teeth.

Someone passed the lamb and said, "Eat! You cannot disobey the imam!"

This drew more laughter. Faraz smiled at the joke at his expense. At least he got a piece of lamb out of it.

Things were going well. He tried to relax, to become Hamed. With different politics and some furniture, this could have been his father's house. These men could have been relatives and friends. Indeed, this scene could have played out any time during the last several hundred years. Only the modern weapons and mobile phones offered any indication that this was the twenty-first century.

Faraz slept that night at the imam's house and went with him to the early prayers in the morning. His wife packed them a breakfast of bread and cheese, and after prayers they made tea in the mosque's small office, which was lined with holy books.

As they ate, the imam asked, "What will you do, Hamed?"

"I do not know, *sayyid*. I must find work." The role was already coming more easily.

"What can you do?"

"Anything, *sayyid*. I will do anything." That meant he could do nothing in particular. Like millions of young Afghan men, Hamed had very little education or training. His entire résumé consisted of looking after goats and learning a bit of Koran when a traveling teacher came through his village every month or so, plus a few odd jobs during his months in the refugee camp.

Faraz did his best to be unfailingly polite and to project an earnest desire to improve his lot in life. That was about all anyone could expect of a poor boy in a war zone.

"Stay here today," the imam said. "Perhaps I will talk to some people."

"Thank you, *sayyid*," Faraz said with all the enthusiasm he could muster. He expected a job like hauling bags of seeds or breaking rocks at a construction site. It would be a start, anyway. The fact was that he had to work in order to eat, while he looked for a way to join the Taliban. He sat with his satchel on the floor in a corner of the mosque to wait.

He would like to have checked his email. He would like to have turned on the news. But here there was nothing to do but sit. After a while he took one of the copies of the Holy Koran from a shelf and tried to read it, but like a true country boy, his Arabic was too poor to get him very far.

* * *

In late afternoon, one of the men from the lunch walked up to him. Faraz stood quickly.

"Hamed, the imam tells me you are looking for work."

"Yes, *sayyid*."

"Come with me." The man turned and left the mosque, and Faraz hurried to catch up.

The man was short and portly. His black beard was neatly trimmed, and instead of a *pakol,* he wore a knitted white *taqiyah,* the prayer cap of a devout Muslim. It covered the top of his head, and had sides that reached down to his ears. He wore a Western-style vest over his traditional clothes. As they wove through the lanes, people offered the man respectful greetings.

After a few blocks, they turned onto a potholed street barely wide enough for a donkey cart and stopped at the tall, heavy gate of a building. The elderly security guard wearing an old Afghan Army uniform, who had been slouching in a folding chair with a shotgun over his knees, sprang to attention, flashed a flat-handed, British-style salute, and let them in with a fanfare of clanging keys.

"Welcome, headmaster," the man said bowing.

"Good afternoon, Wadaan. How is your health?"

"Thank God. And you, sir?"

"Thank God. This is Hamed. He will be working with us."

Faraz and Wadaan exchanged nods as the headmaster led his new employee into the compound.

It was a madrassa, a Muslim school, where young boys were taught Koran, along with basic math, a little agricultural science, the militant version of Afghan history, and a smattering of other subjects. The rectangular central yard was hard-packed from decades of soccer matches. Around it were four two-story buildings, with balconies running along the second floor. The railings were old and rusty, as were the outdoor stairways on the corners. The doors on both floors led to classrooms. Dormitories were behind, with a separate building for toilets and showers, and a kitchen hut next door. Faraz could smell the dinner being prepared.

As the headmaster led Faraz diagonally across the yard toward his office, classes ended. All at once, without any apparent signal, the doors swung open and screaming boys ran out wearing identical blue trousers and tunics and white *taqiyahs*. The ones who had been on the upper level thundered down the stairs, and Faraz and the headmaster were engulfed in the running, shouting mass of boyhood finally free of the day's studies and ready for some *footbol*.

When they saw the headmaster and Faraz, the boys gave way, creating a polite, nodding corridor to his office. As soon as the men passed by, the mayhem resumed.

In the cluttered office, the headmaster sat down hard in his worn and ripped leather chair, breathing fast. The walk from the mosque had exhausted him. His shirt heaved against his chest, and his face was red. He gestured for Faraz to take a chair on the other side of the desk. He poured two glasses of water from a pitcher on a side table and gave one to Faraz.

Once he recovered, he spoke. "Can you read, Hamed?"

The question surprised Faraz. He nearly said "yes," but caught himself in time. "A little, *sayyid*."

"Have you studied Koran?"

"Also, a little. There was a man who visited our village."

"Good. Here, you will learn more."

The headmaster saw the surprise on Faraz's face. "I know. The boys are much younger than you. But you will work, and when there is time, you will learn. You will do cleaning and shopping. You will help me with things. You will live and eat with us. If you are a good worker and you are frugal, you will have a few afghanis left each week to send to your brothers and sisters."

This was more of a job order than a job offer, like in the army. But Faraz was glad to have it. This was easier work than he could have hoped for, and chances were the headmaster had some connections in the Taliban.

He stood and made a slight bow. "Thank you, headmaster. I will not disappoint you." His gratitude and his smile were real.

For the next several weeks, Faraz worked at the madrassa. He cleaned the classrooms and moved furniture, ran errands and brought the headmaster's meals to his office or apartment. He helped organize a soccer tournament, but was careful never to play with the boys, fearing that his lack of skills would blow his cover. He spoke as little as possible and studied the speech patterns of people in the village.

Occasionally, he would sit in the back of a classroom while the younger students were learning to read or studying Koran. He made sure the headmaster knew he was doing that. During his free time, he went to the mosque or wandered the market, trying to get noticed as a lost soul.

He needn't have bothered.

Just as he was wishing that his training had included a class on How to Get Recruited by the Taliban, the headmaster called him into his office. Another man was there, tall and strong with a long beard, a sun-wrinkled face, and an AK-47. Faraz judged him to be in his mid-thirties, and the headmaster treated the fighter with more respect than Faraz had seen him bestow on anyone other than the imam.

"Hamed, this is Abed al-Rahim." Servant of the Merciful. It was a *nom de guerre*, something accorded only to those who had earned it. "He wants to speak to you."

With that, the headmaster lifted himself out of his chair and left them alone with a freshly made pot of tea. Faraz was worried. Had this man come to interrogate him? To arrest him? To take him to a Taliban prison? This was either the beginning of his mission or the end of it.

Al-Rahim smiled and invited him to sit, then poured the tea and started a friendly conversation. The man asked about Hamed's background, and Faraz repeated the story. He probed for details, and Faraz carefully filled them in. Al-Rahim used dialect words from Hamed's home region, and Faraz didn't miss a beat. The man did not say anything about himself, and Faraz didn't ask.

After half an hour, al-Rahim said, "Hamed, are you happy here?"

"Yes, *sayyid*. The headmaster has been very good to me."

"I am glad to hear it."

"A few weeks ago, I did not know where I would find my next meal. Now I have food, a bed, good work to do, and money to send to my brothers and sisters every week. I am also learning to read better and studying Koran."

"That is good," al-Rahim said. "But do you want more?"

"More, *sayyid*?"

"More. More of what a young man wants than stacking schoolbooks and sweeping the yard."

Faraz pretended he didn't understand. He looked at the floor. "What do you mean, *sayyid*?"

"I mean to serve Allah, to serve Afghanistan."

Faraz looked up, "Me, *sayyid*?"

"Yes, you, alongside many others like you."

"*Sayyid*, I dared not dream . . ."

"We will talk further," said al-Rahim. Then he stood, shook Faraz's hand, and left without saying another word.

After that, the headmaster treated Faraz differently. He sent him to more classes, made sure he had enough to eat. One day, he even hinted he might know a girl who could be a good match.

Faraz noticed the changes, and waited. Within a week, he saw two men about his age arrive at the madrassa. They met with the headmaster in his office and then went to the kitchen to get something to eat. The headmaster summoned Faraz.

"Hamed, those men have come to take you to Abed al-Rahim."

"But headmaster, I do not know . . ." Faraz feigned concern, uncertainty, fear.

"Go, Hamed. Pack your things. You will not find your destiny here."

Damn right! Faraz was more than ready to take the next step, to move toward accomplishing his mission and going home—the dream of every deployed soldier.

The madrassa was comfortable and safe. Going with the men was scary and highly dangerous. But it exhilarated him. This was what he had come here for.

Faraz forced himself to hesitate again, not wanting to appear too eager. The headmaster's gaze was steady. The matter was closed. "Yes, *sayyid*. Thank you, *sayyid*. Thank you for everything."

"Peace be with you, Hamed."

"And with you, *sayyid*."

CHAPTER 7

Bridget's BlackBerry rang on her white Scandinavian night table shortly after 0100. She reached for it, knocked it to the floor, and found it, still ringing, under the bed.

"Hello?" Her voice was groggy.

"Ma'am, this is your wake-up call."

It was an emergency signal. Something had happened, and there would be a car outside her building in ten minutes to take her to the Pentagon.

"Got it," she said, and ended the call, sitting up and putting her feet on the floor. Long ago, she had learned that would ensure she didn't fall back to sleep.

What now? The big one everyone's talking about? Please, God no! But there was no time to speculate and no way to find out. She put the radio on, but whatever had happened was not yet being reported. That didn't help her, but it was probably a good thing.

Bridget glanced longingly toward the kitchen, but there was no time for coffee, either. The coffee machine was the most expensive item in her apartment and definitely a worthwhile investment. The rest of the décor was functional, not fancy and certainly not girly. It wasn't exactly an army billet, but it wasn't far off. The furniture held some family photos and a few items she had picked up on her travels, but there was much unused space. Her army insignia, medals, and other paraphernalia were put away in a bottom drawer.

She washed and dressed quickly in khaki pants, a white blouse, blue sweater, and flat shoes. No time for The Look. Then she filled two bowls of food for Sarge, freshened his water, and grabbed her purse.

As she stepped outside, a gray sedan with government plates pulled up. She got in and asked the military driver to put the radio on. But there was still no news.

The driver took her to a seldom-used Pentagon entrance near the DIA offices. Bridget scanned her ID, walked through a metal detector, rode the elevator down, and walked into the Operations Center fewer than twenty minutes after her phone had rung.

"What's up?" she asked, before noticing the night staff's grim expressions.

"Bridget! Thank God," said Elizabeth Michaels, the senior analyst on duty. "There's been an attack in Afghanistan. They hit Carson." Camp Jimmy Carson was a U.S. Army FOB, a forward operating base, in eastern Afghanistan. "At least fifty dead, dozens wounded. They're still dealing with it."

"Fifty! Oh, my God!" Bridget paused as the magnitude of the event sank in. "How did this happen?"

"Truck bomb, we think, huge one, suicide bombers. A 101st Airborne brigade arrived yesterday and the departing unit hadn't left yet, so the place was packed. Transitions are always rough. You know."

"Shit, shit, shit! And again, no intel warning."

"None. Out of the blue, unless you count scattergrams. But God only knows what those mean."

"Dammit! Fifty. Jesus Christ," Bridget said, but what she was thinking was "Please God let Will not be there!"

In her office, Bridget read the stream of updates still coming from Camp Carson, each one detailing more death and destruction. Then she signed into her personal email. Nothing from Will. Chances were he wasn't there, but she wanted to know for sure. She knew he was likely out of touch in a remote location, might not even know about the Camp Carson attack. But still . . .

Girl Left Behind was a new role for Bridget, and she didn't like it. On a day like today, it was particularly difficult to pretend that she was a dispassionate analyst, even to herself.

This was a much more complex conflict environment than Bridget had experienced during her army years. The Taliban was resurgent, new groups of militants seemed to be cropping up daily all around Central Asia and the Middle East, and Ibn Jihad's move to unite them created a whole new level of threat. The terrorists always seemed to have the upper hand.

Well, she thought, you wanted a challenge.

It had been difficult enough to figure out what was going on in Afghanistan when she was there. Now, she was seven thousand miles away and thirty feet underground, and the guy she couldn't stop thinking about was there. As a bonus, she had a young lieutenant's life on her head, with no information about how he was doing and no way to find out or help him if he needed it.

She could only hope that Will was safe, and that Faraz was better at pretending than she was.

* * *

Several hours later, Bridget came back into the DIA workspace from a meeting to find Tommy pounding hard on his keyboard, an all-too-regular occurrence lately.

"If you need a new one, you'll have to pay for it yourself," she said.

"Don't care," he growled.

It was another impossible day in the DIA offices. Burdened by grief and guilt, the team searched for information about the attack and for an explanation of why they had missed any signs. Again.

Bridget had already attended numerous meetings where the intelligence-gathering side was pilloried. It was only 0730, and she had already been at work for six hours. She felt a hefty dose of the same frustration that had ended her army career. So much to do, so little chance of any sort of breakthrough, so devastating they couldn't reverse the tragedy that had hit them so hard from so many miles away.

By mid-morning, Bridget was writing a report for General Hadley to take to the acting secretary. The sad truth was she could have written nearly the same report hours earlier. They had little new information. The troops on the scene and the satellite data didn't provide much, and none of the few informants in the area had called in. Their information would have been suspect anyway.

Most important, the intelligence community was nowhere near answering the question that was on everyone's minds. Was this the MTO, the Big One they had been worried about, or was the Big One yet to come?

The general was not going to be happy. Brigadier

General Jim Hadley, director of DIA Operations, was one of the toughest officers she had ever worked for. His short blond hair and boyish face belied his forty-eight years and his simmering temper. Under the pressure of the terrorist offensive, he more and more often exploded in flashes of flag-officer anger. He was still not a big fan of Sandblast, and made that clear at every opportunity. He needed ops with faster and more certain results. Hadley also speculated that even if Faraz did succeed, whoever came after Ibn Jihad might well be worse.

Bridget's phone rang. It was Hadley. "We're in a White House meeting at 1200."

"What?!"

"You heard me. And I need that report now."

"I'm about to hit send."

"Be outside the East Entrance at 1130," he said, and he hung up.

Bridget hit send, spun around in her chair, and breathed a sigh of relief. Her emergency set of clothes was where it was supposed to be, hanging in a garment bag on a wall hook. This was a tragic day, but she was not showing up at the White House in casual clothes she'd been wearing since 0100.

At 1130, and no closer to answering the key questions about this attack or the previous one, Bridget found Hadley standing next to a car toward the rear of a line of vehicles outside the East Entrance, with Toni Walters from the Af/Pak desk in the secretary's Policy Office. That was the Pentagon's mini–State Department, where academics and military officers analyzed issues and wrote policy advice for the secretary of defense. Their views might or might not coincide with the analysis from the actual State Department, the intelligence community, or the president's in-house policy team, the National Security Council. Toni and Bridget disagreed on nearly everything about Afghanistan.

"Not much new in your report," Walters jabbed.

"Nobody's got anything," Bridget replied, on the defensive.

"Yeah, that's the problem." Walters was tall and thin, towering over Bridget. With her pressed khaki slacks and tweed jacket, she looked like a school headmistress about to slap Bridget's knuckles with a ruler.

Toni was a few years older than Bridget and had been in the bureaucracy much longer. She was what they called a "lifer," a national security wonk totally devoted to her career, who had survived more than a decade of political and bureaucratic shakeups. She had an office right down the hall from the secretary's, and she was certain she could do everyone else's job better than they did.

Toni was a high-level consumer of intelligence, and she was consistently not at all pleased with the product that Bridget, Hadley, and thousands of their colleagues were providing. Bridget hated her a little. She also wanted to be her.

Hadley was scowling. Bridget couldn't tell whether it was his reaction to her report, or to Toni's attitude, or maybe both.

One of the security men on the steps prevented another round of verbal jousting. "Load 'em up!" he said, twirling his right hand above his head. Bridget, Toni, and Hadley got into their car and saw Acting-Secretary Peggy Farnsworth come out of the building and start down the steps. As soon as her limo door closed, the short motorcade pulled out—four DC motorcycle cops, a Pentagon police car, a black SUV with tinted windows for the acting secretary's well-armed security team, the limo, and a couple of cars for staff, with two more motorcycle cops bringing up the rear.

As they climbed the ramp onto the 14th Street Bridge, Bridget gazed out the window. She wanted to avoid more conversation with Walters. She also needed to prepare mentally for what she was about to experience.

Bridget had only been to the White House once, as a tourist. Her father, then still in the air force, and her mother, a school librarian, had taken the family when she was eleven. She remembered how impressed she had been, and how after the tour, her father had talked about the value of service as they munched hot dogs from a street vendor and gazed across the South Lawn at the president's house, gleaming in the midday sun.

Bridget felt a twinge of guilt. She hadn't called her parents in nearly two weeks. She didn't want to field a bunch of questions about her love life and when they might possibly have a grandchild. She asked herself the same questions often enough.

That brought her back to Will, who still had not been in touch. It was evening, now, in Afghanistan, prime time for checking his email, if he had access. She imagined him sitting outside under the stars with his team, sipping nonalcoholic beers and telling stories. Then she imagined him out on a mission, his face painted black, finger on trigger, carefully approaching a target. There could be any number of informants and snipers and booby-traps in his path. Why did she have to fall for a guy with one of the most dangerous jobs in the world? Why did she miss him so much after only three months' being together?

Bridget's thoughts were interrupted by a sharp left turn, as the motorcade left the highway and headed for the Ellipse. Bridget thought she saw the spot where her family had had that picnic all those years ago. Then they swung right, breezed through an open gate, and came to a stop at a side entrance of the West Wing.

Farnsworth and her top aides went right in. The rest of them had to go through security before being escorted to the Situation Room, where they took seats along the wall, behind where their boss would sit at the central table. Hadley made a point of sitting between Bridget and Toni.

The wall at the far end of the room was covered with large flat-screens. One showed a map of eastern Afghanistan, what the military called Regional Command-East, one of the toughest parts of the country. Camp Jimmy Carson was circled in red. Another screen had an aerial photo of the base after the bombing. Others had the TV networks, and a few were blank.

The seats were about half empty when they got there, but they filled up quickly with White House staff, military officers, and folks from the State Department, CIA, Office of the Director of National Intelligence, and other agencies. Bridget nodded at CIA's Mary Larson, who sat across the room looking about as tired, stressed-out, and overwhelmed as she was.

The secretary of state walked in with the president's chief of staff. They were in the middle of what looked like a not entirely pleasant conversation. Then came the chairman of the joint chiefs, a four-star admiral who was the president's top military adviser. It was almost an out-of-body experience for Bridget.

Jay Pruitt of the National Security Council's Central Asia Desk came and sat on her left. She had been in lots of meetings with Jay, and he was a much friendlier presence than Toni.

"I won't ask how it's going," Jay said.

"Yeah, thanks. Won't ask you, either. They serve Scotch here?"

Pruitt stifled a laugh. "No . . . well, not to me. But I know a place."

"I am so there."

One of the blank screens on the wall flashed, and a shot of the commander of U.S. Central Command came on. He was at his headquarters in Tampa, and he was talking to someone off camera. The four-star general was responsible for all U.S. military operations in the Middle East and Central Asia, including Afghanistan. The president's national security advisor was on another screen. He was holding arms talks with the Russians, and joined this meeting from a secure room at the U.S. Embassy in Moscow.

A few minutes later, a marine corps sergeant by the door called, "Attention on deck!" Everyone stood, and the president came in with acting Defense Secretary Farnsworth and Marty Jacobs, the deputy head of the National Security Council.

President Andrew Martelli had been in office for two years, and was gearing up for a reelection campaign that everyone expected to be the political fight of his life. He was a New York liberal in a country that was skewing more conservative by the minute, making his narrow election margin increasingly tenuous. The economy was strong, but his policies on abortion, immigration, health care, and other social issues had angered and galvanized conservatives. And his cautious approach on international affairs had pushed them over the edge.

Bridget understood why the former political science professor and senator was loath to commit military force. He had explained in an Op-Ed in *The New York Times* just a week earlier that he believed "soft power" and "the long game" were the right way to address problems ranging from a rising China to rogue dictators plundering various regions to the ever-present threat of terrorism. He acknowledged that his way was less satisfying to some than military action, but he wrote that it was the only way to achieve true success in the long term.

The election, however, was in the short term, and today's attack gave his political opponents more credibility when they called him "weak" and accused him of hiding behind buzzwords rather than taking action.

"Please, sit," he said, taking his beige plush leather executive chair at the head of the table, with Jacobs and Farnsworth on either side. "Marty?"

"Ladies and gentlemen," Jacobs began, "we have an unprecedented situation. We have two major attacks on America in three months, and indications of more to come. The increased military and covert operations the president authorized after the aircraft attack have hit the enemy hard, but it continues to strike back. We need new ideas, people, new ideas on how to stop these guys."

The president interrupted him. "We've seen all of your plans, and we've already acted on many of them. But I will tell you I'm ready to be even more proactive, to take even more steps to destroy these terrorist networks. That includes more covert ops. I'll be damned if we'll be sucker-punched again on my watch. Is that clear?" He scanned the table.

"And, listen, I'm prepared to consider increasing the U.S. troop presence at the appropriate time. You all know I have resisted doing that, but it might be necessary. I say, might be. Determining that is part of the process we're launching today. We'll put more pressure on our allies to increase their contributions of men, matériel, and money. But we'll likely have to move first."

Bridget had not seen Martelli in person before, but he seemed angry and frustrated, very different from his professorial public persona.

"I want you all to go back to your offices, have your meetings, and bring me a fresh plate of options within the next week. To assist in this effort, I've asked Marty to lead a delegation to Afghanistan to improve our down-to-the-ground understanding of the situation, and to speak to our people there about next steps.

"So, work with Marty. He's the point man. I look forward to seeing your recommendations." The president pushed back his chair, and everyone stood until he had left the room.

Jacobs was talking again, but Bridget was having trouble keeping up. She was awestruck at having seen the president, and she couldn't believe she had witnessed some kind of cross between a presidential pep talk and blowup, not to mention being among the first people on the planet to know that a new, tougher Andrew Martelli was about to be unleashed.

Bridget was surprised by his abruptness. Martelli didn't seem to have the patience to stay for a briefing he'd already heard; and perhaps he wasn't happy with what he would have to do. She barely heard what Jacobs was saying. It was mostly assignments for the various departments, with responses due midweek so they could be churned for the president by the deadline.

Still, she realized, Jacobs knew his stuff. When she was able to focus, his orders made sense, and were pretty clearly pushing in the direction of more military and covert action. She knew he had long advocated such a shift, while the president had resisted it. In fact, some in the media had said the only reason the dovish Martelli kept such a hawk around was that they were old friends from undergraduate days. Insiders knew Jacobs provided some much-needed balance in White House policy discussions, but they also knew the president had most often not followed his advice. That seemed to be changing right before her eyes.

Bridget turned and whispered to Hadley, "They want what we can never provide—more and now." He ignored her.

When the meeting ended, Bridget took one more look around to take it all in, and followed Hadley and Walters to the exit. There was no motorcade. The acting secretary was staying for more meetings.

As they walked along the driveway toward a gate on Pennsylvania Avenue to find a taxi, Toni said, "I don't think we have the capacity for more covert ops."

"We can handle it," Hadley said.

"Haven't seen evidence of that," she countered.

"Maybe you're not paying attention," Bridget said. The exchange was a reminder of why she so disliked Walters.

But she couldn't say Toni was wrong. They should have had enough ops running to see today's attack coming, or at least to put out a general warning to raise awareness at the forward bases. Clearly, they had a lot of work to do if the president was serious about increasing the covert intel-gathering effort.

Bridget was glad they couldn't continue their conversation in the taxi. For now, she avoided further bickering with Toni.

At the Pentagon, Toni said nothing while Hadley paid for the taxi. Inside, the silent treatment continued as she turned for the wide stairway with the ornate wooden railings that led up to the executive suites, the same one visiting dignitaries used to reach the secretary's office. Bridget and Hadley trudged along the hall toward the elevator.

"Wish your boy Sandblast had given us a call about this one."

"Really, General. It's only been a few weeks."

"Yes, yes. I know. But what's the use of having him there if we don't get any benefit?"

"As you know, this is a long-term mission. Any info on imminent threats would be a bonus."

"Yeah, well, we could use a bonus about now. Thing is, Bridget, I don't think this hit on the Screaming Eagles was the big one everyone has been worried about. It's too local, almost like they're trying to throw us off the scent."

"I agree. We'll keep hammering away. And I'm sure if Sandblast gets any intel on something big, he'll call it in."

"Yeah, well, I'm not holding my breath."

Two hours later, Bridget was thinking about going home. It was only 3:30, but she had been working for over fourteen hours. Hadley poked his head into her office.

"You're on the delegation."

"I'm what?"

"With Jacobs. You leave day after tomorrow. I'm sending Tommy, too. I want his perspective. Try to get some clue why we're missing things, and give me a personal assessment. I'd go myself, but there's too much shit flying in the upper reaches. It'd be nice if you could give Sandblast a ring while you're in the neighborhood."

Bridget glared at him, refusing to take the bait.

"Look," he continued, "I know it's a long-term mission, but we have short-term problems to address. If he's in position, if he's alive, maybe he could help. Problem is, we don't have a clue and we can't find out."

Bridget had to respond. "Sir, we knew this mission would require patience. I know that's tough around here, but we're fishing for the big fish."

"Fishing with live bait, putting a young guy out there with no support, no comms. Well, you've heard it all before."

"Yes, sir."

"Don't forget your combat boots," he said, and he moved on.

Bridget sat back in her chair. Well, if the day hadn't been stressful enough. She felt a familiar rush of excitement and anxiety. She had felt it each time she received deployment orders, every time she had boarded a flight to the war zone, whenever she had gone off a secure base.

CHAPTER 8

Faraz woke up on the ground, as he had for the past three weeks, on a thin homemade mattress under a rough blanket. The tent was dark and cold, and he was fully dressed in shalwar kameez—baggy pants and a long shirt—and a sweater. His tent mate, Zahir, was still sleeping, and he did not disturb him.

Faraz stepped into his sandals and slipped through the tent flap, closing it behind him. Outside, it was even colder, but he was used to the chill. He walked the short distance along a dimly lit path to the large, shared outhouse and squatted over one of the holes in the rickety floor. There were nearly a dozen men inside, with no privacy except what their long shirts provided. He was still not accustomed to the stench.

By the time he finished, the muezzin was chanting, and Faraz saw Zahir rubbing his eyes as he walked, still half asleep, toward the toilets. Faraz went to one of the outdoor sinks to wash and joined the flow of men from other tents walking toward the open-air mosque for morning prayers.

The sky was clear and starting to turn from black to

blue. Mountains loomed close by on three sides, snow and ice cascading from their peaks.

At the edge of the mosque, Faraz removed his sandals, grabbed a dusty prayer rug, and took the next available spot, standing alongside a brother he did not know. As the others filed in, he saw the commander, al-Souri, take his spot at the front.

The imam chanted, *"Allah hu akbar."* God is great. There is no God but God.

Faraz chanted with the others as they made the ritual motions to cleanse their faces before kneeling and bending forward, putting their foreheads to the ground in supplication to *"Al-lah,"* "The God," always said that way to emphasize that there is only one.

At the mosque, these fifty or so "brothers" were as one. Moving as one. Praying as one. Seemingly thinking as one. And they were, except for the one they called Hamed.

After prayers, Faraz went to calisthenics, where he lined up next to Zahir. The farm boy was taller than Faraz, but thinner. He had a narrow face that accentuated his large nose, and his long hair overflowed the confines of his poorly wrapped turban. He demonstrated his lack of coordination, his long arms and legs flying in all directions, as another recruit led the group in jumping jacks.

The instructor was a wounded veteran fighter with a bad leg, so he watched from the front with a disapproving scowl, occasionally shouting one-word commands, "Higher," "Faster," "Together!" He wore one of those turbans Faraz imagined must come from the Dirty Turban Store.

Then it was push-ups, stretches, and a series of choreographed lunges, shouts, and chants that Faraz thought would be at home in a North Korean stadium show.

His life as a Taliban trainee had settled into a routine. Prayers, calisthenics, Koran study, and training in basic fighting skills. There were three square meals, which were the trainees' favorite part of each day—perhaps not so different from any other army.

This day, during breakfast at the outdoor mess hall with camouflage netting overhead, Faraz saw some activity across the camp. Instructors and commanders were hurrying toward the headquarters building. He heard men shouting in the distance, but he couldn't hear well enough to tell why.

He and other curious trainees joined the flow on the footpath. "What is it?" he asked one of the instructors who was rushing past.

"A victory!" the man said. "A great victory!"

At the headquarters, al-Souri's security team blocked their way, and the men filled the small open area outside. After several minutes, the commander and his chief lieutenants emerged and arrayed themselves on the porch. This group of gruesome and usually dour men with beards, bandoliers, and assorted guns and knives was quite uncharacteristically jovial.

"In the name of Allah we have struck a deep blow to the infidels!" Commander al-Souri made the announcement, and the men broke into cheers of *"Allah hu akbar! Allah hu akbar!"*

"Our brothers have hit at the heart of the infidel occupiers!" More cheering and chanting. "Here in our homeland, our brave martyrs struck a base of the infidels, avenging their crimes against Islam and killing more than fifty of their soldiers, the cowards called Screaming Eagles!"

The men went crazy now, dancing and cheering, while their officers applauded and fired their rifles into the air. The crowd was pushing against those in front, like Faraz.

He had stopped breathing when al-Souri said the Screaming Eagles had been hit—his division, likely his brigade, which would have deployed about now. His friends. His real brothers.

Faraz felt suddenly cold and light-headed. He thought he might pass out. He crumpled into a crouch, as if he had slipped and fallen. He allowed someone to help him up, and weakly raised his fist to chant with the others, "*Allah hu akbar. Allah hu akbar.*"

When the rally broke up, Faraz headed back toward his tent, still feeling unsteady. Zahir saw that something was wrong.

"Hamed, are you all right?"

"Yes. It is . . . my stomach," he managed.

"Come back to the tent."

Zahir helped him along the path and put him on his mat, then went back outside to join the men congratulating themselves on the attack that they had had nothing to do with, and bragging about how they would soon personally strike such a blow to the infidels.

Faraz tried to wrap his head around what had happened. He felt sick again and rolled onto his side, feeling as if he might vomit.

Then, a second wave of realization hit him. This made his mission even more important, more urgent, more personal, and at the same time even more impossible.

How could he ever reach Ibn Jihad? Security would be tightened, and his position as a trainee seemed more distant from the Supreme Sheikh than before. How could he ever have thought he could do this? How had he let himself be brainwashed by that woman Kylie Walinsky, or whatever the hell her name really was?

He decided he had made a huge mistake. He should be at an FOB fighting terrorists, not at a Taliban camp becoming one. He had known it all along, but it hit him harder than ever now—he was far more likely to die trying than to come anywhere near accomplishing his mission.

At dinner, Faraz sat with the other men on the mess hall's wooden benches. Still in shock, he forced himself to hide it, to act as Hamed would. Al-Souri rose to speak.

"In the name of Allah the merciful, the beneficent. My brothers, today we won a great victory. All of America is crying tonight. Four of our brave martyrs are with Allah reaping their rewards."

The men pounded their hands on the tables. They all knew what those rewards were, including the fabled seventy-two virgins. Al-Souri raised a hand to quiet the crowd. "My brothers, we are part of a great movement. We have struck repeated blows—the Eurostar, the devil Bates, countless battles in our homeland, and now this great martyrdom operation."

More pounding and some shouts of *"Allah hu akbar."*

"And our leader, the great Ibn Jihad, may Allah's mercy be upon him, has more work for us to do. Train hard, my brothers. Study the Holy Koran. Together, we shall bring the True Faith to the world!"

The crowd roared its approval, and the celebration went on and on. Faraz's head hurt, but he joined in as best he could.

The next morning, Faraz's body continued to follow the routine, but his mind was somewhere else. He couldn't stop thinking about his friends. He needed to know who had been killed and who had survived, and who had had their lives changed by traumatic injuries. He imagined the dozens of casualty notifications that would still be going on. And that made him think of his own.

Lost in his thoughts, Faraz began to fall behind in the calisthenics. The instructor shouted at him to focus.

But his thoughts jumped to his other problems. He had blended into the group of farm boys, poor city boys, and mountain goatherds, all looking for something to do with their lives, as well as the three meals a day. But he was not getting any closer to accomplishing his mission, and he couldn't see how it was possible to go from being a fresh recruit to learning the most closely held secret of the organization.

As he tried and failed once again to come up with a plan, the instructor called a break for their breakfast of bread, goat cheese, and tea.

During the meal, the men talked about their training, their home villages, and their families. They made claims about how they would be great fighters for jihad. They told stories from their youth, their exploits on local soccer teams, animals they had raised, things they had stolen from the occupiers. But unlike his American unit, there was no boasting about exploits with women. Most of these men had never met one who was not a family member.

After the meal, Faraz went with one group for Koran study, while others went for tactical training. As he walked into the classroom in the main building, he was surprised to see the camp commander speaking to the teacher at the front.

The commander was Mohammed Faisal Ibrahim, but they called him "al-Souri," the Syrian. He had come to Afghanistan from Damascus as a teenager to fight the Soviets. Al-Souri was known for his bravery, his piety, and his ruthless determination to establish an Islamic Caliphate all across the globe.

He had taken an Afghan wife and learned Pashto. Over the decades, he rose in the Taliban ranks and was *"Qomandan,"* commander of the eastern region. This was his headquarters, and he ran several other training camps in the area. Al-Souri was said to have fought alongside Ibn Jihad many times and to have his respect. He was a military leader, a spiritual icon, and a charismatic figure with few equals in the organization.

Faraz knew the man had given his whole family to the jihad. His wife had been killed in a Soviet airstrike when his two sons were still young. Little more than a decade later, both boys died in the early months of the fight against the Americans, around the same time as Johnny. Al-Souri was rumored to have married again, but by then he had become so careful that U.S. intelligence had never been able to confirm it.

"The *Qomandan* will study with us today," the teacher said as the last of the students came in.

Standing at the front of the small room with concrete floor, wood-slat walls, and two windows, one of them cracked, Al-Souri led them in a lesson on the importance of jihad. Faraz made a point of participating. He wanted to get noticed by al-Souri, but not to stand out by showing off his knowledge and analytical skills. He made sure his questions sounded like they came from ignorance and interest, and he was careful not to challenge the commander's radical interpretation of the Koran.

Al-Souri feigned patience with these young men, but also insisted that they deepen their commitment to jihad, the basis of their willingness to do whatever their commanders asked of them, in the name of Allah. He preached an entirely selfless love of the vision of all mankind ruled by Islam.

"It does not matter if you die, or if I die, or if we all die, or if our families live in poverty for one hundred generations," he told them. "What matters is that we work to do Allah's will, to bring His Holy Koran and His Sharia law to the world." Al-Souri was building suicide bombers.

Faraz pushed his feelings about the previous day's attack aside. He saw the opportunity presented by the commander's visit. It was rare for a trainee to encounter the man in such a small group. He had to establish an identity with al-Souri, had to stand out from the crowd, if he was ever going to gain access to any useful intel. Faraz had to take this opportunity to start the process. But how?

As the lesson continued, Faraz developed a plan, something one of his trainers in Mississippi had mentioned— pull back to be pulled closer. It was risky, but he had no other ideas and no more time.

Class ended. Faraz stayed behind and waited at a respectful distance while al-Souri had a word with the teacher. When the leader turned to leave, Faraz approached him.

"May peace be upon you, *Qomandan*," he began.

"And upon you."

"*Sayyid*, if it pleases you, I would like to have more time for Koran study."

"It is time for your tactical training."

"I want to learn the Prophet's teaching on parents and death."

"You are training to carry on his jihad."

"Yes, *sayyid*. It is my honor."

Al-Souri studied Faraz's face. "Come. Walk with me to the training ground."

Faraz gave way so al-Souri could leave the room ahead of him. Then he caught up on the rock-strewn sandy path through knee-high weeds toward the field where other recruits were starting an exercise in hand-to-hand combat.

"*Sayyid*, both of my parents are dead. The infidels killed my father with one of their drones."

"May peace be upon your parents in the embrace of Allah, and may Allah comfort you and your family."

"I want to carry on training for jihad, *sayyid*. But I am the eldest son. I'm not sure it is right for me to die now, and leave my brothers and sisters even more alone."

"Jihad is the most important thing you can do for your family." Al-Souri's answer sounded automatic. He had clearly heard such concerns from other young men. They walked on in silence.

Faraz would have to improvise. He had to decide whether to back off or press harder. If he backed off, he wasn't sure when he might get another chance to speak to the commander. If he pressed too hard and angered the man, he might never have the chance to speak to him again, might even be sent away or made the next suicide bomber. He only had a few seconds to choose.

"I fear I am not right for jihad," he said. "Maybe I should leave the camp and go support my family."

Al-Souri stopped, and Faraz, walking slightly behind, nearly bumped into him. He righted himself alongside the commander, uncomfortably close on the narrow path. The great man's look was stern. Its message was that quitting was not an option. "Fear is natural," he said. "Acting on fear is cowardice."

"Yes, *sayyid*." Faraz hung his head, worried that his approach had backfired.

"What is your name, my brother?"

"I am Hamed, *sayyid*," said Faraz, looking up.

"Hamed, did you expect jihad to be easy?"

"No, *sayyid*." He lowered his gaze again.

"Are you committed to creating Allah's kingdom on earth?"

"Yes, *sayyid*."

"Good. Now, go to your training."

"Yes, *Qomandan*. Thank you, *Qomandan*."

Faraz turned to walk away, dejected. He thought he had failed, maybe even put himself in danger by being seen as as cowardly and weak, lacking commitment to the cause.

But the commander spoke again. "Hamed, there is much the Prophet can teach you about grief and family."

"May peace be upon him," Faraz said, turning back toward al-Souri and trying to appear hopeful.

It seemed to Faraz that al-Souri was pondering whether he could exploit this recruit's insecurity.

"Perhaps we will find some time to learn together," al-Souri said.

To all appearances, the earnest country boy Hamed was trying to control his excitement at being offered some of the *Qomandan*'s time. In fact, the young lieutenant Faraz was trying to control his excitement at having manipulated the terrorist ideologue.

"Thank you, *sayyid*. I pray the Prophet can help me find my way."

"In His Holy Book, we will find the answers to all of your questions," Al-Souri said, before turning to cut through the underbrush toward the combat trainers standing nearby.

Suppressing a grin, Faraz jogged into the middle of the training ground and got in line for his turn to allow one of his "brothers" to best him at hand-to-hand.

CHAPTER 9

Bridget and Tommy arrived at the VIP departure lounge at Joint Base Andrews at the relatively civilized hour of 0700. Tommy got them coffee from a pot on a table in the corner and put a couple of dollars into the payment jar. Bridget took a plastic-wrapped chocolate chip cookie and tucked it into her backpack for later. She offered Tommy one, but he declined, touching his belly. They both knew there would be plenty of junk food on the plane anyway.

The leather sofas and cherrywood workstations were filling up with members of the delegation. Bridget chatted with Jay Pruitt. For the former senior foreign service officer, the casual dress code for the flight meant pressed khaki slacks, a white shirt, and blue blazer, with a sort of casual yellow knit tie with a flat bottom. Bridget liked Jay, but after nearly thirty years at the State Department and three at the White House, he couldn't shed his diplomatic formality.

Breezing in late was Toni Walters. "Bridget, how *are* you?" she said, waving from across the room as if they were best friends, and then veering off to chat up Bingnan Wang from the Senate Intelligence Committee staff and Clarence Tompkins, his counterpart from the House.

Altogether, there were fifteen of them, representing

the bulk of the U.S. government's surviving high-level expertise on Afghanistan.

The morning sun flooded through the floor-to-ceiling windows looking out toward the flight line. Bridget could see the hulking C-17 that would carry them to Kabul nonstop, with midair refueling over Britain. The crew was loading their bags, piled on wooden pallets and wrapped in heat-shrink plastic. She scanned to the right, where she saw the hexagonal hangar that was home to the two Air Force One 747s. Bridget hoped that someday she'd see the inside of one of those. On the main runway, three F-16 fighter jets did touch-and-goes, one right after the other, the morning sun briefly silhouetting their pilots' profiles under the glass canopies as they pushed the throttles forward and accelerated into the sky.

"Ladies and gentlemen, we are ready for boarding," said an airman near the door. The delegation members filed through, pausing for a final check of their IDs. From the tarmac, the plane looked particularly huge, its four jet engines hanging low from mammoth wings that appeared to bend under the weight. The windowless gray fuselage projected an air of foreboding, lying, it seemed, inches from the tarmac on very short landing gear. Bridget, Tommy and the others carried their computer bags, briefcases, and backpacks under the wing and up a short flight of fold-out stairs into the cavernous interior.

The plane was a shell, eighty-eight feet long and twelve feet high, configured differently for each mission. It could hold battle tanks, helicopters, cars, trucks and all manner of things. Or the tracks on its floor could hold attachments ranging from airline seats to hospital beds. In this case, it was fitted with a galley, toilet cubicles, several rows of economy-class seats, a secure communications cube, and a shiny Airstream camper trailer nearly as wide as the plane. Folks called it the Silver Bullet. The boss had the back half of it to himself, with a desk, a leather chair, and a banquette that turned into a bed. The front of the trailer provided relatively quiet meeting space, compared to the noise of the rest of the plane, and enough room for up to three other senior officials to work and sleep. There was a bathroom in the middle.

Bridget did not rate a spot in there, but she saw her name on a card attached to a front-row seat—extra legroom, but facing the toilets. She moved the nametag to an unlabeled seat in the back row, right in front of the Bullet. Along one side of the aircraft's curved metal walls, there were side-facing seats of metal and canvas for the crew. The reporters would have sat there, too, but there were none on this trip. On the other side stood three towers of first-come-first-served bunk beds stacked four high, and two folding tables piled with snacks. A picnic cooler underneath held cold drinks. There were enough electrical outlets to go around, and a tangle of Internet cables to share. The comms module provided secure data, audio, and video links to the Pentagon.

For Bridget, the most important piece of technology on board was the coffee maker. She grabbed a cup as everyone got settled, and watched through the open door as Jacobs's car and police escort pulled up alongside. He boarded with a few aides, and the aircraft commander led him to the Bullet. Bridget pressed herself against the wall to make way.

Three airmen carried on the VIPs' bags, descended the stairway, and helped the crew fold it into flight position. As soon as the door closed, the plane started to taxi. Bridget moved to her seat as the speaker system came on.

"Ladies and gentlemen, please be seated and fasten your seatbelts. Flight time to Kabul International Airport will be approximately fifteen hours. Thank you for flying with the United States Air Force."

That drew a chuckle from several people. Bridget wasn't sure whether she wanted a comedian for a pilot, but you had to give the kid credit. He was probably twenty-four, and knew he was speaking to some pretty high-ranking officers and civilians. And he was about to fly one of the biggest aircraft in the world nearly halfway around it.

By the time Bridget had her seat belt fastened, the plane was making a wide turn onto the runway and accelerating for takeoff. The deputy national security adviser's aircraft did not wait for other traffic.

Settling in with her coffee, Bridget read some papers she had saved to her laptop and tried not to think about Will. His comms blackout enabled her not to think about him as much as she might have. But when she did, it hit her that much harder. Now, here she was flying halfway around the world to the godforsaken place where he probably was and she couldn't even tell him, much less arrange a rendezvous. This was a new level of all kinds of frustration. She threw herself into her reading.

About five hours after takeoff Bridget ate a surprisingly good meal of roast chicken and potatoes, which somehow came out of the small galley. During the meal, the crew announced the midair refueling, which rocked the plane from nose to tail. It was like trying to eat a meal on a rowboat in rough seas. Thank you for flying with the United States Air Force, indeed.

She spent some time developing a hit list of the key things they needed to get out of the trip. High up was how to improve their chances of stopping the MTO, the big attack that everyone now accepted was on the way. She found Tommy in her old front-row seat wearing a gray ARMY sweatshirt and went over the list with him. He nixed one item as unrealistic and added three more. He might not look the part, but Tommy often had some of the most valuable insights in the office.

"Damn, I should have thought of those." Bridget had to shout at Tommy to be heard over the roar of the engines.

"Hey, that's what you keep the old guy around for," he yelled back. "I've seen this movie several times before. Different actors, different details, same plot."

"Well, thanks. I'm glad Hadley sent you along. We're bound to end up in some scrums with the congressional and White House folks, not to mention Toni Walker."

"Yeah. Like I said, same plot. We experts will figure something out and then someone else will decide we're wrong."

"Cynical much?"

"No, realistic. Anyway, we do what we do, and then we—actually *you*—have to wrestle with the big boys upstairs, you and Hadley, that is."

"Big boys and girl."

"Right, the acting secretary, Peggy. Well, that should be interesting."

"Do you know her?"

"I know everybody. But unfortunately, I don't know her very well. Saw her in meetings over the years, but we came from different corners of the building. Then she shot up the bureaucratic ladder."

"Looks like she'll get the job, don't you think?"

"Naw. They need a heavyweight, a politico, someone with a profile, and, ideally, a military background. Peggy's okay, but no one ever heard of her."

"Well, she and I have that in common."

Tommy laughed. "Yeah, well, maybe, but I'll bet not for long. Anyway, now that some time's gone by, the president will find someone who Congress will accept. Shouldn't be long now."

"You're probably right. Don't you ever get tired of it?"

"Nope."

Bridget rolled her eyes. "Listen, Tommy, I have to talk to you about something." She leaned in so she wouldn't have to speak quite so loudly. "Hadley is pressuring me about Sandblast, wants results now."

"They always do. But there's no way to speed this one up. He only just got there."

"That's what I said. But I have a different problem. A few weeks is starting to feel like a long time for that guy to be out there on his own. Maybe we reached too far."

"Could be. I'm not going to lie to you. This is beyond what we would normally do, especially as green as he is. Or should I say 'was?' He's not so green by now, I guess." Tommy raised an eyebrow. "Although green is the Taliban's color—flags, banners, maybe war paint for new recruits!"

"Can you be serious? We're talking about a young soldier's life."

"Right. Okay. Sorry."

"I worry that, well, I don't know how to put this." Bridget paused, took a breath, then forged ahead. If there was anybody she could say this to, it was Tommy. "I worry that I sent him on this mission because *I* wanted to do it, and now it's his life on the line."

"Well, I'll have to check my personnel file to see if there's a psychiatry degree in there I don't know about. But I can tell you that *you* didn't send him, *we* did, the department did. Lots of people looked at it, including me and lots of people smarter than me, and folks who actually do have psychiatry degrees. And we all concluded it was a Go. Dangerous? Yes. Out there? Uh huh. But definitely a Go."

"True, but it wouldn't have flown if I hadn't pushed it."

"Hey, that's your job—to push for what you believe in. And ultimately lots of folks agreed with you."

"And if he doesn't come home?"

"Let's not get ahead of ourselves. The training report gave him high marks. He could be smoking a hookah with the Taliban high command right now. This mission could hand us the victory we need in this so-called war. We all knew the risks, including the lieutenant. Don't beat yourself up. There's no reason to, and nothing we can do to change the situation. Now, where's that well-grounded, Miss Super Confident in High Heeled Shoes that I've come to know?"

"She's at thirty thousand feet wearing combat boots and dealing with all the shit she thought she left behind years ago, and more."

"She should give herself a break," Tommy said, his fleshy cheeks rising into a grandfatherly smile.

Bridget sighed. "I'll try. Thanks, Tommy." She half-smiled and put a hand on his shoulder. She would have given him a hug if they hadn't been in a crowded aircraft.

A little while later, she and Tommy attended a brief, crowded "signals" meeting in the Bullet. Marty Jacobs wanted everyone to understand how he saw their mission, so as not to get their "signals" crossed. They went over the basic schedule and key people they were going to meet, Americans, Afghans, and allies.

Then Jacobs summed up, simultaneously reminding them he had been deputized personally by the commander-in-chief. "Last night, the president told me he's counting on us. We're there to gather information, assess the operational posture, and come up with ways to make our military and intel efforts more effective. We're not making policy. We're not telling anyone what to do. And when we meet with the Afghans, we are not making promises we can't keep. Clear?"

There was a mumbling of "Yes, sir" around the room.

"All right. Let's get some sleep. We're going to hit the ground running."

Jacobs stood and made a point of introducing himself to everyone he hadn't met previously, including Bridget and Tommy. He spent half a minute or so with each person, asking about their specific roles and mentioning people they might know in common. Bridget had tried the same technique many times, looking for cues to use to remember people's names, while appearing to be genuinely interested in them. Jacobs seemed to be much better at it than she was.

"How did you find yourself at DIA?" he asked Bridget, although she assumed he had scanned her bio in his mission book. When she spoke, he indicated he was suitably impressed with her army career and her Ph.D. "Well, I'm really glad to have you on the team, Dr. Davenport."

"Oh sir, Bridget, please."

"All right, Bridget, I look forward to hearing your thoughts as we go along."

When Bridget and Tommy stepped out of the Bullet, she said, "He's good, isn't he?"

"Yes," Tommy allowed. "But we'll see whether it's sincerity or polish. My bet is on polish. I hear he's a hard-ass."

Bridget shrugged. Tommy was wise in such things, but also maybe jaded.

"You okay?" Tommy asked.

"Sure. Why?"

"You look a little . . . I don't know. Like you're flying into a war zone, I guess."

"I've been there before, you know."

"Yes. Sorry. I know. Wishing you were still in?"

"That's a no," she said definitively, but she didn't really know the answer. She had fought through considerable guilt about deciding to leave the army.

Tommy got himself one of the bottom bunks, while Bridget took out her air pillow and curled up in her seat. He had a point, she thought. When she had served in Afghanistan, Bridget was mainly on secure bases, going to an air-conditioned office for her shifts, socializing in the mess hall, and sleeping in a small trailer she shared with another female officer. But "secure" was a relative term. On one deployment, her "secure" base had been hit with daily incoming fire incidents, when everyone would run into concrete bunkers as enemy rockets landed in a scattershot pattern.

Mostly, Bridget flew in and out of the bases by helicopter. But she also rode her share of convoys. She would stare out the small, bulletproof windows of the armored vehicles, watching people go about their daily lives amid the rubble—shopping, working, going to school. She believed most of them were on her side, but she also knew many of them were not. And she knew most Afghans kept a handgun or rifle at home, and some had grenades and other weapons. You could never really be sure which side they would fight for if they had to use them.

The convoys were terrifying, high-speed, zigzag routes, with lots of security, including drones or choppers overhead, and fighter jets flying Combat Air Patrols in wide circles higher up. On one such ride, the lead vehicle hit a roadside bomb, shaking the road and sending shrapnel into her vehicle's bulletproof windows. That night, she had attended a memorial service for the soldiers who had been killed not fifty feet from her. She remembered that a one-star general spoke, and a colonel looked like he was on the verge of tears.

Such moments engendered an unparalleled feeling of camaraderie. Bridget remembered bowing her head, and feeling that that was exactly where she wanted to be, and at the same time feeling like she wanted to get the hell out of there. She had been to too many of those ceremonies. One was too many, really.

So, she had gotten out, then come more or less right

back—long hours, lousy pay, and more free trips to the war zone.

Bridget inserted some earplugs and put on her eye mask. When she woke up, she would be in Afghanistan. She felt like she knew a lot about the place, and also nothing at all.

As they approached Kabul, the air force flight attendant woke Bridget to ask whether she wanted breakfast. She didn't, but she said "yes." There was no way to know when they would have another chance to eat. She went to the toilet, freshened up as best she could, and changed into a green khaki blouse and tan slacks. On the way back to her seat, she got herself a cup of coffee and went over to look out the little round window in the door, reinforced with steel crosshatches. She saw the Himalayas to the rear, the sandy plains of Afghanistan ahead, and the sun rising through a haze to the east.

Back at her seat, Bridget found a copy of the delegation's schedule—meetings first at the embassy with the U.S. commander and the ambassador, then over to the main U.S. base, Camp Eggers, to talk to operations officers and intel folks. Later, there would be dinner with the prime minister and other Afghan officials at the government complex.

Bridget knew that to call them a "government" was a bit of an exaggeration. They had many of the trappings of government, but they couldn't defend their country and didn't control large parts of it. Where their authority was stretched thin, the Taliban moved in, providing security, healthcare, a welfare system, and its brand of Islamic justice, among other services. For the most part, ordinary people did not get to choose which side to live under. They simply had to go whichever way the wind was blowing, professing loyalty to the government one month and to the Taliban the next, as needed. That was if they could get away with it. Each side would regularly purge the other side's supporters as villages and districts changed hands.

As a government, and as allies, these so-called officials left a lot to be desired. That was the fundamental contradiction of the United States' counterinsurgency doctrine—you needed a strong local partner to succeed, but if there was a strong local partner, you wouldn't need to be there at all. The trick was to find or create a strong enough indigenous political and military force, and then gradually withdraw. "Trick" was the right word. Even after all these years, the United States was proving to be at best an apprentice magician.

It was the second page of the schedule that raised Bridget's heart rate. Tomorrow, they would head for the front—Regional Command-East, the area where the Screaming Eagles had been attacked and where Faraz had been inserted. She wondered whether Will was also in the East, or maybe he was down in Helmand helping the Brits, or perhaps . . . . Bridget put the schedule in her bag and put her focus back on her breakfast.

When the plane came to a halt on the military side of the airport, nearly a dozen U.S. and Afghan officials lined up at the bottom of the stairs to greet the delegation. As the members came to the end of the receiving line, they found body armor on the tarmac with their names written on duct tape stuck to each set. Everyone

got a helmet and a vest of desert camouflage canvas
with inch-thick steel plates front and rear. In training,
they'd lecture you about the importance of properly
fitted body armor. But for visitors, the army provided
a hodgepodge of too big and too small. Some of the
helmets looked particularly comical, leaving Bridget
shaking her head. It really wasn't funny.

Once they were armored up, they climbed into
three Black Hawk helicopters waiting to take them into
the city.

As they circled to land at Eggers, it all came back to
Bridget—the wide main street of the base, the outdoor
restaurant to the right of the main gate, across from the
headquarters building, the PX beyond next to the Aus-
tralians' mess, known as "The Pub." Farther along were
buildings with various bunkhouses, and shipping containers that provided private accommodations for officers. Houses for the top commanders were next, and
then the main mess hall, which was open 24/7. There
was even a small bazaar, where trusted Afghans were
allowed to sell local products as souvenirs. Bridget had
once bought a *pakol* there for her father and a necklace
for her mother.

And there was a rec hall with an Internet café next
door, where troops could email and have video chats
with folks back home. Camp Eggers was the forward
headquarters of a highly complex war-fighting machine.
But it was also home to hundreds of individuals, each
with his or her own story. Bridget remembered doing
personal emails at the Internet Café and hearing mothers
read bedtime stories to their kids seven thousand miles

away. She remembered dads with M-16s on their laps singing nursery rhymes.

There were funny memories, too. One of the strangest things she had ever seen was a ballroom dancing class in the rec hall about five years earlier, in which all the students were wearing camouflage uniforms and sidearms.

The day's meetings were not very illuminating. Bridget already knew most of what was said. It was somewhat useful to hear directly from the two senior Americans in Afghanistan, the ambassador and the commander, and the meetings with the intel guys at Eggers were worthwhile. Otherwise, she thought the day was a yawn, and the evening with the Afghans was particularly useless. They postured and asked for stuff, and made excuses about why their forces and their government were not performing up to expectations.

At least she had gotten some time with Colonel Mike Gallagher, the DIA's liaison in Kabul. Bridget had met him a few times during her army years. He knew his stuff, and he was even more pessimistic than she was.

When she and Tommy met with him in his office, he said, "It's a shit show. We got nothing on the Screaming Eagles attack, nothing on the plane bombing, and not much on stuff happening every day. It's my job to see everything, and I am a blind man."

Bridget remembered that frustration. It was a big part of the reason she was on the visitors' side of Gallagher's desk.

"What about the scattergram surge and the intel on a possible MTO?" Tommy asked.

"You mean the 'chatter' grams?" Gallagher said.

"Load of crap as far as I can tell. Yeah, people are talking. On telephones! But who knows what they're saying? Nothing we have points to anything special in the works, much less a 9-11 type MTO. But then, we probably wouldn't know, would we?"

"Folks back home seem to think it's our job to know," Tommy said.

"Well, fuck them, with all due respect. We're busting our butts out here! If the folks back home think they can do better, tell them to get their asses on an airplane."

"Okay, okay," Bridget said. "We know it's hard. Remember, I had my ass over here for two years, and Tommy's no ivory tower whiner. What we're saying is that there's a lot of pressure for more, so whatever you can do to shake the trees would be appreciated."

"Duly noted," Gallagher said, a good way to end a conversation he clearly didn't want to continue. "Now don't you two have a delegation to catch up with?"

That evening, Bridget and Tommy sat in the Eggers café and reviewed the day. "Pretty worthless, didn't you think?" she said.

"Well, we got a few tidbits. That's about all you can expect from a dog-and-pony show like this. And you need blah-blah to make your report suitably long and boring—fresh, high-level blah-blah, I should say."

"Maybe, but we need to change the way we operate, and we need good information to do that. Gallagher's reaction was a bit over the top, didn't you think?"

"Yeah, but I get his frustration. We have to push, and he has to push back. That's the way the game is played.

In the end, he'll remember we want him to do more, and he'll look for opportunities."

"Doesn't much help for my trip report."

"I know, but be patient. We got seventy-two hours more here, and the most important stuff is in RC-East anyway. Hey, you know Rome wasn't screwed up in a day."

Bridget rolled her eyes, as usual, and got up to get a coffee.

Next morning, they took a small plane to the Regional Command-East headquarters, near the city of Jalalabad. Then it was Black Hawks again, zigzagging at low altitude through the hills to Camp Jimmy Carson, site of the latest attack. Gunners wearing safety harnesses hung halfway out the open doors on both sides of the helicopters, with large machine guns ready to respond to any ground fire.

Tommy nudged Bridget as they came in on final approach, pointing at the view through the doors. Looking past him, Bridget could see the large crater near the main gate, where the truck had exploded. The site had been cleaned up, but the force of the explosion was clear. Several of the base's buildings had been destroyed, and others had whole sections missing or had their corrugated steel walls buckled. She noticed the guard tower was a mobile type, with metal legs that unfolded from a trailer at the base, brought in to replace the concrete one that was now a heap of rubble. She figured there would have been three or four men in it when it was blown apart. She also noticed lots of extra security teams stationed around the perimeter.

They landed alongside the crater, and Marty Jacobs

greeted the commanders and senior enlisted soldiers who had lost men in the attack. The normally buttoned-down senior White House official had left his suit in Kabul and broken out his "mom" jeans, a short-sleeved blue shirt, body armor, and an 101st Airborne baseball cap.

To Bridget, he seemed remarkably softer than he had in the Situation Room and on the plane, in a suit and tie with folders labeled "Classified" in his hands. The harsh sunshine accentuated the crow's-feet by his eyes and the open shirt exposed an age mark on his neck. She noticed he had old-man arms and made a mental note to look up his age. She'd find he was sixty-seven, two years older than the president. Among the brawny combat troops, Jacobs was the slightest man on the base, and the eldest by decades.

After a few minutes, everyone not on duty gathered in a semicircle around him. He stood in front of a concrete security wall with a large American flag painted on it, and waited for an army TV crew to set its shot.

"Gentlemen," Jacobs began, "the president has asked me to tell you he is proud of what you're doing here. This is vitally important work for our national security, and he has authorized more resources to help you get the job done. Our thoughts and prayers are with those we lost and their families. But Americans are also praying for all of you, who remain here with this very difficult and important work to do. May God bless your work here, and all of our fallen comrades."

He put his head down and led a moment of silence. "Thank you, everyone. And God bless you." Then Jacobs shook hands with every man on the base before boarding his chopper and flying away. The delegation was on the ground for less than half an hour, as the security experts had advised.

Bridget was impressed. Jacobs was supposed to be the toughest guy in the administration. But here, he spoke about God and prayer, and she could hear real emotion in his voice. They say there are no atheists in foxholes. Apparently not on FOBs, either. Jacobs looked almost priestly, as he spent a few seconds with each of the soldiers, even as he was on a mission to give them more dangerous work to do.

The next stop was Forward Operating Base Emerson, a safer location, but still a more frontline outpost than such a delegation would normally visit. Jacobs was determined to see things for himself, not just tell the president what the commanders wanted him to hear.

The FOB was a square, a hundred yards per side, protected by Alaska Walls—twelve-foot-high sheets of concrete with a wide area at the bottom so they could stand. They were lashed together with steel cables and topped with razor wire. There was a heavy steel gate next to a parking lot for armored vehicles, and an emergency exit at the back. The army had made sure there was a hill inside the base, and put a concrete bunker on top of it, with narrow slits for weapons and high-powered binoculars that scanned for a mile or more in all directions. The bunker was reinforced with sandbags and rocks, and there was a spiral path lined with white-painted stones that led up to it.

The headquarters building consisted of four shipping containers also surrounded by sandbags. Two more containers marked with red crosses were the clinic, and two rows of tents served as barracks and officers' quarters. The kitchen and dining hall were outside under canvas and camouflage netting, not too different from the ones at the Taliban camp where Faraz lived, and not so far away, either.

The helicopters landed one at a time in an open area that doubled as helipad and sports field. The other two circled above, scanning for threats. As each one touched down, they threw up massive amounts of sand, and they kept their blades going as the delegation members jumped off and ran to get out of the blast, bent at the waist as much as their body armor would allow. Those who were in the know held on to their eyeglasses. As soon as they were clear, a soldier wearing ear protectors and holding a small red flag raised it in a twirling motion. The chopper would lift off immediately so as not to sit, exposed, in such a forward position.

After all three had unloaded their passengers, they flew off to the west to refuel and wait in a safer location.

Bridget squeezed into the back of the base commander's overcrowded conference room and found a spot to lean against the wall. He was a lieutenant colonel. He invited the delegation members to take off their helmets, but advised them to keep their body armor on. He gave them a briefing, speaking loudly over the incessant whir of the air conditioners. Behind him, the wall was decorated with his unit's plaques and awards and a row of portraits of soldiers lost during this deployment.

Even here, there was no avoiding PowerPoint. It was a tough situation, he admitted, lots of bad guys, hard to know whom to trust. But his slides focused on progress—somewhat better security, improvements in the local police force, cordial relations with tribal sheikhs. While she couldn't say he was lying, Bridget knew he was only telling part of the story. It was bad out there. This was exactly the type of area where they had to figure out how to make inroads so they could, as the military said, "find and fix" the terrorist cells.

Toni Walters sat next to Jacobs in the front row and was the most active questioner, showing off her knowledge and her closeness with the acting secretary. But Bridget had to admit Toni asked some pointed questions that would provide useful quotes for both of their trip reports. Her most important questions started with, "How do you know . . . ," challenging various assertions about improving security and the sentiments of the local people. As expected, the answers were based mainly on anecdotal evidence and the claims of local sheikhs and officials. In other words, they were based on not much at all, and Toni let her skepticism show.

Bridget was more sympathetic. She knew how hard it was to get anything done or get any reliable information in that environment. But her understanding didn't change the fact that the commander's briefing detailed a problem they all knew very well—the lack of reliable intelligence. Faraz's mission was designed to address that problem, but it would take time.

* * *

Outside after the briefing, with helmets back on, everyone climbed the hill to look through binoculars. There were a few villages and lots of farm fields, a river with several creeks coming off of it, some wooded areas and more small hills like the one they were standing on—plenty of places to hide, not to mention the mountains that were at most a few miles away. The sun was so bright in the clear, thin mountain air that Bridget reached to put on her sunglasses, only to realize they were already on.

It was lunchtime, and to his credit Jacobs shared combat meals with four senior sergeants at a picnic table well out of earshot of their bosses. In any unit, they were the ones who knew what was really going on. Bridget ate at another picnic table across the field with some mid-grade officers, while Tommy wandered off, as he put it, "to learn the truth" from some junior enlisted men.

Bridget felt like a has-been. All the officers at her table seemed so young and were totally invested in the life she had left behind. The intel officer was a twenty-eight-year-old army captain, her old rank, yet he insisted on calling her "ma'am," and treated her like she was an aging four-star general.

He did provide some insights about what was happening in the valley, complete with an almost impenetrable patois of acronyms, military jargon, and poorly pronounced Pashto. He also agreed with her assessment that they needed more of what they had the most trouble getting—HUMINT, human intelligence, Afghans willing to provide them with information.

Bridget knew there was one "Afghan" out there who would if he could, if he was still alive. She figured he could be fairly close by, but he might as well be a million miles away.

The intel officer saw Bridget staring off into the valley. "Ma'am?"

"Sorry. You were saying?" And off he went, demonstrating more of his grasp of all things Afghan.

Bridget noticed the security team moving across the field. The delegation had been on the ground nearly two hours, the maximum the safety protocol allowed. She saw one of the officers interrupt Jacobs's lunch, apparently to tell him it was time to go. A soldier came to her table and said the helicopters were on the way.

As word spread to gather for departure, the emergency claxon sounded, loud and harsh, almost physically jolting. Soldiers ran for cover or duty stations. Members of the security detail tried to herd the delegation to concrete shelters, but they were eighty feet away and up an incline, and the bureaucrats weren't used to running, especially in body armor under the midday sun.

The first rocket hit less than ten seconds after the alarm had gone off, right in the middle of the sports field. No one was there, but the explosion shook most of the base. The second rocket came almost immediately after, and hit near the table where Bridget had been sitting.

Able to move faster than most, Bridget was nearly at the shelter, but the shock wave knocked her forward and she landed hard. Another rocket came, hitting the hill below the bunker and showering it with rocks and shrapnel. Then another hit, and another. They kept on coming. Bridget crawled the rest of the way into the shelter and lay on the ground with her hands over her helmet breathing hard. Blood from a skinned knee soaked through her trousers, and her head hurt. Several other people were in there with her, lying at odd angles in the small space.

With rockets falling, her training took hold. Take cover. Protect the team. Return fire. She couldn't do that last part, but the procedures and a big surge of adrenaline pushed all other thoughts and emotions aside.

Staying low, Bridget turned her body around so she could see through an opening. There was a big crater between the shelter and her lunch table. Half a dozen people were on the ground, some crying out, some trying to crawl to the shelter, some not moving at all. She slid halfway out to help pull someone in, grabbing them by their body armor, just as another shell kicked up more sand and debris.

It was hard to see, and the close-in explosions made it hard to hear. Bridget felt dizzy and was coughing from the dust. Then another rocket hit, and she pressed her face to the ground.

A moment later, she heard different explosions, the sound of outgoing fire from the base. It went on for about a minute, and then stopped as the choppers that had been coming to get them passed low overhead and banked right along a creek, guns blazing.

Relief swept over Bridget. She had been clinging to the ground with all her might, but now she relaxed her muscles and just lay there for a moment. Jesus, that was close! She looked up when she heard people running through the compound to tend to the wounded.

A voice on a loudspeaker said "RRF Move Out! RRF Move Out!" A dozen soldiers sprinted across the compound toward the armored vehicles. The Rapid Reaction Force was going to try to hunt down any surviving attackers. These were short-range rockets, and the bastards couldn't have gone far.

As Bridget emerged from the shelter, she saw that the headquarters building had been hit. One of its containers was destroyed and the one housing the conference room where they had held the briefing was on fire. The clinic hadn't taken a direct hit, but one of its walls had caved inward from the force of a nearby blast. Another rocket had hit one of the rows of tents.

Bridget's knee was painful and her face was covered with sand. She helped Jay Pruitt to his feet. He had fallen outside the shelter but was okay. She shielded her eyes from the sun and peered down the hill. Three people were still lying on the ground.

"Tommy!" she screamed and took off at a run. He was easy to spot, facedown with his girth rising high off the ground, his sides exposed between the plates of body armor. His ill-fitting helmet had rolled back down to the table where he had eaten. Earth and blood caked his comb-over.

Bridget slid to a stop next to him, kneeling down and grabbing his shoulder. "Tommy!" Then she saw the blood in the sand next to his head. She moved around to the other side so she could see his face. His eyes were open, his pupils dilated. She saw the piece of shrapnel embedded above his right ear.

Bridget had seen death before, but this was so shocking, so personal, and she was so far removed from her hardened military days that she burst into tears. "Tommyyyyy!" she wailed, as she fell to her knees and bent over him, almost in the Muslim prayer position.

Pruitt came to help, his white shirt badly smudged but his tie still on. When he saw what had happened, he tried to get her to move away, but she wouldn't budge. A medic ran over to assess Tommy, then moved on. Other soldiers were administering first aid and carrying people to the clinic, while a team fought the conference room fire.

Eventually, Pruitt got Bridget away from Tommy. Her face was smeared with a mud made of sand and tears. He walked her to a tent where the delegation members were gathering, many of them bruised and bloodied. A lieutenant came to tell them that four of their members had been killed, including Toni Walters.

The young officer reported in clipped tones that the table where Jacobs had been eating took a nearly direct hit. A large piece of shrapnel sheared off Jacobs's right arm above the elbow. He was in surgery at the clinic. Two of the sergeants he had eaten with were dead. Six more soldiers also died elsewhere on the base. Several others suffered serious injuries, and a dozen had minor ones.

Bridget had stopped crying, but she had no ability to function. She was not participating in the conversation about what they would do now. She couldn't believe Toni was dead, and she couldn't get that image of Tommy out of her mind. Then, Clarence Tompkins from the congressional committee staff started complaining that they had been unnecessarily endangered, that their colleagues were dead because of someone's incompetence, that getting them transport out of there should be priority number one. That broke Bridget's daze.

"Bullshit!" she said. She hadn't met Tompkins before this trip, and he was four inches taller than she was, but she got right up in his face like he was a green recruit. "Shut the fuck up, Tompkins. The top priorities are caring for the wounded and restoring security, which they are doing right now. There won't likely be another attack here and now, especially with the RRF on patrol and everyone else at duty stations. Reinforcements and medevac are likely already on the way. Our movement is a low priority, and as far as I'm concerned, we're not going anywhere without Jacobs and . . . and the others."

Her hesitation gave Tompkins an opening to argue, but Pruitt, now the senior official of the group, shut him down. "Enough! I'll talk to the colonel and see what the situation is." He left the tent to find the base commander while Bridget and Tompkins glared at each other.

Shortly afterward, Bridget heard "RRF returning!" on the loudspeaker. The base gate rolled open and the mud-spattered vehicles sped in. They had a prisoner.

The lieutenant returned to the delegation tent to say that the Black Hawks had burned their fuel hunting the terrorists, and were forced to return to base without the extra weight of the delegation. Their flight crews had maxed out their hours for the day, and there was no one else to do the pickup. The visitors were stuck at the FOB for the night.

No one was happy about that, but there was nothing to be done.

Delegation members tried to help clean up and prepare dinner and generally to stay out of the way. All Bridget could do was sit outside against the tent wall. She watched as two medevac choppers landed, delivering the reinforcements and flying out with the most seriously wounded. She saw Pruitt try to speak to Jacobs as they carried him to the helicopter, but he was sedated. He had a huge bandage where his right arm used to be.

The bodies of the dead were packed with ice and put in a shaded tent. They had to wait until morning, too.

Bridget got up to go see Tommy, but the soldiers wouldn't let her. Feeling slightly better, she came up with a mission for herself—to interrogate the prisoner. She went to the command tent to get authorization.

The commander was on the phone with headquarters and dealing with a million things, including his own grief and guilt. "Sure, sure," he said. "Full cooperation." Bridget understood he wanted her to go away, so she did.

She found the young intel officer in his tent working on his report. He had already questioned the prisoner through the base interpreter.

"He didn't say much, ma'am. Scared shitless. Oh, sorry, ma'am."

"Don't worry about it. Not much practice speaking to women out here, eh, Captain?"

"No, ma'am."

"Let me have a go at him."

"Ma'am, I don't think you can do that."

Bridget was trying to be nice, but her fuse was short. "The colonel said to give me full cooperation. I want to talk to the prisoner, so cooperate."

She stared straight at him, hoping he didn't want to take the issue to the colonel in the midst of a crisis. The captain shrugged. They roused the interpreter from his tent and went to the makeshift lockup in a spare shipping container.

The prisoner was sitting in a corner, shackled to the floor and handcuffed. He looked young, and the captain was right, scared to death. He wore ragged clothes and was muddy from hiding along the bank of a creek. His dark eyes widened when he saw Bridget.

"He will not speak to a woman," the interpreter warned. And he was right. The man turned away from Bridget and would not respond to her, or to anyone, as long as she was there.

"Get him to Kabul for interrogation ASAP," Bridget said.

"That's the plan, ma'am."

At dusk, everyone except the soldiers on guard duty gathered near the missile crater on the sports field. In front of them was a row of eight pairs of combat boots, and behind each pair, a rifle stuck into the ground by its bayonet. Helmets were balanced on the rifle butts. There were also four sets of body armor to represent the civilians.

The colonel stepped forward and turned to face the gathering. "We lost eleven brothers and a sister today. They all volunteered to be here. They all did a job most people would not do . . . could not do. Their loss leaves a big hole in those left behind, not only among us, their comrades, but also among their families, their friends, and their communities back home. We will remember them for the rest of our lives."

He paused to compose himself. "But we know . . . we *know* they died doing something they wanted to do, something we all believe in, something vitally important for the future of our country, something brave and good and noble. And for that we salute twelve American heroes."

He turned to face the memorial display and snapped to attention. The other soldiers did the same. The colonel raised a salute in slow motion, and the soldiers mirrored. The civilians put their right hands on their body armor, over their hearts. They held their positions while a recording of taps played on the loudspeakers. An evening breeze lifted some sand and blew it across the field.

Bridget stood at attention, fresh tears etching tracks through the Afghan grime on her face. Her chest heaved under the bulletproof plates. She stared at Tommy's body armor on the ground in front of her. It still had the duct tape label stuck to the front with block letters in all caps, O'REGAN. It was right next to the one labeled WALTERS.

That night, lying on a cot in one of the tents, Bridget found herself wishing Will's SEAL team would fly in to their rescue. She imagined him in full battle gear, commanding his men to take control of the situation, then spotting her and rushing over to give her a passionate kiss and a powerful hug. Somehow, just the fantasy made her feel a little better. She played it over and over in her mind before falling into a deep sleep, exhausted from the trauma of the worst day of her life.

Thirty-six hours later she was back at her apartment in Virginia, staring into her closet and wondering what she could wear to Tommy's funeral.

CHAPTER 10

News of the attack on FOB Emerson caused another celebration at the Taliban camp. Al-Souri was particularly proud that it had been carried out by some of his men. Several had been martyred.

When those who escaped the American guns and the RRF took refuge at the camp the next day, he put on a feast, with speeches and nearly endless chanting and cheering. Everyone wanted to shake the attackers' hands, kiss them on both cheeks, bless them in the name of Allah.

Hamed was among the admirers, although Faraz was finding it increasingly difficult to be Hamed. He allowed himself to be pushed to the edge of the crowd, where at least he didn't have to look at the attackers anymore, see their smug smiles, hear their idiotic stories of bravery and victory. He had met a couple of them. They had been advanced trainees when he first arrived at the camp. One of them had been assigned to help him settle in. The guy had seemed nice enough. Now the sight of him made Faraz want to throw up. As soon as he could, he went back to his tent and pulled the blanket over his head.

It was a week since he had spoken to al-Souri, and

they had not done any Koran study together. He had barely seen the commander, so there had been no opportunity to remind him. Before he drifted off to sleep, Faraz formulated a plan to get his mission back on track.

The morning after the feast, Faraz hung back near the sinks while the others went to prayers. He knew al-Souri always came at the last moment. As the commander passed by, Faraz fell in next to him. Al-Souri appeared to be in a good mood, no doubt the afterglow of the night before.

"Good morning, *Qomandan*. May peace be upon you."

"Good morning," al-Souri replied before looking to see which recruit had addressed him. "Ah." He thought for second. "Hamed, isn't it?"

"Yes, *sayyid*. Good of you to remember."

"How are your Koran studies?"

"Very good, *sayyid*. I find new meaning every day."

"Good," al-Souri said as they reached the mosque, and he turned to take his place at the front.

It was now or never for Faraz. "*Sayyid*, might we study together sometime, um, as you suggested?"

Al-Souri stopped and turned, looking irritated. Then he seemed to remember his promise and the reason he had made it. Faraz hoped the commander was always on the lookout for the next hero, like the boys who were visiting, or perhaps the next martyr, like the ones who died outside FOB Emerson.

"Yes. Come to me after midday prayers and lunch, during the rest hour."

"Thank you, *sayyid*. I will be there!" Faraz walked to a spot in the mosque's last row.

When he arrived at the headquarters building clutching a Koran he had borrowed from the classroom, the guards made him wait. He sat on the steps leading up to the porch and read.

"You. Inside," one of the guards finally grunted.

The *Qomandan*'s office was plain. It had old wooden furniture and no carpet. The walls were bare except for a Taliban flag and a framed Koran verse. Piles of papers cluttered the desk and a side table, and the open drawer of a file cabinet was full to overflowing. There was no computer or regular telephone. Communicating with such devices was too dangerous. But Faraz noticed a satellite phone in a charger and some more in a box on the floor. They would be used once each, for only a minute or so, and then destroyed. Their transmissions were high-value intercepts for folks back in the U.S.

Al-Souri came out from behind his desk and sat at a small table next to a bookshelf crammed with Islamic texts.

"Come sit, Hamed."

"Thank you, *sayyid*."

They studied some of the same verses they had gone over in class the week before about jihad and Sharia law. Then they went on to others that delved more deeply into each man's relationship with Allah, his duty, his total subjugation.

Faraz did not have to pretend he was impressed with al-Souri's knowledge. The man was clearly learned. He moved easily from chapter to chapter, selecting verses that supported his theme and ignoring others that did not. His interpretations were hard to argue with, not that Hamed ever would. Faraz knew there were faults in his logic and fallacies in his assumptions, but they were not always evident. He also knew al-Souri was a terrorist, a ruthless murderer of foreigners and Afghans alike, a man who would stop at nothing, including making him into a suicide bomber, in the pursuit of his apocalyptic vision.

At the same time, Faraz had to acknowledge that al-Souri was a soldier/scholar—the kind of wise, committed leader the U.S. military tried to build in its ranks. American generals would say al-Souri was sick and twisted. He would say the same about them.

After twenty minutes, al-Souri quizzed Faraz on what they had read and appeared to be pleased that he had retained most of it. "Study these passages. We will meet again."

"Thank you, *sayyid*." Faraz took his book, made a small bow of respect, and left.

In the weeks that followed, al-Souri summoned Faraz every few days for Koran study. Faraz heard that the commander also asked for a report on his progress on combat skills. On the fringes of the study sessions, Faraz tried to engage al-Souri in conversation, hoping he would say something about Ibn Jihad. He found that al-Souri was not interested in conversation with Hamed.

Faraz was moving toward the conclusion of his training, but he wasn't at all sure that was good. He worried about what might come next. He didn't want to become a terrorist. He couldn't see how he could make progress on his mission. And there didn't seem to be any way out, any route back to his real life.

As Hamed, he was part of a group of twenty-five trainees who spent much of their time together. They developed a camaraderie, a team spirit, like any military unit. They trained together, helped each other, laughed together. But Faraz had never felt so alone. His comrades thought they knew who he was. But no one for seven thousand miles in any direction knew who he was. He was on a mission of grand scope. But he felt very small.

At night, he turned his concerns over and over in his mind. What the hell had he done? He'd destroyed his life, and his parents' lives, for what?

The guilt over what he had put his parents through overtook Faraz like a desert sandstorm. At first, it was only a wisp in the distance. But it grew and moved closer with surprising speed. Before he knew it, the torrent of sand was sky high and miles wide, chasing him at a speed he could never match. And when it engulfed him, he became lost in a coarse brown fog. He couldn't see clearly. He had trouble breathing. He searched in all directions, but he couldn't get out. He no longer knew where he was. And soon, he wasn't sure who he was.

Between training sessions, Faraz threw himself into Koran studies. It was what he was supposed to do, but it had also become what he wanted to do. He learned much he had not known. He never showed his distaste for the militant ideology al-Souri and his teachers laid over the verses, but he gained a new appreciation for the depth, wisdom, and beauty of the Holy Book.

The Koran became his refuge. Over time, he lost sight of where the classical interpretation ended and the militant interpretation began.

During his private study time, he kept going back to verses enjoining Muslims to "be good to the parents" (Holy Koran, 4:36), and to "show kindness to your parents" (6:151). And the one that haunted him most of all:

We have enjoined on man doing of good to his
parents; with trouble did his mother bear him
and with trouble did she bring him forth. (46:15)

He could not stop imagining his mother's reaction the day the casualty officers visited his house. Did she faint? Did she scream? Surely, she cried. And cried. And cried. She would have put on the black dress of mourning, and never taken it off.

His father would have been devastated, too—all his hopes and dreams for Faraz, and for American grandchildren, gone in an instant. His lifetime of work and hardship, now for nothing.

But it was his mother Faraz could not get out of his mind.

At night, on his mat, he would silently recite the mantra the major had taught him, things he had to remember, to cling to, as his mission took him deeper and deeper into a vortex that daily consumed dozens of young men who were, in the end, not so different from himself.

"202-555-4700, Sandblast, Whiskey-Alpha-5-9-0-Sierra-Sierra-Romeo, 'Go ahead, make my day.'"

It was the phone number of the operations control room at the DIA, his mission name, his ID code, and his response code. He picked that last one, his favorite movie quote. He also recited his evac codes, 1-2-4-7-9-Zulu if all was clear. 1-2-4-7-9-Victor if he was under duress.

He would repeat them over and over. It was the only thing in his current life that connected him to his former life. But as he said the words to himself, he would sometimes slip into something else.

"La ilaha illa-lah, Mohammed rasulu-lah." There is no God but God. Mohammed is the messenger of God.

It was the Shahada, the testimony of Islamic faith, an affirmation of devotion to Islam. Fathers whispered it into the ears of their newborn children. It was supposed to be the last thing a devout Muslim said before he or she died. Faraz had learned it as a child, but now it carried new and deeper meaning for him. He saw its power over men, and he could feel its calling within himself.

In the cold tent under the star-filled desert sky, as the others slept he would pull the blanket over his head and move his lips. "202-555-4700, Sandblast, Whiskey-Alpha . . . ." But often it would trail off and become, *"La ilaha illa-lah . . ."* He would try to focus. "5-9-0-Sierra-Sierra-Romeo. . ." Sometimes, he couldn't do it anymore.

Most often he would turn to "With trouble did his mother bear him and with trouble did she bring him forth. Be good to the parents . . . Be good to the parents . . ."

The army made him commit a grave sin. His parents would never forgive him. Allah would never forgive him.

When he felt his emotions taking over, he would force himself back. "202-555-4700, Sandblast, Whiskey-Alpha . . ." But it was getting almost impossible to stick to that. He would usually fall asleep to the verses of the Koran.

During his mission training, Faraz had been warned that covert operatives sometimes went native, dove so deeply into their cover stories that they lost themselves, surrendered their true identities, believed the lie.

He never thought it would happen to him.

PART TWO

CHAPTER 11

The new secretary of defense placed his left hand on the Bible. His wife Beth was holding it, and she looked at him with a mixture of pride and concern. This was the pinnacle of his career, something he had long dreamed of. But was he up to it?

The couple had a good view over the chief justice's shoulder. The Pentagon's courtyard was packed. There were more than a hundred members of Congress, almost the entire cabinet, the joint chiefs and thousands of soldiers, sailors, airmen, marines, and defense department civilians. Most of the spectators were standing, some craning their necks for a better view through the crowd and the trees.

The VIPs sat in rows of white folding chairs that lined up from the stage, nestled in one corner of the courtyard, all the way to the snack bar in the middle. It was nicknamed the Doomsday Café, and was said to be ground zero for Russian nuclear missiles. Today in particular, there was some irony to that. The Russian ambassador sat in the second row. Bridget and Gen. Hadley sat together, considerably farther back.

Television cameras on the snack bar's roof beamed the event live nationwide and to U.S. military installations around the world.

The man about to take the oath felt a tingle along his left arm. This was something he'd fantasized about since his years as a young marine.

The chief justice's voice boomed over the loudspeakers. "Sir, please repeat after me. I . . . state your name . . . do solemnly swear."

"I, Martin Abraham Jacobs, do solemnly swear . . ."

It had been ten weeks since the attack at FOB Emerson. Marty Jacobs had missed all the funerals and the memorial service at the Washington National Cathedral. He spent more than a month at Bethesda Naval Hospital, where he had several operations and was under sedation much of the time. Once he came around, a press release said he was in good spirits, but that's what people always said.

A few days before he left the hospital, the doctors finally let him have visitors beyond his immediate family. The president was the first one.

President Martelli arrived in a minimal motorcade—the police escort, three security SUVs, an ambulance for any emergency, and one van of reporters, who were not allowed to report anything until the president got back to the White House. When they arrived at the hospital, the limousine stopped right in front of the door. Since the visit had not been announced, there was no crowd to greet him, only a few officers, including the hospital director, an admiral, who took him up to Jacobs's room. The press waited outside.

Martelli entered the room alone, carrying a small paper bag. Beth Jacobs stood, and he gave her a hug. Then he turned to look at his old friend lying in the bed, a fresh bandage on his right shoulder. Flowers, cards, and gifts filled every flat surface, and the president knew that many more items sent from around the world had been distributed throughout the hospital.

"Sorry, I can't salute, Mr. President," said Jacobs.

"KP for a week!" the president said, and they all laughed. "Seriously, Marty, how are you?" He took Jacobs's left hand in his and sat on a chair beside the bed.

"I'll tell you the truth, it was rough. But I'm okay now. Folks here are great, and Beth has been here constantly. Jimmy came from Northwestern a couple of times and Becky comes after school nearly every day. It helps a lot."

"I'm sure it does." The president smiled at Beth. "This'll help, too, when you're up to it." Martelli opened the paper bag and handed Jacobs a bottle of his favorite Scotch, a brand not available in the United States.

"Wow, thanks! How did you manage to get ahold of this?"

"Diplomatic pouch." They laughed again.

"Well, thanks a lot, Mr. President. Once I get the green light, it won't last long.

"Hey, I've told you, when we're like this, I'm still Andy."

"Right. Well, thanks, Andy."

"Just be sure to save a dram for me."

"I will."

"Maybe I'll leave you two alone," Beth said. "Got to powder my nose anyway."

"Thanks, Beth," Martelli said, and he waited until she closed the door behind her before turning serious. "What do the docs say, Marty?"

"Well, they assure me I'm not dead, though for a while there I wasn't sure, myself."

"They are the experts."

"Yeah, well let's hope so. They say it's only the arm, some bruises, and a concussion. Lots of physical therapy ahead, maybe a prosthetic. I've been thinking I should resign. You need a full-time deputy at the NSC."

"Yes, I agree." Martelli's response seemed to surprise Jacobs. Evidently, he thought his old friend would give him an argument. "I need a full-time deputy. You won't be able to do two jobs."

"Um, yeah. I guess this is my full-time job now," Jacobs said, glancing toward what was left of his arm.

"Bullshit! You can lick this during your bathroom breaks."

"Sorry, what?"

"Marty, I want you to be the new SecDef. I *need* you to be the new SecDef."

The small room went silent for a long moment. "Mr. President . . . Andy . . . Jeez, I don't know."

"I'll take that as a yes." Martelli stood, as if to end the conversation before Jacobs could disagree. "Seriously, talk to Beth and the kids, see how you feel in the next few weeks. You're probably on some really good drugs right now, so who knows what you might say?"

"Mr. President . . ."

"There's no need to say more."

"You need a new SecDef now."

"What I need is the best possible person for the job, and that's you. You've been after me to get tougher, and that's what I'm doing. We've increased the op tempo, and we've got fifteen thousand more troops on the way. Military ops aren't a long-term solution, but I'm not going to sit by while these guys rip the heck out of us. I need you at the Pentagon to help."

"I'm not exactly on top of my game right now," Jacobs said, looking toward his bandage again. "Probably won't even get out of here until next month."

"These few weeks won't make any difference. And you'll make up the time by sailing through confirmation. Your reputation as a hawk will stand you in good stead, my friend. By the way, you're the most popular man in America right now, in case you haven't been watching the news."

"I have been. Kinda weird to see yourself on TV. But I guess I don't have to tell you that."

"I'll say."

"But, really, Andy . . ."

"Yes, really, Marty. Look, you've earned the right to take the rest of your life off if you want to. But I don't think that's what you want. We're facing our toughest threat since 9-11, and if we don't handle it right, we could end up living in a very different world, a much more hostile one. I need you to help me with this."

"Well . . ."

"If we don't deal with it, next year the voters will see if the other guys can. And we both know that would be bad news all the way around."

"Yes, yes, you're right. I . . . I haven't thought much about that stuff the last few weeks. My head has been too far up my own you-know-what, I guess."

"Well, you earned the right to that, too. But it's getting to be time to get your head back in the game."

Beth knocked on the door, opened it, and peeked in. "Come on in," said the president. "It's my turn to leave.

Beth, Marty needs to speak to you. I've asked him to be the new secretary of defense."

She gasped. "Oh my God! I hope he said no!"

"Well, I didn't hear him say no, so I'll cling to that. I need him, Beth. The country, and especially the troops, need him. You've got him for a few more weeks, then I want him back."

"Yes, Mr. President," she said in a sarcastic tone, and she flashed a salute. There weren't many people who spoke to him like that these days, and it made them all smile. But she didn't smile quite as broadly as the men did. She seemed to know her husband was not going to turn down this job, regardless of his health or her preference.

Martelli hugged her. "Take care of him."

"I will."

"You get better, now, Marty. Do what the doctors and Beth tell you."

"As if I could ever not do what Beth tells me."

"All right, man." The president took Jacobs's left hand again. "Take care. I'll see you soon, all right?"

"Yes. You take care, too."

"I will." And the president left.

It had been a shock to see his old friend without a right arm. But he was glad Marty was in good spirits, like the press release said. Martelli was sure he would make a great SecDef.

After the swearing in, the new secretary of defense had a series of meetings in the Tank, the secure conference room one floor down from his office. First, he met with the Joint Chiefs. Then, it was the top noncommissioned officers from all the services. Next came his senior civilian aides, the undersecretaries, and assistant secretaries. He listened to what they all had to say, and his message to each group was the same. "We need to turn this thing around. We need to find ways to take the fight to the enemy."

Jacobs had kept on Bates's chief of staff, Tim Harmon, who had missed the ill-fated trip due to his daughter's wedding. Jacobs had never much liked Harmon, but he needed the institutional memory. And he saw Harmon as a bureaucratic strongman, willing to do the dirty work that Jacobs found distasteful. Peggy Farnsworth was gone. The president had appointed her to Jacobs's old job at the NSC. Her replacement as deputy secretary was awaiting confirmation.

Later, Jacobs moved to his wood-paneled office and its adjacent conference room for meetings with key Pentagon agencies. He walked into the office with Harmon and a three-star general who served as the secretary's military aide. Jacobs had been in the office several times, but when he put his briefcase on the desk, he paused. The other men hung back at the doorway to give him the moment.

Jacobs's experience with the military dated back to the month after he graduated from high school in Philadelphia. Facing the draft, he and two friends dared each other to join the marines, and they all did. It was a cliché, but the U.S. Marine Corps made men out of them. Three guys who were mediocre students and had never considered college found themselves working hard to make the grade in the corps. Jacobs went into the infantry and toted an M-16 through the jungles of

Vietnam. He hated every minute of it. Still, he made lance corporal before the end of his tour.

By then, age twenty, he was ready for college. When his hitch was up, he left the marines and cashed in his GI Bill benefits to go to Penn State. That's where he met Andy Martelli, a fresh-faced eighteen-year-old fellow freshman with big ideas and a big ego to go with them. He also met an adorable brunette named Beth.

Jacobs parlayed his BA in international affairs into a series of jobs at universities and think tanks and two advanced degrees. He found he was much better suited to thinking and writing about warfare than he had been to conducting it. Every time he published an article, his old friend Andy dropped him a note, usually to disagree. And now, thanks to Andy, here he was at his new desk in the private office of the United States Secretary of Defense.

He turned toward Harmon and the general. "Last time I was in here, I made a policy pitch to Rod Bates, and I think, if memory serves, he more or less told me I was full of shit." The men laughed. "I probably was." They laughed harder.

"Sir," Harmon said, "he'd be pleased to know you are replacing him. He had a lot of respect for you, and I'm not just saying that. I think, sir, under the current circumstances, he'd be right there with you and the president on the more aggressive approach."

"Well, I'm not sure, but thanks for saying that, Tim." He took a few more seconds to look around and then said, "I guess we should get to work."

They moved into the conference room, where the secretary's policy staff was already waiting. Next came the intelligence team.

* * *

Bridget sat along the wall with other mid-level officials. Hadley had a seat at the table. He and several others had two minutes each to hit the highlights of what their units were working on, and to pitch whatever they needed. The secretary thanked everyone but made no promises.

As the meeting broke up, Jacobs called out to Bridget from across the room. "Ms. Davenport."

Bridget turned and walked toward the head of the table, leaving Hadley waiting by the door.

"Yes, sir," she said.

"How are you?" Jacobs asked in a sympathetic tone, offering his left hand. No one was sure what to do when he did that.

Bridget shook it with her left in a firm handshake. "Well, sir, thank you. And it's good to see you're doing so well."

"Yes, I'm okay," he said, not convincingly. "I'm terribly sorry about your colleague Tom O'Regan. I only met him on the trip, but I hear he was a good man."

"Yes, sir, the best." The hairs stood up on Bridget's arms as the emotions of the last couple of months came back to her.

"I missed all that, the services and all." Jacobs paused. "Made it harder, in a way."

Bridget defaulted to what military people say to fill an awkward silence when they don't know what else to say, "Yes, sir."

Jacobs straightened up, took a breath, seemed to put his thoughts aside. "Your unit has some ops out there and more in the pipeline, right?"

"Yes, sir. It's a tough environment, but we're doing our best."

"Good. This offensive is important, but . . . well . . . we should talk sometime, once I get settled."

"Yes, sir, of course."

"Good to see you, Bridget. Take care."

"And you, sir."

In the hallway, Hadley asked, "What was that about?"

"Nothing, really. It's the first time we've seen each other since Afghanistan."

"What did he mean about talking sometime?"

"I have no idea. Maybe about coming under fire together. I really don't know." They walked the rest of the way to the second basement in silence.

By then, Bridget's scrapes and bruises had healed, and she was no longer expecting to see Tommy at his desk, at least not all the time.

She felt responsible for Tommy's death. She had been his boss, even though he had been her mentor. And she had survived, walked away. She couldn't shake the feeling that when the rockets started falling she should have watched out for him, helped him get out of the kill zone.

At the funeral, when Bridget had gone to the front pew to pay her respects to Tommy's widow, she had barely been able to speak. "Martha, I'm so sorry," she had managed before her voice broke.

"Oh, sweetheart," Martha had said, rising to embrace her, "Tommy loved you so much." Then she turned to her grandson, in his dress air force uniform with the rank of airman first class. "Billy, will you show Miss Davenport to a seat for me, please?" The young man stepped forward, offered his arm, and led Bridget up the aisle, where she found Hadley and took the seat next to his, even though she hated for him to see her cry.

Bridget had also gone to Toni Walters's funeral, and she found herself unexpectedly emotional there, too. Through the eulogies, she learned that she and Toni had more in common than she had ever thought. They were both runners, both Georgetown grads, both doted on their young nephews. And not surprisingly, Toni seemed to have been married to her career, a situation Bridget was so far failing to avoid. Nearly everything she found out about Toni had some resonance with her own life. She felt they should have been friends, or at least friendly. And she was taken aback by how sad it made her feel that now they never could be.

Bridget didn't consider herself much of a crier. But there was a lot to cry about during that time.

For the next month, she had been busy seven days a week. She was setting up new operations and poring over the intelligence data. It was personal now. As Tommy had said, she wanted to "hit 'em back, and hard." Hadley had to tell her to ease off a little, not to force it, and she knew he was right. Theirs was a methodical business. He'd clipped an advertisement from a magazine and taped it to her office door. It said, "Speed Kills."

She had tried to slow down, taking some time on weekends to run on the bike path along the Potomac, south past the airport to a small park that jutted into the river. She would run hard to get down there, then take a break to stare out at the water and soak in the greenery. After a while, she'd have a more leisurely jog home. Bridget never had the patience for yoga. This was as close as she got.

But she had not resumed any kind of social life. Her grad school friend Jen had tried several times to get her to go out, but Bridget was not up for it. And any man at work who made an approach ran into her own personal Alaska Wall.

Bridget was spending a fair amount of time wishing Faraz would call in, hoping he would have coordinates on Ibn Jihad, praying he would tip them off to the big attack, or tell them definitively that it didn't exist. Mainly, she wanted some indication that he was alive. But there was nothing she could do to force any of that, and her other operations demanded her attention.

Will had finally gotten an email out, and she read it over and over.

Hey Kiddo,

I heard about your dustup. Hope you're OK. Sorry about your friend Tommy. I know that's tough.

I miss those mornings.

Will

She had written back.

Thanks Navy,

It was tough but I'm OK. Tommy was a great guy.

I miss the mornings, too.

B.

She knew Will could only write occasionally, but she longed for more. She wanted him to come through her front door and hold her as tightly as those big arms could. And although she knew it was silly, she wanted him to tell her everything was going to be all right.

But that was not going to happen anytime soon.

Bridget liked to think he would never say anything so cheesy, anyway. That was one of the things she had liked about him from the beginning. No bullshit.

She'd had her eye on him since the first time they met at the fortieth birthday party of an old army friend. In a way, she had met a million guys like Will. But there was something she couldn't quite put her finger on, something genuine, that attracted her. Most of the military officers she met were smart and dedicated and patriotic, and many were good looking and in shape. More than a few even had the smile and the bedroom eyes. But every now and then one stood out from the green-, blue- and khaki-clad crowd.

It didn't hurt that fortieth birthday parties were becoming her least-favorite kind of parties, a constant reminder that her own was less than two years away, and that while she had spent the last twenty years advancing her career through the army ranks, grad school, and now at DIA, her personal life had progressed almost not at all.

So, when she got Will's first email, she had been a little bit thrilled.

Hi,

Good to meet you yesterday.

I'll be in your building tomorrow. Have time for lunch?

Will Jackson

She didn't believe for a second that he was going to be at the Pentagon by coincidence, but she agreed to lunch anyway. And that was the start of three of the most pleasant months Bridget could remember. Still, there was always some enforced distance between them— force of habit combined with his looming deployment. They had a mutual need to keep it casual. Now, with everything that had happened, "casual" wasn't cutting it.

By the time Bridget got back to her desk from the meeting in Jacobs's office, there were twenty-seven items in her classified email inbox. She took the plastic container of three-bean salad and tuna out of her backpack, grabbed a fork from her top drawer, and started reading. Shortly after she opened the fifth item, she tossed her lunch onto the desk. The fork flew off and clattered to the floor.

"Holy fucking shit," she whispered. She hit Ctrl-Alt-Del to lock her computer and took off at a run for Hadley's office.

The email read:

To: Ops Dir, DIA, DOD
From: Gallagher / Kabul

TOP SECRET, COMPARTMENTALIZED, NEED TO KNOW

ANA reports det. #TN2082-2708 provides info, unconfirmed: Name is Sabri Shahnawaz; was part of op cell based near Emerson; commander was al-Souri; names of others: Arash Kabuli, Zahir Adamkhel, Hamed Anwali, Nadeem Omarkhel. Interrog continues. END

It meant that the man captured after the attack on FOB Emerson had told the Afghan National Army interrogators his name, his commander's name, and, most important, identified Hamed Anwali as a member of his cell. Hamed Anwali, AKA Lieutenant Faraz Abdallah.

Bridget blasted through the open doorway of Hadley's office and closed the door. He looked up from his computer, "What's this?"

"Faraz Abdallah is in position."

"Who? Oh, Sandblast. Good. How do you know?"

Bridget referred him to the email, and he brought it up on his screen. "Hmm, that's good. Al-Souri is key. Still, no way to know how close he is, or really, Bridget, whether he's still alive. It took them ten weeks to get this out of that prisoner."

"I know. But it's a helluva lot more than we knew five minutes ago. He'd have been a new recruit ten weeks ago. It's a good bet he's still there, probably just finishing his training around now."

"Maybe. But the problem with this mission from the beginning was that there's no way to contact him, no way to get an update or provide any direction."

"True, but he's in the Taliban. I can't believe I just said that. He's in the Taliban, for Christ's sake! And we have an idea where he is. I couldn't have been more than ten, fifteen miles from him at Emerson. Jesus!"

"Maybe he was one of the shooters."

"If he was, I'm sure he was careful to miss."

"Yes, well, I guess this is good news, but I'm not sure what to do with it. If he is where this says he is, he needs to call in."

"I'm sure he would if he had anything worthwhile.

He's supposed to wait until he has IJ or info on an MTO, not risk his position by calling in with little stuff."

"Thing is, we need some big stuff, and we need it now. Maybe we could skywrite him a message to hurry it up."

Bridget left without replying. Hadley's sarcasm irritated her. But it didn't really matter. Faraz was alive and he was in a Taliban camp. He had a shot at accomplishing his mission. Bridget had not been this excited about work, or about anything, in months. But the news also highlighted how perilous Faraz's mission was. The closer he was to his target, the more he was in danger. And there was nothing she could do to help him. She didn't like that feeling at all.

The following week, Jacobs had a lunch in his private dining room for the survivors of the FOB Emerson attack. Bridget thought it would be a somber event, but it wasn't. After a moment of silence for their fallen comrades, the secretary led a discussion of Afghanistan policy. These were, after all, some of the government's top experts.

There was general support for the new policy and a pervasive desire to hit back at the terrorists. But there was nothing particularly new.

Then Jacobs asked the group, "How is this offensive different from others we've done in the past?"

There were lots of answers. This was qualitatively and quantitatively different. But that's not what he meant.

"It seems to me, they hit us, we hit them. They hit us harder, we hit them harder, and on and on and on."

"Well, sir," said Jay Pruitt, "the hope is to make a real, decisive difference this time, to change the balance."

"The 'hope,'" Jacobs said. "You know hope is not a strategy, Jay."

"Yes, sir, I know. But we're doing everything we can to make it happen."

"True. I don't mean to denigrate the herculean effort, but between us I'm starting to wonder whether we can really make a decisive difference by doing the same old things. For every rat we kill, two more come out of the woodwork. You know the definition of insanity, don't you?"

"Yes, sir," Pruitt said, "Doing the same thing over and over, and expecting a different result. But that's why we're trying new things, and doing the old things more intensively."

"Yes, I know." Jacobs paused, then looked up and smiled. "Well, hope is not a strategy, but let's hope our strategy works." There were chuckles around the table. "Thank you for coming, everyone. I *hope* we can do this again. And please, what happens in the secretary's private dining room stays in the secretary's private dining room, all right? Great, thanks."

On the way back to her office, Bridget thought about what Jacobs had said. What was he driving at? "Insanity," indeed! Since Bates's plane had gone down, the whole government had focused on intensified military and covert operations to fight the terrorists. What did Jacobs want? What was he thinking? Wasn't this what he'd been calling for all along? Maybe getting his arm blown off had had an impact on his worldview. Or maybe things looked different from behind the secretary of defense's desk.

But Bridget had to admit she understood what he was saying. Her own war-zone experience had led her to ask the same questions nearly eight years earlier. And she still didn't know the answers.

Shortly after she got back to her office, Hadley stopped by. "What news from upstairs?"

"Not much really. It was more support group than policy council." She didn't like lying to Hadley, but she was bound by Jacobs's request for confidentiality, and she certainly didn't want to share her concerns about the secretary's commitment to the new strategy.

So, she put it out of her mind and went back to work.

CHAPTER 12

Faraz was squeezed between the door of the Land Cruiser and the rather overweight brother to his left. Every time the truck hit a pothole, and there were many, the brother bounced a little more in Faraz's direction. The air-conditioning barely worked, leaving the air in the vehicle heavy with heat, dust, and body odor.

Through the grimy window, Faraz could see a world of dirt. The scene was about as different from his old life as he could imagine. He thought about who must live in that world, in those huts of mud, corrugated metal, and scraps of wood, tending those emaciated goats. Even the trees were skinny and their leaves were dusty, as if they hadn't been watered or rained on in a long time, which was true.

Faraz had been Hamed for more than three months, now. He had gotten to know al-Souri a little, but he had no strategy for accomplishing his mission other than to wait for some opportunity to materialize. He tried not to think about his old life. He did his best to make himself comfortable in Hamed's skin.

As a child of immigrants, he had always felt the split identity of being an "ethnic" American, especially after 9-11 and the invasion of his parents' homeland. Now, he was able to give in to the pull of his heritage, and much of it was comfortable, validating. He had learned a lot about Islam, and for the first time in his life felt a real commitment to his faith.

Now, he faced a new challenge. He was about to see a terrorist operation from the inside. So far, it was only a training exercise, and Faraz had been through many in the army. But his heart rate was through the roof.

He tried to calm himself. They would drive through a country market. Later, the instructor would ask them to describe what they had seen, and to say where they would place a bomb. It was all talk.

But what would he do next time if it was real? As a calming tactic, this was not working.

In the side-view mirror, Faraz could see the sand and rocks the Cruiser was kicking up as it sped along the un-paved road. As far as he could tell, all the Taliban's vehicles were white, but always well camouflaged with dirt.

He glanced toward Zahir, who had the left-side seat, but he was staring out the window. His tent mate had gotten a haircut, and the three meals a day had put some weight on him. He was looking more the part of the Taliban fighter.

When they came around a bend, Faraz saw the town in the distance. It was larger than he had expected, and suddenly the road was crowded with ancient cars dodging donkey carts and people on foot, many of them carrying heavy loads of produce to sell. The vehicle slowed to a crawl, the driver honking and shouting at people to get out of the way.

The market was on the edge of the town. Faraz estimated it was two or three times the size of the market in the smaller town where he had worked at the madrassa.

There were corrals with livestock, long rows of stands selling vegetables, kitchenware, freshly butchered meat, and seemingly all the necessities of life, right down to small packets of tissues and T-shirts with misspelled English words.

And it was packed with thousands of people.

Several stands sold soup or stew and had makeshift tables where men with long beards, wearing soiled clothes, sat to eat and talk about business and politics. A few women sat in other areas wearing chadors. They spent much of their time trying to control their children, overexcited to have such an adventure.

This would not be a little bombing. A bomb here would kill a lot of people . . . women . . . children. He could not be a part of this!

Faraz tried to conceal the fear he felt beginning to show on his face.

Back at camp, there was no privacy—no place Faraz could go to process what he had seen and what he might have to do, or to figure out whether he could avoid it. The only place he was alone was under his blanket, and he wouldn't be there until later.

Sitting cross-legged on the floor of a classroom, he participated in the review of the village visit, enthusiastically as required. The class leader was none other than al-Souri himself. After discussing the relative merits of placing a bomb at various locations in the market, he surprised Faraz and the other trainees.

"But my brothers, there were women and children in the market. Does Allah permit us to take action that could injure or kill them?"

That was the question on all their minds, but they were afraid to ask it. Raising it himself was among the things that made al-Souri so good—acknowledge their concerns, their misgivings, their fears. Then make it all right again. Become their father, and if necessary, their mother.

"It is jihad," offered one of the trainees.

"They are pawns of the infidels," added Zahir.

"Yes," said al-Souri. "They collaborate with the traitorous government."

"They are like animals," said another fighter.

Al-Souri nodded. Dehumanizing the victims was a proven prerequisite for convincing fighters to kill defenseless civilians, particularly women and children.

"The Prophet teaches us, 'Surely from among your wives and your children there is an enemy to you; therefore, beware of them.'" It was Faraz, showing off what he had retained from his study sessions with al-Souri.

The commander had a satisfied smile, and he nodded. "Learn, my brothers. The people in the market—men, women, and yes, children—are worse than the infidels. They are Muslims who love the infidels. They do not deserve to live. And if, and may Allah forbid it, if a loyal Muslim dies, he will be a martyr. Allah will cherish him and reward him for his sacrifice for jihad. We do what we do for Allah. Do not forget that, not even for one second. This attack will weaken the puppet government and move us closer to the day we can establish Allah's law in our country and throughout the world."

As they left the room, al-Souri put his hand on Faraz's shoulder and patted it twice. It was the warmest gesture he had ever seen the man make.

* * *

Faraz and Zahir walked toward their tent together. Zahir had become the closest thing to a friend Faraz had at the Taliban camp. He was a country boy—like Faraz was pretending to be—his father's fourth son, with nothing to inherit and nothing to do back home. He joined the Taliban to have a purpose in life, and at first seemed to be as worried as Faraz about being asked to commit violence.

But as the weeks went on, Faraz had watched Zahir become a true believer. Lacking much Islamic education, he ate up the religion classes and accepted the radical version without question. When they had first arrived at the camp, the two young men would stay up late talking about their lives, and Faraz let Zahir do most of the talking. But as their conversations turned more toward war, politics, and Islam, Faraz could see his new "brother" change right before his eyes. Zahir still had a bit of the country boy inside, but he became a committed fighter, enthusiastic about jihad and reasonably skilled in basic fighting techniques.

Still, he was a good companion, and Faraz needed something like an ally in the camp. He also believed he could manipulate Zahir if he had to, which could come in handy if he ever needed to escape. They spent many hours talking and training together.

That night walking home, Zahir said, "Hamed, this is our moment. This is the reason we were born into this life."

"Perhaps, my brother. But I hope it is not our last moment in this life."

"It would be a great thing to be martyred for Allah," Zahir replied. "It is more than I could have ever dreamed to achieve before the infidels came to Afghanistan."

"Perhaps we should thank them."

"Hamed, quiet! You should not say such things."

"All right, my friend. I know you will always keep me on the right path."

At that, Zahir stopped, grabbed Faraz's arm, and turned to face him. "We must always keep each other on the right path. I call everyone here 'my brother,' but among them all, you are truly my brother."

"And you are mine," Faraz replied, putting his hand on Zahir's shoulder. He meant it, in a way. In this place, he could trust no one. But he could rely on Zahir to have his back in a tough situation. "Come, Zahir, perhaps we can still get some food," he said, and they veered off toward the kitchen.

Later, under the blanket, he could finally be Faraz again. He could finally be Lieutenant Abdallah. As angry as he was with the army, as much as he had been feeling more like Hamed than Faraz, the training run to the village had brought him face-to-face with what being Hamed entailed.

He had discussed this with the shrinks during his training. They had tried to reassure him, to give him tools to deal with moments like this. They told him all soldiers end up killing civilians, intentionally or not, and that doing whatever was necessary was justified if he could get to Ibn Jihad and save countless lives. They told him most of the civilians he would see supported the terrorists anyway, were part of their network, enabled them to operate—the opposite of what he'd just heard from al-Souri.

These were not innocents! They would gladly stone him to death if they had the slightest inkling of who he really was.

That's what he told himself.

You're an American soldier at war with terrorists, America-haters. You swore to defend the country, and it's your job to kill them. Thousands of your comrades are doing exactly that. These assholes killed your brothers, your real brothers in the 101st, and Johnny, too. Yours is the truly holy war. You do what's necessary. Whatever is necessary. Now, let's get back on mission and kick some ass!

A week later, Faraz was running across the training field with Zahir, carrying a satchel filled with rocks. It was mid-afternoon, and they were sweating. At the end of the run, they passed al-Souri, who was looking at his watch. "Good. Better than last time. Now, rest." Then, turning to two other trainees, he said, "Go." And they took off toward a far corner of the field, carrying their own satchel.

It was the third day of operational training for the market attack. Faraz was, to say the least, relieved that it was not a suicide mission, although it was not without risk. He and Zahir would be driven to the market in one SUV, and the other team in another. They would each plant a bomb in carefully selected locations and move quickly back to the vehicles. Controlled by timers, the bombs would go off in sequence, first one, then a few minutes later the other, in an area where al-Souri expected people to flee from the first one.

Faraz kept reminding himself: These people would kill him if they knew. But he felt terrible, sick to his stomach much of the time, in anticipation of what he was about to do.

When the other team came back, al-Souri sent Faraz and Zahir off again for another practice run.

Later, the four trainees gathered in the middle of the field to meet al-Fanni, the Technician. He stood alone, arms folded, behind a tan satchel, like the ones they had been carrying. It was much like the one Faraz had used on his walk into Afghanistan. Many people carried them for travel or shopping. Al-Fanni squatted down and invited the men to do the same.

"This is your tool for jihad," he said. He opened the satchel to reveal an aluminum tube surrounded by plastic explosives, with a digital clock and a battery attached. "Your job is simple, but you must understand," he said. He explained how the bomb worked, how the switch started a countdown, and how the clock activated the battery that triggered the igniters embedded in the explosive. He let them lift the cylinder and heft its weight. It was loaded with nails and scraps of metal.

"This battery is not real," he said. "But its weight is the same as the real one. You will use this for the next phase of training."

The men practiced carrying the satchel. They had to be totally comfortable with it, like it wasn't so heavy, like it didn't contain a bomb.

They worked hard, clearly excited at the chance to make their contributions to jihad. They would no longer be trainees, but fighters.

Hamed appeared to share their enthusiasm.

Faraz felt only dread, and the ticking of the clock counting down to Friday.

When the day came, the two teams left early, each with a driver and two members of al-Souri's personal security detail. Their job was to protect the attackers, and also to make sure they didn't back out.

It was the scariest drive Faraz had ever taken. At every bump in the road, he thought the bomb would go off. The U.S. military called these improvised explosive devices, in other words, homemade bombs. In the army, Faraz had carried hand grenades and been in proximity to a variety of powerful munitions. But until that day, he had never fully appreciated the reassurance that came with using factory-made explosives. This bomb was held together by hand-wound wire, and they were transporting it in the back of an SUV, in a cardboard box sitting on al-Fanni's winter coat, surrounded by bedrolls for padding.

As they approached the village, the other vehicle turned right on a side road toward its designated target area. Faraz's driver went left, and parked on the edge of the market, behind some storage sheds. They waited for what seemed like a very long time.

At midday, when the muezzins called, Faraz and Zahir put prayer rugs on the street next to the vehicle and prayed quickly, while the others stood watch. Then, as gently as possible, they took the bomb from the cargo hold.

As the mosques started to let out, Zahir put the satchel over his shoulder, and they joined the flow of people heading into the market.

Faraz and Zahir wound through stalls selling T-shirts and kitchenware, careful not to talk to anyone or draw attention to themselves. As instructed, they moved at a casual pace and took a detour through a section of butchers, to be sure no one saw them make a beeline for the spot where the bomb would go off. One butcher was already back at work, and Faraz was startled at the *whomp* of his cleaver against a wooden block as he beheaded a chicken.

People were beginning to emerge from the mosques and crowd around the vendors, who shouted their wares in hawkers' rhythms, "Tomatoes, tomatoes, tomatooooooes!" "Ooooonions, Oooooonions." It was a scene repeated in the village every Friday, and in thousands of villages like it all over the world. It felt normal, familiar, safe.

Faraz realized how odd that was. If you offered most Americans a free trip to Afghanistan, they'd refuse. Too dangerous. How could you even ask? Heck, many people were afraid to travel anywhere outside the U.S. these days. But once you reached your destination, even in a war zone, life could seem astonishingly ordinary, even mundane. Right up until it wasn't.

Zahir lowered the satchel to his hand and passed the weight to Faraz. They made the final turn toward their target.

As he carried a bomb through their market, Faraz thought about the people he passed, each of them trying to make it day to day. In spite of what al-Souri and the army had told him, most of them probably didn't have strong political feelings one way or the other. They would have been happy with a job, food for their families, and the simple joy of a kebab and a sweet after Friday prayers. In private, many would have said, "to hell with politics."

But both politics and hell were coming their way.

Zahir yanked on Faraz's shirt to be sure he avoided a man coming toward them with a large tray of bread. They passed a seating area near the prepared food stalls that was beginning to fill up with women and children. One wide-eyed boy took a kebab from his mother and eagerly bit into a chunk of lamb in the middle, allowing the other pieces of meat to slather grease on his cheeks. His older sister shouted at him from behind her veil not to be such a slob.

Faraz checked the watch that al-Souri had lent him. It was time. He took a breath. He could still back out. He could walk away, and then run, try to get out of the village, call in his evac code. It was tempting. But surely, he would not get away. And his mission would be over.

He had made his peace with what he was about to do, as best he could. If he didn't do it, someone else would. It was part of his job. His orders required it.

He heard the girl yell at her brother again. "Idiot!"

In front of him, a vendor called, "Kebabs! Kebabs! Best Kebabs in Afghanistaaaaaan!"

Faraz and Zahir reached their objective, between two popular food stands. Zahir went behind Faraz, reached in, and started the timer. Looking around and trying not to appear nervous, they lowered the satchel to the ground between them. Faraz used his left foot to push it under one of the food sellers' tables. He tried to be nonchalant, but it was hard with his heart pounding and beads of sweat forming on his temples.

When the satchel was set, the two men turned and started to walk away. But they didn't get far. The timer malfunctioned, and a huge blast threw them both forward. Zahir landed hard on the ground, and most of the metal in the bomb flew over him. Faraz was propelled into a food stall, smashing a table and hitting his head on a hot brazier.

The shrapnel caused havoc, slicing people in all directions. The shock wave knocked over tables, canopies, and people. Hot coals, sharp knives, and half-cooked chunks of meat were among the items that became high-velocity projectiles. A moment later, the debris that had been thrown up came back to the ground, and people started screaming and crying.

Zahir sat up and gave himself a quick check. Only cuts and bruises.

It took him a few seconds to find Faraz, out cold, face-down under the debris of the food stall. He tossed aside shards of wood, metal, and singed canvas, and shook him.

"Hamed! Hamed! We must go!" he shouted. Faraz moaned. Zahir turned him on his back and slapped his face. "Hamed! We must go! Now!"

Faraz came to, but felt like he was in a cloud. Zahir tried to sit him up, but he fell back down. His head hurt from the impact, and from a large burn on the right side of his forehead. He looked down and saw he was bleeding from his stomach, where he had hit the sharp corner of the vendor's table. There was also shrapnel in his left leg.

"Hamed! Now!" Zahir said, as people around them started to move and tend the wounded, while others fled the area.

"Who did this?" yelled one man.

"We must find them!" said another.

Zahir lifted Faraz into a sitting position again, and this time he managed to hold it. His head was clearing. "Jesus," he nearly said out loud, but he turned it into a grunt. "We got hit by our own bomb?"

"Quiet!" Zahir said. "We must get out of here." He put his arms around Faraz and helped him to his feet.

A man came over and grabbed Faraz's left arm. "Let me help you," he said. "The clinic is this way." He tried to turn them toward the center of the village.

"No," Zahir said. "Thank you, *sayyid*. I can take care of my friend. Please help the others."

The man hesitated. "Go," Zahir insisted. "It is all right."

"Okay, okay," the man said, and he moved on.

Faraz was still foggy, but he was impressed with Zahir's improvisation. He leaned heavily on him, and they started to make their way back toward the SUV. The air was cloudy with dust and debris. But through the haze he could see the devastation.

They had to step over the vendor's bloodied body to get out of what was left of the stall. Then Faraz stepped on something, and when he looked down he saw it was a hand. Its owner was slumped over a table of kebabs.

They came to the seating area. The blast had blown shrapnel and debris directly at the people eating lunch. They had been mowed down as if by a firing squad, and lay at odd angles on tables and on the ground. Faraz saw a baby's body, its head bleeding from where it had hit the edge of a table. He saw a pregnant woman, injured and trying to stand. He saw a boy screaming, eyes wide, and pointing to where his right leg should have been.

Then Faraz saw the girl. She was maybe fourteen, the one who had been yelling at her brother. Her dress was ripped and her veil hung down. She was kneeling over a woman and wailing, "*Mohr*, wake up! *MOHR*, WAKE UP!!!" The boy with greasy cheeks clung to her, crying. The girl scanned the crowd for help. Faraz could see her fear, her confusion, the pain in her dark eyes, and then, an instant later, a realization. She let out a wail like none he had ever heard.

Their eyes met, but there was nothing he could do for her. Zahir was pulling him forward, out of the market.

As they turned a corner into one of the lanes, they brushed past a man holding up a mobile phone. A minute later, Zahir and the driver helped Faraz into the vehicle. They heard the deep boom of the second bomb on the other side of the market, followed by more screaming and shouting.

"Allah hu akbar," Zahir said. God is great.

CHAPTER 13

Bridget was ten minutes into her workday, and was trying to ignore the noise of the men tearing apart the bullpen of cubicles outside her office door. The place had needed a makeover for years, and Tommy's death prompted her to put in a formal request. She couldn't bear to have anyone take over Tommy's desk, so out it went along with all the others. The new configuration was completely different, and allowed for the addition of two more staff members to deal with the increased workload the new policy created.

She was scanning intercept reports that her team had flagged for her attention when she was interrupted by an urgent email from Gallagher in Kabul. It was the first word of the market attack. Details were sketchy, but it appeared two bombs had gone off after midday prayers. At least a dozen were dead. It was about twelve miles from FOB Emerson. Gallagher was working his sources and would provide more later.

Bridget picked up the secure phone on her desk and dialed.

"Imagery."

"This is Ms. Davenport. You got the email about the attack?"

"Yes, ma'am."

"We need playback from 1200 local time on the coordinates."

"Already working on it. ETA ten minutes."

"I'll be there. Thanks."

Bridget went to get Hadley and they headed for Imagery, the office that had direct, real-time access to satellite photos and videos. The hope was that the satellites had caught the attack, and maybe they could learn something.

In the darkened room, the operator scrolled the video back to noon Afghanistan time. The image was black and white and covered a wide area.

"Zoom in to the coordinates and scroll to 1215," Hadley said.

"Yes, sir," said the operator, and the screen changed to a grainy view of the market. "That's max magnification, sir."

"Now double speed." They watched as the early afternoon played out double time. They could see that the streets were quiet during prayers. There was a trickle of people coming into the lanes when the small mosques finished, and it became a flood when the main mosque let out. The market filled, and they could see wisps of smoke rising from the food stalls. At 1232:37 the first explosion turned most of the image white.

"Slo-mo," ordered Hadley. As the explosion faded, sand and dust still obscured their view. When it cleared, they could see people lying at odd angles, some missing body parts. Blood appeared as dark gray blotches. Then people started to run away. They saw what looked like children kneeling near a body. They saw a man try to get another to his feet. A few people moved toward the area, perhaps to try to help the wounded. It was particularly eerie to watch in slow motion with no sound. Experts would determine the exact force of the blast, but they could see it was a big one.

Hadley took a laser pointer from his shirt pocket and aimed its light at the screen, hitting what he thought was the center of the explosion. "Run it back," he said.

The operator reset the video to the time of the explosion, and then went forward at slow speed. Hadley adjusted his pen. "Go back again, two minutes before the blast, and roll forward in slow motion." The operator complied. They were looking to see whether they could tell who had placed the bomb, or whether it had been a suicide bomber.

The canopies of the food stalls made it difficult. They caught glimpses of many people passing by. But they couldn't tell whether any of them had planted the bomb. It might have been put there much earlier. Again, experts would scour the video for clues, but that would take hours, maybe days.

"Move to the next one," Hadley said, and the operator moved forward at quad speed until they saw the second explosion on the other side of the market at 1241:06. They followed the same routine to see what they could learn, but didn't get much—just carnage and silent chaos.

"Widen out a little," Bridget said. "Let's see if they made a getaway."

The operator widened the shot to include the whole village. As the time code advanced, they saw people running and several vehicles on the move. Some were likely fleeing, others may have been acting as ambulances.

It would take more analysis to determine whether there was anything of value.

"Well, at least we have it," Bridget said.

"Yeah, we'll see if the readers come up with anything," said Hadley, referring to the team that would go over the video in detail. "Let's put a rush on it."

An hour later, back in her office, Bridget's phone rang. It was Hadley. "You got CNN?"

"No. One sec." Bridget grabbed her remote and turned on the TV.

"As you can see in this amateur video, a market in a village in eastern Afghanistan was hit by a double bombing today. Unconfirmed reports say dozens were killed and many more were injured. CNN cannot confirm the authenticity of this video, and we apologize for the quality. We have been told it was shot by a local resident using a cell phone.

"You can see several bodies on the ground, amid some destroyed market stalls. And survivors appear to be trying to help the wounded. There! There you see one young man, apparently injured, leaning on another who seems to be helping him get out of the danger zone. And now the cameraman turns a corner and there on the ground is what appears to be the body of a woman with a young girl and a small child kneeling over her. We can hear them crying.

"This is terribly sad to see in such graphic detail, and we apologize to our viewers for that. And there's the sound of the second explosion in the distance, and that's where the video ends."

"Wow, okay. Lots to do," Bridget said to Hadley.

"Yeah."

She went to the AV room, where technicians recorded all major news broadcasts. "I need the last ten minutes from CNN," she told the lead tech.

"Yes, ma'am. I'll send it to your office ASAP."

Bridget watched the video over and over, until she wasn't quite sure why she was still watching it. But she knew it sometimes took numerous passes to notice all the things in a scene as dense as a marketplace. She was looking for something useful—evidence of exactly where the bomb had been placed, someone fleeing the scene, any of the terrorist faces she had burned into her memory from mug shots and security videos.

Then, on about the tenth run-through, she thought she saw something. Bridget had done this kind of work long enough to know not to ignore her instincts. If her mind clicked on something, it needed to be looked at again, possibly many times, until she could figure out why. It might have been that her thoughts were wandering and there was nothing there. More likely, she had seen something relevant. All she needed to do was figure out what it was.

She hit pause and ran the video back twenty seconds, then forward. Something clicked again. She narrowed the search area to ten seconds and ran through it several times. There it was again, some flash of recognition. But she still couldn't figure out what it was. She stopped to think. What could it be? She was going to figure this out if she had to go frame by frame.

And that's what she did. She was watching the two young men fleeing the explosion. One was looking past the cameraman. He was helping the other man, who was injured, holding him around the waist. The injured man was limping, and had his arm over his friend's shoulder. His head hung down. They were hurrying past the man holding the camera.

She went back again. Then she saw it. It was only five frames. In the first, the injured man raised his eyes toward the camera phone. Then he raised his head with a look of pain and fear, staring into the camera for three frames. In the last, he was half out of shot.

Bridget felt a sudden chill and she stopped breathing. She leaned in toward the screen and ran the five frames forward and back, forward and back. At first, she wasn't sure. She froze the image on the middle frame. He had a beard, his face was burned and bloody, and he was covered with dirt from the explosion. But the more she looked at it, the more sure she was. Bridget sat back in her chair and stared at the screen. Lieutenant Faraz Abdallah stared back at her.

Armed with that information, the satellite image readers focused on Faraz. They figured out that he and the other man had come from pretty close to the center of the explosion. They thought they saw them walk to that location a couple of minutes earlier, but because of the stall canopies they couldn't be sure. That could mean they had planted the bomb. But the more useful information was where they went after they walked out of the amateur newsman's frame. The satellite imagery readers traced them through the lanes to a vehicle that sped off as soon as they boarded. It left the village heading south, toward a Taliban-controlled area, disappeared behind a hill, and went outside the satellite's view.

Bridget's emotions were pinging in all directions. Faraz was alive, and his injuries didn't appear to be life-threatening. She was ecstatic about that, and deeply relieved that she hadn't gotten him killed.

On the other hand, the video had enabled her to peek into his world, and it was indeed a scary place. She'd be going home that night. He'd be in some germ-infested excuse for a clinic, at the mercy of a Taliban doctor who probably mainly treated goats, not to mention a Taliban commander who could send him on a suicide mission at any time. Maybe that had been a suicide mission! Maybe he'd be in trouble for running away. Jesus!

But she had a more immediate problem to deal with. It was pretty clear Faraz had participated in a terrorist attack. They had known that could happen. It had been relatively easy to deal with in the abstract. This was different. This was going to upset some people.

The midday meeting with Tim Harmon was a tense one. As the secretary's chief of staff, it was his job to run interference on all kinds of issues.

"Your man did what?" Harmon boomed. He was standing at the head of the table, and his voice made him appear more formidable than his thin five-foot-ten frame would suggest.

"It appears that he participated in the market bombing earlier today," Bridget repeated.

"As a *terrorist*?" Harmon said that last word with disgust and disbelief.

"As an undercover operative, sir."

"Jesus H. Christ! We'll fry if the media gets ahold of this!"

"How would they?" It was Hadley coming to Bridget's defense.

"Shit, General. You know they do. They always fucking do!" The room went silent. Harmon continued, in a normal tone of voice for the first time, "Can we get him the hell out of there?"

"No, sir," Bridget said.

"And why would we want to?" Hadley had his reservations about Sandblast, but now Harmon seemed to be pissing him off. Bridget knew all too well that no general likes being second-guessed by anyone, perhaps least of all by a political appointee. "Sir, we have a man in position at great personal risk. He's doing what he has to do to accomplish his mission—a very important mission, I would remind you. At this point, we need to let it play out. Could be a big payoff."

"Could be a big shit show! Jesus, Hadley, get a handle on this!"

"Yes, sir," Hadley said.

He had made his point, and it was time to back off. Bridget knew there was no way to get a handle on this.

Harmon glared at them, then stormed out to deal with the next emergency on his list.

A week later, motor drives whirred and shutters clicked in the Cabinet Room. Two big fuzzy microphones on long booms were stretched across the table and lowered to the right height, always seeming to be one jostle away from bopping the president on the head. Members of the press pool rushed in behind the cameras, creating a racket of their own.

President Martelli sat in the middle of the far side of the long table, with his new secretary of defense on his right and Secretary of State Sam Preston on his left. The rest of the cabinet was arrayed on both sides of the table, half of them with their backs to the press corps.

"Mr. President, how does it feel to have Secretary Jacobs here at his first cabinet meeting?" shouted one of the reporters.

"Well," said Martelli, as the thundering horde quieted itself, "We're all thinking about Rod Bates today. It's still a big hole in our lives not to have him with us. But it is great to have Marty here. He's been one of my most trusted advisers on national security for many years, and he has long deserved a seat at this table. Welcome, Marty. I'm looking forward to lots of great work from you—*lots* of work."

Everyone chuckled, especially the members of the cabinet.

"Thank you, Mr. President," Jacobs said.

Another reporter asked, "Mr. Secretary, how's your rehab? Are you ready for 'lots of work?'"

"I am if the president says I am," Jacobs said, and he gave a thumbs-up with his left hand.

"Thank you, everyone." It was the press secretary telling them it was time to go.

"Mr. President," the senior wire service reporter asked from the coveted spot directly facing Martelli across the table. "What can you tell us about rumors of a major terrorist attack on the way?"

"Now, Rory," Martelli replied. "You know I don't comment on rumors. But I refer you to the threat level, which hasn't changed in months."

"Sir, what results can you point to from your new Afghanistan strategy?" shouted another reporter from farther back in the crowd.

"That is our top priority. We are on track and moving forward."

The press secretary came to the rescue. "I said, 'Thank you, everyone.'"

"Yes, good. Thank you, everyone," Martelli echoed. And staff members ushered the reporters and photographers out.

An hour later, when the meeting broke up, Martelli invited Jacobs into the Oval Office for coffee. When they settled on the sofas, the president asked, "How did Rory London hear about the intel on an MTO?"

"I don't know, but if he had solid sources he'd have put it on the wire. He must be fishing."

"Well, that won't last. Even asking the question will get some bounce."

"I think you squashed it as well as it can be squashed."

"We'll see. I meant what I said when this first came up. We can't afford to be blindsided again."

"The intel side is doing everything they can, and looking for new ideas every day."

"I know. Trying is fine. What we need are results."

"Yes, Mr. President."

It always struck Martelli when Jacobs called him that. He looked at his old friend with his right suit coat sleeve pinned to his shoulder. "How you feeling, Marty?"

"Fine, really. The rehab takes some of my time, but my strength is back and I'm ready to go."

"Good. I hope you'll tell me if that changes."

"I will."

"How's Beth?"

"Ticked off at you, I think. She'd rather have me on bed rest. It took a three-star admiral at Bethesda with Stanford Med under his belt to convince her this job wouldn't kill me."

"Remind me to promote that man."

"Yes, sir."

The president took a sip of his coffee. "Marty, what's your answer to that other reporter's question? What impact can we see from the new strategy?"

"Well, the increased bombing and the offensive have forced the Taliban to go to ground, but that won't last. We saw that market attack the other day. That's a soft, domestic target. When they can, they'll hit us again, too."

"Yeah. At the NSC, you always called for stronger military action, and I always resisted. The plane attack forced me to change course. Nearly three months later, the ops tempo is up, but so are our casualties. What have we accomplished, really?"

Jacobs considered the question for a moment. "To be honest, I don't know. How about if I go take a look? I know we said no travel for the first few months so I can do my rehab. But I need to get out in the field, get a fresh sense of how we're doing and where we go from here. I'll keep it short and take one of the docs with me."

"You think Beth is ticked off now . . ."

"Yeah, well, I'll deal with that. Any new SecDef would have left for Afghanistan directly from the swearing in. I've got to show that I can do the job, that I'm not, well, afraid to go back there. And I think a visit actually would be helpful, to the troops in the field as well as for whatever information I can gather."

"You make a good case. Sometimes I feel like a puppeteer whose puppets are on a dark stage seven thousand miles away. It'd be good to have some trusted eyes on the ground."

"I'll make a plan and let you know."

"All right. It's important to get a handle on the impact of what we've done, but more important to figure out what to do next. And Marty, the primary focus of everything we do has to be stopping any MTO that's out there."

"Yes, I agree." He rose to leave.

"And don't overdo it. I need you long-term."

"Yes, *Beth*," Jacobs jabbed as he exited the Oval. "And, thank you, Mr. President."

Chapter 14

At the camp clinic, Faraz was coming out from under sedation. The first thing he noticed was that his left leg hurt like hell. So did his stomach and his head. It took him a second to remember both where he was and who he was supposed to be.

He tried to sit up, but was only able to raise his head a little before collapsing back onto the bed.

"Do not move, my brother." The doctor was across the room, tending to another patient. "How are you, Hamed?"

"Praise Allah, I am alive." Faraz was back in character.

The doctor came over to his bedside and checked his pulse. "You have several injuries, but yes, you will continue to be alive, *insha Allah*." If it is God's will. "Now, rest. Later, you will eat something."

The doctor left the clinic, perhaps to report that his patient was awake.

Faraz closed his eyes. The market attack came flooding back—the people, the carnage, the wounded, and the dead. And the girl—the blood on her dress, the fear in her eyes, her excruciating, plaintive cries for her mother. He moved a little and got a shooting pain from the bruise on his stomach. Good God, what had he done?

Faraz awoke the next morning to the sound of the muezzin calling morning prayers. Zahir was sitting by his bedside.

"Hamed, I am glad you are awake. How are you?"

"Praise Allah, but ooooh." He had tried to move. "It is painful."

"The doctor said you should not move. I am excused from prayers to be with you. Here, drink some water."

"Thank you, my brother." Faraz raised his head enough to drink from a cup Zahir held for him. "Are you all right, Zahir?"

"Praise Allah, only a few bruises."

Faraz was remembering more details of the previous day. "You helped me. Thank you, Zahir. I could not have gotten out without you."

"Do not thank me, my brother. It was my duty and my privilege. You would have done the same for me."

Faraz acknowledged Zahir's words with a nod, and they were silent.

Then the words streamed out of Zahir. "Hamed, you are a hero. You were almost a martyr. We are all praised for the attack. It was a huge victory. But you . . . you gave your blood for jihad. The *Qomandan* spoke to the camp last night. He called you, 'the hero Hamed.'"

Faraz stared at Zahir in shock. Then he raised his hands to cover his face. Faraz intended it to look like a gesture of modesty. But it was really insurance in case

he couldn't suppress a grin. U.S. Army Lieutenant Faraz
Abdallah was a hero of the Taliban.

Then his face fell. How many did he kill?

After prayers, there was an unexpected visitor.

"Qomandan!" said Zahir, jumping up from his chair
and moving out of the way.

Faraz opened his eyes and again tried to sit up, but
he couldn't. "Do not get up, my brother," al-Souri said,
moving close to the bed and holding out a hand for
Faraz to shake. "How are you?"

"Praise Allah."

"You did very well yesterday, all of you did," al-Souri
said, nodding toward Zahir. "We nearly made you a
martyr, Hamed, but Allah was not ready for that."

Faraz smiled.

"You get better now, and do what the doctor says. I
will return tomorrow, and if you are well, we will study
Koran together."

"Yes, *Qomandan*. Thank you."

Al-Souri turned to shake Zahir's hand, a gesture of
respect for the role he had played in the bombing. "Take
good care of him," he said, and then he left.

By the time al-Souri returned the next day, Faraz was
sitting up in bed. They read about duty and sacrifice,
and about the evil of infidels. Then al-Souri asked,
"Have you been thinking about the attack?"

"Yes, *sayyid*."

"And what do you think about?"

"It was a great victory for jihad, *sayyid*."

Al-Souri let that stand briefly. Then he looked Faraz in the eye and asked, "What do you really think about?"

Faraz looked down at the bed. "I think about the people, *sayyid*. I saw so many with blood, so many dead, so many crying . . . ." His voice trailed off, and he did not look up.

"And you feel guilt."

"Yes, *Qomandan*."

"And you worry that these thoughts make you weak, make you unfit for jihad."

"Yes, *Qomandan*." Faraz continued to avoid al-Souri's gaze.

"Hamed, do you remember I once told you that fear is natural, but acting on fear is cowardice?"

"Yes, I do remember." He looked up now, impressed that al-Souri recalled that conversation from weeks earlier. It was a mark of a charismatic leader, the ability to remember names, conversations, anything that might be important to someone he had met, someone he might be able to use.

"In the same way, these feelings you have are natural," al-Souri continued. "But allowing them to control you is worse than cowardice. It is treachery, treachery against Allah." He was speaking quietly, gently, like a wise uncle sharing the secrets of his wisdom. But his words carried extra weight, coming from a man who controlled your life and death. "You must remember, as you said in the classroom, these people were helping the infidels and their traitorous government. This attack will hasten the day when we can establish Allah's kingdom on earth." Now he spoke more passionately, his words dripping with contempt. "That is what is important, not the blood of traitors!"

"Yes, *Qomandan*. I will try to remember that."

"Be sure that you do!" Al-Souri said, seemingly angry all of a sudden. He took the books and left without another word.

The commander was prone to flashes of temper, but Faraz had observed that they were usually orchestrated for a purpose—to inspire the men or to stir up their anger. Perhaps that was the lesson al-Souri had come to teach—not to become weak, not to let guilt affect his commitment to the cause. As usual, the *Qomandan* was operating at a level beyond what Faraz had thought.

It was a lot to process, on top of the stress of the attack. But he couldn't do it now. Now, he needed some rest. The half hour of sitting up had exhausted him.

In the weeks that followed, Faraz found himself becoming Hamed more and more. He knew he should be focusing on his mission, but his efforts to do that had been set back by the physical and emotional shock of the market attack and his own injuries.

As he slept long periods on his pain meds, his dreams evolved from distorted close-up scenes of the bombing to feel-good moments of adulation at the camp. He saw the smiling faces of his fellow trainees leaning in close as they embraced him every time Zahir took him for a walk outside the clinic. He dreamed of al-Souri praising him in front of the whole camp, and of Allah smiling down on him from heaven.

Faraz found himself looking forward to al-Souri's

visits. He was proud that the great man would take time to be with him, and was continually dazzled by al-Souri's knowledge of the Koran and his commitment to his cause.

It was easier this way. If he had been thinking straight, there was nothing Faraz could have felt but overpowering guilt and pervasive anger at al-Souri, at the army, and at himself. But Hamed had only physical injuries to heal. His conscience was clear, and his heart was full after his triumph.

Faraz was allowing himself to feel what his comrades felt—the seductive allure of the commandment to draw closer to Allah through jihad.

Slay the idolaters wherever you find them.
Arrest them, besiege them, and lie in ambush
everywhere for them. (9:5)

His Taliban teachers ignored the fact that the verse referred to the idol worshippers of Mohammed's time, insisting that it required jihad against anyone who rejected their vision of a world under Islamic Law. That included all "infidels" and any Muslim who didn't join the fight to defeat them.

The call to jihad ran counter to everything Faraz believed in. For Hamed, it was a comforting balm.

Many nights, Faraz forgot to practice the emergency codes.

It took two weeks, but Faraz finally returned to light training, taking it easy as the doctor had ordered. After lunch that first day, he and Zahir were told to report for firearms training, a first for both of them and a clear indication they were now more than rookie trainees. Faraz was careful not to perform very well with the AK-47. Luckily, Zahir turned out to be a pretty good shot, so Faraz could also do well without standing out. A week later, they passed a marksmanship test and were summoned to meet al-Souri's head of security in his small office near the front door of the headquarters building.

"Ah, the heroes," the man said in a mocking tone. He was short and had a long, wide, gray beard and a bandolier of AK-47 rounds lying diagonally across his chest. Faraz never knew his name, only that they called him "Balaa." The name came from a massacre at a village in the east years before. It meant Monster, and in the context of his world, it was a compliment. Everyone in the camp, except al-Souri, seemed to be afraid of him, and jumped to carry out his orders.

"You work for me now," he informed them. "We have the most important job in the camp, protecting the *Qomandan*, may Allah help us."

To Faraz, Balaa's words and his body language made clear that he thought there was no way these green recruits with barely decent shooting skills belonged on his security detail. But orders were orders.

Balaa had been a young fighter when al-Souri first arrived in Afghanistan. Both of them were wide-eyed with ideological fervor and brave well beyond the point of recklessness. One day, when their unit was pinned down by a Soviet patrol, Balaa had led a few men who charged the enemy on foot, tossing grenades and firing their rifles. Al-Souri was among them. Balaa was the first to go down in the ill-advised maneuver, and al-Souri had saved his life, singlehandedly dragging him to safety after the rest of their comrades had fallen, and getting shot twice in the process. After that, as al-Souri rose in the Taliban ranks, Balaa was his most loyal lieutenant.

"You will report to me daily after morning prayers," he said to Faraz and Zahir. Then he waved his arm to dismiss them and they hurried out.

Zahir was excited, and Faraz could also feel the warmth of approval, of recognition. Faraz was not receiving any kind of validation from Washington, so Hamed was left to take what he could get.

"This is our chance for greatness," Zahir said. "We will have a big role in the jihad."

"Yes, praise Allah," Faraz said, hearing less irony in his voice than he had expected.

Walking back to their tent, he wondered. Maybe this promotion would give him a chance to actually get some useful information, maybe even to find out where Ibn Jihad was. Or maybe he was on the fast track to becoming a suicide bomber.

For the next several weeks, Faraz and Zahir trained with the security team every day. They were moved out of the small tent for new recruits and into a larger one with better-quality pads on the floor. It was closer to the headquarters building, and farther from the latrine.

When they first walked in, they found brand-new Taliban turbans folded neatly on the mats, the official emblem of their new status.

Balaa's deputy taught them basic skills like how to walk with the commander while watching for threats and how to fan out from a vehicle to create a secure perimeter. Faraz already knew all this and allowed himself to be a quick study. Zahir struggled to keep up, but Faraz helped him during their free time.

"How do you know all this?" Zahir asked.

Faraz demurred. "They just showed us, my brother!"

One night, as they stayed up late talking, Zahir asked, "But what about you? You hardly talk about your village, your family."

"It is true. There is not much to say and it is painful to think about. You know my parents are dead. My brothers and sisters are living with poor relatives. They do not have the life we have or the fulfillment of jihad."

"I understand. Jihad has changed my life. My father used to criticize me for sleeping late, missing the early prayers. But here, I jump out of bed. I am eager to speak to Allah and to begin my work."

"Yes, Zahir. I, too, am a changed man."

During the training sessions, Faraz and Zahir worked hard on their skills, and both improved nicely. At first, whenever Balaa came to watch, at least one of them merited a smack in the back of the head for doing something wrong. But they were doing reasonably well for rookies, and he had his orders to put them on the detail.

As the weeks passed, the head smacks became less

frequent, and one day Balaa said, "Pack some things. Tonight, we travel."

Whenever possible, al-Souri traveled at night, in vehicles with dimmed lights moving at high speed. Faraz and Zahir were in the next-to-last of four SUVs with two other guards. They all had AK-47s, and Faraz noticed they were not too careful about having the safeties on or which way the guns were pointing. Shortly after they moved out, he reached over and pointed the barrel of Zahir's gun away from himself and toward the window. Zahir smiled an apology. They did not know where they were going.

It turned out to be a short trip. They arrived at an unassuming house in a nearby village. Al-Souri went inside, and Balaa ordered the men to establish a secure perimeter. There were several men already guarding the house, who seemed to accept that Balaa was now in charge.

Faraz was teamed with Zahir and two more-experienced men, and stationed along the house's back fence, facing out toward a farm field. During a shift break, he asked one of them, "What is this place?"

The man looked surprised at the new guy's question. "It is the *Qomandan*'s home," he said. On his first outing with the detail, Faraz had been taken to al-Souri's house, where his second wife and their children lived, the family whose existence no one outside his inner circle had been able to confirm. Hamid was truly on the inside now.

In the morning, from his post along the fence, Faraz

saw al-Souri playing in the backyard with his children— a boy of perhaps fifteen, who was quite skilled with a soccer ball, a girl of twelve who tried to keep up with him, and two smaller children, who tugged at their father's tunic, trying to get him to play with them. After half an hour, a woman's voice from inside summoned them all to breakfast.

Faraz could hardly believe what he was seeing. One of the world's leading terrorists was spending tender moments with his family, having quite a normal morning off. Al-Souri would think nothing of ordering the deaths of families like his to advance the cause, and had indeed done so during the short time Faraz had been with him. But the man would love and protect his own family with equal determination.

Al-Souri would say American pilots and drone operators were no different. But Faraz believed they were different, that while they had killed many families like al-Souri's, they did not aim to do so, as he did.

Still, Faraz had to admit, the outcome was the same.

The men guarded the house all day, catching occasional glimpses of the commander and the children, and watching him take one walk around the grounds with his wife, fully covered, during which he admired her vegetable garden.

They left again at midnight. After about an hour they went past the market Faraz and Zahir had bombed, and drove around to a large villa on the other side of the town. One of the men told Faraz it was the home of Qader Khaliki, one of the richest men in eastern Afghanistan and a Taliban financier.

Faraz had heard rumors that Khaliki was playing

both sides of the fence. It was part of the man's role to befriend and bribe government officials, but he had so many dealings with them that his reputation in the Taliban suffered. Faraz figured Al-Souri was going to see Khaliki to make sure he drew the right conclusion from the market bombing only a couple of hundred meters from his house and to demand that he prove it with another substantial contribution.

When they arrived at Khaliki's compound, the financier greeted al-Souri warmly. He looked every inch the rich man, with freshly pressed traditional clothes fitted to his potbelly, a trimmed beard, and an expensive watch. He seemed consumed with his own importance, and pleased that al-Souri's visit was further enhancing his prestige. Khaliki put his arm around the commander and escorted him into the main house. His son took the security detail to a side building that had been turned into a bunkhouse for their visit.

The Taliban's political department had been working hard in the village since the bombing. Its operatives made two simple points in meeting after meeting with local sheikhs, merchants, imams, and bereaved families. They said the attack was not aimed at the people, but rather at demonstrating that the infidels and their puppet government were not as strong as they claimed to be. And the operatives made clear that if the village did not accept that it had played a necessary role in jihad, and that it must now be a bulwark for the Taliban, it would be hit again.

The approach worked, as it had in countless villages before. Knowing what was at stake, including their lives, the sheikhs helped spin the story. Few people believed them, but all understood what they had to do.

In the intervening weeks, complaints about the bombing stopped, government officials fled, Taliban police took control of the village, and money and new teachers flowed to the local schools, along with the militant curriculum.

In the morning, Balaa gathered his men. "My brothers, today our *Qomandan* places great faith in us. He has planned a gathering in the village to show that we are the champions of the people. The attack was a great victory for jihad, and now the village is turning back to Allah. The *Qomandan* will speak to the people. He will rally their support. And in his generosity, he will demonstrate our solidarity with them by providing money and food. But there are still dangers in the village. It is our job to protect him."

By the time al-Souri, Khaliki and their security teams left the villa for the rally around ten a.m., the village was well-primed and bulging with hundreds of visitors, many of them Taliban loyalists to lead the chanting and watch for anyone not showing the requisite enthusiasm. The people lined the streets and shouted as the vehicles wound through toward the market. Women twirled their tongues to ululate, making the traditional *"loooo, loooo, loooo"* sound to signal their adulation. Men held their children on their shoulders for a better view. Taliban flags and banners waved in the morning breeze.

Faraz marveled at the scene. When they got to the

market, he saw that it had been rebuilt, the destroyed stalls replaced. Knowing exactly where to look, he could see some charred tables and a small tree denuded of its leaves. But to the casual observer, it looked as if the bombing had never happened.

In one of the livestock fields, there was a stage framed by green and black bunting and Taliban flags, with a microphone front and center, and loudspeakers on both sides. Villagers streamed in behind the vehicles and pressed toward the front. The security men tried to make a wedge for al-Souri to get to the stage, but he waved them off. He waded into the adoring crowd, shaking hands and kissing babies like a political candidate.

When al-Souri mounted the stage, the chanting reached a crescendo, and it took several minutes for Khaliki to restore order so the commander could speak.

Balaa stationed Faraz at one corner of the stage, looking out into the crowd to watch for any threats. He scanned left and right, near and far, as Balaa had taught him. He varied the angle and distance of his gaze in order to cover a wide area.

Then he saw her. He couldn't be sure. Like all the girls, she was wearing a black hijab that covered her hair and neck. Although she was young, hers was pulled across her face for additional modesty, leaving only her dark eyes exposed. She seemed to be looking right at him. He moved a little and her eyes followed. Like in the market, she had a small boy clinging to her dress.

Faraz felt a coldness in his chest and an overwhelming sense of guilt. He had killed her mother. She had seen him running away. He broke into a sweat.

Did she know he and Zahir had planted the bomb or

only that they had not stopped to help her? Was that sadness in her eyes or hatred? Or both?

There was no woman with her. The man standing next to her was probably her father. He was tall and had a long beard. He was pumping his fist in the air, in rhythm with the cadence of the chanting, but his face and body language told a different story. His eyes seemed empty, fixed not on the stage but on something in the far distance. His shoulders were hunched. To Faraz, he looked broken.

Faraz was having trouble maintaining the image of a Taliban fighter. He looked away. But every time he checked back, the girl was still staring at him. He wished he could do something for her, tell her how sorry he was, give her something that might help. But there was still nothing he could do. And nothing would change what he had already done. Faraz turned away and did not look back in her direction.

Al-Souri's speech was about jihad and the pain that came with it. He said the attack had struck a heavy blow to the infidels and the traitorous Afghans who supported them. He swore that any loyal Muslims who died had been received in heaven as martyrs, and he admonished the community to honor and care for their families, and for the wounded. He spoke of the great Imam Ibn Jihad, who would lead them to victory, and how he would never forget the village's martyrs.

"Together, we shall build Allah's paradise in Afghanistan, and then throughout the world!" he declared to thunderous cheers. "If it is His will, it shall come in our generation. And if it is His will, it shall come after one hundred generations. But I swear in the name of Allah that it will come, as long as we continue to do His will!"

Faraz was not convinced, and he imagined most people in the village were not, either. But there was no denying the power of al-Souri's words. They tapped into the deeply held desire of many people of many faiths, particularly poor people—the desire to be part of something greater than themselves, the need to believe that their suffering had a purpose, a grand, noble, purpose blessed by God.

When the speech ended, the villagers responded with more cheers and ululating. Then they lined up for the money and food, as al-Souri and his security men made their way back to the vehicles and left.

They spent the rest of the day at Khaliki's villa and returned to their camp after dark.

The next day was Faraz's birthday—his real birthday, not the fake one he had given to the Taliban recruiter. He was twenty-four.

Balaa noticed that he was distracted while on guard duty outside the headquarters building. "Hamed! Pay attention! Do not daydream while you are working for me!"

But Faraz couldn't help it. He thought about the meal his mother would have prepared—Kabuli pulao and super-sweet desserts of thin phyllo dough, honey, and nuts, along with his beloved candied dates. He thought about the family gathering his parents would have planned, the stories, the laughter, his father's off-key renditions of Afghan folk songs.

Then he thought about what must be happening at

home instead. In the months since he had left, his parents would have adapted to his death. They would have hung his military portrait on a wall in the living room, draped in black. But by now, it wouldn't hurt them quite as much every time they saw it.

Except today.

Today would throw them back to the beginning. His mother would spend most of the day crying, and his father would alternate between trying to comfort her and staring off into space, not knowing what else to do. Maybe his aunt, Johnny's mother, would come over and the two women would lean on each other, rock back and forth and cry for their sons.

It was horribly, unspeakably unfair. And it was his fault.

That night, Zahir had guard duty. Good thing, too. Faraz had no interest in conversation.

He pulled the covers up over his head and mechanically said his army mantra one time. He closed his eyes and his right hand reached down between his legs. He started the familiar process, but he was close to tears. He tried to put the thoughts of his parents out of his mind, the thoughts of his former life, the life he could be leading instead of killing innocent people and making young girls cry.

Faraz needed to be Hamed. He needed the certain moral rectitude al-Souri provided through the Koran and the jihad—a feeling of surrender, of inner peace. Zahir felt it. Sometimes, Hamed could feel it. But on this night, Faraz could not.

His thoughts went to his happy years at UCLA, his friends in ROTC, the camaraderie they shared. Many of them must now be deployed not far from where he was. Some of them might have been killed or wounded by the same terrorists he was working with. He put that out of his mind and forced his thoughts back again to happier times.

Faraz had been a pretty straight arrow through high school and college. But that hadn't completely stopped him from experiencing the joys of the party life, of late nights and forbidden beer and liquor, and college girls on too many drinks who went weak at the sight of a cute guy with olive skin, dark eyes and a sweet smile.

That made him think of another birthday, his twenty-first. It felt like a long time ago. Everyone he knew had gathered at their favorite nightclub near the campus and drank and danced for hours to the thumping beat. He remembered Kristy, the blonde beauty every guy wanted, in her tiny miniskirt and tank top, French-kissing him on the dance floor and then taking him by the hand into a stall in the ladies' room, leaning in close to whisper "Happy Birthday," and kneeling down to give him the best oral sex he had ever had.

Lying in the bed, he started to get hard. Then his hand stopped. He knew the verse by heart:

And say to the believing women that they lower their gaze and restrain their sexual passions and do not display their adornment. (24:31)

The whore! The fucking whore! She had rubbed up against every guy in the room, practically begging for someone to rape her! The whore! Where was she now?

Probably giving some other guy a blowjob! She was nothing. Nothing!

Nothing compared to that other girl . . . that poor girl in the village . . . oh my God.

The crosscurrents in his mind accelerated into a raging, swirling rapids. He wanted to be a better Muslim, and he wanted his old life back. He hated himself for his past sins, and he ached to commit them again. He hated himself for his recent sins, too, and he desperately wanted to find a way not to commit those again.

Most of all, Faraz wanted to sit in his parents' living room, tell old family stories, and laugh.

He turned over and buried his face in his pillow.

CHAPTER 15

It was a stomach-turning experience for Bridget, climbing aboard one of the three remaining E-4B aircraft. It was identical to the one that had been bombed out of the sky three months earlier. These 1970s-vintage 747s were flying communications platforms, designed to work in tandem with Air Force One to help the president maintain contact with the chain of command in an emergency. Among other capabilities, the aircraft could communicate with submarines, send encrypted orders worldwide, survive an attack by an electromagnetic pulse weapon, and launch a nuclear war.

There had been four of them, and one was always on duty whenever the president was traveling. But they had been retrofitted for another mission—as the secretary of defense's flying headquarters. This was the first time an E-4B was being used for that purpose since the bombing.

It was dark outside by the time Marty Jacobs bounded up the stairs, the last to board, and greeted the crew with a big smile and left-handed handshakes. The senior enlisted man showed him to his small cabin in the nose with bunk beds, a desk, and a secure phone and Internet connection. Outside his door was the old spiral staircase that led up to the cockpit and the area behind it that was designed to be the first-class cabin. On this plane, it was the flight crew bunkhouse. Beyond the stairway on the main deck were a galley, a conference room with secure global communications, and working and sleeping space that on this flight would be used by the secretary's staff and the traveling press.

First stop would be four hours in Brussels for an emergency meeting of NATO defense ministers that Jacobs had requested. The delegation's gear would be transferred to a combat-ready C-17 for the flight to Kabul. As capable an aircraft as the E-4B was, it had no weapons and only limited defensive systems, and all the maneuverability of a double-wide lumbering down an interstate.

Bridget had an airline-type seat at a pod of four workstations fitted with communications and weapons control gear that was turned off. Jay Pruitt was next to her. The familiar ping sounded on the cabin speakers and the seatbelt signs originally put in place for business and leisure travelers flashed on. They buckled in.

"So strange, isn't it," Bridget said.

"Yeah," Pruitt replied. "What can I say? Life must go on."

"I guess. But I'm not sure what we're going to do out there besides show the flag."

"Well, there is some value to that. And you never know, we might actually learn something. Always good to see what's happening beyond the Beltway."

Bridget thought about her conversation with Tommy the last time she had flown to Afghanistan, and felt suddenly very sad. A few months ago, she had never thought they'd be mourning two more major attacks on Americans.

"Ladies and gentlemen, please prepare for takeoff," said a voice on the speakers. Two minutes later they were accelerating down the runway.

At the signals meeting, Jacobs told the delegation members he wanted them to assess the current state of play in Afghanistan and the impact of the new offensive. But he stressed the need to find next steps.

"We can't simply bomb and bomb and bomb," he said. "Eventually, that's gotta ease up, and we need to know what comes after."

There it was again, some apparent dissonance from the avowed hawk. What he said was obvious, but to Bridget it seemed too soon. And Jacobs was said to have wanted such an offensive years ago. She put a big question mark and a big asterisk in her notebook.

At the end of the meeting, Jacobs looked around the table, pausing briefly on Bridget, Pruitt, and a couple of others. "I know it's strange to be going back to Afghanistan. Difficult. I am mindful of that. I feel it, too. But we have to put that aside and do our jobs. That's what our friends would have wanted, and it's what the president is relying on us to do. Thank you, everyone."

Half an hour later, Bridget stood in the back of the press compartment while Jacobs did his first on-board news conference. He defended the new strategy and downplayed any expectations of major results from this trip. He told the reporters he was feeling fine and ready for the rigors of his new job. And he fended off several questions about the now widely reported rumors of a big terrorist attack in the works.

"You all know I won't comment on rumors or intelligence matters. But I will say that the primary focus of this department is to prevent terrorist attacks now and into the future. All right? Now, how about if we all try to get some sleep? Busy days ahead."

Jacobs retreated to his cabin and the reporters started drafting their stories, though they had little to work with.

Bridget and Pruitt returned to their seats. "They keep asking about the MTO," Bridget said.

"Yes, and they will continue to ask about it. It's too good a story to go away. But without anything to back up the rumors, there's not much they can do with it."

"Not much we can do with it, either."

"Yes." Pruitt lowered his voice, even in this secure environment. "That's why you intel folks need to figure it out ASAP, so we can end the threat before it happens, and before anything solid leaks out."

"We're working on it."

Pruitt shrugged.

"And Jay, what did you make of what Jacobs said in the signals meeting, that we can't just bomb and bomb? He's been calling for more bombing for a long time."

"True, but that doesn't mean it's the end of the story. Something's got to come next. Now it's his job to figure that out, and ours, too."

"I guess you're right. But it seems strange to hear it so soon."

"Welcome to my world. Whatever we're doing on anything, let's think of something else to do." Jay stretched and tried to settle into some sort of sleeping position. "But let's think of it tomorrow. Good night, Bridget."

"Good night, Jay." Bridget put her seat back as far as it would go and took a last look around the cabin few people got to see. Welcome to the big leagues, her dad would say.

Bridget closed her eyes, and her thoughts drifted to how she had gotten to where she was. She thought about her decision to leave the army, about how she told herself she would serve at a higher level. Well, this was it, on the E-4B with the SecDef.

In her mind, she saw a picture of herself as a little girl, sitting at the controls of a fighter jet, courtesy of her father and a handsome young pilot. She thought about her first days at West Point, the pride of acceptance squashed under the withering rebukes of the upperclassmen, the determination she'd had to draw on to get through.

And she thought about the day that launched her new life, the day she got her Ph.D., how her father walked from the taxi to his seat with a cane, her mother fussing over him every step of the way, and how he had worn his veteran's cap with rank insignia, which got them an immediate upgrade to the second row.

Bridget smiled and drifted off to sleep.

The first bright spot of the trip was her meeting with Gallagher in Kabul.

"We have a new source," he said. "Just got the info from the ANA. He's untested, but he's saying there's a big attack on the way, something outside Afghanistan against a Western target. Matches what we've been concerned about, but that's all we have. I'm preparing the notification to all agencies now. You're the first to know."

"Who is this new source?"

"He's a guy from the village your man Sandblast attacked. Crazy thing. He got himself detained at a checkpoint. Told his ANA interrogator he'd done it on purpose. Told the whole story of the bombing, that it killed his wife, left him with two kids. Cried like a baby."

"And you believe he's legit?"

"Story checks out. But, you know, we can never be a hundred percent sure."

"Where'd he get his info?"

"He's a gardener. Works for a rich guy in the village named . . ." Gallagher checked his file. ". . . Khaliki. Overheard some Taliban guys."

"So, we can't be sure it's really happening. Might have just been talk."

"True, but we've gotta take it seriously. Tracks with the Israeli report and other tidbits. Not that there's much we can do but keep on keeping our eyes and ears open."

"Where's the source now?"

"Back home, with a little extra cash in his pocket and orders to report ASAP if he hears anything more."

"Well, let's hope he shows up at that checkpoint again soon."

"Roger that."

Other than that meeting, there wasn't much on the trip to impress Bridget, not during the two-day Afghanistan visit, and certainly not in Brussels. Jacobs spent a lot of time showing the flag at events that were open to the media, as Bridget had expected—a town hall meeting with the troops, photo-ops with allied commanders and Afghan officials.

Now, on their final day, the secretary was sitting in front of the mess hall at Camp Eggers under large TV lights. The crew had put up a canopy to protect him from a misty rain. He was doing a series of interviews beamed live into morning television shows back home, during which he said nothing Bridget and the entire world didn't already know.

Bridget was watching the third such transmission when she couldn't take it anymore. She had a few minutes before departure, so she lifted her body armor from the ground and put the heavy vest on—easier to carry that way. She headed off along the main street toward the Bean, the base coffee shop. As she rounded a corner and approached the doorway, three navy officers in camouflage trousers and sand-colored T-shirts came out. One was a tall, light-skinned black man wearing a camouflage baseball cap.

"Will!" she shouted louder than she should have.

"Hey, Bridget! Jeez, how are you?" They hugged—a friendly, in-public hug—and exchanged chaste kisses on their cheeks.

"What are you doing here?" she said.

"I work here. Question is, what the heck are you doing here?"

"I came in with the SecDef."

"I should've figured."

Damn classified travel plans. "I'd have let you know if I could have. And if I'd known where you were!"

"Yeah, well we just arrived in this little garden spot

for some decent coffee and R&R." Will introduced his fellow SEALs. "Guys, I'll catch up with you." They left after giving Bridget a good once-over. Men outnumbered women, even at the headquarters base, by more than ten-to-one.

Bridget and Will looked for somewhere to talk outside the flow of foot traffic on the main road. Privacy was always at a premium in such places. They turned onto a footpath leading to a row of shipping containers that had been modified to serve as officers' quarters. It was raining a little harder now.

"How's it going?" she asked.

"Good, good. Saw some action but no major problems. How about you? You've had a rough patch."

"Yeah, it was rough. And it's strange to be back here. But I have to admit, it's good to see you, Will."

"Good to see you, too," he said. He tossed his almost full cup of coffee into a waste can and grabbed Bridget's arm. She allowed him to pull her into a space between two trailers. He took her in his arms.

Will looked good. Too good. More muscular and tanned than she remembered. But whatever he'd been doing in the gym and in combat hadn't changed the look in his eyes or his grin. She thought she must look terrible, not having had a proper sleep, shower, or make-up mirror for days.

She pushed a wisp of hair off her face.

They kissed, her body armor pressing against his chest. A moment later they heard footsteps on the path, and stepped back, as if they had just been talking.

"This is too weird," she said.

Will didn't answer. He grabbed all three Velcro strips holding her bulletproof vest together and tore them open. Never had that ripping sound had such an electric effect on Bridget.

He slipped the vest off her shoulders and lowered it to the ground. They kissed again, pressing their bodies together. The rain soaked their T-shirts and dripped off the brim of his baseball cap into her hair. His hands explored down her back and beyond. For Bridget, it felt good, really good after so long. But she eased him away.

"Will . . . Oh God, this is so terrible. I have to go. Motorcade muster is in ten at the main gate." She saw the disappointment in his eyes, and it made her want to stay even more.

"Shit," Will said. "That's about a ten-minute walk away." He kissed her again, then leaned back but didn't release her. "You better get moving double time. Can't piss off the new boss. I hear he has a mean left hook."

"Not funny, Will," she said smacking him on the chest. But she was in no hurry to leave.

He took her hand and kissed it. "See you back in DC, kiddo."

She snuggled close. "Yeah. And try to come up with something new to call me by then, okay?"

"Okay, um, sweetie . . . honey . . . lamb chop . . . sugar pie."

"Fuck you, Will."

"No time, muster in eight minutes."

"Too much time, you mean."

Will laughed. "Ouch. I'll get a Purple Heart for that one."

Then neither of them said anything for a moment.

"Better get going before I decide to make you miss that motorcade," Will said. He put his arms around her again. "You don't want to get stuck in this shithole, not even with me."

They kissed, a long, deep, tender kiss, and held each other close. Bridget didn't care if anyone walked by. When the embrace broke, Will reached up to cradle her face with his right hand and wiped a raindrop from her cheek with his thumb. Then he bent down for the body armor and helped her put it on, fastening the strips of Velcro one by one across her chest. He looked at her and they kissed one more time, but voices on the path interrupted them.

She sighed. "I gotta go."

"I know. Go, go," he said, and she turned and ran for the main gate.

Bridget got into the armored van labeled "Staff 2," breathing hard from her sprint. No choppers today due to the weather. They'd be doing a convoy run to the airport. As the last one aboard, she got the best seat, next to the sliding door, with a bit of extra legroom. She closed the door, expecting to leave at any moment, but they waited.

One of the security men came by and opened the door to tell them the secretary had requested another meeting with the ambassador and would be out soon. A few minutes later, the top commander and his senior staff hurried by on foot to join the meeting. It was starting to get dark, and Bridget knew that security would insist they get to the airport in some kind of daylight.

The delay gave her time to think, too much time. It had been a shock to the system to run into Will, and another shock to have to leave him so quickly. She was amazed at how good it had made her feel to see him, to hold him. Her life had been on fast-forward since the day he left, the day of the plane bombing. Seeing him was like the thud at the end of a high-speed run on an old videocassette.

She played those delicious few minutes back in her mind. The touch of his hand on her arm as he pulled her into the space between the trailers, the smell of his soap, the feel of her breasts liberated from the body armor and pressed against him, the stirring tingle when his hands ran down her back. She had pushed that part of her life so far away that she had forgotten what it felt like. And now that she'd been reminded, all she could feel was a deep sense of loss—loss of Will, loss of Tommy, loss of her hard-won sense of invincibility. If she'd been alone, she would have had a good cry.

But she wasn't alone. She had to stare at something through the van's doorway—anything—and summon all her strength to maintain her professional demeanor.

Bridget saw some activity at the front of the motorcade. Jacobs was finally coming out of the meeting. Someone outside slammed the van's door, and the base's heavy steel gate slid to the side. The vehicle lurched, and Bridget's life returned to fast-forward.

Chapter 16

By the time Bridget got home, Washington's intelligence community was well into the shitstorm caused by Gallagher's informant and his info. The president ordered the CIA to take over the running of the new source and to send a trusted Afghan operative into the village to press him to get more information ASAP. There was a near panic to prevent another 9-11.

Hadley told her he had heard there was a shouting match at the White House over whether to raise the public alert level. " . . . from Magenta to Sky Blue Pink," was how he put it, rolling his eyes at what he and lots of others thought was a stupid system. They both knew that such a move would further increase press and public speculation that a big attack was in the works—the last thing the president or anyone else wanted. So the alert level stayed at yellow, the middle of the scale.

Then Hadley lowered the boom. "Listen Bridget, fresh activity on the scattergrams is lending credibility to the new source's info. The jihadis are talking about something, and it's not soccer scores. We can't let this happen. Not like 9-11 or anything close. I want you to figure out a way to reach out to Sandblast. He's best positioned."

"Sure," Bridget said. "I'd love to give him a call. But you know that's impossible."

"What I'm saying is make it possible. Find a way. Get him a message and have him call in. We can't waste that asset. The long game is off the table. We have to address this now."

"But there's no . . ."

"Just figure it out, Bridget!"

Bridget stared at him for a moment. Then she said, "Yes, sir," and left.

Back in her office, Bridget inserted a message into the script that would be used by the Ops Center if Faraz called in, raising the priority on info about any MTO. Finding a way to reach out to him was going to take more time, if it could be done at all.

The threat of a major attack and the increased pressure at work didn't make it any easier for Bridget to get thoughts of Will out of her mind.

Those few stolen moments in Kabul stirred up emotions she had been denying for months. She thought it was almost cruel—no, actually cruel. In a way, she would rather not have seen him at all. But the stronger feeling was gratitude that she had seen him—more than gratitude, thrill really. She only heard from him once after that, before he disappeared back into radio silence.

Sweetcheeks (I'm working on it).

Heading back to Nowheresville. Was good to see you.

Next time, no body armor.

Will

Not much for a girl to work with, but better than nothing. She had responded:

Will,

Keep working on it,

Making you tee shirt: No Body Armor.

Stay safe. Come home soon.

Bridget

Her job had become a grind. There were several DIA operations running under the new strategy, but she thought the whole thing had lost momentum. The official conclusion of the trip had been that the approach was having an impact, but she wasn't sure what difference it would really make in the long term. From her own experience, she knew what Jacobs meant about not bombing forever. Since their return, the secretary had missed some opportunities to restate or praise the strategy, which had some of the savvier reporters speculating. But as far as Bridget knew, things were still moving full steam ahead.

Once again, Bridget was musing about giving it all up, never again answering to a general or seeing a Pentagon corridor, scattergram, or combat zone. She wanted Will to come home so they could escape to someplace that had only beach, sea, and a thatched hut with a king-sized bed, air-conditioning, and a coffee machine. If only she could make that happen, say, tomorrow. She didn't want to abandon Sandblast and her other operations. In the perfect world of her imaginings, they would all end tomorrow, too.

"Silly girl," she admonished herself. "Grow up! This is the life you chose, and it's not a bad one. Now find a way to make it work." She meant, "find a way to be happy." But "happy" had never been a priority. Satisfied. Fulfilled. Those words, she had lived by. But "happy" was not a regular part of her vocabulary. Her grad school friend Jen, whose Ph.D. was in psychology, had once told her, "That's a little project for you and your brain." Bridget was starting to understand what she meant.

But before she could get too far on that project, or too lost in her self-pity, she found out what the last meeting in Kabul had been about.

Bridget and Hadley were summoned to the secretary's office. They thought it was a routine status update, but when they got there the usual cast of twenty-some wasn't there. Instead, it was only the two of them, a lieutenant colonel from the joint staff, and mid-level people from the secretary's policy office and the State Department. Jay Pruitt came in with Jacobs and his chief of staff, Harmon.

"Sit down, everyone, please," Jacobs said. When they were settled, he continued. "Everything said in this meeting is classified Top Secret. Even the fact of the meeting is Top Secret. No one outside this room hears anything about it. Are we clear?"

He scanned the room to be sure everyone acknowledged what he had said. Bridget's mind was pinging hard, trying to think what this could be about. An operation to stop the MTO? Oh, yes, please! But she was wrong.

Jacobs made the announcement short and straight. "The president has authorized us to begin secret talks with the Taliban."

Bridget gasped, and so did some of the others. This was the last thing they expected in the midst of the offensive and the concern about an imminent terrorist attack. Everyone wanted to say, "But, sir . . ." and list all the reasons this was a bad idea, but it was clear the decision had been made.

"This is the team. Jay will lead. Our friends in Oman are making arrangements for you all to meet some sort of Taliban representatives in the coming weeks. These are not peace talks, per se. No one expects a cease-fire or any quick results. These are talks to explore whether we can even talk to these guys, whether there might be some way to lower the temperature and the death toll, whether there might—and I say might—be some way out of this mess in the long term. Initial goals will be very modest: Will they show up? Will they talk seriously? Do they really represent the leadership of the organization?

"If so, maybe we can each take some small steps to build trust. Most important is whether talking to them can get any major terrorist operation off their calendar.

"God," Jacobs laughed at himself. "It might be one of those things that sound crazy when you say them out loud." No one else laughed. Bridget was thinking it actually was crazy. "Anyway, the president has decided we're giving this a try, and I'm with him a hundred percent. It can hardly achieve less than we have in the last nine years. And you're the lucky ones who get to do it.

You're all here because of your expertise and your competence. If anyone can make this work, it's you. I won't ask if there are any questions because I don't have the rest of the day. Work with Jay. Figure out your approach. He'll bring it to the president and me. And again, nobody—nobody—hears word one about this. Good luck and safe travels."

Jacobs slapped his hand on the table in a "that's that" gesture, and he and Harmon got up and left.

Hadley was senior, next to Pruitt, and he spoke first. "Holy Jesus! This is bat shit crazy. You know that, right, Jay?"

"Could be, but we've got our orders. Maybe we'll bring forth peace in our time."

"I wish I could laugh at that," Hadley sneered. "This is going to be a pain in the ass, and pointless. And I hate the idea of sitting across from those bastards. They're supposedly about to hit us in a big way, and we're going to talk to them?"

"We're also hitting them pretty hard," Pruitt said, "Maybe they're feeling pressure to find a way out just like we are. But I get it. This is a lot to digest. Let's reconvene tomorrow at ten in the Old Executive Office Building. I should have more from the Omanis by then."

Two weeks later, Bridget had a window seat on a train in Switzerland, traveling alone under a fake name, with a fake passport, wearing the casual clothes of someone off on a ski holiday and possessing a confirmation voucher for a three-star hotel and a lift pass. She was not a skier. Although she had spent her professional life in intelligence, this was the first time she had ever participated in anything cloak-and-dagger.

The train wound north and east along crescent-shaped Lake Geneva, and in about an hour delivered her to the romantic town of Montreux, where houses climbed up the Alps from the lakefront, almost as far as the eye could see. She checked into the little hotel as the sun was setting over the lake, and told the clerk she was tired and would not be taking the shuttle to the mountain the next morning. Then she went for a walk on the steep, winding lanes to find someplace to have dinner.

Wooden tables, red and white checked tablecloths, fondue, crusty bread, and truly excellent wine, this would have been a fine substitute for her fantasy beach getaway. As it was, it sucked. She thought of an old song one of her army buddies used to say explained everything about being in the military. They'd get up and dance to their own rendition some late nights during her deployments. "Right Place, Wrong Time." The song, by Dr. John, had been around for forty years. Bridget never knew how true it could be until now.

She realized she was humming and tapping her fingers when the couple at the next table stopped staring into each other's eyes long enough to give her a look. She stopped, and offered a weak smile of apology.

Oh, Bridget. Cut the whining. Think of where Will had dinner tonight. Or Faraz!

There was only one thing to do. She raised her right hand. "Waiter, more wine, *s'il vous plaît.*"

The next morning, wearing blue wool pants, a white sweater, and a light blue ski jacket, Bridget walked to the convention center, showed her fake passport at security, and asked for the Travel Agents Association meeting. Upstairs, she found a door with a sign that read "TAA." There were four heavily armed Swiss policemen guarding it—more security than travel agents would normally need. She showed her ID again, a list was checked, a photo compared, and finally the door was opened.

Inside, she found Hadley and Pruitt talking to an Arab man in a dark suit. Jay introduced him as the Omani consul general based in Geneva. As the other members of their group filtered in, including an interpreter from the State Department, the Omani excused himself and went out a side door to check on the other delegation.

The room was bare, with movable walls and floor-to-ceiling windows on one side. The shades were down, and soundproofing panels had been rolled in and lined up along the walls and windows.

"Well, this is it," Pruitt said. He was wearing a black suit and a red power tie, and it almost looked to Bridget like he had accentuated the gray around his temples to add to his gravitas. "Only General Hadley and I will speak. I expect this first meeting won't last very long." Everyone nodded.

A minute later the Omani returned. "Please," he said, gesturing toward the side door. "And phones in here, please." He indicated a box on a table by the door.

Pruitt and Hadley led the way as they filed into a similar room with a conference table in the middle. As they entered, another Omani official was escorting the Taliban delegation and their interpreter through a door on the other side. They were dressed as they would have been in Afghanistan, but without their bandoliers, guns, and knives. The negotiators found their designated places marked with bilingual cardboard nameplates and stood behind their chairs.

The two groups eyed each other with suspicion and not a little hostility. There were no handshakes.

Bridget was in the far-right seat on the American side. The man across from her appeared to be the youngest in the Afghan delegation, probably not much older than Faraz, she thought.

Taking his place at the head of the table, the consul general broke the awkward silence. "Ladies and gentle-men," he began in English, "May I present Mr. Pruitt and General Hadley and their delegation from the United States of America, and Mr. Zaki and Mr. Baloch and their delegation from the Afghanistan Students Association." "Afghanistan Students Association" was a rough translation of Taliban. "Shall we all be seated?" The Taliban interpreter translated his words into Pashto, and the delegations sat.

Bridget forced a smile at the man across the table. He did not return it.

The consul general continued, "In the name of Allah the merciful, the beneficent, and in the name of his royal highness the Sultan of Oman, I bid you welcome and thank you for accepting his highness' invitation. Let us start by each stating the reasons we are here. Speaking for the sultan, may I say we are here to facilitate this dialogue, as an honest friend of both sides. That is all. We are not here to mediate or to offer solutions. It is the sultan's fervent hope and sincere prayer that these meetings lead to an end to bloodshed and suffering in Afghanistan. Thank you. Mr. Zaki, perhaps you can go next."

"In the name of Allah the merciful and beneficent," Zaki began in Pashto. "Thank you Mr. Consul General, and please thank his excellency the sultan on our behalf. We, the delegation of the Afghanistan Students Association, are here as the only true representatives of the Afghan people, who desire nothing more than peace, an end to the illegal foreign occupation of our homeland, and the right to live as we desire under Allah."

"Thank you, Mr. Zaki. Mr. Pruitt?"

"Thank you, Mr. Consul General, and please also convey our thanks to the sultan for helping to arrange these important talks. Perhaps it is auspicious that Mr. Zaki and I start with that point of agreement. We are here to explore whether it is possible to end the fighting and the suffering of the Afghan people, and to give them the opportunity to pursue a future of peace and democracy, under the rule of law, in a country that does not provide safe haven for those who would do us harm."

Bridget noticed he avoided using the word "terrorists." No need to trigger more hostility in the first minutes.

She had done a lot in her career, but she'd never attended a meeting even remotely like this one. The artificial civility was transparent and distasteful, but it didn't last long. Things went downhill about as fast as an alpine ski run.

Each time the Afghans spoke, they increased the anti-American rhetoric, using words like "invasion," "illegal occupation," and "war crimes." They accused the United States of lying, bringing debauchery to the righteous Afghan society, destroying the country with bombs and missiles, and a variety of other sins. Pruitt tried to keep it more positive at first, talking about peace and prosperity. But as the meeting went on, he inserted accusations of oppressing women, trampling human rights, and mistreating prisoners. That drew a fusillade from Zaki about the treatment of Muslim prisoners at Bagram in Afghanistan, at Abu Ghraib in Iraq, and at Guantanamo.

Bridget put it all in her notebook. Reading the transcript later, one could easily assume a fistfight was about to break out. But while the mutual animosity was stated directly, face-to-face, in harsh terms, it was mostly in a matter-of-fact tone without emotion. It was a very strange experience indeed. And the whole thing dragged unbearably because everything had to be repeated by the translators.

As an academic, Bridget absorbed the experience clinically, but she could tell that Hadley was working hard to prevent himself from blowing up. She noticed that Pruitt mostly kept his hands flat on the table, and he seemed to be breathing with unnatural regularity, perhaps a veteran diplomat's technique for keeping cool and calm.

Neither side mentioned the expected attack. Bridget thought of the U.S.-Japan talks that were going on when the Japanese bombed Pearl Harbor. She wanted to check her BlackBerry, but it was in the box in the next room.

After an hour, with the rhetoric heading for its third repetition, the consul general said, "Well, I believe both delegations have clearly stated some important positions. I propose that we adjourn now and reconvene tomorrow at the same time." Bridget was surprised. That was it? Why not continue after lunch? Well, baby steps, she thought, glad she didn't have to deal with such shit all the time.

The delegations stood, nodded their thanks to the consul general but not to each other, and left through the doors on opposite sides of the room.

Back in the side room, there was no breaking news on Bridget's phone. Pruitt spoke quietly to the consul general out of earshot of the rest of the group. Then he walked over to them. "I think that's about what we expected for the first day. They got all that out of their system. The CG hopes for better tomorrow."

"I wouldn't bet on it," Hadley said.

"All right, Jim. Nobody's betting on anything." Hadley's attitude seemed to be starting to annoy him. "I'll take care of the report for DC. Go take a walk on the lake. And remember, not more than two of us are to be seen together outside this room."

Two days later, they left the final meeting empty-handed. "Fucking waste of time," Hadley growled as he and Bridget walked along the lakefront toward their hotels.

"Yes, it seems those guys didn't want to be there any more than we did."

"Assholes. They make my blood boil."

"I got that," Bridget said, getting a smile from Hadley.

The sun was shining off the water to their right and the mountains rose green and misty to their left. Bridget took deep breaths of the crisp, clean air to help clear her head.

They stopped to look at the famous statue of Freddie Mercury, his right fist raised in triumph, as it was at the end of Queen's Live Aid performance in 1985. That performance was a triumph, but Mercury didn't know he was already dying of AIDS, much as these talks were some sort of achievement, but seemed to be already dying, too.

"What the heck is this doing here?" Hadley asked.

Bridget started to answer, but Hadley's cell phone interrupted her.

He looked at the number. "It's Pruitt." He answered, then said, "Okay, see you in thirty," and hung up. He turned to Bridget, "We have another meeting."

"Now what?"

"I don't know. But maybe they didn't want to go home with nothing. Pruitt says it could be a good sign."

"Maybe."

Indeed, the Taliban delegation did have a proposal. They offered to end the siege of two villages near the Pakistani border, where Afghan government troops were pinned down and taking heavy casualties, and the terrain made it difficult for the Americans to come to their rescue. In return, they wanted a hundred prisoners released and a drawdown of five thousand American troops.

That night, on a secure satellite link, Pruitt discussed the proposal with Jacobs, Harmon, and Sam Preston, the secretary of state. Ending the siege would get the U.S. and the Afghan government out of a pickle, and would prove the bona fides of the Taliban delegation. But the price was too high. They settled on a negotiating strategy and a bottom line of ten prisoners and a drawdown of five hundred troops as part of the next rotation in sixty days. Pruitt knew the Taliban would never wait two months for the quid pro quo, but he also sensed that the terms Washington gave him had some wiggle room.

After two more days of bargaining, they agreed the siege would end in forty-eight hours. And once intelligence confirmed that the Taliban had stopped shelling the villages and withdrawn its forces, Jacobs would announce that eight hundred support troops who were scheduled to deploy the following week to replace a departing unit would not be going, at least for now.

The plan worked. The Taliban fighters melted away into the countryside, leaving the two villages in peace, and the Afghan Army was able to send in supplies and reinforcements. A Taliban statement declared that the area had been rid of infidels. The Pentagon called the move a victory for the new strategy. Meanwhile, the deployment orders for a unit out of Fort Bragg, North Carolina, were suspended. The Pentagon spokesman referred to "pre-positioned supplies" and "greater efficiency," but the military audience knew it was double-talk, and the troops and their families suspected they would be heading out soon enough anyway.

Bridget returned home to Sarge the cat and no emails from Will. She knew he couldn't write while in the field, but that didn't make it any easier.

At least the big attack hadn't happened. But chatter continued to crowd the scattergrams.

Chapter 17

In the weeks after Faraz joined al-Souri's security detail, the Taliban fighters increased their operational tempo, finding ways to work around the American offensive, as Jacobs had predicted they would. Faraz had a good vantage point to observe al-Souri planning operations, choosing attackers, and coordinating with other commanders for maximum impact. The man was ruthless. Just as he had sent Faraz and Zahir to attack women and children, he sent other fighters to do the same. Faraz attended several memorial services for "martyrs" who didn't come back.

Al-Souri always attended the services and eulogized the dead men. But to Faraz, he appeared largely unmoved—much more concerned about the need to destabilize the Afghan government, fight its growing police force, and expel the Americans. He clearly didn't care what it took to establish Islamic rule in Afghanistan.

Still, Faraz was finding it easier and easier to be Hamed. The dissonance he had felt ate at him for weeks, until he couldn't take it anymore. For now, Hamed was the path of least resistance. Being Hamed enabled him to get through his days without the guilt and anxiety, and it made him less likely to slip up. He assumed Faraz would always be there if he ever needed him.

For now, he had a cushy job, considering he was in the Taliban, and he didn't see any way he could either escape or fulfill his mission. So, he dutifully repeated his bedtime mantra, but only once or twice, and without any conviction that he would ever need it.

He traveled with al-Souri frequently, visiting other training camps and stopping to see regional sheikhs to solidify alliances or strong-arm them into new ones. Usually, fewer than half of the security men would go on a trip, leaving the others to train and guard the camp. But one day, Balaa gave out travel assignments and doubled the usual guard. Faraz and Zahir were among those going. During the day before departure, Balaa ran extra drills and, without telling them the destination, made sure everyone understood there were special dangers surrounding this mission.

The drive was frightening. Faraz had the middle seat in the back of an SUV, so he could see the road ahead, between the driver and Balaa. The headlights of their three vehicles had been mostly covered with duct tape to make them harder to see from overhead. The lines on the roads were worn and there were no streetlamps. The drivers relied on the light of a half-moon and the occasional farmhouse or village. And they went as fast as possible. They also took a circuitous route, and stopped from time to time under trees or in a darkened village with their lights turned off to try to evade any surveillance from drones or satellites.

It was well past midnight when they pulled into the courtyard of a country villa surrounded by high walls.

There was a main house to the right, and several other buildings were ahead and to the left. The owner was standing in front of his house with a big smile and arms held wide. He was surrounded by half a dozen Taliban commanders in black and silver turbans and traditional clothes, their AK-47s slung over their shoulders, and most with double bandoliers crossed on their chests. All were smiling, and some applauded. Dozens of fighters were arrayed on both sides, and on the porch behind.

"Be alert," Balaa commanded as they jumped out of the vehicle. Some on the team took up defensive positions, but Balaa told them to stand down. "We are among friends," he said, as his men lowered their weapons but held their positions. Then he walked to al-Souri's vehicle and opened the door.

The commander emerged and went straight to his host for a big hug and kisses on both cheeks, and a great shouting of greetings and words of respect. He did the same with the other officers, and the fighters broke out in chants of "Souri, Souri" until al-Souri gestured that they should keep their voices down.

The host took al-Souri by the hand and led him into the house, with the other commanders following. Balaa went up to some of the other fighters and offered greetings, introducing some of his men. Slowly, the mutual suspicion melted and Faraz and al-Souri's other men shook hands with their counterparts and started exchanging war stories.

Al-Souri was clearly the senior man at this gathering. His men got the best quarters in the building closest to the main house, and at breakfast, Balaa sat next to the host's security chief. As a new guy, Faraz stayed quiet, but when the men realized that he and Zahir had helped carry out the market attack and were the ones injured, they were peppered with questions and treated with respect.

Al-Souri and the other leaders spent the whole day in meetings, emerging from the house only for prayers in the courtyard and walks around the compound. Faraz and Zahir took shifts guarding the building or the perimeter, and spent their off time talking to the other men.

At the farewell dinner that evening, al-Souri rose to speak. He thanked the host, and he thanked the other commanders for coming. He made familiar declarations about jihad and their inevitable success, and he praised the commanders for agreeing on new steps to hasten the day when Allah might reward them with victory. Then he surprised Faraz.

"My brothers, our conviction must be unshakable and our labors must never stop. But jihad is not a straight path. Allah will place obstacles in our way to test us, to strengthen us. We must never waver. The Holy Koran provides for us to shepherd our resources, when necessary, even to make temporary peace with our enemies so we may build our forces. But this is not such a time. Our enemies are weak and they lack resolve. This is not a time for us to give up territory we have liberated for Allah. This is not a time for us to show weakness, or to take infidel lies as truth, or to trust the liars to keep their word in dirty deals that serve only their purposes."

The other commanders and their men applauded and pounded the tables.

Faraz realized al-Souri was talking about the withdrawal from the two villages. At the camp, they had been told the Taliban version of the move, that the area had been rid of infidels. But it hadn't rung true. Everyone knew they would normally take over the villages and keep forces there. Now, Faraz understood. It had been part of a deal, a deal with the Americans. He could hardly believe it.

Al-Souri was clearly not happy about the agreement, and apparently neither were these other commanders. As far as Faraz knew, it was rare, perhaps unprecedented, for someone so close to the top of the Taliban to make a fairly public criticism of something Ibn Jihad had done.

After dinner, the other commanders gathered around al-Souri to shake his hand and embrace him. Now the picture was even clearer for Faraz. This was a gathering of the most militant Taliban commanders in the East, and al-Souri was their leader.

Faraz and Zahir went to load the vehicles. "Interesting speech," said Faraz.

"The *Qomandan* is always inspiring," Zahir replied. He had apparently missed the significance of what they had witnessed.

Balaa came over to them. "Quickly, now. We leave to see the Haji in ten minutes."

He was not talking about just any local elder who had made the pilgrimage to Mecca and earned the title "haji." There was only one man in the Taliban he would call "the Haji"—*the* Haji, Ibn Jihad.

From the look on Zahir's face, Faraz could see that even he understood that.

* * *

Under cover of darkness, they drove along narrow roads through the mountains, avoiding highways and villages as much as possible. After more than three hours they arrived at a walled villa at a crossroads on the edge of a town Faraz had never been to before.

Faraz knew Ibn Jihad never stayed anywhere very long, and his preferred residences were either extremely remote or in the midst of friendly villages, where there was little chance of betrayal, and the large number of civilians served to deter American airstrikes.

The SUVs pulled into the compound to a reception far different from the last one. Ibn Jihad's formidable security squad stood in a semicircle with guns at the ready. Balaa got out first. "Karch, my brother," he said, moving toward Ibn Jihad's security chief with his arms wide open to show he was not holding a weapon.

"Karch" was a shortened version of the Pashto word for "Hunter." The man was a legendary assassin. He had a heavy beard, a big belly, and impressive muscles for an older man bulging against his shirt. "Balaa, my little brother," he responded, and hugged his old friend and rival, perhaps a bit too hard.

Then al-Souri got out of his SUV, and Karch went over to greet him with a handshake and kisses on both cheeks. "You are most welcome here, my old friend."

"It is good to see you," al-Souri said. "I hope you are well."

"Praise Allah. He keeps old men like us fit for jihad!" The three men laughed. To Faraz, it seemed forced, but Karch's security detail relaxed, and al-Souri's men got out of their cars.

While Karch led al-Souri and Balaa into the house,

his deputy showed the visitors to their quarters in another building. Balaa had designated a few men to stand watch, along with some from Karch's team, and the others were told to get some rest.

Although Faraz was deep into being Hamed, he was not in so deep that he had forgotten why he was there. Now, as he lay on a mattress in the side building, his target, Ibn Jihad, was likely in the house across the courtyard.

Everything he'd done—all the horrible shit—had led him here. The question was: did he care anymore? And if he did, was there anything he could do about it? Could he kill IJ or call in an airstrike? Would he end up dead either way? And did he even care about *that* anymore? Officially, he was dead already. Most of the time, he could not imagine Faraz Abdallah coming back to life.

But if the lie to his parents led to the destruction of the Taliban . . . wow! If killing that girl's mother helped set her free from these assholes . . . .well, that would be something, anyway. And if he survived, could he someday—someday soon, maybe—walk down that tree-lined street to his parents' house again?

It was all too much to contemplate. But just by thinking about it, he was starting to bring Faraz back from the dead.

Faraz closed his eyes.

All right, all right. Procedure. First, rest. Then confirm IJ is actually here. Then figure out what to do.

Damn! I never thought I'd be anywhere close to this

position. Kylie Walinsky's insane fucking plan actually worked! All right, breathe.

Faraz took a deep breath and let it out. Then did it again.

Maybe this is what it was all for. Whatever happened led me here, right here, to this compound in . . . in . . . Damn! I don't even know where the fuck we are!

Okay, calm down. Find out tomorrow. Meanwhile, try to get some sleep.

202-555-4700, Sandblast, Whiskey-Alpha . . . ."

In the morning, Faraz got his first look at Ibn Jihad.

Everyone gathered at dawn for prayers in the courtyard. Ibn Jihad and al-Souri emerged from the main house together, hand in hand. Faraz had seen grainy old photos of Ibn Jihad, the only ones in existence. He recognized the man, but barely. What he saw was not at all what he had expected.

Ibn Jihad was nearly a head shorter than al-Souri, thin and unimposing. He had a trimmed salt-and-pepper beard and wore a shiny clean white cotton tunic with matching trousers and a large white *taqiyah* on his head. He had the appearance and bearing of a seminary teacher. Looking at him, Faraz would never have imagined he was the leader of a global terrorist network responsible for tens of thousands of deaths, and held a visceral hatred for anything Western, especially anything American.

The two men took their places at the front of the small gathering and prayed. Afterward, they all went into the main house for breakfast. This was a show of amity. Ibn Jihad and al-Souri were demonstrating to their most trusted, and most dangerous, aides and security teams that they were still friends, still united in jihad, even though al-Souri didn't like the deal with the Americans.

After breakfast, Faraz saw Karch talking to Balaa. Then Balaa came and told them there would be joint security teams to protect the leaders as they continued their meetings during the day. More Taliban commanders would be arriving, and there was much to do.

Faraz's turn outside the meeting room came a few hours later. For two hours, he heard bits of Ibn Jihad and al-Souri's conversation about operations, strategies for ousting the Americans, and issues related to various sub-commanders and regional sheikhs. Then he heard a heated exchange. The tone was clear, but he could only catch a few phrases, " . . . no surrender . . . ," " . . . strategic maneuver . . . ," " . . . too many concessions . . ." Then they lowered their voices. Whatever they were saying, they wanted to keep it to themselves.

When they all gathered for lunch in the villa's great room, Ibn Jihad rose to speak. "In the name of Allah the merciful, my brothers, we all share the mission of jihad, the desire to see Allah's Law supreme throughout our land and in the entire world. But we must be patient. We must adjust to the actual situation, and sometimes we must step back, just a little, in order to move forward with great force. We must fight Allah's enemies with our brains as well as our weapons."

It was an obvious criticism of al-Souri. The room was silent. Faraz saw several men slowly alter their posture and move their hands to be able to grab their weapons quickly if needed.

Then al-Souri stood. "Of course you are right, my brother. Surely, we shall see victory together, *insha Allah*." The two leaders embraced.

There was a general grumbling of approval, and Karch led the men in a chanting *Allah hu akhbar*. The tension passed. The hands moved back to their eating utensils. There was no rift. The leaders had agreed to disagree, and al-Souri had reaffirmed his fealty to Ibn Jihad. There would be no bloodshed in the villa today.

As he headed out for his next guard shift on the perimeter, Faraz passed Karch's office. The door was open. He saw a satellite phone in a charger on the desk.

His heart was pounding as he walked across the courtyard. Now he had confirmation that Ibn Jihad was there, and he had comms.

During his watch, several more regional commanders arrived, along with their security details. These were some of the same men they had been with the day before, along with some Faraz did not recognize. This was a major gathering of Taliban leaders to cement their support for Ibn Jihad and the secret talks. Faraz could not believe his luck. There was no other way to describe it. This was a golden opportunity.

After his guard duty, Faraz was assigned to help set up tables and chairs in the courtyard for a banquet. There was a fair amount of chaos, as Karch and his deputy organized teams to get the job done. Karch's men lit small lanterns that would provide enough light for the dinner, and strung ropes to suspend a camouflage netting over the courtyard. After considerable effort, it was all arranged, and the fighters stood behind their chairs.

When the commanders emerged from the main house, al-Souri was in second position, behind Ibn Jihad. Despite the lingering tension, it was a festive event, with the commanders telling war stories and the younger men cheering and shouting at every story of attack and victory.

Faraz took a turn serving, and as he went around to the other side of the table, he came up behind Karch's deputy, who was talking to one of the visitors. His paunch strained his tunic, and it rode up a bit on the sides. Faraz saw that he had the satellite phone clipped to his belt. He tried not to react, but if anyone had been watching they would have seen him ogle the thing, wide-eyed.

Later, when the commanders went inside, the security men stayed at the table and told their own war stories. Faraz and the other younger men listened and delivered their adulation on cue.

"It was some of our men who attacked the infidel base not far from here," Balaa bragged. "They killed fifty and shook the enemy to its core!"

There were cheers and pounding on the tables. Faraz remembered the rage and guilt he had felt on that day, how it had made him physically ill.

"Yes," said Karch in a tone more dismissive than laudatory. "That was a good tactical strike. Soon, we shall see the value of a real strategic blow on all our enemies."

The men murmured their approval, and one of the

commanders started a chant of "*Allah hu akhbar*." But Faraz saw Balaa shoot a look of disapproval in Karch's direction.

Faraz felt a jolt of realization and the courtyard seemed to blur and sway. Had Karch just referred to a major attack yet to come, a disclosure that earned Balaa's rebuke? What was it Karch said? "A real strategic blow on all our enemies." Faraz gripped the table and tried to breathe normally. Any doubt about what he had to do faded away in that instant.

Karch's deputy and the man next to him got up to go to the toilet. They left their weapons behind, and the deputy took the phone off his belt and put it on the table. Faraz knew this was it. He looked at the phone. Was he Faraz or was he Hamed? The answer came with speed and certainty.

He got up and grabbed a rag to help wipe the table and clear the dishes. When he got to the deputy's place, he put the rag over the phone. Then he picked up the rag and phone together, put them on some plates, and headed for the kitchen.

He put the dishes in a pile by the sink, but took the phone, wrapped in the rag, and went out a side door toward the barracks. He made a quick right, into a dark passage between buildings, and emerged behind the kitchen, next to the dumpsters wedged into a narrow space between the building and the compound wall. The stench was awful, almost unbearable, but he had no alternative. He crouched down and unwrapped the phone. Faraz had seen satellite phones before, but not this model. He pushed the power button. It beeped.

In a panic, he covered the phone with his hands,

hoping it wouldn't make any more noise. He found the volume control and turned it all the way down.

The phone's small screen came to life, showed the phone company's logo and then an hourglass to indicate it was booting up.

Hurry! Hurry!

A smiley face appeared on the screen with the words, "Enter PIN," and four blanks to fill in.

Shit, now what? Okay, okay, what could it be?

Faraz entered "1, 2, 3, 4," and pressed the green button.

The smiley face went serious and shook from side to side. The screen read, "PIN Incorrect. Enter PIN."

Damn! Faraz was breathing in short, rapid gasps. He worked to slow it down.

He entered, "1, 1, 1, 1," and pressed green again.

The smiley face bounced and went out of frame. The screen read, "Welcome! Searching for Satellite."

Thank God! Faraz waited and watched the graphic of a satellite dish rotating.

He could hear the activity in the kitchen, the clattering of plates, and the men shouting. The deputy would be back at the table soon, Faraz could only hope his first thought was not of the satellite phone.

The screen read, "Raise Antenna."

Damn! Stupid mistake! Should have known that. Faraz raised the phone's antenna and held it away from his body.

The screen showed the satellite dish swinging again. There was nothing Faraz could do but wait. If they were looking for the phone, there would be a commotion.

Maybe he'd have time to toss it into the bin and join the search. Maybe not.

The back door of the kitchen opened, and Faraz made himself as small as he could behind the dumpster, covering the screen with his hand. He held his breath. Two men came out and one opened one of the dumpsters, while the other threw two bags into it. They were talking loudly and joking. One offered the other a cigarette, and they lit up.

Faraz was sweating. He had to breathe, so he tried to do it quietly and slowly, but he was only building the oxygen deficit in his body and his urge to take big gulps of air increased. The smell from the dumpsters was overpowering, but he couldn't move. He was only a few feet from the men.

Faraz's hands were starting to shake. He was either going to fulfill his mission or die. Or both. If he made the call, what did he do next? How did he get out of there? Or just forget it. Let it happen. Remember, you're already dead anyway.

It was much harder being Faraz than being Hamed.

It felt like hours, but it was only a couple of minutes until the men, still smoking their cigarettes, went back into the kitchen and closed the door. Faraz took a deep breath and used his sleeve to wipe the sweat from his forehead. He uncurled his body a bit and looked at the screen.

It read, "Signal Acquired," and it offered him a list of choices of satellites and networks. He picked the first one.

The screen read, "Accessing Selected Network."

After another excruciating thirty seconds, he saw the prompt he was looking for, "Enter Number."

Faraz worked hard to control his hands. His thumbs sought out the right buttons—001-202-555-4700, send.

The screen read, "Dialing . . . Requested . . . Awaiting Response . . . Call Failed."

What!?

Then immediately, the screen read, "Redialing."

This time, it held on that. Maybe this was a good sign. Then came, "Requested . . . Awaiting Response . . . Awaiting Response . . . Awaiting Response."

Faraz wiped his forehead again and involuntarily shook the phone, as if that would make it work faster.

Come on! Come on!

At last came the beep-beep of a distant phone ringing.

Faraz's adrenaline was pumping so hard he could not even sigh with relief. He raised the phone to his ear.

"Operator."

The abrupt answer startled him. "Um." Shit, not very professional! "Sandblast," he whispered. Damn, he hoped they could hear him!

"Repeat."

"Sandblast," he said a little louder.

"Continue."

"Whiskey-Alpha-5-9-0-Sierra-Sierra-Romeo."

"Continue."

"Go ahead, make my day."

"Confirmed. Report."

Faraz swallowed hard. "Tango Alpha. Repeat, Tango Alpha." TA, the abbreviation for "target acquired."

"10-20," came the response, the standard code for "identify location."

Faraz had thought of that. He held the satellite phone in front of him, with the microphone close to his mouth, but the screen far enough away that he could see it. He read the longitude and latitude coordinates from the top line. The operator repeated them back.

"Roger," Faraz said. "Navigate to this signal."

"Understood. Further?"

Faraz wasn't expecting that. He would love to have given the evac code, but he wasn't in position. That would be his next project, after the airstrike, if he survived. "Negative," he said.

"Stand by for message ex Kylie Walinsky."

"Ready."

"Request urgent confirmation and details, reported upcoming MTO. If unavailable, pursue and report ASAP."

"Hmmm," Faraz said. "Yes. I have heard mention of a strategic-level strike, possibly with multiple targets. I have no details at this time."

"Roger. Repeat, message requests urgent confirmation and details."

"Understood."

There was a very brief pause, and then the operator said, "Foxtrot Hotel." FH, Fire in the Hole. It meant, "get the heck out of there, pal."

"Roger. Thank you." But by the time Faraz said the words, the line had gone dead.

Faraz sat there staring at the phone. The screen read, "Enter Number." Oh, how he would have loved to call his parents. But that was clearly not a good idea. He sighed as he realized there was no one else in the world he could call.

Faraz dug a hole in the ground with his hands and put the phone into it, still turned on, with its antenna sticking up out of the ground. He covered it with the rag. The pilot or drone operator would be able to lock on to the signal to make a precise strike. Then he stood, brushed himself off, and came back around the kitchen. Making sure no one was watching, he reemerged onto the path.

He saw the deputy talking to some other senior men. For the moment, he had forgotten about the phone.

CHAPTER 18

At the U.S. Air Force Tactical Control Center in Nebraska, Master Sergeant Remy Delacruz received a flash order on a red banner at the top of the main screen centered on his desk. It was flagged, "Priority Tasking." He was required to click on it within five seconds.

When he did, and entered his password, it gave him the coordinates Faraz had called in minutes earlier. Delacruz clicked and dragged them into his Target Vector window. Immediately a screen to his left showed the course to that location from where his MQ-1A Predator was currently flying over eastern Afghanistan. He looked up at the three screens mounted above the others, showing a panorama from the aircraft's nose camera. He clicked to accept the route, and saw the barren, moonlit hills appear to tilt right as the craft banked left and automatically accelerated toward its target. The navigation software put the flight time at twenty-two minutes, seventeen seconds.

The joystick Delacruz could use to fly the Predator was moving on its own, with the computer in control of the flight. Now, he checked the lower right screen of the six-screen array. It showed the aircraft gauges and a graphic of the plane's underside, with its two Hellfire missiles. Delacruz ran a weapons status check, but he knew he didn't have to. The server would not have given him the mission if his drone had not had enough fuel and a green light on its weapons system.

Each missile was sixty-four inches long and seven inches in diameter, and they packed a wallop. The explosive charge from either one, delivered to a precise location on the globe using satellite tracking and laser homing, would destroy anything and kill anyone within at least a fifteen-meter radius. The missiles could be fired from a distance of nearly five miles.

The watch commander, a lieutenant, walked through the dimly lit room, past half a dozen other workstations like Delacruz's, and stood over his shoulder. "You good for your 1752, master sergeant?" she asked. Each mission was designated by the time, in GMT, that it had been given to an operator.

"Yes, ma'am," he said. Delacruz didn't know what the target was, and he didn't want to know. He and the dozens of other operators received several such taskings every shift, sometimes for airstrikes, sometimes for reconnaissance, sometimes, it turned out, for nothing. These missions, once done by men with years of training and officer ranks flying at considerable discomfort and personal risk, were now done by enlisted men and women on the other side of the world, sitting in swivel chairs in air-conditioned control centers working normal shifts, with lunch breaks.

The watch commander reached down and changed the view on the lower left screen to show a close-up satellite photo of the target—the best available from the air force's supply of pictures of that location. "Looks like a residential compound. Good distance from other civilians. Clear of obstacles except that one hill to the southeast. There's a phone signal to follow, and we'll get you a live satellite feed."

"Thank you, ma'am. I'll come in from the northwest and fire from standoff distance, standard attack altitude. Out of sight, out of mind, ma'am." It was the unit's unofficial motto.

"Roger, that," said the lieutenant, and she headed back to her desk.

Bridget was coming back into the DIA offices from a meeting when Liz Michaels ran over to her, clearly excited about something. "Sandblast just called in."

"Jesus! What?"

"He called it in, Bridget. Your boy called it in!"

"Holy Mother of . . ."

"Tasking has gone out. ETA twenty minutes. We'll need Level One approval."

"Ibn Jihad?"

"He called 'TA.' IJ was his target. Not a lot of chitchat on the call. By the book."

"And we have confirmation it was him?"

"ID codes and voice recognition."

"Wow. You call Hadley?"

"Yup. You two have a secure conference call in ten. Congratulations, Bridget. This is huge!"

"Thanks, but let's not jinx it." Bridget went into her office and logged in. She listened to Faraz's call. Wow. That was him. She had thought she might never hear his voice again. She noticed he did not give the emergency extraction code. Apparently, he wasn't set up for that yet. Then she got a chill. Maybe he was there, on the target. Jesus!

Her heart started hammering away at her ribcage. The United States could be minutes away from killing the world's most notorious terrorist, in an operation she had put together. It could also be minutes away from killing the man who made it possible, a soldier she had sent into harm's way. Get the hell out of there, Faraz!

Her phone rang and she put on the headset. "Davenport."

"Stand by, ma'am."

"Bridget." It was Hadley on the line. "We'll be waiting a while. This is a big one. Jacobs and Harmon are coming on. Maybe others."

"Roger, sir."

"Sandblast said he's heard talk of an MTO, but no details," Hadley said.

"Maybe he's not high enough in the organization."

"Or maybe it's just talk. Or maybe it's happening today. Or who knows what. A more experienced operative would have provided more detail."

"Well," Bridget said. "A lot is about to change. The long-term objective seems to have overtaken the short-term one."

The operator announced that the Nebraska control center was on the line, so Bridget and Hadley had to suspend their conversation.

While they waited, Bridget studied the data on her screen, the route of the drone, details on the target, and a transcript of Faraz's call. Her fear had been right. The coordinates of the call were the same as the airstrike. Faraz, go now! Blow your cover, do anything, but get out of there! Hellfire at your location in ten minutes!

Her headset clicked. "This is Harmon. The secretary will be with us in a moment. This is your 'terrorist,' Bridget?"

"My operative, yes, sir." She hoped her flash of anger flowed through the phone line.

"This is Secretary Jacobs."

"Sir," Harmon said, "Everyone is on."

"Thank you. I understand Sandblast has called in a tasking. What's our level of confidence?"

"One hundred percent, sir," Hadley said. "We have ID codes and voice recognition. The call was less than fifteen minutes ago, so we believe the information is good."

"And the operation?" Jacobs asked.

A senior officer from Nebraska answered. "On track, sir. We are now seven minutes out."

"Thank you." He paused. "Folks, I'm going to put a hold on this."

"Sir?" It was Hadley, clearly surprised.

"We need to take this to the president. It's too big a step to take without his sign-off, especially now."

"Timeframe is key, sir," Hadley said.

"I know that."

Bridget could hear that Jacobs was annoyed.

"Operations, what's the fuel status?"

"Plenty, sir. We can stay on station for several hours if needed, and I have other assets to take over at that point."

"Good. Do that until further notice. The rest of you, East Entrance in ten minutes. I'll get us some face time." He hung up.

"Jeez, Harmon, you gotta talk to him," Hadley said.

"You heard the man. See you in ten." And Harmon hung up.

* * *

An hour later, while the drone circled high above Khaliki's compound, they were waiting in the Oval Office, along with the president's intelligence adviser, the chairman of the joint chiefs, and Jay Pruitt. An aide got the secretary of state on a secure speakerphone from a hotel in Singapore, where it was four in the morning.

It was another out-of-body experience for Bridget. She made a point of scanning the room. They were on an off-white sofa facing another identical one, with a colonial-style coffee table in between. The oval carpet had the presidential seal. There was a portrait of Washington in front of her and a bust of Lincoln behind. The office was designed to impress and intimidate, and it did.

She forced herself out of her reverie. There was no time for tourism. She checked her watch. It had been more than an hour and a half since Faraz had called in. The mission could have been completed within twenty-two minutes, which was the kind of timeframe they needed. Human targets tend to move, especially if they know they might be targets. Too many times, the bombs had come too late, missing their intended victims and killing innocents.

They all stood when President Martelli came in with his chief of staff, Greg Capman. "Good afternoon, everyone."

"Good afternoon, Mr. President," Jacobs said. "Sir, this is General Hadley, head of operations at the DIA, and Ms. Davenport, his director for Central Asia."

"Good to meet you both," Martelli said, as he and

Capman shook their hands. "Ms. Davenport, you were with Marty and Jay at FOB Emerson, weren't you?"

"Yes, Mr. President."

"Well, it's good to see you here, safe and sound." Martelli looked straight at her and for that moment, Bridget felt as if she were the only person in the room.

"Thank you, sir," she managed.

The president scanned the group. "Let's sit down, shall we?" Martelli sat in his chair at one end of the coffee table and crossed his legs. Jacobs sat at the opposite end of the table and the others were arrayed on the sofas, sitting up straight with their feet on the floor, except Capman, who sat to the side and took notes. Bridget took out her notebook, too, fighting the impulse to do nothing but stare at the president.

Martelli raised his voice a bit. "Sam, you on the line?"

"Yes, sir."

"Good. Well, I know we have a drone circling based on some pretty credible information."

"Yes, Mr. President," Jacobs said. "This comes from one of our own working in deep cover inside the Taliban."

"This is the man from the market bombing video, right?"

"Yes, sir."

"Extraordinary. You've got to give the guy a lot of credit. Must be difficult as hell."

"Yes, Mr. President," Jacobs said. "This is a high-risk, high-reward operation, a direct response to the plane bombing. Frankly, sir, many folks thought it was foolhardy, could never work. But here we are."

Martelli looked at Jacobs down the length of the coffee table and said, "Yes, here we are in the middle of talks with the Taliban and one of our drones has a bead on their leader."

No one in the room said anything. After a few seconds, Secretary of State Sam Preston spoke through the speakerphone, "Mr. President, I would have jumped at the chance to hit IJ a month ago, but this is the worst possible time. If nothing else, the talks seem to have put a hold on their big operation. Killing IJ could unleash it."

"Or it could end the threat," Jacobs said. "Problem is, we just don't know, as usual. What is *not* usual is that we have a chance to take the initiative in an unprecedented way. Look, I agree the timing is not ideal, but we have to understand this is an opportunity that is not likely to come again. I helped engineer the talks, but this is a chance to strike a truly meaningful blow, something, if I may say, on a level with the killing of Rod Bates."

"Mr. President?" Greg Capman wanted in on the conversation.

"Yes, Greg," Martelli said, twisting in his chair to face him.

"If we hit IJ and then the big attack comes, we'll be blamed for provoking it. You'll be blamed. For now, the threat of an attack is down, and so is the media drum beating about it."

The room was quiet again. Martelli did not respond and turned silently back toward the others. He looked like he disapproved of Capman bringing politics into the discussion, but he didn't dispute the point.

Bridget's impatience was rising. She had expected this would be a routine briefing and sign-off. She had thought the missile would be speeding toward its target by now. She had been so focused on the operation that she hadn't thought about the talks. Still, in her mind a clear win was by far preferable to the deep uncertainty of diplomacy with terrorists, even with the MTO in the mix. Jacobs was right. Hitting IJ could end the threat. Or, if not, well, the attack was coming anyway.

Bridget turned her wrist subtly on her notebook so she could see her watch. It was now more than one hundred minutes since the call. She tried to stay still, but couldn't help looking back and forth from the president to Jacobs, trying to assess the state of play. Were they all just going to sit there?

Again, Preston broke the silence from the speakerphone. "Mr. President, not to put too fine a point on it, but you need to decide whether we are escalating or de-escalating." Preston let that sink in before continuing. "And this information is over an hour-and-a-half old. IJ might not even be there anymore. Also, I understand this house is on the edge of a village. We could end up killing a bunch of civilians while IJ is miles away. Sorry, but this could be bad all the way around."

Jacobs shuffled his papers. "Mr. President, we now have video and photos from the drone." He held up an image. "It clearly shows several vehicles in the compound and no movement in the last hour. Infrared indicates numerous guards on the perimeter. That means someone important is there. And with our targeting technology, the villa is far enough from other houses."

In her notebook, Bridget wrote, "Current intel good. LET'S DO THIS!!!"

"General," the president said, turning to Hadley.

"What are the implications for your man if we don't do this?"

"If we don't do this?" What? Bridget wanted to jump off the sofa, but she calmed herself. She had never been to such a meeting before. Makes sense they would cover all the angles.

"Unknown, sir," Hadley said. "We don't know if he bugged out after the call or whether he's still there on the target."

"So, we could kill him, too, if we proceed?"

"Yes, sir, possibly. That would have been his decision on what to do after he made the call. And sir, if he did run, we can't say when we might get another chance on IJ. He's very good at being invisible."

Bridget stared at Pruitt and pleaded with her eyes. Jay, say something! But he didn't.

Martelli put his right hand on his chin and rubbed it back and forth. "Admiral?" He turned to the chairman.

Bridget shifted her stare. *Tell him it's a slam-dunk!* But the admiral disappointed her, too.

"This is good info, sir," he said. "We're well within the parameters to believe the target is good. Our soldier will have taken steps to get out of the kill zone. He's had plenty of time. But, Mr. President, it's a tough call for a different reason. This could affect how long our troops have to be there, and what they have to face. Killing IJ would hurt the Taliban. But they'd likely come back with a fury, possibly under a more hard-line leader. Certainly, there would be no more talks. This is a strategic decision, sir, not a tactical one."

Bridget's fingertips were white from holding her notebook so tightly. The admiral had a point, but she agreed with Jacobs—unique opportunity, huge impact. And after all the work we did, all that Faraz did. Jesus!

President Andrew Martelli shifted in his chair and gazed out the windows toward the Rose Garden. It was only the most difficult decisions that came to the president. As any president often did, he faced two extremely imperfect options. And this decision involved life and death, today, for dozens of people, maybe including an American soldier, as well as the future course of the war, with thousands more lives in the balance.

So, kill IJ, throw the Taliban into disarray, end the talks and brace for a new torrent of violent attacks in Afghanistan and in the West, maybe including an MTO? Or abort the airstrike, press ahead with the talks, and rely on the world's leading terrorist to help end the war?

Nothing prepared a person for decisions like this. And Martelli had to decide right now. Too much time had already gone by. All eyes were on him. The only sound was the secretary of state's breathing ten thousand miles away, amplified by the speakerphone.

Bridget started to lean forward in anticipation, but she stopped herself. She glanced at her watch again—one hundred eleven minutes since the call. C'mon!

To her, the president looked grim, unhappy. It seemed like a long time passed, but she thought it must have been only ten or fifteen seconds. Then, his face changed. He pursed his lips briefly and made an almost imperceptible nod. The president had made his decision.

He looked back toward Jacobs and the others. "Folks, I think we need to stay on the course we've set. The Taliban—IJ, really—lived up to his side of the agreement. Jay and his team are heading back to Switzerland next week to see what else we can accomplish. If we make this strike, we'll slow the Taliban down for a while, but it won't end the war. And it would likely be years until we could be back in a position to de-escalate and maybe disengage. Meanwhile, how many would die?"

He paused. No one answered. Bridget realized her mouth was open in surprise. She closed it.

"Marty, let's abort this strike. General, I hope your man gets out okay. Do whatever you can to help him and keep me posted, will you please?"

"Yes, Mr. President," Hadley said automatically.

Jacobs gave the cue to leave, "Thank you, Mr. President."

They all stood. Bridget felt a little unsteady. They mumbled their thanks and the president made brief eye contact with each of them as they filed out. "Thank you all very much," he said.

In the outer office, Jacobs said, "Well, that's one I'm glad I didn't have to decide. I think I'd have been unhappy either way." Hadley's face was turning red. Bridget averted her eyes and gazed, unfocused, at the floor.

The general spoke in a stage whisper, "We sent a young lieutenant into harm's way, serious harm's way, and now politics screws him!"

Jacobs raised his eyebrows at Hadley's vehemence. "Look, I understand how you feel, General, but this isn't 'politics.' There's more to our Afghanistan strategy than

Operation Sandblast. A lot has changed in the months since you launched this guy. It's a tough situation for him, but that's the way it is. Like the president said, do what you can for him. I'll see you across the river."

He turned and walked with Pruitt toward the NSC offices, where he could make a secure call to cancel the airstrike.

Bridget couldn't speak. She thought she might throw up right there in the wastepaper basket with the presidential seal on it. Her shoulders were slouched. She realized she had her hand on her heart.

A marine in a dress uniform came to escort them to the exit.

"What just happened?" Bridget asked Hadley as they emerged from the West Wing and walked along the driveway toward the gate.

"We got fucked, that's what happened," Hadley said. "Especially your man Sandblast got fucked. Jesus! I wish I'd never approved that mission."

Bridget was silent. She wished she'd never proposed it. Lieutenant Faraz Abdallah was out there, waiting for an airstrike that wouldn't come. She hoped he was miles away, heading for a secure location where he could call in the evacuation code. If so, he might not know the airstrike had been aborted. On the other hand, if he was still there or nearby, he'd be confused and angry, to say the least, and rightfully so. But really, Bridget knew she couldn't imagine what he was going through right about then.

Well, at least he wouldn't be killed by the U.S. Air Force tonight. What a fucking horror show!

Hadley hailed a taxi and told the driver to take them to the Pentagon.

In Nebraska, another urgent message flashed onto Master Sergeant Delacruz's screen. "Abort 1752. Abort 1752."

Delacruz raised his eyebrows and then shrugged. This one felt real, somehow, but . . . whatever. He took a last look at the live video of the villa compound spinning on the upper screens as the drone circled at fifteen thousand feet in a wide arc. Then, on his keypad, he punched in the code for Return to Base and sent the command.

The joystick tilted and the Predator banked right, boosted its throttle, and made a beeline for Bagram Air Base like a fighter jockey with a hot date.

Thirty-four minutes later, another operator would handle the drone's landing. Delacruz would be on the way to his daughter's soccer game.

Back in her office, Bridget was still feeling as if she'd been kicked in the stomach. She was supposed to be helping destroy the Taliban, but her best plan had been shot down by the President of the United States, at the very moment it was about to succeed. At the same time, she couldn't figure out what the heck she was doing on a team negotiating with the Taliban. Everything she knew about them told her that at best the U.S. would get some short-term gain in return for long-term pain, while the Taliban would use any easing of hostilities to build for the future.

Is that what happened in the Oval? Did IJ play Martelli and win a reprieve on his life, and not even know it?

Meanwhile, Faraz was essentially lost in Afghanistan. And she couldn't even remember how many weeks it had been since she'd heard from Will.

Hadley came in carrying his briefcase. He looked like he had recovered better than she had. Bridget knew he'd been in the bureaucracy longer, and although as a military commander he surely hated what had happened, it wasn't his first time being thrown from the bull.

"Okay," he said. "Which one of us is going to talk the other out of resigning?"

That should have gotten a chuckle out of Bridget, but it didn't. "Maybe neither," she said.

"Here, we deserve this." Hadley opened the briefcase and took out a bottle of Scotch. The alcohol ban was the most widely violated rule at the Pentagon. "I thought we'd be celebrating, but I think we can repurpose it."

Finally, he got a resigned smile out of Bridget. "Okay," she said reaching for her bottom desk drawer, "if you don't mind plastic cups."

"I do mind," Hadley said, taking two cut-glass tumblers out of the case. He put them on her desk and poured the drinks. He handed a glass to Bridget and raised his. "Your health."

"Faraz's health," Bridget said. He nodded. They clinked glasses and sipped their Scotch.

The warmth of the drink spread through Bridget and she sighed, relaxing a bit for the first time since she had entered the Oval Office. "That helps. Thanks, General. But it doesn't really help Faraz."

"Well, let's think about what we can do on that. We need to find a way to bring him home." Hadley took another sip.

"I'm sure that's the number one thing on his mind right now, although he's gotta be pretty pissed if he's close enough to know what happened . . . what didn't happen. Anyway, not much we can do unless he calls in the evac code and tells us where he is."

"True. Let's make sure everyone up and down the line is ready in case he does."

"Will do."

"And Capman was right. The threat is down and the media is looking elsewhere for stories. That gives us more time to figure this thing out."

"You think there's something to the scattergrams and the bits of intel on an MTO, don't you?"

"I don't know anything you don't know. But my gut says 'yes.'"

"So does mine, especially after Faraz said he heard about it, too."

Hadley leaned back in his chair and downed the rest of his drink. "I've got another little shocker for you."

"Oh?"

"I'm shipping out."

"What?!"

"Yeah, G2 in Kabul." G2 was the military acronym for chief of intelligence at a major military command.

"Jesus, General! Congratulations, I guess. I thought you were done with deployments."

"So did I. Guy got sick. I head to training in two weeks and then directly downrange."

"Jeez. Well, second star, I presume."

"Yes, there is that. Comes with a one-way ticket to Kabul, though."

"Well, round trip eventually, let's hope."

"Yes, let's hope. And speaking of promotions, Bridget, you're acting."

"What?"

"Acting Director of DIA Operations, effective next Monday, so I can get some time off."

"Me? Why?"

"Because I told them to, and for a change they listened. It's only interim, but you know what they say."

"What's that?"

"Around here, few things are as long-lasting as a temporary solution."

"Ha!"

"Especially true on this," Hadley said. "They didn't know it was coming. Could take months to get a military person with the right rank and experience in here. We're kind of a high-demand item at the moment."

"Well, I know you're the one going to the war zone, but I can't say I'm at all happy about this."

"Yeah, well, you should talk to my wife."

CHAPTER 19

In the hour after he made the call, Faraz was in a silent panic. His heart and his mind were racing as the other men talked and joked into the night. He kept looking toward the sky. He tried to calm himself.

Let Faraz die with Hamed. It was too crazy to imagine he could get out of there. He would die a martyr for two causes. He said the Shahada to himself.

Balaa saw that he was the odd man out amid the revelry. "Hamed, go!" he ordered. "Take a watch."

"Yes, *sayyid*." Faraz got up, took his weapon and went toward the gate. During the short walk, he realized what a favor Balaa had done for him.

Maybe Hamed and Faraz were not dying tonight. But where would he go? Well, worry about that later.

At the gate, he reported to the senior guard on duty and said Balaa had ordered him to do perimeter duty, outside the wall. The man told him to relieve a fighter stationed at a corner of the compound, where it backed up to some woods and the hill.

Faraz headed that way and relieved the other fighter. The man thanked him and moved quickly to join the party in the compound.

Once he was gone, Faraz was alone. It was dark, so the men on the wall couldn't see him. He went through the trees and climbed the hill. It had been over an hour, so he didn't think he'd get far before the airstrike, but maybe far enough. When he reached the crest of the hill, he found a small clearing that gave him a view of the compound. He sat down to wait. This should be a good show.

It was getting cold as the time approached midnight. The town was quiet, and the war stories had finally ended in the compound. Faraz listened to the crickets, and he thought he heard a wolf in the distance. He scanned the sky, but he knew he wouldn't see anything until the last second. He listened for the whistling of the missile, the last thing its victims would hear before *boom*.

But it never came. He speculated on reasons for the delay, but none made sense. Was there something wrong in the call? Had his mission been canceled? Were there no air assets available? Surely that could not be the reason, not for this target!

He sat on the hill for an hour, not knowing what to do. He could leave, but that might be more dangerous than staying. In Afghanistan's tribal society, strangers were noticed, and al-Souri's men would be searching for him, wondering why he had run away. He could go back to his post and wait for someone to relieve him, then reenter the compound and . . . what? Become Hamed for real? Look for another opportunity to call and ask what happened or give the evac code? That would mean getting to somewhere he could be picked up. Seemed unlikely.

SANDBLAST   269

As much as he was a respected member of al-Souri's personal guard, Faraz realized he was also a prisoner. His commander knew where he was supposed to be at all times. No deviation from routine or orders was tolerated.

He sat with his knees up, his arms wrapped around them, his chin perched on top—as if waiting for the executioner.

Then he heard footsteps on the hill. He grabbed his AK-47 and pointed it into the darkness. Someone was searching for him. It looked like he was going to go out shooting. At least he'd take one of these motherfuckers with him.

His body was tense. His army training took over. Instantly, Lieutenant Faraz Abdallah was ready to shoot his way to freedom, or death. His finger tightened on the trigger.

"Hamed! Hamed!" came a voice from the darkness. It was Zahir. "Hamed, is that you, my brother?"

Faraz exhaled and his body relaxed. He was Hamed again, and his opportunity for escape had ended. "Yes, I am here," he said, lowering his weapon.

Zahir came to the edge of the trees. "What are you doing? You are too far from your post!"

"Toilet, toilet," Faraz said.

"Okay, okay, but too far." Zahir waited until Faraz came to him. "You are lucky the commander did not see you. Go now and get some rest. I will take over."

"Thank you, my brother." Faraz slapped Zahir's shoulder. Could mean "thank you." Could mean "farewell."

The two men walked down the hill, and Zahir took up the post at the corner of the wall.

Even though Faraz was going back into the compound, he was still hoping for an airstrike. That'd be the easiest. He'd accomplish his mission and be done with all this.

What the hell was going on?

PART THREE

CHAPTER 20

The president's decision to stick with the Taliban talks was not working out. The new acting Director of DIA Ops found the next round even more painful than the first had been. Their negotiators seemed to be playing for time—making proposals and then pulling back when the Americans made reasonable counterproposals. And there were long waits for responses from the Taliban command to any American ideas.

After the aborted airstrike, Bridget's heart was not in it. And her new duties had her working half the night to keep up. Charming Montreux was starting to look like a bad joke. She'd had quite enough fondue to last a lifetime, and she concluded that there was little worse than being in a romantic European town alone.

After three weeks, Pruitt got permission to give the Taliban an ultimatum—deal seriously with one of the proposals or they would go home.

The response took several more days. Finally, back in the negotiating room, the senior Taliban delegate, Zaki, said, "Perhaps we should consult with our leaders and return here in a month to continue."

Bridget looked up from her note taking.

"A month?" Pruitt replied.

"We must be patient in such a process," the Omani consul general said.

Bridget glanced toward Pruitt. He was staring straight at Zaki. Bridget knew of no specific guidance on how to respond to such a suggestion. He would have to improvise.

Pruitt leaned forward in his chair. "We will not return in a month," he said. "We will return only if and when there is something concrete to work with. We remain open to constructive responses on any of the pending issues, but we will not return to waste time for another round of talks."

He waited for the translation and watched for Zaki's response. The man revealed nothing, but turned to the consul general. "Thank you, sir. I believe we have concluded our business for now."

The break in the talks created a problem for the president. He had based his Afghanistan strategy more and more on the secret effort, not only aborting the IJ airstrike but also holding back on several military moves that would have escalated the fighting. Martelli's actions were making less and less sense to the press and the public. Congressional and media criticism was rising, as there didn't seem to be progress toward either winning or ending the war.

Worse, there was rising concern among those in the know that if the talks were finished, IJ would turn his attention back to striking at the United States or another Western target. As weeks passed with nothing from the Taliban and no indication from the Omanis that anything would be coming, patience with the process was running thin.

The president called Jacobs, Pruitt, and Secretary of State Preston to the Oval Office for an assessment, along with his chief of staff. "I'm not waiting for these guys forever," he said. "I'm willing to talk to them, but I'm not a patsy."

"Let me speak to the Omani foreign minister," said the secretary of state. "I'll tell him we need to know whether this is a break or a breakdown."

"I think we need more than that," Martelli responded. "It's too easy for them to say 'it's a break.' Let's set a deadline."

"Not usually a good idea in such situations, as you know, sir," Preston said.

"Then, what? How do we move this forward?"

"Mr. President, it's been several weeks," said Jacobs. "I don't think it's unreasonable to ask whether we are in talks or not. Especially with guys like these, maybe it's good to show some impatience, some toughness."

"Could easily backfire," Preston argued. "This is the long game, and if we play it short we could end up right back where we started—in an offensive that grinds on with heavy casualties and doesn't get us any closer to the finish line, and potentially in the crosshairs of an MTO we haven't been able to pin down after months of trying."

Chief of Staff Greg Capman spoke for the first time. "Sir, I know it's not your favorite subject, but we do have a campaign coming up. We need to show some results one way or the other. We can't have no results from both the offensive and the talks six months from now."

"You're right, not my favorite subject. But you're also right that we need something to run on. I won't be paralyzed by fear of an attack. IJ is alive because I wanted to protect the talks. But if these guys are conning us, it ends now." He turned to the secretary of state. "Sam, tell the Omanis we need a response to our latest proposals within a week or we're not going back to Montreux."

"Sir, IJ will think it's a bluff and he'll call it," Preston said.

"Then he will. And we'll get on with the offensive before the extra troops come to the end of their deployments. If IJ sends something a week later, or a month later, well, we'll read it anyway."

"And we'll be in a stronger position to make a tough response to whatever it is," Jacobs said.

"Maybe," said Preston. "But my gut says this is going to go poorly."

"Best to know sooner rather than later," Martelli said.

"Yes, sir," Preston said. "Thank you, Mr. President."

With fake ski trips off her schedule, Bridget immersed herself in work, running operations and trying to squeeze more out of the intelligence data. Her new status put her in more meetings and forced her to rely on other people to do the actual work. It was a down period for her. Her life was starting to feel a lot like her years in Afghanistan—slogging away with little to show for it.

She still hadn't heard from Will and was starting to dread his return, rather than look forward to it. He was due home in a few weeks, as far as she knew. But her fantasies about taking what happened at Camp Eggers to the next level had given way to visions of an awkward and brief encounter, culminating in a final farewell. She thought that was more likely, particularly because he was due for an extended period stateside. It would be more difficult to have a relationship that could be long term than to have one with a fixed end date.

Bridget also knew it could take him months to decompress from a combat tour, and there was the chance, if he had seen tough action, that he might never be quite the same.

She thought about Faraz less and less, because whenever she did, she got depressed. What must he be going through? Was he still with al-Souri? Was he on the run? In custody? Was he even alive? She could think of no good scenario for Faraz. She imagined him in a basement, tortured, interrogated, and then executed. It was a rabbit hole of ugly nightmares, and she tried to avoid it.

She had never come up with a way to reach him as Hadley had ordered. Now, with the talks in trouble, the need for information on any change in Taliban activities, particularly any big attack, was greater than ever. But Faraz's status was unknown, and his ability to help was questionable. If she had been able to contact him, Bridget would have told him to abort and evacuate. He should have figured that out already. But if he had, where the heck was he?

Bridget was alone with her thoughts quite a lot these days, and they were not good company. Evenings, she would most often be sitting on her sofa with a glass of Scotch and Sarge on her lap, reading a paper on counterinsurgency or the ethnography of Central Asia.

So this time, the call from Jen was a welcome diversion. At thirty-two, Jen was still a party girl. Bridget had turned down about ninety-seven percent of her invitations over the years and mostly regretted accepting the others.

"Bridge! Haven't seen you in ages!" Jen was over the top but sincere. Although they were very different, the grind of grad school had created a bond. And since Jen was now a clinical psychologist, if nothing else, Bridget could get a free session—potentially useful, especially if alcohol was involved.

"Now, listen before you say no," Jen admonished like an evil twin beckoning her to some new form of transgression. "I know you hate the bar scene, but this is a *restaurant*." She said the last word as if it were a revelation. "And it's not downtown, it's on the Southwest Waterfront, very chill and sophisticated. It's their grand opening Friday, so everything's half price, including the tequila. And, Bridge, they have two hundred kinds of tequila. Two hundred!"

"Okay, Jen. To be honest, I really do need to get out. You had me at half-price tequila."

"Excellent! Wow, that was easy. I planned twenty minutes of badgering."

"Well, enjoy your free time."

"Oooo, aren't we the sarcastic one? Dr. Jen says something is going on with Bridget. I will bring my shrink license."

"Then I better bring my checkbook."

"Ha! The entertainment value will be more than enough, I'm sure. Is this about the Sea Lion?"

"SEAL, Jen. He's a . . . Oh, never mind. This is about the tequila."

"Yeah, right. Okay, I'll round up the usuals. See you there at, say, nine-ish? That's 2100 hours or something to you. Should be early enough to get seats at the bar."

"I thought you said it's a *restaurant*."

"It is! It is! Don't worry. But I suggest you eat something beforehand. Did I mention the tequila?"

Bridget laughed. "Okay, Jen. I'll be there, stomach properly lined."

"And look hot. This is a Look Hot Occasion. No fucking bureaucrat pinstripes, Okay, Bridge?"

"Okay, okay. I won't embarrass you. See you tomorrow." Bridget had second thoughts as soon as she hung up. Besides being a psychologist, Jen was a self-proclaimed relationship expert and also still single.

The restaurant was lovely—white tablecloths, liveried waitstaff, and a view of the Potomac. The bar was solid wood and oval shaped, with hanging glassware above, a mountain of tequila bottles behind, and tiny light bulbs set on dim, hanging down on bare wires.

When Bridget arrived at 9:15, the tables were packed and the bar was crowded. She found Jen and her friends around the other side, near the windows. They had saved her a bar stool.

"Bridget!" Jen said a bit too loudly. She had apparently already tried the tequila. Bridget knew the other women from Georgetown or previous outings, so it was kiss-kiss all around. Jen looked Bridget up and down. "Girl, you are the hottest. How do you do it?"

Bridget was wearing a red mini, a white silk blouse open three buttons to tease with a hint of cleavage, sheer stockings and her highest heels. She'd even had her hair done.

"You are two behind, so better get going," Jen said. She handed Bridget a shot from the row lined up on the bar. Each was on a small plate with some salt and a wedge of lime.

"Cheers," Bridget said, and she downed the drink straight.

"All right! Good start," Jen said, leaning one elbow on the bar. "The doctor will see you now."

"Oh, Jen. I thought this was supposed to be a fun night."

"It will be, but I'm at my best on two shots. By the time I hit four everyone seems schizo, especially me."

Bridget laughed. "By Jove, I think you've got it!"

"Really, Bridge, what's going on with you and the Sea Lion?"

"I don't know. Work sucks. Will's due back soon and . . . I don't know . . . I need a change, I fear a change, I want . . . I don't know what the hell I want, except for another shot. I definitely want another shot."

Jen went into a fake German accent. "Vhat ve have here is ze excessive buildup of ze vital bodily fluids, requiring ze release. I prescribe a swim with ze Sea Lion, or any fish, really. Ze water may be cold, but it will feel zooooo gooooood. After zat, all vill be much clearer."

"Thank you, doctor. Um, are you sure you're really a doctor?"

"I'll send you a bill if you want."

"How about if I pay you in tequila? Bartender!"

After a couple of shots, Bridget started relaxing. The women were funny, and the bartender was way too cute. They analyzed the various tables of men near the bar, and fended off approaches by a few of them, but it was all good banter and they got some free rounds out of it. Bridget ordered some appetizers for the group and a glass of ice water. She didn't want the alcohol to get too far ahead. But she had to admit this was actually fun. Probably, it was the tequila talking.

As she scanned the room her eyes kept stopping on one particular guy. He had short brown hair, brown eyes, and an easy smile. He was laughing with his friends, and briefly seemed to be making headway with one woman, before her friends dragged her away. He looked young, but he was undeniably cute. Then he caught her looking at him. He raised his eyebrows and tilted his head as if to say, "Me?" He smiled, took his drink from the table and walked over.

"Hi, I'm Richard."

Bridget was pleased that he hadn't used a pickup line. Problem was, up close it was clear he was even younger than she had thought.

"Bridget," she said, and they shook hands.

"Can I buy you another, um, water is it?"

"Very funny. I'm taking a short break."

"Tequila, then. They must be tried," he said, making a sweeping gesture toward the bottles.

"Sure."

The conversation flowed easily. He was a congressional staffer, of course, but he wasn't pretentious and didn't dwell on work, like so many men and women in Washington did. When he touched her arm making a joke it didn't feel creepy. It felt rather nice, as a matter of fact.

"Another?" he asked.

"My round," she said. She wanted to extend this little flirtation, but on her terms. Her friends were involved in their own conversations, but Bridget saw Jen keeping an eye on her, as if she might need help. She didn't.

Bridget was dying to know how old this guy was. "Where did you go to school?" she asked.

"Georgetown. Graduated three years ago."

Holy shit! Okay, point one: They were there at the same time. Point two: He's freaking twenty-five!

Bridget remembered taking the Pledge several years earlier, when she was in grad school. After a wild night, she and a friend had sworn off twentysomething men. They could be fun, but ultimately they were disappointing, and she hated herself for succumbing to their charms all too frequently in those days. The campus was full of them.

But by the end of her second drink with Richard, her resolve was wavering. Best to break the spell those eyes were casting. She had a boyfriend, after all. Well, sort of.

"Excuse me," she said, getting off her bar stool to go to the ladies' room. "Be right back."

There were only two women in the small hallway outside the restroom, but the wait felt endless. She had wanted to get away from Richard for a few minutes, but now she was worried he might not be there when she got back. Finally, it was her turn.

When she came out of the bathroom a few minutes later, Richard was standing in the small hallway.

"Hi," he said. "I thought you might have bugged out on me."

"Oh. No." The little hairs on the back of Bridget's neck were standing up, but she tried to be cool. He put his hand on her arm and gently pulled her toward him.

Oh, why not, said the tequila, and it seemed to be making excellent sense.

It was a lovely kiss, soft but probing, and he held her

close but not hard. They were interrupted by a woman heading for the ladies' room, who said, "Oh, sorry. Why don't you two get a room?"

"My thoughts exactly," Richard said, looking Bridget straight in the eye and venturing into the cheesy for the first time that evening.

Bridget looked at him. He was cute. And he seemed like a nice enough guy. And she needed this. Good God, she needed this! It was pretty much doctor's orders.

She took him by the hand and led him out of the restaurant.

When she woke up in his bed, it was 3:30 in the morning. Her head hurt and she felt a powerful urge to leave immediately. She looked over at him, his hair tousled on the pillow. Not a bad choice. But, really, Bridget! She sat up and felt a shooting pain in her forehead, but she powered through.

She checked her surroundings. It was a studio apartment. Oh, for God's sake! Bridget hadn't seen the inside of one of those in decades. She eased out of the bed and went to the bathroom to wash up and get dressed.

Not bad for a guy's place. He must have cleaned up, hoping to get lucky. That's me. Some teenager's lucky break. Jeez.

Now she had a decision to make. Wake him? Slip out? Leave a note? Retreat would be sensible but cowardly. She found his shopping list and a pen on the kitchenette counter, turned over the list, and took the pen in hand. Now, what? Everything she could think of was corny. She settled on, "Thanks for the tequila, Bridget," and her phone number. She thought about altering a digit, but this had been fun. She could decide later whether to do it again. Was she really that desperate? Yeah, maybe.

She closed the door as quietly as she could on the way out.

Back home, Bridget took a shower and put on a gray sweat suit with ARMY on the front. The hangover was intense. Or maybe it had been so long since she'd had one that she was out of practice. She megadosed ibuprofen, found some eggs in the fridge for breakfast, and drank all the water she could stomach. Then she and Sarge assumed their usual positions on the sofa and she tried to read.

But she found it hard to focus. She kept playing parts of the previous night over and over in her throbbing head. And she liked it. She thought that feeling must be pleasure, but, again, it had been a long time. She smiled and put her nose back into the book.

Unfortunately for Bridget, the book was about Afghanistan, and when she got to a chapter about Special Operations, she suddenly remembered what her mind had walled off for the last twelve hours. Will.

She was a sorry excuse for a human being! Bridget sat up, forcing Sarge to jump to the floor, where he gave her a look of reproach. "Yeah, I deserve that," she said. Oh, Bridget, how could you?

Then, she pivoted to defend herself. She and Will had only dated for a few months. He'd been gone for longer than that. Logic was on her side. Still, she felt guilty. She guessed that meant something. Damn.

She got up and went for a run.

* * *

Monday's text from Richard flashed onto Bridget's BlackBerry when she caught some signal walking to the courtyard snack bar on her lunch break.

"Hope this is your real number. You like Chinese food?"

She tried to ignore the little surge of excitement. Arrgh! She wished she had given him a fake number. She put the BlackBerry back into her purse.

Two days later, he wrote again. "If not B, whoever you are, like Chinese food?"

Why? Why did he have to be so good? She decided to write back. "Sorry. Can't." Without the help of the tequila, she was settling back into her old pattern.

Richard responded immediately. "Can't like Chinese food? Bet you can if you try."

True that. Suddenly, "Chinese food" had taken on a whole new meaning. It wouldn't take all that much trying for her to get into the mood for some "Chinese food." She thumbed her BlackBerry, "Okay. Sunday 2pm Mr. K's in Chinatown." Sunday lunch, less pressure than Saturday night, easier to bail. Good plan.

"Cool," he wrote. He seemed to know enough to quit while he was ahead.

CHAPTER 21

The past month had been at least as frustrating for Faraz as it had been for Bridget. In the early days after the meeting with Ibn Jihad, he was still hoping for an airstrike, that somehow the military had tracked him from the compound by the hill back to the camp. Faraz fantasized that that was what they had been waiting for, the chance to take out the headquarters and all the fighters in it. When that didn't happen, he thought maybe Washington didn't want to kill their own man. Could the whole thing be on hold because of him?

But there was no way to find out. Al-Souri's paranoia about being targeted by the Americans had increased. The *Qomandan* had banned all cell and satellite phone use in the camp, and in any compound he visited. The phones were kept under lock and key, with their batteries and SIM cards removed. Whenever one had to be used, Balaa or one of the other experienced fighters took it miles from camp to make the call, then destroyed the phone and buried its pieces in several places. Faraz went on a couple of those trips, but couldn't see a way to get the phone short of trying to kill the other half-dozen men on the mission. And he knew if he started shooting he'd be dead before he could get all of them.

Faraz had thought a lot about trying to escape. If he'd had a good opportunity, he would have done it. But he was trapped by his own competence. He had become one of al-Souri's favorites, and even Balaa accepted him as a full member of the security detail, no longer a trainee. As a result, he had almost no downtime. He always had a key assignment and was often close to al-Souri.

He frequently overheard al-Souri, Balaa, and other senior officers planning attacks on villages and on government forces, especially the poorly armed and trained local police. They had no qualms about killing civilians and were most gratified when they caused the maximum amount of pain, misery, and chaos. He never heard them plan an attack on Americans, though. If he had, he knew he'd have to go into the room shooting.

But most of the men who came to see al-Souri were relatively low level, capable of carrying out only local operations. Al-Souri also had a few meetings with other commanders and emissaries from Ibn Jihad. But if something big was in the works, they were keeping it very quiet.

He was still invited into al-Souri's office occasionally for Koran study—some of the commander's few breaks from his duties. A couple of times, he tried to draw him out.

"*Qomandan*," he asked one day, "The Holy Koran commands us to make jihad against all our enemies. Yet we are doing only these local attacks? Will we strike again at the foreign infidels?"

"Patience, Hamed," al-Souri replied. "Jihad is a long road." That was all he had said. And he turned back to the book with a more serious look on his face.

Faraz couldn't tell whether that meant a big attack was coming or whether it meant al-Souri was frustrated by the policy that was keeping the attacks small. Based on Al-Souri's leadership of the militant faction and his tense meeting with Ibn Jihad, Faraz suspected the latter. And the more he watched al-Souri, the more he saw bad moods and a short temper in place of the zealot's enthusiasm for war.

None of that helped Faraz figure out the Taliban's next move. He had made great efforts to get to where he was. He could be Hamed now effortlessly, but the appeal of the role had been lost that night at Ibn Jihad's villa. His original mission seemed to have been terminated, and for a while he was obsessed with finding a chance to escape. But he had not, and he didn't see any prospect of doing so. Meanwhile, he was making no headway getting info about an MTO. Washington could reasonably expect he was in a great position to report on any attack plan. But he had nothing. His frustration seemed to reach a new high every day.

During one work detail, he found himself alone with Balaa. The security team was repairing some fencing at the back of the camp, and Zahir had cut himself on a piece of razor wire. After he went to the clinic, Faraz was working alone, and fell behind the others. Balaa came to help him.

Faraz had to think quickly to come up with an approach. He knew Balaa was always eager to show how important he was, how far above the foot soldiers. After a few minutes, he said, "This is a great time for jihad, *sayyid*."

Balaa seemed surprised Faraz would try to make small talk with him, or maybe he was just not good at small talk. "It is always a great time to fight for Allah," he responded.

"But *sayyid*, we have not hit the infidels for a long time. I feel something . . ." He lowered his voice. "I feel something big is coming, maybe to defeat the infidels once and for all."

Balaa gave him a dismissive shrug. "Why would you say that?"

"I just . . . I do not know. I have heard talk. That is all."

"Do not listen to 'talk,' my brother. Listen to orders!"

"Yes, *sayyid*."

"And do not repeat this 'talk' ever! Do you understand me?"

"Yes, *sayyid*. I am sorry, *sayyid*."

"You have been doing well, Hamed. Do not let that change. Tomorrow, we travel. Focus on your duties. Do not worry about things that do not concern you." Balaa glared at Faraz for a moment to let his words sink in, then he turned and went to check on the other men.

For Faraz, Balaa's reaction was as close as he was going to get to a confirmation of an MTO. But what good was it? He had no way to report it and no useful details anyway. All he knew was that he had to try harder to get the information he needed, and that the wall around it would be very tough to penetrate.

It was all very demoralizing for Faraz, and made life as Hamed feel pointless. He was going through the motions as if in a daze, like any long-term inmate exhibiting good behavior while keeping his anger in check and harboring dreams of freedom.

He tried to hide his feelings, but Zahir noticed. "You are not happy these days, Hamed," he said that night as they settled into their beds.

"Why do you say that, my brother?"

"Because it is obvious." Zahir looked at him across the tent, waiting for an answer. Faraz had watched his tentmate become more assertive lately, clearly drawing confidence from his stature as a member of the security team, and from his deepening faith.

Faraz sighed. He had to come up with something to say. "You are right, Zahir. I thought jihad would be more . . . fulfilling, I guess. But our lives are the same every day—guard duty, training, trips outside. We are not fighting the infidels, exactly."

"Hamed! How can you say that? We will have our chance to attack again. In the meantime, we have two of the most important jobs in the camp. Do not forget that. Our commander is nearly as important as Ibn Jihad."

"You are right, Zahir. Perhaps I am missing my family. Maybe I am tired. I do not know."

"Sleep, then, and try to remember that we all have our role in jihad. It should fulfill you every day."

"Yes, yes. You are right again. Good night, my brother."

Faraz turned over, away from Zahir. What the fuck was he going to do? He needed to get out of there. He should just find a chance and make a run for it. Maybe during this trip. If he didn't make it, well, tough shit. He adjusted his pillow and put his hand over his face, as if he were praying.

202-555-4700, Whiskey-Alpha-5-9-0-Sierra-Sierra-Romeo . . .

CHAPTER 22

The next morning, Bridget's third cup of coffee was interrupted by a call from Jacobs's secretary.

"The boss wants you in an Oval Office meeting. Catch a ride at the South Entrance in thirty minutes."

"What's this about?"

"That's going to be well above my pay grade. I'm sure he'll fill you in."

A quick touch-up in the ladies' room, a fresh notebook in her purse, and an email to her staff, "Out for a meeting. Back in two," and Bridget was heading for Jacobs's motorcade.

He did not fill her in. She was two cars behind him. At the White House, Jacobs went straight in to meet with the president. Bridget was left in the Oval's waiting room with several officials she didn't know, and she was reluctant to show her ignorance. Then, Mary Larson from the CIA came in.

"Figured you'd be here," Larson said, like Bridget was the black sheep at a family wedding.

"What's that supposed to mean?"

"We have a problem, an opportunity and a problem. And your man is the problem."

"What are you talking about?"

"No one told you?"

"No."

"What the hell goes on over in that ridiculous building of yours? We have good info that al-Souri is at the home of a regional sheikh in eastern Afghanistan."

"And?"

"And, we're going to hit him. Drone is on the way. Problem is, your man Sandblast might be there."

"Jesus!" Bridget paused to process. U.S. intelligence agencies got such "hits" on the whereabouts of various terrorist leaders from time to time, but the sourcing was usually suspect and the information out of date. "We know this, how?" she asked.

"It's solid. HUMINT from an informant in the village. This is the town al-Souri bombed a few months ago. Our man lost his wife, and none too happy about it, as you can imagine."

"We know about this guy," Bridget said. "He came in through the Afghan military."

"Right. We've been pressing him to deliver, and he came up with this."

"You know, the president put the kibosh on a similar op a month ago."

"That was then, this is now," Larson said. "That was the top dog. This is a lesser dog. All kinds of ops are up. And maybe this will get Ibn Jihad's attention for your talks.

"My talks?"

"Whatever. Word is al-Souri opposes them. Remember, he's from Syria. Known to be more militant than IJ. We could be doing IJ a favor."

"I doubt he'll see it that way."

"Doesn't matter. Your talks are about dead. This will either revive them or put a fork in them. And jihadi chatter is up again on the scattergrams. If these guys aren't negotiating, they're going to blow something up. Maybe, we hit them first this time."

"That's a good sales pitch," Bridget said. "We made it ourselves a month ago."

"This is different. We've been cultivating this sheikh for years. Khaliki is his name. Now, we find out he's been financing al-Souri and feeding him information all along. This could be a two-for-one."

A marine in a dress uniform came to the doorway. "Ladies and gentlemen, please follow me."

Bridget let Larson and the others go ahead of her, using every second to try to think through the problem. In the Oval, the marine directed her to a seat just behind the inner circle. Larson was on the sofa, closer to the president.

They all stood when Martelli and Jacobs came in with their top aides.

"Please everyone, sit," the president said, and he took his chair at the end of the coffee table. "Ms. Larson, what is the CIA's level of certainty that the target is on-site?"

"Very high, sir. Our source is watching the compound as we speak. He's supposed to call in if anything changes."

"It's unusual to have that kind of real-time intel, isn't it?"

"Yes, sir. That's why we want to move on it."

"Where is Ms. Davenport?" Martelli scanned the outer ring of seats. "Ah, there you are. Is your man there, too?"

Bridget was not prepared for that. She wasn't prepared for anything. Damn you, Jacobs!

"We don't know, Mr. President. His last contact was calling in the airstrike. When that was aborted, we don't know whether he stayed with al-Souri or went on the run."

"How could he still be there?" Larson asked, turning to face Bridget. "After making the call, he must have bugged out."

"We would have heard from him if he had," Bridget countered. "He'd need evac."

"If he's alive all these weeks later."

"All right," the president took back control of the conversation. "I understand the situation. I tend to agree with the CIA. We need to expand our campaign against these guys. By now it's clear. They screwed us on the talks, and now we have solid intel on the whereabouts of one of their key leaders—one of their most militant, according to you all. We can't keep a hands-off posture forever. I think Ms. Larson is right, much more likely our soldier is on the run or . . . well . . . lost, I'm sorry to say."

Bridget was shocked. Just four weeks ago Martelli had aborted the airstrike out of concern for Faraz and for the talks. Now, he seemed willing to send in a drone to kill them both.

As the president turned to other officials for their comments, Bridget tried to get Jacobs's attention. He saw her. But if he understood that she wanted him to speak up for Faraz, he ignored her. An air force general was saying how clean a strike could be, minimizing and maybe avoiding civilian casualties, even though the villa was on the edge of a village.

Martelli scanned the room. "All right. We seem to have consensus, and I agree. Let's proceed."

Bridget felt a wave of nausea, or was it adrenaline, or both. Jacobs was avoiding her looks, now. People were shifting in their seats, ready to stand when Martelli did.

"Mr. President!" Bridget said more emphatically than she meant to.

"Yes, Ms. Davenport."

"I'm sorry, sir, if I'm speaking out of turn."

"Go ahead, please."

Now it was Jacobs who was giving Bridget a look, and this one could have penetrated an Alaska Wall. She couldn't avoid it, because he was sitting right next to the president, but she refused to be deterred.

"Sir, there is another way. We could send in a Special Ops team. Make the hit and try to protect Sandblast, if he's there."

"The drone is only a few minutes out," Larson said, clearly angry that Bridget was trying to derail the plan the president had just approved. "Gearing up Special Ops would cause a significant delay."

"Some delay, yes," Bridget said. "But I'm guessing it could still be done tonight. We can check that for you, Mr. President."

Martelli turned to Jacobs. "Marty?"

"It's possible, sir," Jacobs said. He was trying to hide it, but Bridget could see he was about as angry as Larson. "There's not only the delay, but it puts more American lives at risk."

"Well, we need to do this tonight," Martelli said. "But if there's a way to protect our man, if he's there, that would be the way to go."

The chairman of the joint chiefs spoke up. "A hit-and-rescue with almost zero prep time is a tall order, even for our Special Ops guys."

"Tall orders are their specialty, though," the president said. "Isn't that what you always tell me, admiral?"

"Yes, sir. We'd need some time to take a look at it."

"Well, we don't have much time. But let's take an hour or so to explore Ms. Davenport's proposal. Marty, I'll expect to hear from you."

"Yes, Mr. President," Jacobs said, and stood to signal they should all leave.

Jacobs let his anger out in the hallway. "Who asked you to throw a wrench in?" he boomed in a stage whisper, with Larson glaring at Bridget over his shoulder.

"Sir, that's our man out there. We have a responsibility . . ."

"Don't lecture me about responsibility! We have a responsibility to stop a major terrorist attack. Thousands of lives are at risk. If we lose this opportunity because of you, you can take that 'acting' promotion and flush it down the toilet. In fact, we'll cut your ID card into little pieces and flush it down, too. Don't you ever, ever, undermine me in front of the president, or in front of anyone! Frankly, it's unlikely I'll give you the chance."

Bridget was taken aback by the intensity of Jacobs's anger. They were all under a lot of pressure, but she'd never seen that before. She hesitated, giving Larson the chance to jump in.

"Don't screw this up, Bridget. Go do your homework, and let's move on this thing. And if our informant sees so much as light go on in that villa, CIA will demand that the drone fire immediately!"

Larson's tirade gave Bridget the time she needed to

come up with an answer to Jacobs. She nearly edited herself, but didn't.

"Sir," she said, "next time you don't want me to speak, don't invite me to a meeting where someone's deciding to kill one of my operatives. And if that's the plan, please at least let me know. What did you expect me to do?"

"It all came together very quickly this morning. Jesus, Bridget, it's not my top priority to keep you informed."

Bridget looked at him in disbelief. "I'll look at the possibilities and report back. And sir, any time you want my ID card, you can have it." She surprised herself with that last comment. Maybe she shouldn't have said it. But as she thought about it, she was glad she had.

Without giving Jacobs a chance to respond, Bridget turned and walked toward a secure workspace where she could find out what was possible.

The reply to Bridget's urgent request to Special Ops command came in minutes.

TO: DIA / Ops / DoD
FROM: JSOC / Kabul

Per request, mission capability confirmed for this date.
SEAL Team 22, LtCdr Will Jackson, within range and standing by . . .

There was more, but Bridget had stopped reading. Her blood ran cold, and she felt like her heart stopped. Holy Jesus!

Faraz had been her priority. She had only been thinking about Special Ops in the abstract. Idiot!

Bridget's small, temporary White House cubicle seemed to spin around her. She stared at the message on her screen, and summoned all her experience to try to come up with a way out.

She could ask for more options, but she knew that if there were any, Special Ops would have offered them. She couldn't lie and say there was no team available, because other people would see the email. Perhaps she could say she'd had second thoughts and decided to support the airstrike. But that wouldn't ring true, and Bridget felt guilty even thinking about it.

She couldn't trade Faraz's life for Will's.

She reread the email and wiped perspiration from her forehead. She had set this in motion, and now she was stuck. More to the point, so was Will.

Bridget forced her hand to reach for the phone. She asked the White House operator to connect her to Secretary Jacobs. He took down the information and hung up.

Waiting for his callback, Bridget still felt woozy. She thought about her first date with Will, about that last morning before he deployed, about their all-too-brief encounter in Kabul. She remembered the sadness in his eyes when she told him she had to leave.

She jumped when the phone rang.

"All right, Bridget," Jacobs said. "The president has authorized the Special Ops raid. But this better work. Damnit! An airstrike would have happened already. Now, it'll be a long day for us, a long night for them, and an uncertain outcome."

"These guys are good, sir. They'll get it done," Bridget said, trying to convince herself as much as Jacobs.

"They better," he said, and he hung up without saying good-bye.

Bridget felt very alone. The Special Ops email was still on her screen. The blinking cursor seemed to be mocking her. She tried to calm herself, but it was difficult.

This would, indeed, be a long day. Bridget could only hope Will was as good at his job as he was supposed to be.

CHAPTER 23

Lieutenant Commander Will Jackson had the night watch for SEAL Team 22, now based at FOB Emerson, which had been rebuilt following the attack several months earlier. Will was in the new, blast-proof command center, sipping a coffee to prepare for a long shift. He was five weeks from going home, and starting to think about it more and more. That was dangerous, he knew, but hard to avoid. The communications blackout on this tour had been particularly difficult. He would have liked to be in touch with Bridget, although not being able to write relieved him of the burden of figuring out what to say.

And he had been busy. The SEALs and other Special Operations units deployed across Afghanistan performed a variety of missions for which they had unique skills. Some of them grew beards and put on local clothes to embed with Afghan forces and provide advanced training. Others, like Will's team, performed counterterrorism operations, attacking specific buildings, neighborhoods, or towns to root out and kill al-Qaida or Taliban fighters. These were called "cordon and clear" missions, meaning "seal off and capture or eliminate the terrorists."

The communications sergeant interrupted Will's thoughts. "Commander Jackson, urgent comms, sir."

Will went over to read his screen. "Tonight?"

"Yes, sir. Looks that way."

"How far?"

"About an hour by road, sir."

"Can you get me HQ on a secure line?"

"Yes, sir."

While the sergeant worked, Will read the message again. It had map coordinates, and then:

Cordon and clear. High Value Target. Expect
heavy resistance. Lethal force authorized. Watch
collateral damage. Possible friendly inside. Code
name: Sandblast.

Will touched the arrow key and saw satellite and drone imagery and a map of the village. He immediately understood the warning about collateral damage. Other houses butted up against the walled villa on the east and south sides.

The compound was at a crossroads at a corner of the village. It had three gates, but one of them led directly into the village. They would have good access to the other two from the roads, away from the civilians. But the Taliban lookouts would also have good fields of view. This was going to be a tough one. He hoped this alleged friendly stayed out of the way when the shooting started.

But he had another worry. His team was always ready to go on a moment's notice, but an operation like this, against a strong force in a fortified location they hadn't scouted, would ideally have more lead time. Good planning was essential.

"Sir, HQ on that phone." The sergeant pointed to a phone in the corner.

"Thanks. Send someone for Chief Weston, will ya?"

"Yes, sir."

Will picked up the phone and asked for his commanding officer. The conversation was brief.

"Will, I share your concerns. But this comes from the top, and it's a Very High Value Target. You'll have details shortly. Take whatever you need. You'll have air support for surveillance, but to avoid collateral damage, air fire is to be used only in an emergency. Radio silence until contact. Good hunting, Will. Best get going."

There was nothing to say except, "Yes, sir."

At Khaliki's villa, Faraz stood guard outside al-Souri's bedroom door, while the commander slept. He had a view of the courtyard through a hallway window.

It had been a busy day. They arrived before dawn, and Al-Souri spent many hours in meetings with several local sheikhs. The compound was crowded with various tribesmen, most of whom seemed suspicious of one another. Faraz had taken no particular note of the gardeners working on the narrow border of greenery along the outside the compound walls.

At sunset, there was no grand dinner in the courtyard, as there had been at Ibn Jihad's villa. When the leaders came out, there was a brief show of unity and the men left quickly. Then, al-Souri huddled with Khaliki and his son.

It was nearly midnight when Balaa gathered the security detail for a briefing. They would be spending the night at the villa, and there would be more meetings the next day. That was unusual, but not unprecedented. Balaa said al-Souri had gone to bed. He gave out the assignments for the first night shift, putting Faraz outside al-Souri's bedroom. The remaining men went to the bunkhouse to sleep for a few hours before taking their turns on duty.

Ninety minutes later, Bridget was sitting with her team in the DIA's Field Operations Center at the Pentagon. Because it was nighttime in Afghanistan, the live video feed from the drone was infrared. This was even stranger to watch than the daylight satellite video of the market attack had been. They could see the vehicles and the body heat signatures in the compound, and vague outlines of the wall and buildings, but nothing was very clear.

Bridget was expending much of her energy trying to look normal. Apparently, it wasn't working. Mary Larson from CIA came in, took an empty seat next to Bridget, and said, "What the heck is wrong with you?"

"Nothing, why?" Bridget said, without taking her eyes off the screens.

"Because you look . . . I don't know . . . scared shit-less, I guess."

Bridget turned toward Larson. "Don't be ridiculous. We've got guys about to engage the enemy. Sorry if we're not as detached as you are up the river."

"Hey, this was your idea. If you'd kept your mouth shut, we'd all be celebrating by now."

"Or mourning the loss of one of our own."

"We might end up doing that anyway."

Bridget swallowed a "fuck you."

The only sound in the room came from a speaker that carried the hiss and crackle of the SEALs' radio frequency.

Will was riding shotgun in the lead vehicle speeding along a dark country road. Chief Petty Officer Charlie Weston and another SEAL were in the back seat, and the team's newest member was driving. There were two more up-armored Humvees behind them, with Will's second-in-command, Lieutenant Jorge Martinez, in the last one.

"Sir, five minutes out," Weston said.

"Okay, let's stop here."

The vehicles pulled to the side of the road and the men got out to gear up—full high-tech body armor, to allow maximum movement while providing maximum protection, and lightweight helmets, with built-in night-vision goggles, communications gear, and video cameras. Everything was black. They did weapons and comms checks.

There were twelve men in all, a highly trained, highly efficient, and highly coordinated team. Everyone knew his job and had proved many times in tough situations that he could do it well. They had been together for this entire deployment and for three months of training beforehand, nearly nine months in total. And this was the first combat tour for only two of them.

They gathered around Will. "Okay, just the way we diagrammed it. Martinez's team turns right on the next road and goes around to approach the main crossroads from the east, heading for the pedestrian entrance. The rest of us go straight in from the west and hit the main vehicle gate on the corner. Stay quiet and be careful about those civilian houses to the east and north. Radio silence until Martinez announces ready. He'll need the most time. Last intel from the drone indicates target is still on-site with lots of security. Heads up for the friendly, but mission comes first. Questions?"

There were none. "Okay, let's go, nice and slow and quiet, drivers."

They loaded up and continued. Martinez peeled off on a side road, skirting around the market Faraz and Zahir had bombed. Will and the rest of the team continued straight toward the crossroads. They stopped before the last bend in the road, two hundred yards from the villa. The men alighted quietly and formed their teams. Two stayed behind with the vehicles, as the rest walked toward the villa. Will led the men on foot, walking in a gully by the roadside along a row of hedges. The road was almost completely dark. There were about a million stars visible, but they were fortunate there was no moon.

As the compound came into view against the night sky, Will and his men could see the ten-foot-high walls, capped with shards of glass embedded in cement. The solid steel gate sat at a forty-five-degree angle to the intersection.

Fifty yards out Will, Weston, and their team crouched

in the gully and waited. For Will, this was the hardest part, these final minutes before an assault. They could be detected at any moment, and he had time to think about everything that could go wrong. The enemy force could be twice as large as they thought it was. They could have RPGs. They could have a howitzer in there, for God's sake.

He signaled his men to stay put, and he inched forward. He could see three guards on the roof of the main house and two in the street on his side of the wall, walking back and forth. All were armed with AK-47s, and from what he could tell they were reasonably well trained, as expected. He used hand signals to convey the information to the team.

Just then, a guard on the far side of the roof shouted, "*Dussman! Dussman!*" Enemy, enemy! He fired his rifle on automatic in the direction of Martinez's team.

Will raised his left hand for his men to keep their positions. His right was on the trigger of his M-16. They were supposed to attack simultaneously, but now that the guards' attention was directed to the other side of the compound, he wanted to use that.

The guards on the roof all moved to the far side and joined the firing. One of the guards on foot patrol in front of Will ran toward the corner of the compound to see what was going on. Before he got there, Martinez's team blew the pedestrian gate. One of his men shot the guard as he came around the corner.

Will raised his left hand, and counted down, 3 . . . 2 . . . 1. Then he thrust his arm forward in a "Go" motion and ran toward the compound, taking out the one remaining guard with gunfire.

Will stopped in a crouch, ready to fire at anyone who

appeared above the wall. Petty Officer Bobby Krauss ran past him and placed a backpack-sized bomb at the base of the metal gate. It was a one-way charge, designed with legs to be pushed into the ground and a metal plate to focus the blast in one direction. Krauss retreated, and he, Will, and the others turned their backs. Krauss pushed a button on a remote control.

The explosion buckled the gate and broke its latch. The SEALs turned and ran through, firing as they went.

Bridget tightened her already tight grip on the arms of her chair and hoped Larson didn't notice.

They saw the SEAL vehicles split up to approach the compound from two sides. They saw the men get out and move slowly toward the villa. They saw the guards start firing, and they saw Martinez's team blow the pedestrian gate. Then they saw someone from the other team run forward and shoot the guard, just before Krauss blew the main gate.

They didn't know who was who, but they could see these guys knew what they were doing. So far, so good.

The few seconds' warning provided by the rooftop guard had made a difference. Al-Souri's men in the barracks had time to grab their weapons, so when Will and his team came through the gate, they faced gunfire from two sides. One of Will's men fired a rocket-propelled grenade through a window of the main house with devastating effect. But the Taliban fire forced the SEALs to disperse and take cover.

* * *

Inside the house, the RPG caused widespread damage and injuries. A piece of the hallway ceiling came down on Faraz, knocking him to the floor. He came up slowly, bleeding from a head injury.

As the gunfire continued outside, he heard al-Souri call, "Help me! Help me!"

What should he do? He assumed this was an American raid, but he couldn't be sure. It could be a rival Taliban faction. If they were Americans, they might be here to kill al-Souri. But al-Souri wasn't Faraz's target. He might still be his ticket to another shot at Ibn Jihad, if anyone cared anymore.

Then Faraz had another thought. If these were Americans, maybe they could take him home. That would be something! But if he went home now, what was it all for? Damn! He needed an update on his mission. And what if the commandos didn't make it out? There were a lot of Taliban men in the compound, and the fighting outside was intense.

There was no time to consider so many permutations. Faraz's instincts took over. He went through the bedroom door and saw al-Souri bleeding badly. He grabbed a shirt from the rubble on the floor and pressed it to al-Souri's wound, a large gash in his side. The man cried out in pain.

"Quiet, now, *Qomandan*," he said.

He took some other clothing and made a wad to press on the wound, then wrapped a turban around al-Souri's torso and tied it as tightly as he could. Al-Souri moaned in pain and passed out.

Faraz went to the doorway and looked into the hall. To the right, just beyond a side door, Khaliki's bedroom had taken a direct hit. He turned left toward the front door, bending low so he couldn't be seen through the windows. He passed one of his Taliban colleagues, dead or unconscious on the floor. He could hear the gunfire outside, but the main house wasn't taking any hits for the moment. Faraz stopped at the last window and looked out. He saw that the fighting was concentrated on the other side of the compound, near the barracks where the bulk of the Taliban force was.

Faraz jumped as an explosion went off in the middle of the attacking force. One of the Taliban fighters had made an accurate shot with an RPG. The assault team intensified its fire, but Faraz could see that two of its members were wounded.

He heard someone in the courtyard shout, "Six down! Six down!" "Six" was the American military designation for a mission commander.

Okay, they were Americans, but their commander was wounded or dead. Their chances of success had dropped significantly. If Faraz was staying on mission, this was his chance to help al-Souri escape.

When the RPG hit the assault team, Bridget was not the only one in the Operations Center who gasped. But when they heard Chief Weston break radio silence to call "Six down," she was the only one to say, "Oh, God, no!" It was only a whisper, but Larson heard her and was about to say something. Bridget raised a hand to shut her up.

They could just about make out Will leaning on two

men and limping toward the main house. "Thank you, Jesus." Bridget mouthed the words, succeeding this time in not saying them out loud.

The lack of gunfire in the house was good news. With luck, all the Taliban fighters inside were dead or injured, and the three Americans could wait there safely until the team and the vehicles came to get them.

The next thing they heard was Martinez, now leading the force fighting in the compound. "Vehicles, evac, evac, evac!" He was aborting the mission. The speaker clicked and the drivers acknowledged.

"Yes! Go! Go! Go!" Bridget's brain tried to project halfway around the world.

Faraz returned to the bedroom to rouse al-Souri. "Commander, we must go!" He helped him up and was about to take him into the hallway when he heard the crash as Chief Weston broke through the front door. Faraz peeked into the hall and saw Weston and Krauss help Will into the relative safety of the living room.

Faraz lowered al-Souri back to the floor, where he passed out again, and went down the corridor as quietly as he could.

He turned a corner and paused just outside the living room. "American coming in," he said. It sounded strange to hear his own voice speaking English. "I repeat, American coming in."

Will was lying on the living room's Afghan carpet bleeding, but Weston looked at him for guidance. Will nodded.

"Code word," Weston demanded. The SEALs would say one word if all was well, another to signal danger.

"Don't know it."

Will was bleeding and in pain, but he managed to call out, "What's your code name?"

"Sandblast."

"It's okay," Will whispered. His voice was weak. and he leaned back on his elbows while Krauss worked on his wounded left thigh.

"Show your hands and come ahead slowly," Weston said, keeping his M-16 pointed at the doorway.

Faraz leaned his weapon against the wall, opened the living room door, and stepped inside. He held his hands up high.

"Lieutenant Faraz Abdallah, U.S. Army, undercover."

He was everything the SEALs expected to see in a Taliban fighter—dark skin, beard, turban, bandolier, traditional clothes.

They couldn't help staring at him.

The body heat signatures inside the house were faint, obscured by the wooden roof, and the SEALs had their mics off, so the action was hard to follow. But when the team in the Ops Center saw someone join the men in the living room, they assumed it was a member of the assault team.

Almost as if they were choreographed, Bridget and the others held the arms of their chairs and leaned in toward the big screen, even Larson.

* * *

Weston kept his rifle on Faraz and looked at him with suspicion. Krauss looked up wide-eyed.

"They told us you might be here," Will said. "It's okay, chief. You can stand down. Jesus, Lieutenant, you okay?"

"Yes, sir," Faraz said, lowering his arms. He could see that Will's blood was soaking the carpet.

"You're bleeding," Will said, pointing toward Faraz's head.

Faraz reached up and felt the blood caked on his turban. "It's okay, sir, only a bump on the head."

"So, you want to come home with us?"

"Is that what they told you? To take me out?"

"No, they only told me you might be here. I have no orders on what to do if we find you, other than not to kill you. My orders were 'cordon and clear.' That's blown now, anyway."

Faraz had a decision to make. He had Will's target in the next room badly wounded. But al-Souri was not his target. He could kill the man anytime. No need to do it now, unless he wanted to go home with the SEALs.

"Sir, I need to know if my mission is on or off," he said.

"Sorry, Lieutenant. Can't help you." Will winced as Krauss tightened his bandage.

The gun battle was raging outside. Faraz looked toward the front door. "You have egress?"

"On the way," Weston said.

Faraz turned to Will. "All right. Tell Washington . . ." He still wasn't sure what he wanted to say, but he was out of time. "Tell them I need to stay. Tell them I need to stop the MTO or at least find out what it is."

"You've got info on an MTO?"

"Yes sir, more vague confirmation. Something big, multiple targets, I think. But I don't know details. Same as when I called in an airstrike a few weeks ago. What the hell happened with that?"

"Sorry, again I don't know."

Faraz shook his head in frustration. He didn't know whether he was supposed to stay or go, and this SEAL had no info to help him.

"Look, I need to speak to Kylie Walinsky. Kylie Walinsky, okay? I'll find a way to call in. Tell them she should sit by the goddamn phone until I call."

"All right, Lieutenant," Will said. "Kylie Walinsky. Hey, our targets were al-Souri and a guy named Khaliki, who owns this place. Do you know if we got them?"

"You hit Khaliki's bedroom hard, but I can't confirm. Al-Souri's wounded but I'm taking him out of here. I need him for my mission."

"Command wants him dead today."

"Sorry, sir. I need him until I speak to Walinsky. I'll kill him for you some other time."

Faraz could see Will was not happy.

Will could have ordered Faraz to give up al-Souri, or even had Weston put his gun back on Faraz and try to force him to comply. But that would have taken time he didn't have. And at this point, Will had bigger things to worry about than killing one terrorist. He had to get himself and his team out of there alive.

"I'll hold you to that, Lieutenant," Will said. "Good luck."

"Thanks," Faraz replied. "Good luck to you, too, sir. You should be safe here until your men come for you."

* * *

Faraz closed the living room door behind him, picked up his gun, and rounded the corner to return to al-Souri. He saw Balaa and Zahir coming along the hallway toward him from the back door.

"Hamed! Where is the *Qomandan*?" Balaa demanded. They were only a few feet from the living room door, and Faraz knew the SEALs would have their rifles trained on it.

"Oh, praise Allah!" Faraz said. It struck him how quickly he could change his identity, and then change it back again. "I have been looking for you. The commander is here." He took them back down the hall to the bedroom.

When Balaa saw al-Souri wounded and unconscious, he fell to his knees and tried to bring him out of it. He failed. Faraz had never seen Balaa upset about anything, but he saw it now.

Balaa jumped to his feet. "You must get him out of here," he ordered. "Go through the side door. There is a vehicle in the alley. I will create a diversion." He grabbed Faraz by the shirt and shook him. "You must do this! Save the *Qomandan*!" he shouted.

Faraz was momentarily shocked, but he recovered and said, "Yes, *sayyid*."

"Pick him up! Be ready!" Balaa said. He checked the hallway, moved to the front door, and paused. He looked back to see Faraz and Zahir carrying al-Souri into the hallway. He nodded at them and they turned for the side door.

"There is no God but God. Mohammed is the messenger of God," he whispered. Then he shouted, *"Allah hu akhbar!"* and he ran into the courtyard shooting, drawing the attention and the gunfire of the Americans outside.

Balaa zigzagged across the compound. The Americans cut him down with M-16 rounds. After he fell, he continued to fire, keeping his enemies pinned down and distracted for a few more crucial seconds.

The group at the Pentagon couldn't figure out what was happening. At first, they thought all the people in the house were members of the assault team. But now, nothing made any sense.

The man who was killed running through the compound was clearly a terrorist. But who was the man who appeared to go from the Special Ops team in the living room to join the terrorists in the hallway and then escape out the back?

Bridget gasped. Could it be? Could it fucking be?

Faraz got into the back of the SUV and dragged al-Souri in behind him, with Zahir pushing from the feet. Zahir moved to the driver's seat and found the key on the sun visor. He fumbled as he tried to get it into the ignition, and it fell to the floor.

"Hurry! Hurry!" Faraz said.

Zahir picked up the key and got the vehicle started. It lurched forward and stopped. Zahir had driven only twice before.

"Go! Go!" Faraz yelled.

"But, the gate . . ."

"Go fast! The lock will break."

Zahir floored the accelerator. The SUV kicked up gravel and sand as it leaped forward and crashed through the compound's one remaining gate, speeding directly into the village. Zahir braked and turned left, skidding and sideswiping a wall. He floored it again and sped through the town at high speed.

Balaa was now dead in the compound and the vehicles were outside the main gate. Martinez ordered the SEALs to gather on the front porch of the house, including the other wounded man, who emerged from behind a shed, a medic helping him.

With Will injured and their mission blown, and the Taliban fighters still firing at them, this certainly constituted an emergency. Martinez made the radio call. "Air support, SOS! Building, west side of compound. Fire! Fire! Fire!"

High above them, the drone banked hard and sped toward them from the east. Fewer than ten seconds after Martinez's radio call, the rocket engine on one of its Hellfire missiles ignited and the clamps holding it under the drone's left wing released. The missile streaked past the village houses and descended rapidly, its GPS and laser tracking systems steering it toward the midpoint of the side building, where the Taliban fighters were holed up. The SEALs crouched down and turned their backs. They heard the missile's signature, high-pitched squeal right before the huge explosion shook the compound.

As soon as they stood back up, Weston and Krauss came out of the house, supporting Will between them. The SEALs formed a protective wedge and moved quickly through the gate and into the vehicles, returning fire from a few surviving fighters.

As they sped away, some of the Taliban men ran through the gate and chased them on foot, firing wildly. But they didn't go far. They were exhausted and most of their comrades were dead.

With the drone focused on the barracks, the folks at the Pentagon didn't see Faraz, Zahir, and al-Souri escape. After the aircraft fired, it shifted its attention to providing air cover for the fleeing SEALs. It would be half an hour until Bridget's team could get the satellite video to have a wider view.

In the SUV, Faraz tightened the bandage around al-Souri and cursed himself for not bringing more material to work with. He took off his own shirt to make a fresh dressing.

Al-Souri came around. "Go to Kadikiya," he said.

"Where is that, *Qomandan*?" Faraz asked.

"I know the place," Zahir said, driving with more confidence now. "It is not far from my village. I will take us."

"Ask for Doctor Zia," al-Souri whispered, before passing out again.

* * *

The doctor at FOB Emerson replaced the field dressing that Krauss had put on Will's left leg. The wound was bad, but not life-threatening. The medevac chopper would get him at first light, and he would be on a flight to the army's Landstuhl Medical Center in Germany by midday. From there, when he was stable, they would transfer him to a navy facility stateside. His tour would be ending a few weeks early.

It fell to Martinez to write the after-action report, with help from Weston. The chief gave him the conversation with Faraz word for word, as well as he could remember it. Martinez slugged the report "Urgent, Critical, Top Secret," and sent it off on the secure network.

"God fucking damn it!" Larson said. She was in Bridget's office, reading Martinez's report over her shoulder.

AFTER ACTION REPORT: Target 1 not neutralized Target 2 fate unknown. Team commander and one other injured. Awaiting medevac. Sandblast is on Target 1, location unknown. Reports possible multi-target MTO. No further details. Sandblast will call Ops Center ASAP. Requests Kylie Walinsky stand by for direct. Timing uncertain.

"Your boys screwed the pooch on this one. Now we're all fucked, especially you."

"How about you get the fuck out of my office, Mary?"

"Absolutely," Larson said, gathering her things. "Best to be as far away from you as possible when this shit hits the fan." She paused at the doorway. "Seriously, Bridget, this was a big missed opportunity. We're all in for it now." She left looking as much dejected as angry.

Bridget reread the report. The main thing was, Faraz was alive. And he wanted to talk to her. No kidding. But why hadn't he come out with Will's team? Still trying to crack the MTO even after the aborted airstrike? Unbelievable. And he's on "Target 1," al-Souri. That should blunt some of the blowback, at least.

Bridget stared at her screen and thought of Will. He was okay. Focus on that. But he had been injured on a mission she had ordered. It was serious enough that he was being flown out of the war zone. And she saw him get injured. Jesus! And he'd met Faraz. Holy Christ! This was too much.

She calmed herself and emailed Gallagher in Kabul asking for a standard after-action call with the assault team. Then she went to the ladies' room and splashed some water on her face.

As Bridget dabbed her cheeks with a paper towel, the woman she saw in the mirror was not the one she expected to see. You've gone soft, she thought.

She replayed the day in her mind, as if she had been there. She saw Will get injured, not a blurry body-heat signature. She saw Faraz escape out the back, not a faint shape on an infrared video feed. He had voluntarily gone off with al-Souri in spite of the orders to kill him. Faraz was sticking with his mission, even though the airstrike he called in on Ibn Jihad had never happened.

What must Faraz be thinking?

Bridget had more than a dozen operations running in Afghanistan, and she had watched many unfold on the screens in the Ops Center. Having been in the field herself, she knew very well that these were real people risking their lives, sometimes getting injured or killed. And she was always aware that she had a safe desk job, far from the front lines. She could think of the operations, the agents, the informants as parts of an apparatus—a machine she was building and operating to help defeat the terrorists. Seven thousand miles, the Pentagon walls, and the secure steel doors of the DIA offices gave her some separation. And that was essential. It enabled her to do her job.

What she had just seen changed all that, put her back on the ground in Afghanistan, where she and her army friends had been at risk every day. She thought of that convoy run, the casualties she saw come into the base, the memorial service that night. And she thought of the attack on FOB Emerson, Tommy and the others lying dead in the sand.

When she had been in uniform, and experiencing these feelings all the time, she had developed emotional callouses. But now, her callouses were as long gone as her rank insignia and desert camouflage uniform.

Staring at her formidable-woman "Look" in the mirror, she felt not very formidable at all.

Thank God at least there won't be a memorial service for Will tonight.

Another woman came into the bathroom. Bridget went into one of the stalls and locked the door. She leaned against the wall and put her face in her hands.

* * *

Back at her desk, Bridget received a reply from Gallagher. Will was sedated and the docs wouldn't wake him for the call. The intel officer at FOB Emerson was debriefing Weston and the other members of the team to try to get more details, and would send a report ASAP.

Bridget consulted with the comms guys. Would she have to live at the Pentagon until Faraz called? The short answer was yes, in fact she would be restricted to the small area between her office and the comms room. She sent Liz Michaels to the apartment with a list of things to bring her, called the cat-sitter to take care of Sarge, and ordered a bunk to be delivered to her office before the end of the day.

She was all set if Faraz called. But the one she really wanted to talk to was Will, and not on the after-action call with a dozen people listening.

The president was about as unhinged as Jacobs had ever seen him.

"They let al-Souri get away? Did they not understand the orders?" the president was fuming and pacing in front of the fireplacc in the Oval Office.

"One man had different orders," Jacobs said, trying to adopt a contrite posture as he stood near the middle of the room. "The SEAL commander didn't want to point a gun at Sandblast to get his cooperation. It was an unfortunate set of circumstances."

"Unfortunate? It was a major flying fuckup! I wanted al-Souri dead to send a message and try to get these talks going again. 'Remove IJ's biggest rival,' you told me. Now, we've got nothing. Worse than nothing! We've got the Taliban leaders going to ground, no chance for progress in the talks and probably a bunch of suicide bombers heading our way. This was the worst possible outcome. I should have sent in the goddamn airstrike."

Jacobs rubbed the stump of his arm. It ached when he was under stress. "Sorry, Andy. Let's talk about what we can do to fix it."

"There's not shit we can do, as far as I can figure! Understand, Marty, this is a big setback. A new list of strategy enhancements, or whatever the hell you call them, is not going to do the job. We need to up our game."

"You've become quite the hawk, haven't you?"

"Oh Christ, Marty! You've been after me for years to do stuff like this. Now, you're defending the people who fucked it up. We've got talks going nowhere, military ops going nowhere, and now Special Ops going nowhere. You want me to accept that?"

"No, of course not. We'll get to work on it. And don't forget, Sandblast is still in position."

"For all the good that's done us. Go on, get back to work."

"Thank you, Mr. President." That was the first time Jacobs had been kicked out of the Oval. And he left not having any idea what he and his team might come up with.

It would likely be some version of the so-called New Strategy, the aggressive approach that was still the public face of the administration's policy. Neither Jacobs nor Martelli wanted to do that. They had been looking forward to the day when they could reveal the secret talks and announce some results that would be the beginning of the end of U.S. involvement in Afghanistan. That would have been a worthy accomplishment, something the president could take to the voters. Now, they would have to make do with more fighting and a "Tough Guy" approach that wasn't working, and that everyone knew wasn't really Andrew Martelli.

In the hallway, Jacobs told Harmon to convene a meeting at six p.m. to brainstorm options, and to tell people to be prepared to stay all night.

That suited Bridget well enough. She was spending the night in the Pentagon anyway.

She checked the suitcase Liz had brought and found everything she needed. The bunk looked pretty uncomfortable and took her back to her army years. Technicians had installed a two-way speaker in her office that would sound an alarm to wake her, and enable the comms officer to speak to her, and to hear her confirm she was on the way. She hoped Faraz called soon, and Will, too.

Shit! Bridget remembered her date with Richard on Sunday. She'd probably still be stuck at the Pentagon, and with Will brought back to the forefront of her mind, she had lost all interest. Will was coming home. The anxiety she had been feeling was no longer there. She was excited. Happy, even. Well, Dr. Jen, there it was.

She logged into her personal email and sent a message to Richard's phone, "Have to cancel. Working Sunday."

He wrote back, "Next week then?"

"No. Sorry. Can't." She hit send, and in case he didn't get the message, she took her phone out of her purse and blocked his number.

CHAPTER 24

As Zahir drove the dark country roads, Faraz worked on al-Souri in the back seat. The wound was bad, and Faraz didn't know how far the village was. If it took much longer, he thought al-Souri wouldn't make it.

"How much farther, Zahir? The *Qomandan* is dying."

"Not far now, just in the next valley. Help him, Hamed!" Zahir's voice was desperate.

"Do not worry. I will keep him alive until we get there. After that, it is in Allah's hands."

Faraz was covered with al-Souri's blood, as were the seat and the carpet. But the flow had slowed. That told Faraz that Al-Souri's blood pressure was down and he didn't have much more blood to lose. His pulse was weak, and Faraz could barely detect his breathing.

It was nearly three a.m. when they got to the village. Zahir stopped at the first house, ran to the door, and pounded on it. "Wake up! Wake up! Emergency!" he shouted several times.

"Who is there?" asked a man inside, who was likely pointing an AK-47 at Zahir through the door.

"I am sorry, brother. We have an injured man. Which house is Dr. Zia?"

"Zia is last house on the left at the other end of the

village. You must be crazy! Coming to a door like that at night you are lucky I did not shoot you."

By the time the man finished, Zahir was running back to the vehicle.

He repeated the same routine at Zia's house, but the doctor was more accustomed to such wee-hours intrusions. He came out to the car and shined a flashlight into the back seat. Zia gasped. "Commander al-Souri! Oh, Allah! Bring him in! Bring him in!"

Zahir and Faraz carried al-Souri inside and put him on an examining table in the doctor's home-office.

"What happened?" the doctor asked.

"We were attacked by the infidels," Zahir said. "They fired a grenade."

"Go. Put the car behind the house." As Zahir went to move the car, the doctor unwrapped the makeshift bandages and examined the wound. "He is lucky to be alive." He packed the wound with gauze to stop the bleeding and glanced at Faraz. "You helped him?"

"Yes, doctor."

"You did well. You saved his life. How did you know what to do, how to create a pressure dressing?"

Faraz hesitated. "I do not know the name," he said. "My uncle was a healer in our village. I went with him sometimes."

The doctor looked up at him. He seemed doubtful but didn't press the point. "Go, wash off the blood. My wife is in the kitchen. She will give you some clean clothes. I will tend to your head afterward." Then he turned his attention back to al-Souri.

* * *

Three hours later, as the morning light was coming over the mountains, Faraz, Zahir, and the doctor said the morning prayers and sat down to have tea and bread at a small table in the living room. Al-Souri was stable but still unconscious on the examining table.

"It was dangerous to come here," Zia said.

"The *Qomandan* ordered it," Zahir replied, "before he became unconscious."

"I suppose he knew his life depended on reaching me, but Ibn Jihad has forbidden all fighters to come here. It is safer if I travel to them. Coming here endangers me, and there are not so many like me."

Zahir and Faraz had nothing to say. They followed al-Souri's orders, but he had apparently broken Ibn Jihad's

"Never mind," the doctor said. "Get some rest. The *Qomandan* will sleep for several more hours."

As he settled in on the floor of the doctor's spare room, Faraz finally had a chance to think about the last twenty-four hours. He had nearly been killed and, a few minutes later, nearly taken a ride home. He had recommitted to his mission and then saved a leading terrorist's life. He could be on his way to another promotion in the Taliban, after which, at the right time, he would try again to kill its leader, and al-Souri, too.

Or the doctor's house could be hit with an airstrike at any moment.

It was hard to sleep. He couldn't be sure he had made the right decision, but there was no point worrying about that. He had been Faraz for about two minutes. Now, he was Hamed again, and for the foreseeable future.

It seemed to him more important than ever to find out

about the MTO. Maybe killing Ibn Jihad and al-Souri would stop it. But how could he find IJ again? And did anyone in Washington care anymore? He needed to find a phone.

He rolled over to face the wall. "202-555-4700, Sandblast, Whiskey-Alpha . . ."

When al-Souri came around that afternoon, he asked for Faraz and Zahir. The doctor called them in. "I will leave you three to talk. I must go to visit another patient. The men can stay a few minutes, then you must rest, *Qomandan*. Do not try to get out of bed."

"Thank you, doctor," al-Souri said. His voice was raspy, and he could not raise his head from the pillow. When the doctor was gone, he continued. "You two have done well. Now we must summon Balaa to bring some men and take us back to the base."

Faraz and Zahir looked at the floor.

"What is it, my brothers?"

Neither spoke up immediately. Finally, Faraz said, "Commander Balaa is with Allah. He is a martyr for jihad."

"He sacrificed himself to save us," Zahir added. "He ran into the infidels' bullets so we could escape, with you."

Al-Souri was silent. He turned his head toward the ceiling and recited, "He is Allah, alone in the heavens and on the earth. He knows what you conceal and what you reveal, and He knows what you have earned." (6:3)

The two young men repeated the verse.

"He was a great man," al-Souri said. "I fought with him for many years. I was nearly martyred to save him.

And now he has been martyred to save me. He has earned his place in paradise." Then, after another silence, he turned to Faraz and asked, "What of our other men?"

"We do not know, *sayyid*. Many were martyred, but some survive, I think. We took you out the back of the house, so I cannot be sure."

Al-Souri considered that. "Then my men at the villa and at the camp do not know whether I am alive." He paused again. "We must get word to them. And we need more men here." Al-Souri stretched his neck to be closer to the two men. He appeared to realize something, and he spoke quickly now, in a whisper. "This is very urgent. We are exposed here, in danger. Zahir, you must leave immediately. Do not tell the doctor you are going. Get to the camp as fast as you can, and return here with half a dozen men."

Faraz was surprised at his urgency, and Zahir looked confused. It seemed safe at the doctor's house. Maybe al-Souri's paranoia had been increased by the attack. Or perhaps he knew something they didn't know.

"Yes, *Qomandan*," Zahir said. "Do not fear. I will do it."

"Be back before morning prayers, Zahir. Do not fail."

"*Insha Allah*, I will not fail you, *Qomandan*."

"Good, good." Al-Souri settled back into the bed. "Go, now. Leave me. I must rest." He closed his eyes, and the two fighters left him alone.

Back in their bedroom, Zahir retrieved his rifle. "What is going on, Hamed? Why is the *Qomandan* so worried?"

"He wants the men to know he is alive. He wants more of his men around him. That is all I can see."

"I hope you are right. But it felt like more than that. In any case, I must go immediately."

Faraz gave him some bread that was left over from their lunch, and a bottle of water. They went out the back door and found the keys where Zahir had left them in the SUV's ignition. The back seat was caked with dried blood.

"Be safe, my brother," Faraz said, and the two embraced. Zahir got in and drove away.

When the doctor came home, he was not happy that Zahir had gone to get more men. "I told you no one is to come here!" he said.

"We followed the *Qomandan*'s orders," Faraz replied.

"He is not my *Qomandan*!" The doctor was angry, but there was nothing he could do.

CHAPTER 25

Bridget saw Jacobs; his chief of staff, Harmon, and their entourage barrel into the DIA workspace and take over the conference table at the far end of the room. Because of the restrictions on Bridget's movements, this would be the venue for the all-night meeting the secretary had called.

Once he had dropped his briefcase on the table and given his staff some instructions Bridget couldn't hear, Jacobs came straight into her office and closed the door. She stood facing him and held out her ID card.

"Oh, put that away. Don't be ridiculous. This was a major screwup, and I wish you'd kept your mouth shut. But I need you to make it right."

"I am sorry about how things turned out, sir," Bridget said. "I thought it was the best plan at the time."

"I know, I know. But we have a mess on our hands now, and the president is, frankly, pissed as hell. He nearly took *my* ID a little while ago. Let's hope Sandblast calls in soon. His orders will be to kill al-Souri, and then bug out."

"Yes, sir. But he did say he had wind of an MTO."

"Exactly why this is such a disaster. We need to strike now to try to derail it."

"We give up on IJ?"

"Yes. We take the win and get our man out. Then we resume the talks. If that doesn't work, we find another way to go after IJ."

"Got it, sir." Bridget thought it was a mistake. They had no other way to go after IJ, not in the foreseeable future. But she had more than used up her day's allocation of freedom to challenge her bosses.

The cubicle area outside her office filled up with officials from around the building. They took over the new desks, or perched on credenzas, or leaned against the walls.

First item on the agenda was a clip from the video shot by Chief Weston's helmet camera. Now, Bridget actually saw Faraz come into the living room. She got a glimpse of Will lying on the carpet soaked with his blood. She heard Faraz say her fake name and decline the offer of a trip home. And she watched him turn and go back to the mission she had sent him on, a mission Jacobs had just changed.

Mary Larson was back, having ejected one of Bridget's staffers from a seat in the front row. While Bridget felt like she'd been on a three-day drunk, Larson looked fresh as a hothouse daisy, if hothouse daisies wore herringbone suits, sensible shoes, and loads of attitude. She complained about the SEALs' failure to kill al-Souri, and went pretty close to ballistic over Faraz's direct refusal to do so. She also presented new intelligence indicating that al-Souri was the leader of a militant faction within the Taliban that was trying to sabotage the talks.

"Taking him out would have been a game-changer,"

she said. "Might have blocked the MTO. If Sandblast calls in, he must be ordered to kill al-Souri immediately."

This was Bridget's chance to ask the question she had decided not to ask Jacobs earlier. From the back of the room, sitting in her desk chair in the doorway of her office, she raised her voice to be heard. "You really think killing his Number Two will stop IJ from moving forward with the MTO and bring him back to the table?"

"The talks are not the agency's priority," Larson shot back over her shoulder. "Al-Souri is a key operational commander and a lightning rod for the worst of the Taliban's worst. He needs to be taken out. Killing al-Souri might not stop the MTO, but it would likely delay it and give us more time to figure out what it is. As things stand, the botched raid could speed up the MTO timeline."

Bridget knew others would share that view, and it was a direct rebuke of Will and Faraz. She spoke up again. "That's a bit strong, Mary, don't you think?"

"No, I don't," Larson said, turning to glare briefly at Bridget as if her question was a childish interruption. Then she turned again to Jacobs. "Sir, with all due respect, that's the way we see it at Langley. This is an opportunity to have a real impact on Taliban/Al-Qaida joint operations."

"The president and I agree, and I've already issued the order." Jacobs said. "But Ms. Larson, how long does CIA think it will it take them to replace al-Souri? Forty-eight hours? Seventy-two?" he asked.

"Perhaps. But with a man of much less experience and stature. We are not convinced that Ibn Jihad is more moderate than al-Souri. But if he is, killing al-Souri will make it easier for IJ to resume the talks and delay the

MTO. If that doesn't happen, we'll have proof that the 'moderate' act is a sham."

Jacobs had no argument with that last point, and the meeting moved on to other issues. The secretary approved an increase in the alert level at U.S. military facilities worldwide, and he announced that the president would sign off on the same for all embassies and stateside transportation facilities in the morning. Homeland Security guys with Uzis would be on patrol at airports and train and bus stations, and that would likely spark similar moves around Europe and Asia.

The heightened security was a good deterrent for hard targets, but it was the soft ones they had to worry about—sports stadiums, shopping malls, movie theaters, anyplace where people gathered. Those were virtually impossible to defend. They needed to somehow shift the momentum of the fight, and fast, before the terrorists scored another major victory. Lives were at stake, and so was the future of the Martelli administration.

Harmon reported that the attack on Khaliki's house was in the news, along with rumors it had been an unsuccessful hit on al-Souri. The story had stirred the pot about the secret war both sides were waging while the world focused on the relatively insignificant details of the public war. Every pundit on every network seemed to be asking what else was happening that the public didn't know about. And they duly dredged up and rehashed the old unconfirmed reports of an impending major terrorist attack. Although she hated politics, Bridget could see that if it came now, the president would be blamed for having sparked the escalation.

The meeting went on for several hours. At first, Jacobs seemed angry, frustrated, shooting down ideas and demanding more creative thinking. But as the evening wore on, he warmed to the task, and appeared to be pleased with the action memo for the president that was taking shape in Harmon's notebook.

A little after one a.m., Jacobs said, "All right. This is a good start. Keep the ideas coming. We'll present this to the president in the morning. Now, everybody try to get some sleep."

He and Harmon headed for the third floor to finalize the proposals. Larson shot Bridget a final glare before heading out to tell her bosses she'd gotten their message across. Everyone else went home, except Bridget, who worked in her office for a while before spending her first night on the cot.

The document Bridget reviewed at 0700 and President Martelli received on top of his morning intelligence briefing book at 0730 basically called for a return to all-out warfare against the Taliban. It declared the talks dead, at least for now, and said the U.S. and its allies should increase ground and air operations, including hits on Taliban leaders, and launch a new effort to disrupt the group's communications and its use of the Internet for recruiting and coordination.

It also recommended another increase in combat brigades and Special Operations units in Afghanistan, along with a public "get tough" stance, which the president's campaign advisers would certainly welcome.

By 0740, Bridget had a secure email confirming that the president had approved all the recommendations. In addition, at a second meeting outside her office door that afternoon, Jacobs signed half a dozen new covert-mission authorizations. Bridget was close enough to see he could do little more than scribble with his left hand.

When everyone else left, Jacobs went into Bridget's office. "I spoke to the president and he wants to be sure the orders are clear this time. He wants Sandblast to take out al-Souri ASAP—either kill him or give the coordinates for an airstrike. If Sandblast has a location for IJ, the president will decide if we strike or not. Frankly, I think we'll get the green light on anything your man calls in. After the call, Sandblast is to get the heck out of there. End of mission."

"Got it, sir," Bridget said. But what she really wanted to say was, "Could have used a fucking green light a month ago!"

CHAPTER 26

Zahir returned to Dr. Zia's house before dawn with three Land Cruisers and six other men. They drove slowly to the back of the house, trying not to make too much noise. But Zia heard them arrive and met them in the back hallway.

"You are welcome here," he said without enthusiasm. "Zahir will make you tea. You will have to sleep on the floor of their room." He went back into his bedroom and closed the door.

Faraz emerged to greet them with hugs. "My brothers! Praise Allah you are here. The *Qomandan* will be happy to see you."

The men stayed at the doctor's house for three days while al-Souri recovered from his injuries. On the fourth morning, al-Souri said to the doctor, "I am feeling better. I will return to my base tomorrow."

"No," the doctor said.

Al-Souri was not used to having anyone contradict him, and he showed it. "Why not?" he demanded.

"Our leader, Ibn Jihad, may peace be upon him, has ordered you to report to him as soon as you are well enough to travel. His men should be here tonight to take you."

That afternoon, Faraz supported al-Souri as he struggled to walk around the doctor's small back garden.

"Ibn Jihad's security men will arrive tonight," al-Souri said.

"Yes, *sayyid*. The doctor told us."

"Do not worry. You did nothing wrong. You followed my orders. The sheikh may not be happy that we came here, but he and I go back a long way. We did not endanger the doctor. If the infidels had followed us with their drones or their satellites, we would all be dead by now."

But Faraz was getting anxious. Maybe he should have gone with the SEALs. "Do you think we will be punished for coming here?"

"I think it will be all right. But be on your guard," al-Souri said.

"Yes, *sayyid*."

Shortly after midnight, Ibn Jihad's security chief Karch pulled into the doctor's driveway with four vehicles and a dozen men. Karch emerged. The big man was sweating and clearly angry. "Get your things! Carry Commander al-Souri to the vehicle! We leave immediately!"

The doctor protested. "Give him one more day. Two would be better."

"No!" Karch snarled, showing disrespect for the doctor that surprised Faraz.

"It is okay," said al-Souri. "It is time for us to go. Thank you, Dr. Zia. May peace be upon you."

Two men helped al-Souri into an SUV they had configured so he could lie down in the back, while Karch took the doctor into the examining room. Faraz could hear Karch grilling Zia on the extent of al-Souri's injuries, how he had survived the attack and why so many of his men were at the house. He seemed to be in a hurry, but he wanted all the details. Faraz couldn't hear every word, but he heard his name and Zahir's mentioned several times.

Karch emerged from the examining room apparently even angrier than before, and ordered them all out of the house. Once they were outside, Karch's men raised their rifles. "Give me your weapons," Karch said to al-Souri's security team.

"What? Commander . . ." Zahir protested, but Karch cut him off with a wave.

"Your weapons. Now!"

They were outnumbered, and Karch was a senior commander very close to Ibn Jihad. They complied. They boarded their SUVs and fell in with Karch's convoy, separated by vehicles carrying his men, whose guns were ready in case al-Souri's guards gave them any trouble.

They left less than ten minutes after Karch and his men had arrived.

Two hours later they came to a different compound from the one where they had seen Ibn Jihad several weeks earlier. This one was in a large town that extended onto the first slope of foothills leading to the mountains.

It seemed to Faraz that they drove about halfway up the main road, nearly to the central square and mosque, before turning left onto a small lane through a residential neighborhood. At the end of the street, they drove through the gate of a walled compound that backed up to some woods.

The trip did not go well for al-Souri, and Karch's men immediately took him to a bedroom, where they said a doctor would tend to his wounds. Al-Souri's men were taken to an outbuilding and put under guard in two locked rooms. Faraz and Zahir were together, along with two others.

"What is going on?" Zahir asked.

"I do not know," Faraz replied. "They seem to be angry that we went to Dr. Zia's house. Do not worry, my brother. Our commander will speak to Ibn Jihad after prayers." Faraz did his best to sound confident.

The men lay down in the beds and tried to sleep. At dawn, they heard the village muezzin in the distance. They got up, and Faraz knocked on the door. "My brothers, toilet and prayers, please."

The door opened and two of Karch's men marched them, one at a time, down the hallway to the bathrooms, AK-47s pointed at their backs. The bathrooms were old, with cement walls, cracked white floor tiles, and a thin baseboard of black dirt. There were two squat toilets in open stalls and one working sink with a leaking faucet. There were no towels or toilet paper, only a short cut-off hose attached to a spigot next to one of the toilets for washing oneself, if needed.

When they had finished, Al-Souri's men prayed in

their locked bedrooms, and afterward Zahir said, "This is not good, Hamed."

"I agree. But we must wait for the commanders to speak. It will be all right. This is only a precaution." Neither of them was convinced, but there was nothing to do but sit on the beds and wait.

The morning passed with no news.

After midday prayers, Faraz and Zahir were taken to the main house, where they found al-Souri sitting on an easy chair in the living room, in obvious pain.

Zahir rushed to him and knelt down. "*Qomandan*, how are you?"

"Praise Allah, I am all right," al-Souri said, putting his hand on Zahir's shoulder.

"What is happening? We are being held like criminals."

"Be calm. Soon my brother in jihad will join us and all will be well."

"He is not here? He will come in daylight?" Faraz asked.

"Yes, soon."

Faraz understood Ibn Jihad must be in a big hurry to get there if he was traveling during the day. They sat in silence, with four armed men guarding them, and waited.

Less than an hour later, there was a commotion in the courtyard as Ibn Jihad arrived with his security team.

Karch met him in front of the house and whispered in his ear. Ibn Jihad nodded and gestured toward the house. Karch mounted the steps, opened the front door, and shouted. "Stand up! El Haji is coming."

As he came through the door, Ibn Jihad saw Faraz and Zahir stand, with the guards' rifles still pointing at them. Al-Souri could not stand, but he straightened himself as best he could.

"How are you, my old comrade?" Ibn Jihad said.

"Praise Allah."

"You should not have gone to Dr. Zia. You know this. Perhaps it was your day to be a martyr."

Al-Souri was silent. Finally, he said, "We will all have our day."

Ibn Jihad nodded. "Leave us, and take these men with you," he said, tilting his head toward Faraz and Zahir. All the men left, trailed by Karch, who closed the door.

Ibn Jihad moved a chair so he could sit and face al-Souri. He leaned in close. "The doctor is the least of it," he whispered. "You were hit. How were you hit, with all the precautions we take?"

"I believe it was Khaliki. He would do anything for money. The scum!"

"Nonsense! Khaliki is dead, killed in the raid, and his son, too." Ibn Jihad was suddenly angry. His eyes widened. He spat when he spoke. "That is not the act of a traitor! He was martyred, as you should have been."

"I did not know," al-Souri said quietly. "May peace be upon him in the arms of Allah."

"This was your fault, Faisal," Ibn Jihad said, leaning even closer and calling al-Souri by his middle name, the name he had used before earning his nom de guerre.

"My fault? How? I took all the steps. There must be a traitor in the village. We will teach them not to betray us!"

Ibn Jihad stared at him.

He had already sent men to the village to investigate. They had terrorized the people for three days with threats, interrogations, and beatings. But no one knew that the man whose wife had died in the market bombing had become a CIA informant. No one knew that when he sent the children to live with relatives in the mountains it was to protect them in case he was exposed. And no one knew how good a liar he could be to honor his late wife and protect his children, even when the Taliban men beat him.

"No. The village is loyal," Ibn Jihad said, leaning back in the chair, still looking directly at al-Souri.

"How do you know?"

Ibn Jihad cut him off with a wave of his hand. "You have a spy in your ranks."

"My brother, how can you know that? Let me send men to the village . . ."

The top commander waved his hand again. "You have become careless. You have allowed the infidels to get close to you."

"My brother, no." Al-Souri tried to lean forward but was stopped by the pain. He fell back into the chair, while Ibn Jihad watched him with a mix of pity and scorn.

"Now, of all times. Now, when we have used their weakness to strengthen ourselves. Now, when we are ready to strike another great blow for Allah, as you have been demanding. You have put it all in jeopardy!"

"You are wrong, my brother. My team is loyal and our plans are intact."

"You have no idea!" Ibn Jihad exploded again. "No idea!"

"My brother . . ."

"The men will take you to rest now," Ibn Jihad said. Then he stood, moved quickly to the door and opened it. Karch was there. "Take the commander to his room," he said. "Then come to me."

CHAPTER 27

It was Bridget's third day camping out in her office, and she was not a happy camper. She had coped with much worse conditions in the army, but she wasn't used to it anymore. She didn't think of herself as particularly concerned about creature comforts. Still, she missed them now that they were gone.

She was not allowed to be more than thirty seconds away from the comms room, so no meetings in other part of the building, no walking out to the courtyard café, not even any workouts in the Pentagon gym. She only ventured out of the secure area once a day to use the nearest shower, in a three-star general's office suite two minutes' run away. There was always a female Pentagon Police officer with her, on an open line to the comms room, who could, in theory, yell "Call! Call!" and then help her on with her robe and run interference for her as she sprinted down the hallway in flip-flops, maybe with shampoo in her hair, through the pre-opened security doors to the comms room.

It was a terrible plan, but Bridget was at the point where she would prefer that, and the lifetime of humiliation that would follow, to spending another night on the cot.

But she was looking forward to the next item on her calendar—the after-action conference call with Will and Chief Petty Officer Weston. Several DIA officials were squeezed into her office to listen. She had contacted Hadley at his new post in Kabul and asked him to run the call. She gave him some gobbledygook about wanting a military officer to lead the conversation, and he bought it. Larson was on the line with a team at CIA, and there were folks from Special Operations and the White House.

There was a beep, and the DIA comms operator came on. "General Hadley, I have your call with Landstuhl, and we should have FOB Emerson on in a moment."

"Thank you. Commander Jackson, can you hear me?" Hadley asked.

"This is Dr. Samuels, head of trauma surgery," came the reply. "Other than one brief chat with immediate family, this is the first call we've allowed Commander Jackson to take, and only because of the high priority we understand is attached to it. Still, General, ten minutes max."

"Thank you, doctor. We understand the restriction. Commander, this is General Jim Hadley. How are you?"

"I'm all right, sir, thank you."

Will's voice sounded different to Bridget. Maybe it was the distance and the scrambling of the secure line, but Bridget couldn't help thinking that he must be in pain. She felt her heart beating hard, and tried not to let her emotions show. She crossed her legs and adjusted her notebook on her knee.

"Glad to hear it," Hadley said. "We're waiting for Chief Weston to come on from Afghanistan. We have folks on from across the agencies, including the mission coordinator Bridget Davenport at DIA."

There was a pause, and Bridget could almost hear Will processing that information. He said, "Hello, ma'am." Bridget could see his grin, and she pretended to reach for something in her purse on the floor so others couldn't see she was grinning, too.

The only thing she could think about was the last time Will had held her, wedged between the shipping containers at Camp Eggers, his big muscles pulling her in, the taste of his coffee breath. In spite of her best efforts, she came up smiling and let the others wonder why.

The phone line beeped again, and the operator said, "We have FOD Emerson now, sir. Please go ahead."

"This is Chief Weston, sir."

"Hello, Chief. I'm General Hadley, and we have Lieutenant Commander Jackson on from Landstuhl, with a cast of thousands listening in. Now, gentlemen, we've seen the video, but tell us your impressions of the encounter with our man."

It took all the acting skills Bridget could muster to maintain her composure as Will and Chief Weston told the story. She used her pen and notebook to keep her hands from shaking, and stared down at them as she wrote, working hard to focus on the information. She was also trying to come up with something she could say that would send a message to Will that the others wouldn't understand. Hadley carried the conversation, but there wasn't much beyond what they had seen on the video.

Then Larson piped up, without identifying herself. "Commander, why didn't you order Sandblast to kill al-Souri? That was your Priority One."

"Ma'am, I've thought about that a lot since the raid," Will said. "I mean, there was this jihadi standing there. He was one of ours, but he had clearly been on his mission for a long time. I felt it was beyond my authority to alter his orders. I respected his judgment in that situation, ma'am. Looking back, maybe I should have pulled rank, given my mission the priority. But frankly, with my team shot up, I was focused on getting us all out of there. He said he could hit the target at any time. Seemed to make sense to let him carry on."

"Thank you, Commander," Hadley said, blocking Larson from pressing the point.

Bridget knew he would be irritated that a civilian would question a SEAL officer's judgment under fire.

"We're not here to second-guess you, Commander," Hadley continued. "Thank you for your insight. Ms. Davenport, any questions before the doctor pulls the plug?"

"Oh, um, yes." She hesitated. "Yes, thank you, General. Um. Commander, how did Sandblast seem to you?"

Will paused. It was the first time Bridget's voice had been on the call. "Uh, well, he seemed fine to me, um, ma'am. He was confident, knew what he was doing. Appeared to be in good health, aside from the bruise on his head. It was strange, though. Looked like a jihadi, talked like a trooper."

"Good. Thank you." This was Bridget's chance to say something. "Commander, we look forward to the day that you're home safe."

Bridget imagined Will was grinning again. "Thank you, ma'am," he said. "Me, too."

* * *

After the call, Bridget was surprised at how good she felt, almost gleeful. It was Will's voice that had done it. Even though he didn't sound great, hearing him speak had an enormous impact, after everything they had both been through.

She tried to read her notes. They were almost illegible, but she managed to type up a summary of the call. Her conclusion was that Sandblast was in position and on mission, and should be able to deliver al-Souri at any time, with a second chance to hit Ibn Jihad also possible. Between the lines, the message was that Lieutenant Commander Jackson had made the right decision. Bridget felt quite pleased with herself as she read it over. When she sent the email, she copied Jacobs directly. She thought he was likely to forward it to the president.

It was evening now, and she was alone in the office, except for the cleaning crew. She had changed into her U.S. ARMY sweat suit and a pair of warm socks. The office was cold at night, without all the bodies to counteract the seemingly constant flow of air-conditioning.

The excitement of Will's call was still with her. She imagined him in his bed with his shirt off, one hand behind his head, smiling at her, waiting for her to . . .

Oh, what was the use? *He's four thousand miles away, wounded and probably wearing a polka-dot hospital gown. And you're in your office, with the cleaning crew vacuuming outside your door.*

C'mon Faraz, call! Move this mission forward. Bridget needs to get the fuck out of here!

CHAPTER 28

Ibn Jihad ordered Faraz and Zahir held in a shed, separate from the other men. It had nothing in it except two bedrolls, and the floor was hard-packed dirt. There were no windows, so the only light came from gaps in the wooden walls. It would not be pleasant to be held there for very long.

Zahir was in a panic, pacing back and forth across the small space. "Hamed, why are they doing this to us?"

"It will be all right. Ibn Jihad does not like when his orders are disobeyed. Perhaps it is an example to the others."

Zahir sat on the ground and put his head in his hands. "Honestly, Hamed, I am afraid. Yesterday, I was a brother in jihad. Now . . . now, I do not know."

"You are still a brother, Zahir. Do not worry so much. Are you suddenly a farm boy again?"

That seemed to jar Zahir out of his self-pity. He looked up at Faraz. "I hope you are right, and we are not in real trouble. But did you see Karch's face? He is angry. He will kill us if he thinks for one second that we are not loyal."

"But we are loyal," Faraz said, trying to sound like it was true.

It was only a few minutes later that Karch came into the shed, flanked by two of his men. He pointed at Zahir. "Come with me!" he ordered. Zahir jumped to his feet, and the two guards grabbed his arms and marched him toward the side building.

Faraz was left alone in the shed. He felt sorry for Zahir. The man had come to fear the brutality of the brotherhood that had only given him comfort and strength before. He would do anything to restore his position. He would certainly have exposed Hamed as an infidel spy. But he didn't have the slightest clue. Sadly for Zahir, having nothing to tell them, he would likely face a long interrogation.

But Faraz was more worried about his own future. Surely, all this couldn't be because they took al-Souri to Dr. Zia's house. They were clearly in serious trouble, and he didn't know why. If they suspected he was a spy, well, that was the nightmare scenario. But why would they?

After half an hour, Faraz decided he might be able to get some more information if he could hear even a little of Zahir's interrogation. He knocked on the door of the shed. "My brothers, toilet please."

"Wait," came the reply. A few minutes later, the door opened and one of the guards handed him a bucket and some old newspapers.

Faraz protested, "But my bro . . ." The guard slammed the door in his face, and he heard the bolt slide home.

Now, it was Faraz's turn to pace the shed. He had not thought about his backstory in months. He repeated it to himself now, with the name of his home village, the name of the sheikh he had met that first day in the mountain village, and his family history, with all the made-up details. He reviewed the interrogation survival skills he had learned, steeling himself for the pain that was to come.

An hour later, the bolt slid again and the two guards came in. They grabbed Faraz and took him to a room in the side building. It was empty except for two chairs. They put him in one of them and left.

There was black cloth on the windows, and when the door closed it was quite dark. As the minutes dragged on, the room became hot, and the air got stale.

After what seemed like a long time, Karch and two of his men burst in, closed the door, and shined lights in his eyes. It was primitive, but effective. Faraz closed his eyes and turned his head.

Karch put the other chair in front of Faraz and sat on it. He leaned in close. "Look at me!"

Faraz turned his head and blinked his eyes to try to get used to the light.

"Who are you?" Karch shouted at close range.

Faraz paused. He had not expected such a basic question. "I am Hamed Anwali, *sayyid*, member of . . ."

Karch slapped him hard across the face. "Liar!" he boomed. "You are a liar! You are a traitor, a spy for the infidels!"

Faraz recovered from the blow and played his part. "Please, *sayyid*. I am not . . ."

Karch slapped him again. "Quiet! I will not hear more of this!"

Faraz's head hurt and his mind was swirling out of control. Did Karch know who he was? If he did, he'd have already killed him. No, he would want to break him, to find out about other spies. But he was probably just fishing. God, please let him be fishing!

Faraz hung his head. He tasted blood in his mouth. He dared not move or speak. Karch got up and stood over him for a long time, as if he might hit him again. Then he stepped back, sat in the chair, and said, "Let us start at the beginning."

Karch led Faraz through his cover story, insisting on the name of every sibling, every relative, every village. He pressed Faraz on the sequence of events, trying to trip him up. He took the names of the sheikh in the first village Faraz had reached in the mountains, the imam in the town, the headmaster he had worked for, and other people he had met. All of the details matched what Faraz had already told the Taliban recruiters. The lack of new information seemed to fuel Karch's anger as the session wore on.

Finally, he exploded. "You are a spy for the infidels! You tell them our secrets!"

"No, *sayyid*."

"Stand up!" Karch took the rifle from one of his men and hit Faraz hard in the stomach with the butt. Faraz doubled over, and Karch hit him in the back of the head. Faraz fell facedown on the floor. Karch put his foot on the back of Faraz's neck. "You betrayed Commander al-Souri and led the infidels to him!"

"No, *sayyid*. I was injured. I saved . . ."

Karch kicked him in the side, then put his knee on

Faraz's back and kneeled down to be nearly face-to-face with him. "Liar! How did you save your *Qomandan*'s life? Where did you learn such skills?"

"My uncle. I told the doctor, my uncle . . ."

Karch jumped up and kicked Faraz again. "Liar! No one learns such skills from a village medicine man."

"But, *sayyid* . . ."

Karch picked Faraz up by the neck, pushed him back into the chair, and choked him. "You are a traitor to Allah!"

"*Sayyid*, I have never . . . I am a loyal servant of Allah. I have shed blood . . ."

Karch released his throat and punched him in the face, propelling Faraz and his chair to the floor. Karch loomed over him. "Fuck you and fuck your blood! You do not know what it is to shed blood for jihad!"

"*Sayyid*, I . . ."

Karch picked Faraz up and punched him again. He fell back and hit his head hard on the floor. His nose was bleeding. Karch kicked the chair away and jumped on top of him, with a knee in Faraz's stomach and his hands around his neck. He leaned in close and whispered, "If you are lying to me I will personally cut your fucking balls off. Do you believe me?"

"Yes, *sayyid*." It was not difficult for Faraz to appear to be scared to death.

"I will choke you with my own hands in front of all the men, while you beg for mercy like a woman!"

Faraz stayed silent. He believed Karch one hundred percent.

Karch stood up and brushed himself off. "We shall see if you are telling the truth. We shall see if you survive another day." He turned and left quickly with his men. They shut the lights, leaving Faraz on the floor breathing heavily in the darkness.

Karch's words echoed in his mind—*We shall see if you survive another day.*

Faraz stayed on the floor for several minutes, then lifted himself onto the chair and assessed his injuries. Nothing too serious, but his face and his side hurt, and he had a bump on his head. He thought Karch's kicks had broken a rib or two.

He waited an hour, sweating and breathing the stagnant air. Then guards came and took him to another room, where he found the bucket and newspapers, a pitcher of water, a small plate of rice and beans, and a mat and blanket on the floor. He assumed Zahir was in a similar room elsewhere in the building. He also assumed Karch had sent men to recheck his story. He knew it would only hold up as far as the mountain village. Beyond that, there was no Hamed Anwali.

A week ago, he could have driven away with the SEALs. He could have gone back to the army, back to San Diego, back home. Now, Karch was right. He might not survive another day.

The next morning, the guards gave him cold tea, stale bread, and a prayer rug. They changed out the bucket, and gave him a second one with water in it so he could wash. No one spoke to him, and he did not try to speak to them.

Faraz washed and prayed, as he was supposed to. Then he ate, and sat against the wall to think. He took inventory of the positives first. He was not seriously injured. He had eaten. He was not tied up—that was an important one. His room had a window for light, but it was locked and barred, and looked out on a narrow passageway between the building and the side wall of the compound. If he crouched down, he could see a slice of sky. If he looked to the left, he could see a gate with a heavy chain and lock on it. To the right, he saw only wall.

The list of bad things was shorter but more significant. He could figure no way to get out of there. And if he didn't come up with one, he was a dead man within a day, two at the most.

The routine at midday was the same—a change of buckets, a small meal. There were always two guards at the door while a third came inside. His odds of overpowering them were slim, and he knew there would be more men in the hallway and at the building's doors. He was starting to panic. He fought it by pacing the room. He did squats and push-ups, solved mathematical problems and played word games with himself. He tried to stay occupied and sharp, ready for whatever was to come and alert for any chance to escape, as he had been trained to be.

But as the afternoon wore on, and the air in the room became stifling hot, he found himself sitting in a corner, sweating, waiting for the worst. He slapped his face, jumped to his feet, and ran around the room a couple of times. He needed to stay in control. He needed a plan.

That night, as nightmares troubled his sleep, two men burst into the room and grabbed him by the arms. They marched him down the hallway toward the interrogation room. When they passed the bathroom, he pulled back. "Please, brothers. Please."

One guard glanced at the other, who shrugged. They let him go to the toilet.

Faraz squatted in a cubicle and looked around for something he could use. There wasn't anything, really, only the small hose attached to the spigot on the wall.

"Hurry!" ordered one of the guards from the hallway. "Commander Karch is coming."

Faraz came out swinging the hose. The metal connector hit the nearest guard in his right eye, and the man cried out. He raised his hands to his face and bent over. Faraz gave the other man a karate-style chop to the throat, collapsing his windpipe, and then hit him with two short, quick punches to the face. He took the man's gun and stabbed him in the stomach with the bayonet, sending him to the floor doubled over and screaming. Faraz pivoted to the other man and hit him in the back of the head with the rifle butt. He went down hard in the bathroom doorway.

But the ruckus had drawn the attention of Karch's other men. Faraz turned and saw one of them running down the hallway toward him. He fired the guard's rifle and the man went down. Faraz ran the other way, toward the building's side door. Before he got there, it opened and a guard stepped into view. Faraz fired again and killed him.

At the doorway, Faraz stepped over the guard's body and looked out. To the right, he saw men running toward him. To the left, there was no one, only the side wall and the passageway. He stepped out, spraying fire from the AK-47 toward the men, then turned and ran around the corner of the building into the alley. He stopped short of the gate and fired at its lock and chain. They broke, but behind him two men had reached the beginning of the passageway and one fired.

A bullet hit Faraz's left arm above the elbow. He turned and sprayed the men with bullets, stepped to the gate, pulled it open, and ran into the woods beyond.

He took cover behind a tree and turned to face the gate. A man emerged, and Faraz shot him. Then another tried to come out, and Faraz fired again. He knew the Taliban men would realize they could not follow, but he also knew they would go out the front of the compound and come around, probably from both sides. He had to move.

His arm was bleeding, and it hurt like hell. Faraz pressed his shirt to the wound. He removed the gun's nearly empty magazine and flipped it over to insert the spare that was lashed to it. He turned and ran through the woods, along the outskirts of the town.

Faraz heard Karch shouting at his men from inside the compound. They wouldn't be far behind. He reached the edge of the woods and turned right onto a small lane between houses. Then, before reaching the main road, he swung left into a winding alley that provided some cover from his pursuers. He was moving as fast as he could, but it was an uphill run.

Karch had gone to the right from the front gate with several men, sending his deputy to the left with another team. They met in the woods behind the compound and realized Faraz had gotten away. Karch was livid, screaming at the men for their incompetence, and ordering them to return to the compound, mount the vehicles, and find the traitor.

Karch took his deputy and went into the barracks building. He found the two men he had sent to get Faraz, one dead from the bayonet wound, the other injured and lying on the floor. He grabbed the wounded man by his shirt and punched him hard in the face. "Idiot!" he shouted. "Incompetent!" He punched him again. "You are as bad as the traitor!" Karch hit the man repeatedly until his face was unrecognizable and he could barely breathe. Blood flowed into his windpipe. He choked and died, with Karch still holding him by the shirt. Karch pushed him to the floor in disgust and went to the room where Zahir was being held.

"Your friend is a traitor!" he shouted.

Zahir cowered in a corner. The deputy's AK-47 was pointed at his head. "Hamed? No!" But Karch's look and the gun barrel convinced him not to argue. "Commander, I did not know . . ." His voice was weak.

Karch went to him and lifted him by his hair. "Fool! How did you not see? Or did you help him?"

"No! Commander . . ."

"Ach!" Karch pushed him against the wall. "Where will he go?"

"I do not know, *sayyid*, please . . ."

Karch grabbed Zahir by the shirt with both hands. He leaned in nearly nose-to-nose, "You will help us find him, or you will share his fate! Do you understand me? There will be a gun on you at all times. One move and you die." Karch pushed him toward the door.

Zahir stumbled, then steadied himself as one of

Karch's men grabbed his arm and led him out of the room.

Two minutes later, Zahir was between two fighters heading into the village on foot. The other men had AKs. He did not.

Zahir still couldn't believe what was happening. Hamed, his friend, his brother in jihad, a traitor? If this was true, he should have known. He was as guilty as Hamed. He had failed the jihad, failed Allah. He felt tremendous guilt and a wave of intense fear. He would be executed as a traitor, and he deserved it. There was no place in heaven for men like him.

Still, Karch hadn't killed him on the spot. Maybe Karch knew he believed deeply in jihad. Maybe there was a chance for redemption if he helped find Hamed. Maybe he could reclaim his place in paradise. Maybe. Somehow.

As Faraz neared the end of the village, he stopped and leaned against the alley wall, breathing hard. He checked his arm again and pressed a clean part of the mostly blood-soaked sleeve against the wound. He had to keep moving, had to find a vehicle or a hiding place. He pushed off the wall and rounded a corner to see that he was in front of a mechanic's shop.

He used the butt of his rifle to break the rusty lock on the garage doors, pushed them open, and went inside. As his eyes adjusted to the darkness of the shop, his heart jumped. In the middle of the garage was the best thing he could have found, if it worked.

"Who is there?" came a voice from behind the equipment.

"Come out!" Faraz said, raising his rifle.

A young man emerged, then stopped abruptly when he saw Faraz and his weapon. "Please do not shoot me!"

"Quiet!" Faraz ordered. Then he switched to a whisper. "Show me your hands. Who are you?"

"I am Sharafat, the mechanic's apprentice," the young man replied, his hands now high above his head. "I was sleeping. Please, *sayyid* . . ."

"Do you have a telephone?"

Sharafat seemed surprised at the question, and did not answer immediately.

"Telephone!" Faraz demanded.

"Yes, yes. Over there." Sharafat pointed to a flip phone in a charger on the workbench. Faraz took it.

"What is the name of this village?"

"This village?"

"Yes!"

"It is Kibley Baad, *sayyid*, Kibley Baad." The name meant "Western Breeze."

Faraz stepped forward and pointed his gun at Sharafat's head. "Do not lie to me."

Sharafat held his hands higher, shaking. "I am not lying! Please, my brother! It is Kibley Baad."

"Over there," Faraz said, indicating a corner of the garage. When Sharafat turned to comply, Faraz hit him in the back of the head with the rifle butt. He went down, unconscious. The blow sent a sharp pain along Faraz's injured arm and he felt dizzy.

He squatted against the workbench to steady himself and opened the phone. It booted up and the display indicated he had two bars of signal. He listened to try to determine whether any of Karch's men were nearby. He heard nothing, so he dialed the number.

"Operator."

The speaker alarm sounded. "Ms. Davenport to the Comms Room! Ms. Davenport to the Comms Room! Confirm."

It was early evening in Washington, and Bridget was still at her desk working. She jumped up so quickly she nearly fell over. "Yes, coming," she said. Her heels were lying under the desk, which was good. She took off at a run in her stocking feet.

"Go ahead, make my day," Faraz said.

"Confirmed. Report."

"I need to speak to Walinsky," Faraz said.

"On the way," said the operator. "Report."

"Okay. Tango Alpha, repeat Tango Alpha."

"10-20."

"Village called Kibley Baad, repeat Kibley Baad. Compound in southwest corner of village, approximately one kilometer southwest of my current location. Also on-site, al-Souri, repeat al-Souri. Confirm."

The operator was repeating the information as Bridget ran into the room breathing hard. He held up a hand for her to wait until he had finished. He turned on a speaker, and Bridget heard Faraz say, "Confirmed." Then the operator nodded at her.

"This is . . ." She paused. "This is Walinsky."

It took a moment for Faraz to respond. "Ma'am, I . . . I . . . What happened last month? Do I still have a mission?"

Bridget had seen the video of Faraz as a jihadi, but hearing him on the speaker, she pictured the young, idealistic lieutenant she met at Fort Meade—the guy who wanted the tough mission, who did the unthinkable to get it, who reminded her of herself.

"Al-Souri is now the priority. Can you take him out?"

"Negative, ma'am. I'm blown and on the run."

Bridget was reading the operator's notes over his shoulder. "But he's with IJ?"

"Yes, in the same compound, as of a few minutes ago."

"Excellent. Leave the rest to us. I'm sorry about your previous TA call. Not my decision. Your orders are to bug out ASAP. Are you ready for evac?"

"No. Can't stay here. Gotta keep moving."

Faraz grunted from a shooting pain in his chest where Karch had kicked him.

"Are you all right?" He could hear the concern in Bridget's voice from across the world, from a different world, in a way.

He shifted his position to ease the pain. "Yes. I'm injured, but I'm okay."

"Nothing more on an MTO?"

"I believe there is one. But they keep a tight lid on comms and planning."

"You have timeframe? Location?"

"Negative. Sorry. One commander called it something like 'a strategic blow on all our enemies.' When I asked about it, I nearly got my head bit off."

"All right. Get to a safe place and call again. We'll do everything we can to get you out."

"I'm heading toward the insertion point. I'll call when I can."

"All right, Fa . . . Sandblast." She had nearly called him by his name on an unsecure line. "Be careful."

"Yes, ma'am. Please make sure this isn't all for nothing."

"I'll do my best. Good luck. Stay safe."

Faraz had nothing more to say. He knew the Taliban had equipment to scan for cell phone calls, and this conversation was already too long. He also knew Karch's men would reach this end of the village at any moment.

"Yeah, thanks," he said. "Gotta go." He ended the call and put down the phone.

Faraz took hold of the workbench and stood up. The dizziness had passed. He looked toward the middle of the garage. The motorcycle he had seen when he first entered must have been thirty years old. It was a Russian make, and he had never seen one like it. It was rusty and its seat was ripped, but it had a big engine. That would be helpful in the mountains.

With his rifle slung over his shoulder, Faraz got on and stepped down hard on the kick-starter. Another sharp pain shot down his side. The motorcycle sputtered and died. He tried again, cursing the pain and the noise but having no choice. The engine came to life, and belched a cloud of foul-smelling smoke into the garage. He shook the bike and heard gasoline slosh around in the tank. He couldn't tell how much he had, but it would have to do.

He pushed down with his left foot to put it in gear and released the hand clutch. The machine jumped forward and stalled. Damn! He tried again. Same result.

Come on! Come on! Maybe the Russian shifter didn't work like he remembered Johnny teaching him all those years ago.

Faraz had to put pressure on his side yet again to restart the engine. The pain was intense. He tried to think about how to get the thing to move. He pushed up on the shifter and eased off the clutch. Success. Thank God!

He rolled to the doors, pushed one open with the front tire, the other with his right arm. He leaned forward to check the road, just as two of Karch's men came around the building and stopped right in front of him. They were as startled as he was, which gave him the split-second advantage he needed. Faraz swung his rifle into position, put his foot on the ground, and fired a short burst, killing them both.

As they fell, a third man came into view. Zahir.

"My brother, what are you doing?" Zahir asked. His tone indicated he still found it hard to believe that Hamed was a traitor. Zahir knelt down to check on one of the fighters. The man's rifle lay next to him.

"Stand up!" Faraz said, pointing his AK-47 at his friend and still straddling the motorcycle.

Zahir unfolded his lanky frame slowly and held his arms wide.

"Where is your weapon, my brother?" Faraz asked.

"I am not allowed. I am your friend, and they say you are a traitor."

"And what do you think?"

"I . . . no. But you ran away, and you killed these men. Hamed, why?"

"Walk away, my brother."

"What?"

"Walk away. Do not run. Walk down the hill. Tell Karch I shot these men but did not see you. Go now!"

"Hamed, no. I cannot . . ."

"Do as I say. I must leave this place."

Zahir appeared to be frozen where he stood. He looked again at the dead men on the ground, then back at Faraz. "You were my friend, my brother."

"Go! Now!"

Zahir's confusion turned to anger. "Curse you, Hamed! You are a traitor!"

Faraz tightened his finger on the trigger, took a short breath and held it. His eyes met Zahir's. Faraz tried to will him to run. But he didn't.

Zahir reached for the rifle, and started to shout, "*Qomand* . . ."

Faraz moved his finger ever so slightly. Two bullets exploded out of the barrel and struck Zahir in the chest. The force of the high-powered rounds threw him onto his back. Faraz was close enough to see his eyes wide in pain and disbelief.

"Say the Shahada, my brother," he said.

Faraz put the gun back over his shoulder, threw the

motorcycle into gear, and lurched through the doorway, carving a path between Zahir and the other two men. He got a last glimpse of his friend as he sped by. He would be pleased, Faraz thought. They will give him a martyr's funeral, after all.

CHAPTER 29

At the villa, al-Souri was startled awake when Ibn Jihad flew into his room shouting. "Your man is a traitor! Your man!" He slammed his fist onto the bedside table. The fist would have hit al-Souri if he had been anyone else. The blow toppled everything on the table—the lamp, a glass of water, and a copy of the Koran.

Ibn Jihad bent to pick up the Holy Book. "You see? You see what you made me do?" He put the book on another table.

"My brother . . ." started al-Souri, sounding weak and still half asleep.

"Quiet, Faisal! You have done this!" He moved closer, leaned in toward al-Souri's face, and whispered, "Anyone else would be dead by now. But you . . . I need to think about this. You will stay here, for now." Ibn Jihad paused.

Al-Souri sighed. "Which man?"

"Hamed. One of your favorites, I hear. We will find him, and he will pay."

Al-Souri knew he would pay, too, if Hamed was a traitor. But he found it hard to believe.

Ibn Jihad turned to leave but stopped at the doorway and looked back at al-Souri. "How could you let this happen . . . after all these years?" His tone was disappointment tinged with resignation. The man did not show sadness or remorse. He turned again, and left.

Alone in the room, al-Souri tried to think it through. *Hamed? No. Hamed came to the camp as a simple country boy. I made him a committed fighter for jihad. I made him!*

Al-Souri replayed his relationship with Hamed. Maybe he should have known. Maybe Hamed was too smart for a country boy. Maybe he asked too many questions. Damn him! But Ibn Jihad could be wrong. After thirty years of jihad—thirty years of killing infidels and evading their spies and their drones—al-Souri was not so foolish. Surely, he would have seen it.

But he knew it didn't matter whether Hamed was a traitor or not. What mattered was that Ibn Jihad thought he was a traitor. And that put al-Souri in danger.

In the hallway, Ibn Jihad ordered his men to move al-Souri to the building across the compound where his security team was being held, and to prepare to leave the villa.

He could have left immediately with a few men and one old SUV parked across the compound. But Karch and most of the men were still out looking for the traitor, and they had most of the vehicles. He decided it was too dangerous to travel without more protection. He would wait for them to return.

In Nebraska, the tasking order had been on the drone operator's screen for several minutes. She had already dragged the coordinates of the villa in Kibley Baad into the aircraft's navigation vector window, and watched as it banked and accelerated toward the target. This would be a quick one. At five-hundred miles an hour, the drone only needed eighteen minutes to get within weapons range.

The operator ran a systems check. All lights were green. The computer automatically communicated that fact up the chain of command. She took a sip of her coffee and ripped open the wrapper of an energy bar. Just another day at the office.

The village streets were empty. The shooting and shouting had awakened the whole town, but the people knew enough to stay indoors.

When Karch got to the garage, he found three of his men standing over the bodies of Zahir and the others, doing nothing. He saw the motorcycle track.

"Idiots!" he shouted. "Return to your vehicles. Follow him!" The men turned and ran for their SUVs, with Karch behind them.

The search teams sped through the village and checked the surrounding roads, but Faraz had made the most of his brief head start. One by one, they gave up, and returned to the villa empty-handed. Karch was in the last vehicle to arrive.

Ibn Jihad came out of the house. He wanted to send forces from across the region to search for Faraz, but he dared not use a phone.

"Karch! You take two vehicles and five men to search for the traitor. We will send more from the base.

Leave six men here to guard al-Souri and his men. The rest will come with me."

"Yes, *sayyid*," Karch said, "We will be ready to go as soon as the vehicles are fueled." He shouted orders at his men to get the jerricans of gasoline stored behind the house, and to prepare to go out again and search a wider area.

Bridget was in her office when the call came through. Hadley was on from Kabul. Jay Pruitt was at the White House. And a one-star general joined them from the Nebraska control center. They had all seen a rough transcript of Bridget's conversation with Faraz, generated by voice-recognition software.

"Secretary Jacobs will be with us shortly," said the operator.

A beep announced someone had joined the call. "This is Harmon. The secretary is with the president. Please stand by."

They waited in silence.

Three minutes later, another beep. "This is Secretary Jacobs. Is everyone on?"

"Yes, sir," Harmon said.

"Good. I spoke to the president. This is not what we expected. Sandblast is blown and cannot take out al-Souri. We have to hit both or neither. Correct?"

"Yes, sir," Bridget said.

"All right." Jacobs paused. "The president agrees this is a unique opportunity. We can't give them another pass. Do I have the duty commander at the control center?"

"Yes, sir. This is General Campbell."

"Very well. This mission is a Go. I repeat, we have a Go from the National Command Authority to proceed with this strike. You will receive coded electronic confirmation shortly. General, are you hearing me?"

"Loud and clear, sir. Mission is on course and will be completed in approximately six minutes, pending electronic confirmation."

"Thank you, General. We are aware that this target is in a civilian area. You are to take all precautions to avoid collateral damage. But success in this mission is vital."

"Yes, sir. We have already plotted the optimal weapon trajectory to minimize civilian casualties."

"Good. I think in this case we'll stay on the line and wait until you have the electronic orders. Bridget, what's the status of Sandblast?"

"He's wounded, sir. He sounded, well, scared, to be honest. He was being pursued. But from what I could gather, his injury is not life-threatening."

"Good. Have you put an evac plan in motion?"

"Not yet, sir. He needs to get to a safe place and call again. But we're ready to move as soon as he does."

"Keep me posted. Interesting line he had—'A strategic blow on all our enemies.' That's a quote we'll remember. But nothing behind it."

"No, sir," Bridget said. "Unfortunately, he got shut out when he tried to get details. They're clearly holding this one very close."

"And now we've lost our best-positioned inside man. Damn! We need to crack this thing."

"Yes, sir. Already working on it. Could be we'll derail it with this strike."

"Mr. Secretary?" It was General Campbell in Nebraska. "We have received coded electronic confirmation for the mission, sir, and we have acknowledged. We estimate completion in approximately four minutes."

"Thank you, General. Get me the After-Action Report immediately."

"Yes, sir."

"Well, thank you everyone. This is a big night for us, a major turning point. Lots of work ahead. We'll convene in my office at 0700. General Hadley, we'll get you on a secure line. Thank you all again. Good night." He hung up, and the operator ended the call.

Suddenly, Bridget was alone again—no one to talk to or share the moment with. She headed for the Field Operations Center.

In the compound, Karch's men were refueling the SUVs from the large containers. It was a slow process. Another team loaded bags into the vehicles. Karch designated the men to stay behind to guard al-Souri and his security detail, and he chose the five who would go with him in the first two vehicles that were ready. That left ten men to accompany the commander.

Karch hugged Ibn Jihad and kissed him on both cheeks. "You will be safe with these men. I will see you soon at the camp."

"Be sure you bring that traitor with you," Ibn Jihad said. "Alive or dead." He went back into the house to wait for the other SUVs to be made ready.

Karch boarded the lead vehicle, and his team sped through the village, past the bodies of Zahir and the other two fighters that still lay in front of the garage.

There were no men to spare to tend to them. The people of the village would take care of it in the morning.

In the Operations Center, Bridget saw the compound in grainy infrared on a live satellite image. She could see that there were vehicles and people in the courtyard, but she couldn't make out any details.

She saw two vehicles leave. Damn! "What was that?" she asked the operations team.

"Two vehicles have left the compound, ma'am. Do you want to request an abort?"

"Negative. Dammit!"

A map on another screen showed the surrounding area, with the villa in the middle marked by a red dot. To the south, a blue dot representing the Predator flashed as it circled to attack from the east, so its missile would be pointed away from the village.

"Firing point in thirty seconds," said one of the Ops Center officers. "All systems are green. Operation is a Go. Operator will fire at maximum range."

Bridget watched the body heat signatures in the compound, some moving back and forth to an area behind the building, others standing near the vehicles. She saw someone come out of the main house and move toward the convoy. This time, it was all clinical; none of the angst of her last visit to this room.

A voice came over a loudspeaker. It was the drone operator in Nebraska. "The weapon is armed," she announced. "Systems on automatic."

On the map, Bridget saw the drone turn left to point toward the villa.

"Missile launch in 10 . . . 9 . . . 8 . . . ."

·Bridget felt the skin of her arms and legs tingling. She held her breath.

"3 . . . 2 . . . 1 . . . weapon release confirmed. Time to target fifteen seconds."

Bridget fixed her eyes on the satellite image. The people appeared to be gathering around the vehicles, perhaps preparing to leave. She squeezed the arms of her chair, willing the supersonic missile to go faster.

"Weapon track is good. Stand by for impact," said the voice on the speaker.

Ibn Jihad bid farewell to the men who would stay behind, and left them inside the house. As he came out and approached his vehicle, his guards stood at attention. He put one foot on the side rail and prepared to lift himself in. He heard a high-pitched whine in the sky.

The global terrorism mastermind looked up. He knew what was about to happen.

Through the drone's nose camera, Bridget and the others in the Ops Center saw the missile hit right in front of the main house, incinerating Ibn Jihad and all the other men in the courtyard. As the initial flash faded, they could see that the explosion had destroyed much of the house and part of the compound wall. Earth, debris, and parts of vehicles had been thrown into the air and were now strewn across the compound. What was left of the house was on fire. They saw some survivors run out through the flames.

But because the angle of attack was designed to limit collateral damage, the building across the courtyard, where al-Souri and his men were being held, was only partly destroyed.

Jolted by the explosion but still in bed in a locked room, al-Souri heard some of his men calling for him. He raised his voice as much as he could. "I am here. Come and get me."

Two men broke down the door to his room. *"Qomandan,"* one said, "part of the wall is down. We are free, now."

"Get the others, quickly."

They went out to follow his order.

It was difficult, but al-Souri managed to sit up. He heard the whine of the drone's second missile and looked out the window. It hit with a blinding flash, only ten feet from the first one, killing the men who had run out of the house to help their comrades.

The blast knocked al-Souri to the floor. The window shattered, and broken glass and other debris rained down on him.

As soon as he could, he called out again, "I am alive! Who is with me?" There was no response. Then he heard footsteps in the hall.

The two men appeared again in the doorway, along with two others.

"Qomandan, are you all right?" asked the senior man, a fighter named Gul. He helped al-Souri back onto the bed.

"Yes. Find us a vehicle. We must leave at once."

"Yes, *Qomandan.*" Gul and another man ran to comply.

A few minutes later they pulled in front of the barracks in an old Land Cruiser they had found on the far side of the compound. All four men carried al-Souri to the vehicle.

Ibn Jihad's few remaining men were distracted, trying to help the wounded and searching frantically for their boss or his body. Al-Souri's vehicle sped past them unchallenged and exited the compound through the gap in the outer wall.

They didn't go far before al-Souri shouted, "Wait! Return to the compound."

"But *Qomandan* . . ." said Gul.

Al-Souri cut him off. "Now! Do it!"

Gul turned the SUV around and drove back.

"Get out! Get out!" al-Souri ordered, and he made them help him get out, too. "Weapons! Get the weapons!" he said.

The men collected four undamaged AKs from the edge of the bomb crater. Al-Souri demanded one, taking it with his right hand and putting his left on the vehicle for support. He wedged the rifle butt into his hip.

Ibn Jihad's men came out of the rubble to see what was going on. Al-Souri opened fire on them. "Fire, you idiots!" he shouted, and his men did. They mowed down all of the survivors. Al-Souri personally dispatched the wounded.

"Check the compound." he ordered. "No one lives to tell what happened here." Al-Souri leaned on the SUV until the men came back.

"They are all dead, *Qomandan*," Gul reported.

"All right, now we go," al-Souri said, his voice weak from the exertion.

They drove southwest, toward their base. Al-Souri was in pain, but his mind was clear. Everyone who knew Ibn Jihad had turned against him was dead, he thought, except his own loyal men . . . and Hamed. Oh, Hamed. What have you done?

But al-Souri was wrong. He didn't know Karch and his search party had left before the attack.

Bridget watched al-Souri's departure and return with some confusion. She saw the flashes of gunfire, but she didn't know why it happened or who was who.

"Can we hit the vehicle?" she asked the operations officer.

"Negative, ma'am. Drone is out of missiles and we have no authorization. But we can follow it for a while."

Bridget had known he would say that. She also knew they'd likely lose the SUV on the dark mountain roads.

Back in her office, Bridget went over the video of the attack and the latest satellite photos of the compound. She also listened to her conversation with Faraz several times, trying to read between the lines. How was he, really? Wounded and on the run, that's how he was. Jesus! Please let him call in the evac code.

It was late, now, and quiet in the office. She jumped when the phone rang. It was Hadley from Kabul.

"How's it look?" he asked.

"A bit unclear. Seems to be a clean hit. No collateral damage. Anyone in the courtyard has got to be dead, but we don't know who they were yet. Two vehicles left before the first strike. Don't know who they were, either. Then there was that shooting. Some survivors in a side building apparently fled, then came back to finish the job for us, then left again. Very strange."

"Could be the IJ/al-Souri rift was worse than we thought."

"Maybe. As usual, there's a lot we don't know."

"We're working our sources out here, and monitoring Internet and comms traffic."

"So are we. If IJ and al-Souri are dead, they won't be able to keep it secret for long."

"You know, Bridget, you could actually go home now."

"Yes, but I think I'll stay here tonight to monitor the comms traffic and in case Sandblast calls again."

"Well, up to you. Try to get some sleep at some point."

"Roger that, sir."

"Good night, Bridget. And good job."

"Thank you, General. But it won't be a good job until Sandblast is home safe."

"Roger that, too." Hadley hung up, and Bridget went back to her work. She was pretty sure she wouldn't be able to get any sleep.

CHAPTER 30

After an hour riding the country roads, Faraz's arm was throbbing and he was getting weak from loss of blood. He knew he wouldn't be able to evade the Taliban for long in this part of Afghanistan. He needed help.

It was dawn, now, and the old motorcycle was struggling as the foothills got steeper. Faraz was concerned it might overheat, so he stopped behind some bushes over the crest of a hill and turned it off. He opened the fuel cap and gave the motorcycle another shake. There was hardly any gasoline left.

Faraz surveyed his surroundings—scrubland and woods. But in the distance, on the rise of the next hill, he saw some cultivated fields and a farmhouse. It was his only option. He coasted down the hill, then restarted the motorcycle and gunned the engine for one last climb.

The bike sputtered and died on the last stretch of road leading up toward the house. He walked it into the gully by the roadside, laid it down, and covered it with tall grass.

As he climbed up out of the ditch with the rifle over his shoulder, he startled a teenaged girl walking down the hill wearing a long skirt and tunic that looked like a school uniform.

At the sight of the man, she tightened her hijab across her face. "Good morning, *sayyid*, may peace be upon you."

"And upon you. Good morning, miss. I am sorry to scare you."

She was petite and had a soft voice. All he could see were her dark eyes, which widened as she took in the sight of him. "You are a fighter," she said. Then she gasped, noticing his bloody arm. "And you are wounded! What happened to you?"

"It is all right," Faraz said.

"No, you must come to the house. My mother will tend to your wound."

"You are very kind, but . . ."

"No 'but.' Please, come." She was more assertive than her age and appearance suggested. She turned and started up the hill, stopping after a few steps to look back and motion for Faraz to follow.

As Faraz and the girl turned onto the gravel driveway toward the farmhouse, she called out for her mother. "*Mohr! Mohr!* A man needs help. Come quickly!"

First out the door were two barefoot young children, a boy and a girl, eager for a diversion. But they stopped, shrieked, and retreated back into the house when they saw Faraz, bloodied and carrying his gun.

"What? What is it, Zareena?" her mother called from inside the house. Faraz had to smile. "Zareena" meant "Golden."

"*Mohr,* I met this man on the road. He is injured. We must help him!"

Her mother reached the doorway, lifting her hijab across her face after the warning that there was a man outside. Seeing Faraz, she took a step back.

"*Salaam alaikum, sayyida.* I am sorry to intrude." Faraz put his right hand over his heart and bowed his head in greeting. "If it is too much trouble, I can go." He knew the unwritten code of Afghan hospitality would force her to let him stay.

"No, no," she said, recovering. "*Alaikum salaam.* Please come in. We must help you. Wait here, in the living room. Please, sit." She indicated a wooden chair. "Zareena, come with me."

In the kitchen, her mother admonished Zareena in a whisper. "Why did you bring him here? He is a fighter."

"I know what he is. I had no choice. He is injured. He left his motorcycle by the road. He was coming here anyway."

"All right. All right," the mother said. "Give the man some water and then go get your father. He is in the northern field."

Zareena poured a glass of water and took it to Faraz. Then she went out the back door, gathered her dress up over her ankles, and ran as fast as she could toward her father.

The living room was spare but clean. There was a settee with a thick, carved dark wood frame and home-made upholstery, likely reserved for guests, and a matching chair, which was certainly the father's usual spot. The rest of the furniture was simple and handmade. There was one nice, but ancient, Afghan carpet, probably a wedding gift, and there were some rustic mats covering other parts of the floor. A few bowls and vases sat on white doilies on some of the tables, and there were two small embroidered panels on the walls depicting plants and flowers. A wood-burning stove in one corner would have provided some warmth in winter. A table ran along the wall to the left of the front door.

The farmer's wife came back into the room with a bowl of water, some clean rags, and a knife. The children came in behind her and cowered in a corner, keeping their eyes on the fascinating visitor. The woman was plump and her clothes were dirty. She had tightened her hijab to be sure her hair and neck were covered and readjusted the piece that hid her nose and mouth. To Faraz, her eyes looked tired and a little scared. She put a rag over the upholstered chair and invited him to move to it.

He rested his gun on the carpet and leaned it against the wall where he could reach it easily. He sat in the chair, suddenly grateful for the break and the treatment.

The woman cut off his bloody sleeve and washed the wound. The bullet had gone right through. "Oh Allah, you have been shot!" she said. "A fight with the infidels?"

"Yes, *sayyida*." He was pleased she had assumed the lie he was going to tell.

"And where are your brothers?"

"We were separated. They must be back at our camp by now."

If the woman doubted his story, she did not let on.

Faraz winced several times as she finished her work and dressed the wound with some clean cloths. "Is it painful?"

"A bit, yes," Faraz said.

"We have no drugs to give you, but I will send Zareena to fetch the doctor from the village."

"Oh, no. Please don't do that," Faraz said, looking straight at her.

She seemed to understand that she should not argue with him. "All right. My husband will be here soon. You can discuss it with him."

"Thank you."

As the woman gathered her rags and bowl, Faraz heard Zareena and her father come through the back door. After a moment, the farmer appeared in the living room doorway with Zareena behind him. He was skinny and suntanned. His sweaty turban was loose and his clothes were muddy. His beard was untrimmed. He held an AK-47 pointed at the floor.

The man's eyes took in Faraz, then moved to his gun against the wall, then back. "*Salaam alaikum*. You are welcome here, my friend," he said, as he had to.

"*Alaikum salaam, sayyid*. And thank you. Your family has been very kind."

"We shall send for the doctor."

"No," said his wife. "Our guest has asked us not to."

The farmer furrowed his brow. "Leave us," he said, and she did, taking the children and Zareena with her.

The man sat on the wooden chair opposite Faraz with his gun across his knees in a nonthreatening posture. "Now, tell me please, my brother, how did you come to be here?"

Faraz repeated the story he had told the man's wife. The farmer stroked his beard. "A battle with the infidels, near here?"

"Yes, *sayyid* . . . not far." Faraz could tell the man was not buying the story. He leaned toward his gun, but it seemed far away.

Responding to Faraz's movement, the man rested his right hand on his rifle. "We have not had infidels in this area before, only their bombs."

Faraz did not respond.

"You are wounded, but you do not want a doctor. You tell a story that I find . . . well . . . unusual." The man paused and they stared at each other. "I think you have problems even greater than the infidels."

"*Sayyid* . . ." Faraz said, shifting even closer to his rifle.

"Do not move!" the man said, taking his AK in his hands and pointing it at Faraz. Then he shouted, "Zareena!"

The girl came to the kitchen door.

"Take his rifle and put it next to me."

"Fahr!" she protested.

"Do it!" he yelled.

Zareena complied, keeping her eyes glued to Faraz.

"Now, go," her father ordered. She returned to the kitchen. The farmer relaxed a little, but kept the rifle pointed toward Faraz. "Now, my friend, I will ask you again. How did you come to be here?"

Faraz tried a new approach. "My brother, I urge you not to hurt me. My comrades will be looking for me. Be careful. You have three children to think about."

"I have four children. Now answer my question."

"Four? Where is the fourth?"

"My eldest son. Your . . ." He searched for the right words. "Your heroic brothers took him last year." It was the right formulation of respect, but Faraz could hear that the words were heavy with disdain.

"And you have not heard from him since then?"

The man nodded, and his body sagged a bit. But his hands were steady on the rifle.

Faraz understood this could be his way out or maybe not. The farmer could be lying. This could be a test.

But it didn't matter. The Taliban would be searching for him, and the farmer would have to alert them that he was there. Otherwise, he would be considered an accomplice. Faraz looked at the man's face, his body language. He was going to have to take a chance.

"I, too, have had problems with my brothers," he said.

"I thought so." The farmer leaned back in his chair. He gestured with the rifle toward Faraz's arm. "And this wound? It is from your . . . brothers?"

"Yes, *sayyid*. I am in grave danger. And you are in danger as long as I am here. I must go now. Perhaps you have some fuel for my motorcycle."

"I would do better to give you to your brothers," the farmer said.

Faraz looked at the man, trying to read what was behind his eyes. "But I do not think you will, *sayyid*. Am I right?"

The farmer didn't answer.

"Your anger is deep, my friend. You want to protect your family, but you do not want to sacrifice another young man to the Taliban."

"They have brought nothing but fear and death to

this land," the farmer said. But he kept his gun pointed at Faraz.

"I am your guest, *sayyid*. I will do whatever you say. But, please help me. Give me fuel and send me away. Your family will be safe when I am gone."

Faraz could see that the farmer was considering his request, perhaps trying to come up with a better option. But his thoughts were interrupted by the sound of vehicles turning into the driveway. They both looked out the window to see two SUVs coming toward the house. Faraz could see through the dirt-spattered windshield. It was Karch.

"Quickly!" the farmer said. "To the back of the house! Zareena! Hide him. You know where." The man took Faraz by his good arm and pulled him up. Zareena appeared in the doorway and quickly turned to lead him out of the house. Faraz grabbed his rifle and the rag from his chair, and followed her through the kitchen and the back door.

There was a shed against the back of the house. Zareena opened it and pulled out some tools. Then she crouched down and lifted the wooden floor to reveal a small crawl space in the earth below.

"Get in, quickly!" she said. "This is where we hid my brother. It did not work for him. Perhaps you will be more fortunate."

Faraz stepped into the hole with his rifle and lay down on his good side, pulling his knees up toward his chest to fit. Zareena closed the floorboards and shut the door. The tools were still outside, but she had no time to correct the mistake.

* * *

The farmer leaned his rifle against the wall, out of sight of the front door, and greeted Karch. *"Salaam alaikum, sayyid."*

"Alaikum salaam."

The conversation was polite, at first. Then Karch said, "We must search the property."

"My brother, that is not . . ." Karch pushed the farmer into the house. He staggered back.

Karch came in, saw the rifle and took it. "My brother," he said in an admonishing tone. "You greet us with your weapon at hand."

"We are alone, far from the village, *sayyid*. You can understand . . ."

One of the children started to cry.

Karch moved close to the farmer. "Tell your family to come out here. Then we will search your house and your farm. If you are telling the truth, you will have no problems. But if you are lying, it will not go well for you."

"We are not lying, *sayyid*. We are simple people. We love Allah and his jihad. My son is a fighter. Please, *sayyid*, search as you like."

The man's wife emerged from the kitchen, the small children clinging to her skirt. Zareena was behind them. Karch's men came in through the front door. The Taliban men were large, bearded, fearsome—all clearly tired and angry and all armed with AKs, pistols, and knives.

The farmer did not like the way they were looking at Zareena. He put her behind him.

"Search!" Karch ordered, and he pushed the family to one corner of the room.

* * *

From his hiding place, Faraz could hear everything. Karch, of all people. He was the most volatile. Damn! Faraz wanted to surrender himself to save the family. But he knew that if he did, Karch would kill them all anyway. He wanted to come out shooting. But he knew his chances were slim against Karch and his hand-picked team. There was nothing he could do but wait and hope and pray.

He heard two men stomp down the hall to the bedrooms while the others moved furniture and opened cabinets in the living room, looking for anything to incriminate the family. Then, he heard one of the men speak.

"Commander Karch, look here."

The farmer's fear turned to panic as Karch crossed the living room and the fighter showed him a brown spot on the floor, next to the chair where Faraz had sat. Karch crouched down and touched it. It was sticky. He rubbed his thumb and finger together and smelled them. He looked at the farmer. "Are you injured, my friend?"

"No, *sayyid*."

"Is someone in your family injured?" Karch asked, his voice rising.

The farmer did not answer. Karch crossed the room and slapped the man hard across the face. "Traitor!" he boomed. His men raised their weapons.

"No!" shouted the farmer's wife. But one look from Karch, and she cowered in the corner with her children.

"Why do I find blood on your floor?"

"Maybe from the farm . . ."

Karch hit him again. "Where is the traitor, Hamed?" he demanded.

"I do not know, *sayyid*. I swear by Allah!"

Karch grabbed him by the throat and squeezed. "Do not lie in the name of Allah!" he shouted, inches from the man's face. "Where is he?"

The farmer did not answer. His look turned from panic to heartache. He knew all was lost.

Karch looked around. His gaze settled on Zareena. He released the farmer's neck, shoved him to the floor, and grabbed the girl by the arm. He ripped the hijab off her face and turned her so she was facing her parents and the children. Zareena's eyes were wide with fear, and she was shaking. Karch took the knife from his belt and pointed it at her.

"Look at your daughter's face for the last time, traitor, or tell me what I need to know!" He put the knife against her throat. Her brother and sister were crying.

The farmer was still gasping for air from the choking. He sat awkwardly on the floor, his body showing his defeat. He knew they would all die, now. He had done his best for his family, and now it was over, whether he gave up Faraz or not.

His wife screamed and pushed the children's faces to the floor. She covered them with her skirt so they could not see. Her husband looked at Karch in surrender and despair.

"Please, *sayyid*, for the sake of my son, the fighter," he pleaded. He turned his gaze toward Zareena. She might have been able to save herself by telling them about Faraz, but she didn't. Her father had never loved her more or been more proud. He tried to say all that with his eyes.

Karch ran out of patience. "Aach!" he said in disgust, and he slit her throat with one deep slash of the knife.

Zareena collapsed to her knees. She grabbed her neck with her left hand and reached toward her mother with her right, then she crumpled to the floor. Her mother shrieked, "Zareena!" and fell on her sobbing. The children looked up and burst into tears again. The farmer said the Shahada.

"Tell me now or you all die!" Karch shouted.

"You will kill us all anyway!" the farmer screamed back. "Animal! There is no place in paradise for the likes of you!"

Karch raised his AK-47 and fired one bullet into the farmer's forehead.

"No!" screamed his wife.

"Whore!" said Karch, and he turned his weapon on the woman and her children.

In the dark hole, Faraz flinched at each scream and shot. He felt as if his blood had gone cold. It all happened so quickly. There was nothing he could have done, but that didn't ease his guilt. And now it was over. The last cohoon of the gunfire faded, and the house was silent.

"Search the farm," he heard Karch order.

Faraz heard the five men come through the back door and past the shed as they fanned out to search the fields and gullies. Then he heard Karch's heavy footsteps come through the kitchen and down the back steps.

He moved left first, away from the shed. Faraz heard the sound of his bayonet slashing at the bushes along the back of the house.

Then he heard Karch's footsteps come back toward him and stop in front of the shed, by the tools Zareena had left outside.

As Karch opened the shed's door, Faraz pushed the floorboards up and started shooting. He hit Karch in the legs and he fell hard, coming even with Faraz. Faraz shot him in the face at point-blank range.

The noise drew Karch's men back toward the house. Faraz used the hole and Karch's body for cover, and fired his AK-47 on automatic. He killed the first two men quickly, but the others were smart enough to stop and hit the ground.

Faraz raised his voice. "Your commander is wounded," he lied. "Leave now and I will spare his life." The men did not respond. "I give you five seconds!"

One of the men sprang up and ran toward Faraz, firing wildly. Faraz cut him down with a short burst, then reached over and took a fresh magazine of bullets from Karch's rifle.

"Who will be the next martyr?" he shouted, reloading. "Or you can turn and run away. Save yourselves to die for Allah another day!"

The two men rose together and ran toward Faraz firing more accurately than their comrade had. One bullet hit him in the right shoulder and another grazed his left side. He would have been killed if not for Karch's body and the ground absorbing most of the rounds. He returned fire, and with the attackers in a more exposed posture than he was, he was able to shoot them down.

When the gunfire stopped, Faraz was breathing hard. He was bleeding from his new wounds, and his old one had soaked through the homemade bandage the farmer's wife had put on. He sat back in the hole to recover, his gun ready in case there were any more of Karch's men.

He stared at the body of Ibn Jihad's security chief, overweight and bloody, his long beard sagging to the side and his one remaining eye wide open. Faraz spat at him.

Then he stood up, stepped over Karch, checked to be sure the other men were dead, and turned for the back door of the house.

In the kitchen, he washed his wounds and tied them with fresh rags. As he started to go into the living room he hesitated, knowing what he would find.

Still, when he went through the doorway the carnage stopped him short.

The farmer sat on the floor, lying back against the wall. A single gunshot wound on his forehead was clean and neat, but the exit wound behind had splattered blood and gray matter on the wall. His chest was riddled with the additional rounds Karch had unleashed. The man's wife was facing away from Faraz, lying sideways in a final effort to protect her children. She had been shot numerous times in the back. Her babies lay dead next to her.

Then there was Zareena. She lay twisted, half on her stomach, half turned to the side toward her mother. Her blood soaked the carpet. Her eyes were open and looked horribly, hopelessly sad. Her hijab hung down onto the floor, and Faraz saw her face for the first time. She appeared younger than he had thought, with beautiful, perfect olive skin, marred only by the slit from Karch's knife.

Faraz had seen much death in the past several months, much more in the last few hours. But seeing Zareena made his breathing flutter. His heart pounded as if it might explode out of his chest. Everything that had happened to him flooded through his mind.

It seemed insignificant now, compared to this.

Faraz swallowed hard and knelt down. He wanted to comfort the girl, to thank her, to do something. He had never felt so woefully inadequate in all his life. He reached down and picked up the loose side of her hijab, laid it across her face, and put the string behind her ear. Now, she was perfect again. He could see only her dark eyes, not the sweet face she hid from the world or the awful gash across her neck.

He closed her eyes, and recited the words that had been said at Johnny's funeral.

"Inna lillahi wa inna ilayhi raji'un." We surely belong to Allah, and to Him we shall return.

Faraz wanted to stay longer, but he knew he should go. Although the farmhouse was remote, someone might have heard the gunfire, and there could be more of Karch's men in the area. He stood and surveyed the scene one last time.

Then he turned and went to the front door. Raising his weapon, he went out cautiously, making sure there were no more Taliban men around. He went to the SUV closest to the road and got in. The key was in the ignition and he started it. It had half a tank of gas. Thank you, Allah, for that at least.

Faraz put the vehicle in gear and made a U-turn through the farmhouse's front yard. He turned left onto the road and continued his journey into the mountains.

CHAPTER 31

The 0700 meeting was in Jacobs's conference room, and the atmosphere was oddly festive. When Bridget came into the room, officials from other Pentagon offices went over to offer congratulations. Mary Larson from CIA even gave grudging kudos, and the chairman of the joint chiefs shook her hand. Bridget saw that Hadley was there, in the form of a green light flashing on a speakerphone in the middle of the conference table.

In the hours since the attack, the news had all been good. Terrorist communication channels lit up with chatter that Ibn Jihad was dead. Gallagher in Kabul passed on a report from one of his contacts in the area, who said he'd never seen such chaos among local officials as they rushed to the scene and wailed for the Taliban's propaganda cameras.

Within the last half hour, the Taliban's website had been draped in black, with one word written across the center in large type: MARTYR. An official announcement was expected at any moment. CNN was already calling it an "American Victory in the War on Terrorism."

The fact that they couldn't account for al-Souri was a relatively minor irritation. And the continuing concern about an impending MTO was smothered under the elation that for once the "good guys" were on the offensive.

Even Tim Harmon was smiling as he came in from the secretary's office and gave Bridget an awkward hug. He moved on to accept undeserved congratulations from others in the room. After a couple of minutes, he said, "Everyone, please find your seats."

As folks were settling into their places, Jacobs came in and stood at the head of the table. The crowd quieted. "I just got off the phone with the president," he said. "He wanted me to congratulate all of you on striking a major blow for our nation. Special thanks to Ms. Davenport, and her team at DIA." Everyone applauded.

Bridget smiled, and remembered she had nearly been fired less than a week ago.

Jacobs continued, "Bridget, any update on Sandblast?"

"No contact since last night, sir. We have units standing by for evac."

"Good. He did a helluva job." He paused, then picked up his coffee mug with his left hand. "Folks, it's a bit early for making toasts, but please join me." Everyone stood, and those who had coffee or water raised their drinks. "Sandblast," the secretary said.

"Sandblast," everyone replied.

"And Tommy," Bridget said to herself.

When the meeting ended, Jacobs called Bridget into his office.

"You did well," he said from behind his desk, with Harmon standing to the side. "You stepped out of line a couple of times. But I admire that you stuck by your man. It brought us here, and you get a big chunk of the credit."

"Thank you, sir. I appreciate your saying that. But it's not about . . ."

"I know. It's not about the credit. But, still . . ."

"Yes, sir."

Jacobs looked at Harmon, then back at Bridget. "We want more of this."

"Sir?"

"We want more ops like Sandblast, and we want you to run them. We'll continue doing the short-term stuff—military, covert, all of it. But the president has authorized me to set you up with a new unit to develop and run high-priority, long-term operations with big potential payoffs."

"Sir, Sandblast was high-reward, but also high-risk. We can't count on a string of successes like this."

"We know. But we're going to give it a shot. You know we're trying to think outside the box, find new tactics. Well, this is one." He glanced at Harmon again. "Tim, here, doesn't like it, but we're going to call it Task Force Epsilon."

"Epsilon?"

"I guess you don't know I studied Greek in college, became a bit of a Greece nerd for a while."

Bridget saw Harmon make big, mocking nods of his head. And he was smirking, which was unusual.

Jacobs continued. "Epsilon is the first letter of both words in the Greek phrase, *Epíthesi Ekdíkisis*."

Bridget gave him a quizzical look.

"It means Revenge Attack," he said.

* * *

Mohammed Faisal "al-Souri" Ibrahim woke up in early evening in bed at his base. The camp doctor was with him. Al-Souri struggled to sit up.

"Easy, *Qomandan*," the doctor said, but al-Souri insisted and made it into a sitting position.

"How long did I sleep?"

"Only a few hours," the doctor replied. "Your wounds are serious, but of course Dr. Zia did well treating them. You will recover, but you should rest now."

"Nonsense! There is much to do. Send Gul to me."

"Yes, *sayyid*. Please, drink some water." The doctor gave him a glass and went out to follow his orders.

A few minutes later, Gul came into the clinic. "How are you, *Qomandan*?"

"Praise Allah. But do not worry about me. We have work to do. There will be a meeting of commanders to choose a new leader. We must find out when and where the meeting will be."

"Yes, *Qomandan*. We have already received word. The meeting will be here, out of consideration for your injuries. Our brothers will arrive tonight."

Al-Souri leaned back against his pillow, relieved. His wounds made him weaker than he wanted to admit, and he was pleased to avoid another long car ride. "Very well. Make the preparations. Be sure I am awake by the time the last of the brothers arrives."

"Yes, *Qomandan*," Gul said and left the room.

Al-Souri stared at the ceiling and his lips moved silently, "Allah, your power is far beyond what mere men can understand. You brought Hamed to me. Was he a spy? Was he a test? No matter. What is done is done.

And You have shown me what I must do now. *Allah hu akhbar*." God is great. He closed his eyes and fell back to sleep.

The new head of Task Force Epsilon got up from her seat on the Metro as the train pulled into Medical Center station in Bethesda, Maryland, just outside DC. At last, her anticipation would be rewarded and her anxiety would come to an end. Bridget was hoping for another reunion like the one in Kabul, without the five-minute time limit. But Will had been through a lot. And now that he was back for the long term, she wasn't sure what their relationship would be. It was Get Serious Time. Or not.

She had shared her concerns with Jen, who warned her, "Anticipation is always more intoxicating than reality. Best to keep expectations in check." Thanks again, Jen.

The tone sounded and the train's doors slid open. Bridget joined the crowd passing through the turnstiles and moving toward the long escalator up to street level. When she emerged into the daylight, the fifteen-story central tower of the Naval Hospital loomed in front of her. She crossed Wisconsin Avenue and headed for the main desk.

A clerk gave her a visitor's pass and directed her to the proper wing and floor. Bridget passed the gift shop and realized she should have brought something. She knew Will wouldn't want any silly knickknack or flowers or balloons. She'd promise him an extra-large bottle of bourbon as soon as the docs would allow it.

A few minutes later, she emerged from the elevator

into the off-putting hospital smell. Walking along the hallways and trying to follow the room numbers, she could feel her heartbeat quicken.

Then suddenly, she was standing outside his door. She stopped to compose herself. The shade was drawn inside the window between the room and the hallway, and she could see her reflection. Bridget ran a hand through her hair and straightened her jacket. She replaced her worried look with a smile.

All right, you're as ready for this as you'll ever be.

She went over what she had come up with to say, knocked on the open door, and went in. "So, the navy doesn't believe in body armor, eh?" She stopped to look at him, sitting up in bed with his bandaged leg exposed. Her imagining had been right. He was wearing a frumpy hospital gown.

"Hell no!" he said with that broad grin. "Body armor's for army wimps!"

She moved to the side of the bed, dropped her purse to the floor, took his hand, and leaned in for a kiss. It was a long one, and when their lips finally parted she asked, "Will it hurt if I hug you?"

"Don't care if it does," he said, pulling her in. They held each other for a long time, then kissed again, more deeply. Finally, she stood up to get a good look at him, still holding his hand.

"Will, it's so good to see you," she said. What she didn't say was that she was overjoyed beyond words and beyond all expectation. Like that morning he'd left, she could hardly think of anything to say. She wished she had planned her second line as well as she'd planned her first. She went with, "Sounds lame, but I'm really glad you're okay."

"Thanks. It's great to see you, too. And I'm the one who's lame." He pointed at his leg.

"What do the docs say?"

"Well, they say I'll walk. But they won't make any promises beyond that. Looks like I'll be riding a desk for a while."

"I know it's not what you want, but it's not all bad."

"Only a bureaucrat would say that!"

Bridget smiled. "Who knows? Our desks might even be on the same continent."

"Now wouldn't that be something?"

They smiled at each other.

"Sorry, I didn't bring you anything. I don't think they allow booze in here, but there will be a big bottle with your name on it at my place when you get out."

"Sounds good." He frowned. "But I was hoping for a teddy bear."

They laughed.

"What's the latest on your man Sandblast?" Will asked.

"You heard about the strike on IJ last night?"

"Yeah. We got TV in here and everything."

"Well," she lowered her voice. "That was his info. He was already on the run. We haven't heard from him since."

"He seemed to have his shit together. If there's a way out, I'm guessing he'll find it."

"I hope so. We're standing by for evac. All he has to do is call in the code."

"He promised to kill al-Souri for me. Did he do that?"

"No, it seems not, but we can't be sure yet. That may have to be a project for another time."

"Count me in."

"Sure. You can hit him with your desk."

"Aw, you know how to hurt a guy!"

They were about to embrace again, but a nurse came in to check Will's blood pressure. They waited while she did her work. "Commander, we'll be taking you down for another X-ray in a minute," she said.

"Okay, thanks," Will said, as the nurse left the room. "Sorry," he said, with a little shrug.

"That's okay. I need to get back anyway. I'll come see you tomorrow."

"Yeah, do that . . ." he said taking her hand again. He chuckled. "I almost said 'kiddo.' I don't know what to call you anymore."

Bridget smiled. "Call me Bridget. Stupid navy!" They kissed again and didn't care that the orderly caught them when he came in to get Will.

Bridget watched as he was wheeled down the hall, and surprised herself by choking up. She put her right hand over her face to hide it. When the double doors into X-ray swung shut behind Will's gurney, she stared at them for several seconds before collecting her bag and heading for the elevator. As she walked, her shaking lips relaxed and curled into a smile.

It was well after midnight when Gul helped al-Souri walk from his room to the outdoor mess hall, set up for the meeting of Taliban commanders. He insisted on walking the last bit, in view of the others, with only a walking stick. The men applauded, cheered, and stomped their feet when he reached the front. The senior commanders were on benches, their security teams standing around the outside, along with al-Souri's remaining force. The scene was lit by gas lanterns set on dim.

One of al-Souri's allies in the Taliban's militant faction rose to speak. "My brothers. It is a sad day for all of us. Our leader, the martyr Ibn Jihad, may peace be upon him, is with Allah. But we need to move quickly to avenge his murder. He would want us to choose a new leader and move forward with speed and decisive force for jihad." The men applauded again. "And we all know who that man should be." He turned to al-Souri and the men cheered and chanted, "Al-Sou-Ri, Al-Sou-Ri!"

Al-Souri soaked in their adulation, then raised a hand for them to stop. "My brothers, in the name of Allah the Merciful, the Beneficent, and in the memory of our beloved, martyred leader Ibn Jihad, I thank you for the honor you offer me. Jihad is the mission Allah has given us, and we have all committed our lives to it. This is as it should be, and Allah shall have his victory." There was another round of applause and foot stomping.

"But, my brothers . . ." He coughed and leaned on a table for support. He brushed away Gul, who came to help him. "My brothers, I must decline this honor."

Men gasped, and some shouted, "No! No!"

"Yes, I must decline. There are many of you who can take on this duty here in Afghanistan. It is time for me to return home to Syria. In my country, there is a corrupt dictator who is ripe for defeat, a Shi'a who cloaks himself in Islam while raping the country. While the great infidel powers are busy here, we will defeat the scoundrel in Damascus and establish our Islamic State in Syria. From there, we will join with you and spread Allah's law around the world." The men were shocked and did not respond immediately. Then cheers broke out, and the commanders moved to the front to embrace al-Souri and kiss his cheeks.

When the mayhem eased, his friend addressed the crowd again. "My brothers, we are reminded that our comrade is not only a fighter but an imam. Tonight, he has taught us yet again. He will lead from the West and we will lead from the East, and Allah shall be the ultimate victor. Tonight, al-Souri is once again the Syrian, and also the global warrior for jihad!"

As the men launched into sustained cheering, al-Souri gave a wave of acknowledgment and allowed Gul to help him back to his room. They would continue their meeting without him.

When he was settled in bed, Gul asked, "Anything else, *Qomandan*?"

"Yes." Al-Souri raised his head. "You must listen carefully."

"Yes, *sayyid.*"

Al-Souri gave Gul the combination to the safe in his office. "Inside, you will find a green notebook. Go to the page with today's date and memorize the phone number next to it. Leave the notebook in the safe and take a new satellite phone far from camp. Call the number and say the proverb, 'If you do not recognize Allah, at least know him by his power.'"

"Yes, *sayyid*. 'If you do not recognize Allah, at least know him by his power.'"

Al-Souri nodded and thought for a moment. Ibn Jihad had turned on him, but they had been brothers in jihad for more than thirty years. Their final plan must go forward. It was Ibn Jihad's legacy, and his own revenge. The infidels had cracked his inner circle, killed his friend, and nearly killed him.

By this, they would surely know Allah's power.

"Arrange my travel," al-Souri said, laying his head on the pillow. "I will leave tomorrow night."

When the phone rang at the safe house in London, Mahmoud jumped. He had spent many nights sitting beside phones that never rang, and then destroyed them with the now well-worn hammer, discreetly distributing their remains among several dumpsters on his daily walks.

In the months since he killed the bellboy and placed the bomb in the luggage room at the Marriott, Mahmoud had moved up in the organization. The killing of Defense Secretary Rod Bates had thrown the American war policy into chaos. First, they had committed more resources and intensified their operations, sacrificing the lives of more of their troops. Then they had scaled back as soon as Ibn Jihad dangled a shiny trinket in front of them—the possibility of an easy exit from the giant-killing quagmire of Afghanistan. Fools! Now, they were left more exposed to what was to come.

Mahmoud had been given an important role in preparing that next great step in the jihad, a complex operation conceived by the leader himself and shepherded by his close comrade, the legendary al-Souri. This would surely hasten the day when Allah's law would reign. It would be something the entire world would notice, and from which the infidels would never recover.

But when the rumors had started a few hours earlier that Ibn Jihad was now a martyr, Mahmoud's shock and grief had been accompanied by concern. He thought the operation was even more urgent, a way to show decisively that the movement survived. But would the order ever come? How would the jihad continue without its leading light?

Now, of all nights, the phone was ringing.

He stared at it and waited for the second ring to start. Then, Mahmoud picked it up, his hand shaking. He pushed the green button, raised the phone to the side of his head, and said only, "Yes?"

He heard Gul's voice from a hilltop thirty-five hundred miles away, "If you do not recognize Allah, at least know him by his power."

The line went quiet for a moment, then Gul started to recite the proverb again. But Mahmoud was already lowering the phone, staring at it as if he might see the image of Ibn Jihad on its small screen. He pushed the red button to end the call, and got the hammer out of a drawer. His heart was suddenly racing. He had much work to do in the coming hours, much of Allah's work.

The call was what Bridget and her colleagues would have labeled "actionable intelligence," information they could use to bust a terrorist cell and prevent an attack. But none of them heard it. And if they had, they wouldn't have understood its significance. Hours later, the call would be nothing more than a small dot among hundreds on a scattergram.

Faraz drove all day, stopping only to wash his wounds and bandages in a river and for a brief rest in a wooded area. Returning to the road, he convinced a man to give him some food and gasoline. It wasn't difficult. No one was going to refuse an armed fighter with obvious injuries. He told the man he was going home to recuperate, so there was no need to report the encounter. The man seemed to believe him.

Now, the sun was setting, and he was exhausted again. He had lost a lot of blood, but he couldn't stop.

As he drove on, he found himself thinking about Zahir. "You were my friend," he had said. Those were among his last words. Zahir had pulled Faraz out of the village after the bomb nearly killed him. Zahir had covered for him on the hill, the night of the aborted airstrike. They had trained together, stood guard side-by-side countless times, shared a tent for more than half a year.

Faraz had killed many people that day. He had been trained to kill, and to deal with it, by two fighting forces. But he had never been trained to kill someone he knew, someone who called him friend, brother. He thought about the Zahir who had arrived in camp a few days after he had, the simple farm boy who couldn't do a decent jumping jack. But that was not the Zahir who reached for the weapon outside the garage, the Zahir who would have killed him one second later. The truth was, they were not friends or brothers.

Faraz was fighting off his emotions, trying to keep the car on the road.

He'd had one true brother. Johnny. He was the reason Faraz was there, on a remote mountain road in eastern Afghanistan. Johnny would be proud of me today, he thought.

"Wish you could have been here, brother," he said out loud.

At last, through the dusk, he saw the lights of the town he was looking for, the town where he had worked at the madrassa. He could see the minaret of the mosque where he met the imam, and the ring of buildings around the market square. He tried to make out the madrassa, but other buildings blocked his view.

Faraz turned left to skirt the town, and the SUV climbed the hill onto the upper road. After a few minutes, he came to the intersection where the boy had left him. It was dinnertime, and the street was quiet. He drove on, climbing all the way. Halfway to the village, he saw a good spot and steered the vehicle to the edge of the road, facing the drop-off into the valley. He set the emergency brake, turned off the engine, took the keys, and got out.

The cool mountain air revived him. He took his gun from the passenger seat and used the bayonet to remove the license plate. Then he released the brake and pushed the SUV over the edge.

Faraz watched it gain speed as it rolled down the hillside, bouncing over the rough ground until it smashed into a large rock near the bottom. They'd find it in the morning, with blood on the seat, and wonder what happened to the poor driver.

He smiled for the first time that day.

Faraz looked back toward the town and the foothills beyond. It almost seemed as if he could see all of Afghanistan from there.

He remembered thinking about his parents the last time he was on that road, and how proud they would have been to know he was in Afghanistan fighting the terrorists. What would they think now? God, he wanted to go home.

Faraz took one last look and sighed. Then he slung

the rifle over his shoulder and started walking up the road.

When he crossed a stream a few minutes later, he threw the keys as far as he could and watched them drop into the water. Half a mile farther on he buried the license plate in the soft earth at the edge of a farm field.

As the moon rose over the mountains, Faraz climbed with renewed energy. The village wouldn't be far, now. He hoped the old sheikh was still on the payroll.

ACKNOWLEDGMENTS

My transition from attempting to write facts as a journalist to attempting to write fiction as a novelist was aided immeasurably by many good friends and professional mentors, including several people who fit both descriptions.

I must first thank "The Two Barbaras," my fiction writing teachers—author and editor Barbara Cronie, who directs the Writers' Colony at Old School Square in Delray Beach, Florida, and author, editor and graphic artist Barbara Flores, whom I first met through the Palm Beach Community Educator program. They were the linchpins of my early fiction education and supporters throughout the process.

My developmental editor, Lourdes Venard of Comma Sense Editing, wielded her electronic machete with surgical precision to slash out the undergrowth and overgrowth and help me find a story in my first draft. Without her clear thinking, deft touch, and positive approach, I would still be lost in that thicket. In addition, Lourdes was unendingly generous with her time, guidance, and contacts, and even performed emergency synopsis resuscitation.

Sandblast's early readers were also invaluable, including my first reviewer and fan, my wife Audrey Kahn, as well as other members of my family and numerous personal friends. My friends in journalism, the military, and academia were particularly instrumental in correcting my mistakes and sharing their broad experience to help deepen the story. A big, big thank-you to Daphne Benoit, Col. (Ret.) Steve Boylan, Marvin Diogenes, Andrew Gray, Capt. Greg Hicks (USN), Ambassador Ali Ahmad Jalali, Kathleen J. McInnis, Thom Shanker, Adm. (Ret.) James Stavridis, and Heather Williams.

I must also acknowledge the contribution of the countless members of the U.S. armed forces at all levels, as well as defense department civilians, national security experts, and fellow reporters, who taught me so much and inspired me during my time covering the Pentagon, and traveling to the war zones and U.S. military facilities around the world. In addition, during my years as a foreign correspondent, I relied heavily on local staff members and freelance translators to be able to at least glimpse into the cultures I encountered. Without those people and those experiences, *Sandblast* would not have been possible.

Many writers join critique groups to help improve their craft and stay focused. I have been part of several over the years, and I thank all my fellow members for their comments and support, most especially my current group, Porter Beermann, Caryn DeVincenti (Dana Ross), Jane Kelly Amerson Lopez, Marcie Tau, and Lou Ann Williams.

Any aspiring author knows the tribulations of the query process. My spreadsheet is 162 queries long. It is said that all a writer needs is one good "yes." Michaela Hamilton at Kensington Publishing was mine. Once she read *Sandblast*, she was ceaselessly enthusiastic and supportive, patiently guiding me through the process and providing essential advice and the benefit of her experience. At this writing, I look forward to working with Michaela and the rest of the Kensington team as we launch this series.

Finally, thank you for taking a chance on a new author. You can find more about me through online retailers and Goodreads, and at www.alpessin.com, where I hope you'll use the Contact Al form to let me know your thoughts on Sandblast and the issues it raises. Please follow @apessin on Twitter and alpessinauthor on Instagram, and "Like" the Al Pessin Author page on Facebook. I'll keep you up to date on events and new books, and I promise not to bother you too often.

Don't miss the next exciting thriller from Al Pessin

BLOWBACK
A TASK FORCE EPSILON THRILLER

Coming soon from Kensington Publishing Corp.

Keep reading to enjoy a preview excerpt . . .

The six-man Special Ops team slipped into the village at two a.m., walking almost silently along the edge of the road, past the ramshackle one-room houses, trying not to disturb the sleeping dogs. The men were all in black, with night-vision goggles protruding from their helmets and M-4 assault rifles at the ready. The thin mountain air was cold, and their breath turned to fog as they breathed, steady and even, in spite of the long climb. Clouds obscured the moon, always a good thing.

GPS indicated their target was thirty yards ahead.

At the same time, thirty-five hundred miles to the west, a young man walked along a very different road in a nondescript residential neighborhood of South London.

It was well into a cold, drizzly evening as he rounded the corner he'd been looking for, twenty-minutes from the Underground station where he'd gotten off the train. Mahmoud wore black jeans, a dark green T-shirt, and a black jacket. His baseball cap and backpack were gray, and the cap bore no team logo. He pulled it down to his eyebrows as he turned into the wind.

He found the spot he had scouted, between the light circles of two lampposts, and checked his phone. Three bars, just as before. Mahmoud turned into a dark alcove between two houses and wedged himself into a small space behind their dumpsters. He dialed the international number from memory.

The distant phone rang once, twice, and the beginning of a third ring. Someone picked up and blew a small puff of breath through the wires, satellite links, and cell towers into Mahmoud's ear. He understood—all was clear.

Mahmoud recited the Muslim proverb in Arabic, as it had been recited to him on another call a few hours earlier. "If you do not recognize Allah, at least know him by his power."

The line was silent for a second, as if out of reverence—not for the wisdom of the proverb, but rather for its power at that moment.

Then the programmed response came, *"Allah hu akhbar."* God is great.

The sergeant leading the Special Ops team raised his right fist to signal Stop. He turned toward his men, checked his weapons, and adjusted his goggles. The others did the same. He looked at each man in turn, and each one nodded to indicate Ready.

The sergeant turned forward again and resumed the advance.

* * *

Mahmoud touched the phone's screen to end the call, took the back off, and tossed the battery into the dumpster. He took out the SIM card and crushed it in his hand as he resumed his walk, planning a circuitous route to a different tube station on a different line.

At a public ash can, with a tall neck and a small opening for cigarette butts, he disposed of the SIM. He dropped the rest of the phone in a trash can a few blocks away.

The rain was heavier now, dripping off his jacket onto his shoes. He had another ten minutes of walking ahead of him.

The Special Ops team's target was sleeping on a homemade mat on the dirt floor of a small hut in the center of the village, a few steps off the road behind an animal shed. He was alone. Blood from his wounds had soaked through the makeshift bandages and stained his freshly borrowed shirt. His dark beard was scraggly. His wool cap lay next to him. His traditional Afghan trousers and tunic were filthy from one interrogation, two gunfights, eight hours on the road—some of it walking—and a day in this hut.

His right leg jerked, and his right hand moved as if to raise a weapon. He woke up in a sweat and nearly cried out. It was the third time that night he'd had the same nightmare: The Taliban search party caught him. He was in a fight for his life. He lost.

Awake now, the young man heard footsteps. He reached for his AK-47 for real this time, and pointed it into the darkness.

Someone opened the door slowly and quietly. The red lights of laser targeting sights swept the room.

A voice said in foreign-accented Pashto, "Lower your weapon." He did, but he kept his hand on it. He thought he knew what was happening, but here, one could never be sure.

Three men entered with practiced speed. The first grabbed his AK. Another pointed a rifle at him. The third approached and shined a light in his eyes. He winced and turned away, then blinked and turned back, looking straight into the light. The man behind it twice compared the face he saw to a photo on a small tablet computer.

"State your name," he whispered in English.

The man on the floor swallowed. It had been a long time since he'd said his name. He took a breath. His tone and his identity strengthened as he formed each word. "Lieutenant Faraz Abdallah."

"Codeword and authentication please, sir."

"Sandblast, Whiskey-Alpha-5-9-0-Sierra-Sierra-Romeo."

The man nodded and put the tablet back into his pocket. "Master Sergeant Murphy, sir. We're here to take you home."

A twentysomething Arab man didn't stand out on the London Underground, especially not in this neighborhood. Mahmoud had a seat and he played a game on his phone, as he settled in for the long ride back to the safe house. He didn't much like electronic games, but playing helped him blend in with the crowd. And it kept his eyes down under the baseball cap.

His backpack was lighter than it had been that morning. He had no more spare clothes. And he had three fewer mobile phones, having used each one once in far-flung parts of the city, and then dismantled and discarded them.

Mahmoud had been remarkably calm for most of the journey. But every time he thought about what he had set in motion, his heart raced and beads of sweat formed at his temples. The infidels would truly know Allah's power. And with His help, they would see the futility of their war on His people.

Less than forty-eight hours earlier, the enemy had scored what they saw as a great victory. They had committed the cowardly murder of Ibn Jihad, leader of the newly unified global movement to end the infidel occupation of the Holy Lands and establish Allah's law throughout the world. By these acts, the holy fighters would begin their revenge. The infidels would realize that their victory was hollow, that no drone could crush the believers, that time and right and numbers were on their side.

Mahmoud's stomach grumbled. He hadn't stopped to eat all day, hadn't spoken to anyone or purchased anything. He had scanned a different travel card for each train and bus ride. He had changed his shirt, jacket, and baseball cap in public restrooms several times and trashed the used ones. He was certain that no one knew who he was or what he had done.

Hunger pangs were a small price to pay, especially compared to the price the brothers would be paying tomorrow. He still thought of them as "brothers." Tomorrow, they would be "martyrs," like the great Ibn Jihad, may Allah grant him the highest place in paradise.

In his blessed memory, tomorrow would be the greatest day ever for the jihad.

Faraz walked to the helicopter under his own power, surrounded by the Special Ops guys. It was a strange sight—American troops with blackened faces, body armor, helmets, M-4s, and night-vision goggles walking with an Afghan in sandals and traditional clothes.

It looked like he was their prisoner. But he had called them in to rescue him.

On the chopper, they had Faraz lie down on a gurney so a medical team could check him over. He protested when they lashed his chest and legs down, but they said it was for safety.

He threw a look at the medic when he started the IV. The man said, "Hydration, sir." But those were the last words Faraz heard before he went under.

The Black Hawk stayed low and banked hard, descending the Hindu Kush into Pakistan.

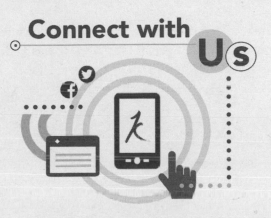